THE OPIUM PURGE

Lady Fan Mysteries
Book Three

Elizabeth Bailey

SAPERE
BOOKS

THE OPIUM PURGE

Published by Sapere Books.

20 Windermere Drive, Leeds, England, LS17 7UZ,
United Kingdom

saperebooks.com

ISBN: 978-1-912546-49-7

CHAPTER ONE

The cloak splashed red against the pristine snow. Arms uplifted to the heavens, bare fingers catching at fresh flakes, the girl twirled on the vanished lawn of the Dower House, her countenance alight with pleasure.

Watching from an upper window, barefoot and inadequately clad for early January, Ottilia Fanshawe was struck by the ethereal beauty of this dawn trespasser. Who she might be was a mystery, for Ottilia's mother-in-law had made no mention of a stranger so worthy of notice. Although this was no surprise, with the Dowager Marchioness of Polbrook's concentration centred upon the perfidy of her elder son.

The tirades, endured with ill-concealed chagrin by Ottilia's long-suffering spouse for the duration of their stay, showed no sign of letting up. The sheer delight of the scarlet-clad girl in the garden was thus refreshing to Ottilia's jaded patience.

If one were to imagine a fairy princess, this creature embodied the vision to perfection. The hood of her cloak had fallen to her shoulders, revealing a cluster of fair curls framing a glowing face fit to set a painter groping for his brushes. A row of pearly teeth showed within the luscious open mouth and a pair of sparkling eyes were just visible.

Yet even as she enjoyed the sight, Ottilia's innate common sense could not help but deprecate the lack of gloves and the foolhardy excursion into the cold of a winter's day without proper protection. She doubted the billowing cloak offered much by way of warmth, especially since the girl had apparently donned a diaphanous gown more suited to an evening party. Its folds twinkled in the light, suggesting a spangled confection nestling beneath the concealing cloak.

All at once it was borne in upon Ottilia that the girl had ceased her twirling dance in the snow, and had discovered herself to be observed. She was looking directly up at the window, with an intent stare that was oddly disturbing.

Obeying a half-formed impulse, Ottilia lifted a hand and waved. The girl's features exploded into life, opening into a huge smile that could not but draw an answering one from Ottilia. Two bare hands came up, and the fingers waggled in a fashion that reminded her irresistibly of a toddler's attempt at waving.

Laughing aloud, Ottilia watched as the girl abruptly turned and darted away. She was quickly lost to sight around the corner of the house, and Ottilia found herself leaning into the glass in an effort to catch a last glimpse.

"What in the world are you about, Tillie?"

Lord Francis Fanshawe's sleepy voice caught Ottilia's attention and she straightened, turning her head. Her husband had partly emerged from between the bed-curtains on her side, which Ottilia had left closed. She threw him a darting look of mischief.

"I've been watching a fairy dancing in the snow."

"At this hour?" And then her words seemed to sink in. "A fairy?"

"A girl. A stranger, I think. She seemed a childlike creature, but very beautiful."

Francis swung his legs out of the bed, and a frown creased his brow as his gaze dropped. "You'll catch your death, standing there in your nightgown."

Ottilia shivered, belatedly becoming aware of the cold in her limbs. She looked about for her shawl, but her spouse was already on his feet and moving to seize it off the back of the daybed where she had left it last night. He crossed to the window and draped it about her shoulders, his arms enwrapping her from behind over the top of its woollen folds.

"There. Though I'd prefer you to snuggle between the sheets with me. Even if we are pledged to be circumspect for a space."

Ottilia sank into the warmth of his embrace, but she could not withstand a spurt of irritation. "An old wives' tale, Fan."

One of Francis's hands slipped down to cradle the swell at her abdomen, slight as yet. "When Patrick gave much the same warning?"

"I shall have something to say to my brother when he arrives," Ottilia said on a slightly acid note. "Between you and him, I shall be driven demented before ever I get through the next six months."

Francis held her tighter and she felt his lips caress her cheek as he mouthed tender endearments that could not but damp her rising annoyance. She sighed a little, aware of the unaccustomed emotional turmoil that seemed to attack her more as her pregnancy advanced. Her usual calm had deserted her, and although she was no longer nauseous, she was apt to be snappy and prone to unwarranted distresses. Ottilia was becoming wearied with apologising already, and the weeks ahead of her seemed to stretch into eternity.

Francis relaxed his hold. "Tell me about your fairy."

"Oh, the girl in the snow!"

The memory sprang back into Ottilia's mind, and she at once realised that the girl's joyous appearance of freedom had spoken to the deeps within her, where frustration was king and life had lost something of its savour.

7

"She's exquisite. A picture book doll; or a princess. I wonder who she is." She turned a little, surveying her husband's strong-featured countenance, with the untied lush brown hair falling attractively about his lean cheeks. "Sybilla has not spoken to you of any odd neighbours, has she?"

"What, with every second word that comes out of her mouth a fresh curse for Randal? I doubt she has room to notice." Francis released her, moving to locate his dressing-gown. "The only girl I know of that lives around here is young Phoebe."

"You mean the girl Giles is supposed to marry? Lady Phoebe Graveney, is it not?"

Her husband shrugged on his robe and tied it. "That's the one. Hemington's daughter. The family was away over Christmas, I believe, but I daresay she'll be in evidence shortly."

"What does she look like?"

"She's well enough, as I recall."

Ottilia clicked her tongue. "A trifle more detail, if you please, Fan. Is she blonde?"

He frowned in concentration. "Dark, I think."

"Then it cannot have been she." Ottilia glanced out of the window, her mind's eye supplying the missing image of the girl she had seen. "Besides, I can hardly suppose a girl foolish enough to run around in the snow in a spangled evening gown is likely to be the future Lady Polbrook."

"Lady Bennifield, to begin with," corrected Francis, adding feelingly, "And I wish you would not mention that name, Tillie."

Ottilia had to laugh. "Yes, it hardly bears repetition after the manner of your Mama's saying it."

The dowager had formed the habit of laying savage emphasis on the title now borne by her new daughter-in-law, which had made a marchioness of her son's erstwhile French mistress. Randal had married the moment his year of mourning for his unfortunate first wife had come to an end, in secrecy and without reference to his afflicted family. Upon being apprised of the deed, his mother had vented her scorching fury in a letter to her younger son. Francis had sworn there were flames coming off the paper. The letter had ended with a peremptory summons for Ottilia and Francis to spend Christmas at the Dower House, Sybilla declaring that nothing would induce her to share Polbrook's board for the festivities.

In the event, Ottilia had succeeded in persuading her mother-in-law at least to attend an invitation for dinner on the twenty-fifth, if only for the sake of her grandchildren, who had both been present.

"Giles at least appears to have become reconciled." Ottilia moved to join Francis, who had flung aside the bed-curtains and was sitting on the edge of the bed. "We have not seen him since New Year's Eve."

"Reconciled? Don't you believe it! I suspect it will be long before he forgives his father. As for being saddled with a French half-sister and brother —"

"Half-French."

"Don't quibble, Tillie."

"And they are scarcely to blame, poor things."

"No one is blaming them, but Giles's objections are perfectly understandable."

"Until your brother has legitimised them," she pursued, unheeding, "they had as well be orphaned waifs."

"You may be sure Randal has had the matter in hand for months." His tone was hard. "I imagine Jardine was instructed long since."

The family's man of business had been instrumental in locating the marquis when he had gone missing in France after his wife was brutally murdered in the autumn of '89. The ensuing scandal had rocked the family to its foundations, compounded by Lord Polbrook's reappearance in company with Madame Guizot and her two children, whom he had rescued from the vengeance of a populace gone mad. Francis, left to pick up the pieces during his brother's absence, had been sorely beset.

Ottilia reached to set her hand over his where it rested on his knee, lacing their fingers. "You have not forgiven him, have you?"

Her spouse shifted his shoulders in that way he had when confronted with uncomfortable truths. "I think he might have waited."

"Well, you know why he did not, for he told you so."

Francis snorted. "Yes, he wanted to secure his precious Violette's future. It does not appear to have occurred to him to think of the effect upon his son and daughter. Or that Harriet had to postpone Candia's come-out again until the scandal dies down. I know he does not give a fig for Mama's disapproval, provided he is not obliged to listen to her complaints."

The deep discontent in her spouse's tone moved Ottilia to slip an arm about his back and lean her head on his shoulder. "My poor darling. There is no question but you have borne the brunt of it."

For answer, Francis drew her closer in a convulsive hug and pressed a kiss against her forehead. Then he sighed a little. "I could wish Patrick and his family could have come here sooner."

"Indeed, so do I, for I'm afraid the snow may prevent them coming altogether."

"My God, I hope not!"

Ottilia laughed. "Well, let us be sanguine for your sake. Their presence must at least stop Sybilla's tongue temporarily. And I defy even your mother to rival Sophie's ability to prolong a recital of her sufferings."

Francis cast up his eyes and Ottilia remembered how vocal he had been on the subject of Patrick Hathaway's wife, after the few days spent at her brother's house from where they had been married in June last year.

"If you will tell me how Patrick is able to tolerate her whining, I may take a leaf out of his book with Mama. Has he some secret herb he uses? A potion to render one deaf for a space?"

Ottilia's mirth bubbled over. "He merely retires to his surgery. Or invents a patient he must instantly visit. At least, I assume he invents it, by the number of times a message has arrived opportunely."

"Well, I can't use that excuse here. I could almost wish you might stumble upon another adventure, if it could divert my mother's attention."

This remark served to remind Ottilia of the strange girl she had seen. She got up abruptly. "I'll ask Sybilla about my fairy. That may give her thoughts another direction."

Francis caught her hand. "Now? Aren't you coming back to bed?"

Ottilia sagged. "I cannot, Fan. I shall go mad if I have to lie there doing nothing."

"Still so restless?"

"Yes! I shall dress and go for a walk, I think." Francis let her go and made to rise, but she quickly set a hand to his shoulder. "I'll be all right on my own, Fan. You need have no apprehension. I promise I will take the greatest care."

11

He squinted up at her. "Very well."

Ottilia knew that look. "You mean to dress in any event and follow me, do you not?"

Francis quirked an eyebrow. "I won't sleep again now. But I'll have to shave, so I've no doubt you'll be well ahead of me."

Despite a cheerful fire in the grate, the front parlour gave off a chill as Ottilia entered the room. She had barely taken in the fact when she was brought up short by the sight of the stranger in the scarlet cloak standing bang in the middle of the room.

"Lord above!" Ottilia stared blankly at the creature, whose china blue eyes turned swiftly towards her.

"There you are!"

"Yes," agreed Ottilia, moving into the room. "But how in the world did you get in?"

It was then borne in upon her that the Dowager Lady Polbrook's companion was also present. Teresa Mellis was standing a little to one side, evidently struck dumb by the appearance of the unknown visitor.

"Miss Mellis?"

The woman turned towards her, a countenance edged with tension. This was not unusual with her, as Ottilia knew, for the companion was possessed of a nervous disposition, apt to be thrown into play by trifles. For answer, she pointed towards the French window, which Ottilia realised was open.

"No wonder it is cold." She moved across with the intention of remedying the matter.

Miss Mellis intercepted her. "Wait!" Once more she pointed. "Look."

Ottilia glanced briefly at the girl, who had not again spoken, but whose oddly fixed stare was following Ottilia as she moved. Miss Mellis took a couple of steps in the direction of the window, her finger stretched out towards it. An oddity in the glass pane imprinted itself upon Ottilia's vision. It was splintered, with a jagged hole that had scattered shards upon the carpet underneath. A startled question leaped into her mind, and she turned back to the girl even as Miss Mellis's low-toned warning sounded.

"You may well stare. See her hand? She broke the glass."

By now Ottilia had caught sight of the girl's bloodied fingers. Without thought, she went up to her and seized her wrist, lifting the hand for inspection.

"Heavens, child, how in the world did you come to do such a thing?"

The stranger's gaze, still fixed on Ottilia's face, shifted to take in her own hand. A pair of fine brows rose. "How did I do that? I don't remember cutting myself."

Behind her, Ottilia heard Miss Mellis let out a protesting whimper. Ottilia looked round, taking in the fright in the pallid face. On the shady side of fifty, Teresa Mellis was prematurely lined due to the possession of delicate skin with a tendency to dryness, and every distress, of which there were many as Ottilia had noted, showed in her thin features. She spoke little unless spoken to, and was in the habit of making terse pronouncements if called upon to answer.

"She punched her fist through the glass."

The girl made no comment, but merely watched the interplay as Ottilia looked from her and then back to Miss Mellis. "Did you see it?"

The companion shook her head. "I saw her put her hand through to unlatch the door."

"To the detriment of your poor hand, young lady." Ottilia turned back to the girl with a smile. "I think our first task must be to wash your wounds and make sure you have no pieces of glass embedded in your flesh."

The girl's pretty mouth opened and a tinkle of high-pitched laughter came out. "Like a pin cushion."

From the corner of her eye Ottilia noticed the shiver that shook Miss Mellis, and privately could not blame her. The stranger was decidedly odd. But first things first. Releasing the girl's wrist, she went to close the door and pull the curtains across to cover the hole.

"Let us at least try to keep in the warm." Turning again, she addressed the companion as she moved to the bell-pull and tugged upon it. "Would you be so kind, Miss Mellis, as to find lint and bandages? A pair of tweezers too, if you will, and perhaps a magnifying glass. Do you have one?"

Miss Mellis let her breath go in a shaky sigh. "I will get them."

Watching her limp from the room as fast as she was able, Ottilia suspected Miss Mellis was glad to remove herself from the girl's presence. Her acquaintance with the woman was slight, but sympathy prompted her to make a particular effort to understand the companion, for Ottilia's introduction to the family had been as the creature's temporary replacement when the woman had sustained a broken leg over a year before. She would never admit as much, Ottilia guessed, but it was obvious the winter cold was creating problems with her lingering disability.

Returning her attention to the unexpected visitor, Ottilia summoned a smile and kept her tone even. "Won't you sit down? I will have one of the servants bring a basin of water and a towel, and then we may see what can be done."

The girl made no move to sit, nor to look for a chair, but remained just where she was, her eyes playing over Ottilia's features.

"You are not beautiful."

Ottilia laughed out. "But you are."

"Yes."

There was no pride or conceit in the one word. It was merely agreement, Ottilia decided. She set a hand to the girl's back and moved her gently towards a long sofa upholstered in blue-striped brocade, which was set to one side of the fireplace. She obliged the girl to sit.

"What is your name?"

"Tamasine."

"How pretty. Do you live near here, Tamasine?"

The visitor made no reply to this, but continued to watch Ottilia as she removed the warm, hooded cloak she had donned for the purpose of taking her walk and set it aside on a convenient chair. She then placed herself next to the visitor.

"Who are you?" the girl asked suddenly.

Simplicity seemed the better part of discretion. "I am Lady Fan."

Tamasine's countenance lit with another of those lightning smiles. "Lady Fan, Lady Fan, Lady Fan. You are not like a fan at all."

"Well, I should hope not. It is a nickname."

There was no direct response to this as Tamasine continued to regard her for a moment. Then she opened an entirely new subject. "They will be looking all over for me."

"Who will?"

"My guardian. And Lavinia."

"Who is Lavinia?"

Tamasine made no answer. Instead her glance shifted off Ottilia for the first time as she looked about the room. It was a large apartment, which managed to feel cosy nevertheless, done out in a faded blue with white-painted Adam curlicues surrounding each of the faux panels, in several of which were hung portraits of past dowagers who had inhabited the house in their years of widowhood.

"I like it here. Can I stay?"

Taken aback, Ottilia eyed the girl, trying to read her expression. "But surely you have a home of your own?"

"Oh, yes. It is not far." Her gaze returned to Ottilia's. "I found the garden."

"So I saw. You appeared to be enjoying the snow."

"I wasn't cold," said Tamasine, as if this was disputed.

Ottilia remembered the glimpse of a spangled gown and glanced down. Sure enough, the cloak had fallen away as Tamasine sat, revealing a diaphanous garment, ill-suited both to the weather and the time of day. Had the girl even been to bed?

"Were you attending an evening party last night?"

"I don't attend parties. They won't let me."

Ottilia was beginning to have an inkling why this might be so, but she refrained from speaking her thought aloud. "Who is your guardian?"

"Joslin."

Ottilia tried again. "Does he have a second name?"

The bell-like tinkle sounded. "Of course he does."

She strove for patience. "What is his full name?"

"Sir Joslin Cadel." Tamasine sighed, suddenly dejected. "He is trying to stop me being married, you know. But I shall outwit him."

"How will you do that?"

"I shall escape with Giles."

It was perhaps fortunate that a servant chose this moment to enter the room in answer to the summons of the bell, for Ottilia scarcely knew what to reply to the revelation Tamasine was on terms of intimacy with Francis's nephew.

"Biddy," she said, addressing the plump-cheeked youngster who had entered and was staring with unconcealed curiosity at the newcomer, "would you be so kind as to bring a basin of warm water and a couple of towels? Miss Tamasine has had the misfortune to hurt her hand."

To Ottilia's surprise, this request had the effect of causing the maid to start, her eyes popping at Tamasine, who was staring back.

"What is the matter, Biddy?"

The maid bit her lip, and wiped her hands down her apron. "I think as it's Miss Roy, my lady, from Willow Court, the neighbour's house across the way."

Ottilia took in the information along with the strange look that told her Biddy was privy to more information on the matter, but now was not the moment to investigate.

"Thank you, Biddy. Fetch the water and towels straight away, if you please."

The maid started, dropped a curtsy and withdrew. Ottilia turned to Tamasine.

"Is that your name? Tamasine Roy?"

"The sugar princess, Miss Tamasine Roy," said the girl with an air of reciting a well learned lesson.

"Sugar princess? How charming. I have always wanted to meet a princess."

Laughter tinkled from the girl's mouth. "I am not a real princess, silly. That's what they call me over there."

Over where? But Ottilia did not pursue it. "And how old are you, Tamasine?"

"Two and twenty, I think."

Ottilia began to wonder if the childlike responses merely signalled a backward mind, or if there was a darker significance. One thing was certain. Tamasine Roy was no ordinary female.

Before she could prosecute any further enquiries, Miss Mellis re-entered the parlour, armed with the necessary implements to take care of Tamasine's bleeding hand.

"Thank you, Miss Mellis. Biddy is bringing water and towels, so we had best wait for that first." Noting the older woman's reluctance to approach the visitor, Ottilia tried for a way to give her thoughts another direction. "What do you suppose can be done about that window?"

Miss Mellis had laid the things she carried on a convenient small table near Ottilia, and she went with obvious relief towards the French windows. Pulling aside the curtain, she inspected the damage to one side.

"Grig must be sent for. He will have it repaired in no time."

"Are you talking of that old fellow who works for Lord Polbrook?"

Miss Mellis nodded, but Ottilia could not help being dubious. From what she had been privileged to observe, the fellow Grig, who seemed to be a sort of handyman, was one of these grumbling old retainers who was apt to protest that every task was impossible. As if she read Ottilia's mind, Miss Mellis spoke up.

"He is perfectly disobliging, but he knows how to do and he likes Sybilla."

For all her reticence, it had more than once struck Ottilia that Miss Mellis was credited with a deal less shrewdness than she possessed.

"Well, I will leave that in your capable hands," she said, noting the faint flush that crept into the companion's cheek. "Meanwhile, allow me to present to you the sugar princess, Miss Tamasine Roy, whose guardian Sir Joslin Cadel is no doubt hunting for her at this very moment." She turned to the girl and found her watching the other woman without expression. "Tamasine, this is Teresa. She is going to help me clean you up and get rid of any remaining splinters of glass."

The girl's sudden smile showed. "Thank you."

Ottilia was agreeably surprised to hear her speak so naturally. Perhaps her malady, whatever it might be, was not total. Before anything further could be said, the maid returned, accompanied by her older colleague, who bustled in, shaking her head and tutting.

"What's all this, pray?"

It was evident from Biddy having been moved to bring in reinforcements that her tongue had been hard at work.

"Agnes, this is Miss Roy, who has been unfortunate enough to suffer an accident with the window."

Agnes, a buxom dame with a vein of strong common sense, looked across at the window where the curtain was once again drawn back. She stared for a moment, and then looked back to the visitor briefly, before her gaze passed on to Ottilia.

"I see, my lady. Where would you like this basin putting?"

Ottilia directed its disposition. About to dismiss the maids, she was forestalled by Miss Mellis. "Agnes, pray send to Grig at the big house to come and mend this window immediately."

The older maid glanced once more towards the window. "I should think I'd better, ma'am. Young Toby may ride over at once."

Clicking her tongue the while, she departed with her colleague, no doubt with the intention of instructing the lad who served nominally as Sybilla's footman, but in reality as general help whenever a strong male arm was needed.

Ottilia at once requested Miss Mellis to sit on the other side of Tamasine and hold her hand over the basin, for she could place no reliance on the girl doing what was needed without assistance. That Teresa Mellis was reluctant was obvious, but she obeyed.

"Now then, let us see what we can do here."

Adopting a cheerful manner, she set about the task of cleaning the hand, making sure not to touch it for fear of causing glass fragments to embed more firmly. Instead she cupped water and poured it over the fingers until the blood was sufficiently washed away to enable her to see where the cuts originated.

"Dear me, I am afraid there are several places where you have damaged yourself, Tamasine. Where is the magnifying glass, Miss Mellis?"

The companion did not release her grip upon the girl's wrist, but she reached to the little table and lifted the batch of lint, which proved to have been covering the glass. Ottilia thanked her and took it up, along with the tweezers.

"Now then, keep your hand as still as you can, if you please."

"Oh, I can be still for hours," said Tamasine airily.

"Excellent," Ottilia murmured as she applied herself to the tricky task of locating splinters of glass.

"I used to sit in the canes, you know, hiding from the black fellows. I kept very still so they would not see me and chase me away."

This confidence set Ottilia's mind afire with conjecture. The image it conjured spoke of a place other than England. The canes and black people? Could the girl have lately arrived from a sojourn abroad? She had no chance to explore the interesting possibility for Tamasine spoke up again.

"Giles said I must be still while he kissed me."

The hand Ottilia was working on jerked, and she threw a reproachful look at Miss Mellis, who was wide-eyed, her jaw dropping. Ottilia could not altogether blame her, for this alarming little piece of news was enough to send anyone into shock. Was young Lord Bennifield courting Miss Roy? Leaving the matter of canes, Ottilia probed gently as she extracted a minute sliver of glass from the girl's hand.

"How did you meet Giles?"

"He is quite handsome."

Did she not remember, or did the question have no meaning for her? Ottilia tried another tack. "Did Giles come to your house?"

"Joslin said he must not. I told him to come."

"When did you tell him?"

"In the woods." The high-pitched laugh sounded. "He nearly fell off his horse."

Ottilia could well imagine it. The unexpected sight of Tamasine's extraordinary beauty might be counted upon to stun any young male. But Lord Bennifield was spoken for, and if he had not the wit to recognise that Tamasine Roy was clearly unfit for dalliance, it did not augur well for his future with Lady Phoebe Graveney. There was some excuse for Miss Mellis's dour look of disapproval.

Setting aside another splinter she had extracted, Ottilia deftly turned the subject. "Have you been many weeks in your new house?"

Tamasine set her head on one side as if she considered the question. Having deliberately phrased it in a way to make it easy for her to grasp and answer, Ottilia was gratified to find her responding in a more natural fashion.

"The leaves were falling when we came. The woods are pretty when the trees are red."

"Indeed, yes. I am fond of autumn myself."

This was productive of nothing more than a blank stare. Did she not understand the seasons by name? Ottilia began to wonder just how much this girl was able to fathom of life. She seemed to inhabit a world of her own, and it was doubtful anyone had been able to instil much into her mind by way of education.

Intrigued, Ottilia determined to discover what she could, but was frustrated in this design by the entrance into the parlour of her mother-in-law, the Dowager Marchioness of Polbrook.

"What in the world is happening here?"

The tone instantly set Miss Mellis trembling so that Tamasine's hand shook and Ottilia had perforce to cease her labours. She looked across as Sybilla came up, her black eyes snapping from one to the other of the women grouped on the sofa. Mindful of the dowager's currently lacerated temper, Ottilia rose swiftly, catching her mother-in-law's gaze.

"Sybilla, are you acquainted with Miss Roy?"

An arrested look came into the dowager's features and a frown creased her brow. "Roy?"

"Tamasine Roy, yes. From Willow Court. She had the misfortune to cut her hand on the glass in the door."

Ottilia gestured towards the French windows as she spoke, infusing meaning into both eyes and voice in hopes of arresting Sybilla's attention. The dowager, like the maid before her, looked across at the damaged glass and back to the girl on the sofa, who was staring up at her with unaffected interest.

"I am sorry you were injured in my house, Miss Roy," Sybilla said, throwing a questioning look towards Ottilia.

Tamasine's glowing smile appeared. "You are Giles's grandmama."

Ottilia noted the stiffening of the dowager's straight back and the tautness that came into her cheeks, and swiftly stepped into the breach. "Quite right, Tamasine. It seems Miss Roy became acquainted with your grandson in the woods while he was out riding, Sybilla."

The dowager's direful glance came to rest upon Ottilia's face. "Indeed?"

"Giles comes to see me every day," announced Tamasine.

A grim sparkle in the black eyes as they turned back to the girl made Ottilia cut in quickly. "Tamasine's guardian has warned him off, however."

"But I told Giles to come. I like him to come."

Hoping that it would not occur to Tamasine to mention the kiss, Ottilia flashed an apologetic look at her mother-in-law and gave an infinitesimal shake of her head. Sybilla's gaze narrowed, but she did not speak. Ottilia let her breath go and quickly sat down again, taking up the tweezers and magnifying glass.

"I must continue my task, ma'am."

A little of Sybilla's thundercloud look abated. "She has glass splinters?"

"Several, I am afraid."

"Then make sure you find them all, Ottilia."

She watched in silence for a moment, standing over the group and doing little to aid Ottilia's concentration. Then she burst out in a tone of irritation, "You will never manage it in under an hour at this rate. Teresa, you hold the magnifying glass while I take Miss Roy's hand."

"An excellent notion, ma'am."

Ottilia gave up her place to the dowager, moved the little table to one side and instead knelt on the carpet, which proved a much better position from which to see the splinters. Tamasine made no objection. Indeed, she appeared to relish the attention, although she turned away from the operation on her hand and stared openly into Sybilla's face. The dowager, evidently disconcerted, fidgeted with her free hand, apparently trying not to return the stare. Ottilia was just wondering how much she knew, when Tamasine spoke up.

"Why is your face full of furrows?"

Ottilia was almost betrayed into a laugh at Sybilla's astonished look.

"Is it?" was all she could find to say.

"Yes."

Sybilla's black eyes turned towards Ottilia and a faint grimace crossed her features. Ottilia gave her a tiny conspiratorial smile. In fact the dowager was relatively unlined, but Tamasine's literal approach to life clearly did not allow for gradations.

"Well, I suppose it is because of my age," Sybilla offered at length.

"Is this your house?"

The abrupt change of subject might have thrown a lesser woman, but the dowager took it without a blink. "It is indeed."

"I like it."

"I am happy to hear you say so. Especially as it has been the means of such a sorry accident."

Tamasine's head turned swiftly and she was suddenly confronting Miss Mellis. A faintly malevolent look in the china blue eyes put Ottilia on instant alert.

"You said it was not an accident."

The unfortunate Miss Mellis shrank a little and Ottilia felt compelled to intervene. "Do sit still, if you please, Tamasine." She waited for the girl's eyes to turn towards her, and smiled. "I wish you will tell Lady Polbrook all about your dancing in the snow."

As she had hoped, a peal of her peculiar laughter was drawn from the girl. "I wasn't dancing, silly Lady Fan. There was no music."

"Pardon me, my error." Ottilia looked to Sybilla. "I saw her from my window, you must know, and thought a fairy had come into the garden."

Tamasine laughed again. "It was me."

"Indeed it was, and I can see very well you are not a fairy after all. But I cannot blame those who call you the sugar princess, for you look just like one."

She was treated to the girl's huge smile. "Simeon says I look like a china doll."

Ottilia noted the introduction of this new name, but she did not make the mistake of asking for enlightenment. "Does he so? Well, I can understand that."

Sybilla was mouthing at her and Ottilia caught the query as 'Who is Simeon?' She wanted to know herself, but she took a roundabout way of enquiry.

"Does Simeon live at your house, Tamasine?"

"When Joslin is dead, he will come."

CHAPTER TWO

A gasp escaped Miss Mellis's lips, which drew a sharply rebuking glance from her employer, whose gaze then once more centred on Ottilia, question in the delicate raised brows. Before Ottilia had a chance to make any response, a voice was heard calling from somewhere outside the house.

"Tamasine! Tam, where are you?"

Ottilia looked towards the French windows and saw that her mother-in-law and Miss Mellis were similarly riveted. The girl did not appear to have heard, her attention being still on the ministrations to her hand. The voice was male and Ottilia drew the obvious conclusion.

"I believe your guardian is calling for you, Tamasine."

"Oh, yes. I knew he would come."

"Tam? Tamasine!"

This time there were two voices, coming in one atop the other. The second was female and Ottilia recalled the girl mentioning the name Lavinia. Ottilia set down the tweezers and scrambled up.

"I will go and tell them you are here."

"Let Teresa go," said the dowager.

But Ottilia had no intention of surrendering the opportunity to waylay the guardian, from whom she might well discover more information about the girl. She picked up her cloak and began setting it around her shoulders. "No, no, ma'am. Poor Miss Mellis will take cold. I am well equipped for the weather for I had intended to take a walk in any event."

She was moving as she spoke, and was out through the door, closing it behind her before the dowager could make any serious objection.

It did not take many minutes to locate the source of the voices, for she had only to follow the sound as they both continued to call for the errant Tamasine. Rounding the corner of the building, she caught sight of two people at a little distance, walking just within the grounds of the Dower House. Ottilia cupped her hands to her mouth and hailed them.

"Sir Joslin!"

She had to call again before he halted, turning in her direction. Ottilia waved and kept walking towards him, calling out as she did so. "We have Tamasine safe, sir."

He put up a hand in acknowledgement, called out to his companion, who was standing some feet away from him, and immediately set a path towards Ottilia.

After Tamasine's extraordinary remarks about her guardian, Ottilia was agreeably surprised to see as he neared that he was a personable man, with a significant tan to his skin which lent credence to the notion of the party having been recently abroad in a hotter climate. Sir Joslin was a good deal older than his ward, rather loose-limbed and tall, and wearing just now an expression both dour and exasperated. A sheen of sweat upon his brow, despite the cold, indicated the energetic hunt in which he had been engaged. Ottilia's sympathy stirred. Young Tamasine must be a trying burden.

The woman who accompanied him appeared to be more harassed than upset, an intense look of concern visible in an otherwise pleasant countenance of indeterminate age. She was clearly mature, but not yet of middle years. Ottilia put her on a par with herself at thirty. Her complexion was a trifle sallow, but not tanned, which suggested either that she had not been with the company in a different country or that she took sensible precautions to keep her face out of the sun.

"I hope my ward has not proved a nuisance to Lady Polbrook, ma'am," said Sir Joslin as he came up.

He sounded a trifle out of breath and seemed to speak with a little effort. Ottilia hastened to disclaim, putting out a hand in a friendly way.

"Nothing of the sort. How do you do, Sir Joslin? May we dispense with formality? I am Lady Francis Fanshawe."

He dipped his head in a bow and Ottilia was impressed with the firmness of his handshake, but faintly dismayed by the slight dampness of his ungloved palm. He gestured to the female who was with him.

"Miss Ingleby, Tamasine's companion."

Ottilia smiled at the woman. "I wish I might wholly reassure you, but I am sorry to say that Tamasine has suffered a slight accident."

"Oh, no, what now?" Miss Ingleby sounded despairing.

A frown creased Sir Joslin's brow. "Is she much hurt?"

"She cut her hand. I was just removing some splinters of glass when we heard you calling." Inviting them both with a gesture to accompany her, Ottilia turned for the house. "If you don't mind waiting, perhaps it might be best if I complete the task before you take her home."

"You are very kind.'

A mechanical tone. Was Miss Ingleby's mind on other matters?

"To tell you the truth, I am afraid I may be a little to blame. I saw her from my bedchamber window, you see, and waved. I think she may have taken it for an invitation to come and find me."

There was no reply to this, but Ottilia saw the two exchange a glance which she was at a loss to interpret. It had not occurred to her to pretend ignorance of the evident peculiarities of the girl's character, but she sensed unease. Were they merely embarrassed? Or could they possibly imagine Tamasine's condition might be concealed? She tried again.

"I take it she gave you the slip, Miss Ingleby?"

The woman reddened, and it was Sir Joslin who answered, his tone repressive.

"Tamasine is fond of early morning outings. I have spoken to her before about going out unaccompanied, but girls, alas, are too often headstrong."

The absurdity of this was patent. Headstrong? The child was no ordinary girl, to be coupled with flighty behaviour. Nor could Ottilia believe that Tamasine had the slightest notion of the shibboleths governing the conduct of young ladies, even had she been previously under a laxer rule than obtained in England. She had the mind of an infant, if indeed she had any normality of mind at all. She chose her words with care.

"I imagine you must be anxious to keep her protected, as lovely as she is."

Sir Joslin had stiffened at the first part of this speech, but at this he relaxed a little. "Indeed."

"She is not yet out, you see." Miss Ingleby spoke on a note of apology. "We cannot have all the young bucks after her before she has been presented."

Ottilia was at a loss how to reply to so blatant a lie. How in the world could a female with Tamasine's obvious disadvantages possibly make her debut in polite society? Irritated, she was moved to blast this nonsense.

"Dear me. I daresay the advent of my nephew Giles into Tamasine's life is most unwelcome. Although at two and

29

twenty, as Tamasine confided to me, she must be anxious to spread her wings."

She had expected Sir Joslin to be effectually silenced, but he proved to be made of sterner stuff.

"Lord Bennifield is naturally welcome in our home, but I cannot sanction any further meetings with Tamasine. I accept his lordship's explanation that he encountered my ward by chance."

And there the matter rested, for they were approaching the French windows to the parlour. Thoroughly disappointed to find Tamasine's guardian so foolish as to attempt concealment, Ottilia could almost wish the girl would confound the fellow with a series of untoward remarks. With some relish, she pointed out the broken pane of glass.

"I'm afraid poor Tamasine put her hand through there."

Miss Ingleby gasped out, but Sir Joslin frowned her down. "I trust you have not been burgled? Did it happen during the night?"

"No one saw the glass in the process of breaking, if that is what you mean."

Aware she was being as evasive as the guardian, she found him tight-lipped as he stared at the jagged hole. Had a trifle of pallor entered his features under the tan? Satisfied at these signs of discomfiture, Ottilia opened the door.

"Do come in, both of you, but be careful of the broken glass on the carpet."

Entering ahead of them and taking care where she stepped, she saw that Teresa Mellis had taken over the task she had abandoned, no doubt set thereto by Sybilla, and the company had been augmented by Francis.

Ottilia caught his expression as his gaze rested on Tamasine before his head turned in her direction. The frank admiration in his face caused her an unexpected pang and it was a moment before she could speak. By the time she had recovered herself, both Miss Ingleby and Sir Joslin Cadel were in the parlour and Tamasine's bright smile was in place.

"I knew you would find me, and I was not cold at all, and Lady Fan mended my hand."

She was pointing at Ottilia with her free hand, the other still firmly grasped by the dowager, who inclined her head towards the newcomers.

"Sir Joslin."

Then Sybilla was acquainted with the man. It was evident she had heard something of Tamasine before, although clearly not from this source.

Sir Joslin bowed. "Forgive this intrusion, my lady. I think you have not met Miss Ingleby, my ward's companion."

Sybilla acknowledged the presence of the woman with a nod, and returned her glance to the guardian. "I am glad to have the opportunity of speaking to you, sir, for I must offer my regrets that such an accident should befall your ward in my house."

At this, Miss Ingleby spoke up. "It is for Tamasine to apologise. She should not have trespassed in your grounds."

The dowager raised her brows. "No apology is necessary. Miss Roy is welcome to wander here if she wishes."

"Your ladyship is uncommonly forbearing," cut in Sir Joslin, "but my ward will not trouble you further, I believe."

"It is no trouble. Besides, I daresay Miss Roy must feel a restriction in our limited estates here. I gather these sugar plantations are substantial properties. Barbados, was it not?"

Ottilia's ears pricked up. That explained the nickname. Then the child must have been referring to sugar canes. She made a mental note to quiz Sybilla on the subject the moment the visitors had departed.

"Indeed, ma'am. My cousin's plantation was extensive and it is true that Tamasine was able to roam free. There were slaves enough to look out for her."

The mention of slaves brought about a dismaying silence, and Ottilia looked swiftly towards her husband. Francis's eyebrow quirked and he flashed a glance at his mother, whose views were known to Ottilia. The dowager was a staunch abolitionist, as evidenced when her tone became icy.

"Teresa, have you done?"

Miss Mellis sat back with a nod, and Ottilia went across to the group on the sofa, relieved to be able to promote a change of subject. "Have you found all?"

"I can see no more, but perhaps you had best check, Lady Francis. Your eyes are younger."

She stood up as she spoke, effacing herself into a corner as was her custom. Ottilia thanked her and took her place on the floor.

With one of her characteristic laughs, Tamasine piped up. "I was a pin cushion, Lavinia."

"I hope not, my dear," said her duenna in a tone that showed clearly she did not appreciate the humour of this remark. "We will bandage your hand presently."

"Let me do that." Ottilia indicated the lint and bandages Miss Mellis had brought down.

Miss Ingleby came towards the sofa. "No, indeed, ma'am, you have been incommoded far too much already. If you are satisfied there are no more splinters, pray leave the rest to me."

It was plain she was anxious to be gone, which was unsurprising, Ottilia thought, considering the evasive manner of their earlier discourse. Glancing across at the guardian, she saw Sir Joslin was leaning on a chair back as he waited. The pose was nonchalant, but an oddity about it slipped into the back of Ottilia's mind.

She laid down the magnifying glass with which she had been subjecting Tamasine's hand to a minute inspection. "I cannot see any more splinters."

"Then come, Tamasine," said Sir Joslin in a voice of authority, straightening up.

The girl rose with alacrity. "Lady Fan said I was a fairy dancing in the snow."

Ottilia forgot the reserve exhibited by the guardian and his companion. "And so you were. It gave me a deal of pleasure to watch you."

Miss Ingleby had taken hold of the girl's wrist, and Ottilia noted the tightness of her grip. She turned her charge towards the dowager. "You must thank her ladyship for taking care of you, Tamasine."

Tamasine remained where she had been put, but she did not address Sybilla, instead directing her remarks towards her companion. "You didn't catch me, Lavinia. I have had a lovely time, and now you may take me back to my eyrie."

It was said on a note of gaiety, but Ottilia, watching closely, saw the same faint look of malevolence in the blue eyes that the girl had worn earlier in addressing Teresa Mellis. An impulse to prolong the departure came over her and she used the first excuse that came to mind.

"Before you go, Sir Joslin, allow me to present my husband, Lord Francis Fanshawe."

The two men exchanged bows, and Francis then inclined his head to include Miss Ingleby, who dipped a slight curtsy.

"Forgive me, sir, if we hurry away."

Ottilia caught her husband's eye and he rose immediately to the occasion.

"You must do as you see fit, ma'am. But may we perhaps offer you some refreshment before you go?"

"Breakfast perhaps," came tartly from Sybilla, and Ottilia knew her scheme was frustrated.

Sir Joslin bowed. "We will not impose upon you any further, ma'am." He glanced at the two females and gestured to the door. "Lavinia."

Thus adjured, Miss Ingleby said a hasty farewell and drew Tamasine towards the French window. The child made no effort to speak a word of farewell or thanks to anyone in the room, but in the silence left behind, her voice was clearly audible from outside.

"Why did we not have breakfast? I am very hungry, you know. I hope you may have something better for me at home than bread and water."

Francis waited a moment for the echoes to die away, and then fixed his gaze upon his wife. She was looking a deal brighter than she had done earlier, undoubtedly due to her interest in the present rigmarole with these strangers and that peculiar girl.

"Tillie, what in the world was all that about?"

But his wife was forestalled by his mother. "You may well ask." She gestured to the window. "You will note the wretched fellow made no offer to have the glass mended."

"Oh, I have sent for Grig, Sybilla."

Teresa's intervention went unheeded. "If this is a sample of West Indian manners, I shall soon be wishing the fellow otherwhere."

To his relief, Tillie put a question. "You have met him before?"

"He had the decency to make a courtesy call, but I've not seen hide nor hair of the fellow since."

"Is he one of these sugar barons?" Francis cut in before his mother could launch into a tirade.

"Not he, but his cousin was. Tamasine's father."

"Is he dead?" asked Tillie. "Who was he?"

"Matthew Roy. One of the Cornwall Roys, I believe."

This was puzzling to Francis. "Why in the world did they not settle in Cornwall then?"

Tillie's clear gaze came back to his face. "By Sir Joslin's attitude, I imagine they were anxious to conceal Tamasine's condition from the family."

"You think there is something seriously wrong with her?"

A jerking movement drew Francis's attention to his mother's companion and he saw her give a distinct shudder. The dowager had also seen it.

"What in the world is to do, Teresa?"

"Something wrong? You have only to look at the window!" She turned to Francis. "Is there nothing we may do while we wait for Grig to repair it?"

He was provoked into flippancy. "Remove to the drawing room upstairs."

"Pull the drape across, Francis."

He went to the window to do his mother's bidding, but again looked to his wife. "Yes, but what is all this about the window?"

"Miss Mellis thinks Tamasine deliberately broke the glass so that she might get in."

"Great heavens! That little slip of a thing?"

"My thoughts exactly, Mama." Francis paused as he set a hand to the curtain, looking back to where Teresa was perched in her usual prim fashion on the edge of a chair near the fire. "It takes a deal of strength to smash through glass."

"She punched it."

"With her fist? Are you sure, Teresa?"

"I saw her put her hand through the hole."

As much astonished by this sudden garrulousness on Teresa's part as by what she had said, Francis wordlessly brought his gaze to bear again on his wife.

"If she did not do it, how was the glass broken, Fan?"

A thought occurred to Francis and he pulled the curtain aside again, searching about the debris on the carpet.

"What are you looking for?"

"Unless the girl's hand was severely bruised," he answered, turning his attention to the area further afield from the French windows, "I suspect there will be a stone in here somewhere. It may have rolled some distance."

"A stone?" His mother's tone was arctic and Francis inwardly groaned. "You are saying that mindless child deliberately took a stone and smashed the glass just to get into my parlour?"

A fragment of grey beneath the escritoire near the door caught Francis's eye. "Aha." He crossed swiftly towards it and bent down. "There we are. The wall must have stopped it." Seizing the object, he rose with it in his hand, hefting it for weight. It fitted neatly into his palm.

Tillie came to meet him, looking closely at the offending missile. "It looks quite small."

"Small but serviceable." He met his wife's searching glance. "Not the work of a mindless child, Tillie."

"No, indeed."

He noted the worried frown between her brows. "What did you make of her?"

An odd look flashed in her eyes and her tone was strangely brittle. "Apart from her extraordinary beauty, you mean?"

Taken aback, Francis wondered what in the world this signified. Some instinct warned him to refrain from asking in company. Instead he held her gaze. "Yes, she is ravishing. But it does not take a genius to see how weirdly she behaves."

"I should think not indeed," came tartly from his mother. "Anyone can tell there is something amiss, as Teresa says."

Francis ignored this. "Tillie?"

The odd look had vanished and his wife's expression now was merely troubled. She did not answer but instead moved away towards the sofa, her gaze going to Teresa. "Miss Mellis, what do you really think?"

Surprised, Francis looked quickly across at his mother and caught her eye. That she was as much astonished to hear Teresa's opinion being sought was plain enough. But he had not become acquainted with his wife's mental powers for nothing. If Tillie turned to his mother's companion for her views, she had a sufficient reason. But Francis was unprepared for Teresa's terse response.

"I think she is deranged."

Predictably, his mother exploded. "Deranged? That is all I need! It is not enough for my son to scandalise society by marrying his mistress in unseemly haste. Now my grandson must needs make a fool of himself over a girl who is fit for Bedlam."

This was news to Francis. "Giles? How so?"

"According to that idiotic girl, he dances attendance on her every day. And I have no doubt the whole affair is clandestine."

Francis sighed. "Like father, like son?"

"Not in the least," came the snapping response. "Such conduct is far more in the vein of his mother than of Randal. And right on Phoebe's doorstep too."

Since his deceased sister-in-law's amours had been all too public, this comparison seemed unfair and Francis did not hesitate to speak his mind. "You can hardly blame the boy for being bowled over. And I have yet to learn that Giles is in the habit of chasing after every petticoat who comes within his ken."

His mother's expression told him she was ready to argue the point, but she was forestalled by Tillie.

"But you might blame him for not recognising her condition."

"But what is her condition? If Teresa is right — and I must say that the servants have heard rumours —"

Tillie's eyes lit with interest. "What rumours?"

Once again, Teresa surprised Francis, a definite quiver in her voice. "They say she is kept in an attic. For her own safety. They say she flies into rages without warning. Some even say she is dangerous." Teresa's hands were twisting in her lap. "It is too bad of them. To allow a girl of that stamp to be running around the country. Who knows what might happen?"

Francis was unsurprised to hear his wife's sharpened tone as she immediately took this up. "But it is only rumour?"

"I wish you will be quiet, Teresa," his mother snapped. "Of course it is rumour. No one knows anything for certain."

"Except that we have met her, Mama." He refrained from throwing his mother's own earlier words back in her face. "I must say she didn't strike me as dangerous."

"But one can't know," said his wife.

He bent a questioning gaze upon her. "Do you think she's mad?"

"I don't pretend to guess at it. There was a certain look in her eyes once or twice that made me wonder. She is certainly naïve, childlike in her speech. Her mind is like a butterfly and she cannot be relied upon to respond to a direct question. But I don't know, Fan. There is, I think, intelligence there."

"But it is overshadowed by naivety?"

"Something of the sort. Did you remark how she spoke of going back to her 'eyrie'? And it seemed to me that for the most part she did follow what was said."

"Follow what was said?" His mother sounded indignant. "When every sentence that came out of her mouth was utterly non sequitur?"

"Ah, but that does not necessarily mean she did not understand the trend of the conversation."

"Why, Tillie?" asked Francis, intrigued. "What makes you say so?"

"I suspect Tamasine chooses not to respond in sequence." Tillie put up a finger in a typical gesture of caution. "Which does not infer she is at one with what is going on. It is obvious that she lives in a world of her own. But it is equally so that she recognises others who live in her world."

The dowager brought the flat of her hand down onto the seat of the sofa beside her. "But you are painting the very picture of a madwoman, Ottilia."

"Yes, I rather think I am. But madness may take many forms. We do not know that Tamasine's particular insanity could be of any real danger to anyone else."

Francis was just digesting this when the sound of running feet squeaking in the snow outside came to his ears. He moved back to the window. "What the devil is it now?"

Within a moment, a scarlet figure came into view. Tamasine Roy began tapping on the glass. "Help me! Help me, pray!"

His mind a sea of conjecture, Francis opened the door. As the girl tumbled into the room, all three women rose in a body, shifting towards the window. Tillie reached her first.

"What is the matter, Tamasine?"

The girl's lovely features were flushed with exertion, and her blue eyes were wide, her cherry lips parted as she panted a little. Her voice was a squeak.

"Joslin!"

"Your guardian? What is amiss with him?"

The girl's head whipped round and she looked blankly at Francis, as if she did not expect to hear him speak. He was glad when Tillie intervened, coming to the girl and seizing her uninjured hand.

"Come, Tamasine, tell me what has happened to Joslin."

The girl's eyes turned to Tillie and she blinked rapidly several times. At last she spoke, her voice empty of any vestige of emotion. "Joslin is dead. I have killed him."

In the stunned silence that followed this announcement, Ottilia was guiltily conscious of a thread of excitement running through her. But the seriousness of the situation swiftly rose to the fore and she did not hesitate, putting out a steadying hand to the young girl's shoulder. "Where is he?"

The blue eyes met hers. "He fell down the steps."

"Where?"

"In our garden."

"Are you certain he is dead?"

Tamasine blinked. "I pushed him."

Ottilia took this in without comment. "Have you left your companion there? Lavinia?"

"Lavinia said to get help."

Relief ran through Ottilia. She was glad she'd had no time to divest herself of her outer garments as she was ready for immediate action. So also was Francis, attired in a greatcoat and boots for the purpose of following her on the walk she had perforce abandoned. She turned to him at once.

"There is no time to lose. He may still be alive."

He nodded. "I'll go on ahead. You bring the girl." He added as he stepped through the door, "And keep well wrapped up in that cloak, Tillie."

"But you don't know where to go," Ottilia called after him, shifting quickly into the aperture.

"Of course he does." The dowager's testiness was again in evidence. "Francis grew up around these parts, don't forget. He knows the house."

A new thought caught at Ottilia's attention. "Sybilla, do you have a physician you can trust?"

"Doctor Sutherland. I'll send for him at once. A pity your brother is not yet arrived."

"He could not usurp the province of the local man, in any event." She turned back to the girl. "Come, Tamasine, lead the way, if you please."

"Take care, Ottilia! Remember your condition."

Acknowledging her mother-in-law's parting shot with a slight wave, Ottilia pulled Tamasine through the doorway and shut the French window. "Can you tell me what happened as we go?"

She kept a firm hand on the girl's arm as the latter darted forward, setting a good pace across the snow-packed lawns.

"Joslin fell."

Ottilia could hear a note of excitement in her voice at the repetition. "Yes, but what happened before he fell?"

"He was laughing."

41

They rounded the corner of the house and Ottilia saw that Francis had already reached the boundary of the dowager's land and was pushing through to the road beyond.

"And?" Ottilia pursued, keeping a wary eye where she trod.

"He held his head. Like this." Tamasine put her hands to her temples at either side and swayed a little.

Could it be headache? Ottilia's mind swept across the possibilities. Had he been taken suddenly ill? Any number of conditions might have overtaken him. Then she recalled Tamasine saying she had pushed her guardian. She locked onto the point.

"Why did you push him, Tamasine?"

The girl's odd laugh sounded. "So he would fall."

A dead end. Ottilia cast about for another way to get at the facts, slowing a little as the snowbound ground under her feet began to dip. "Did you say something to make Joslin laugh, Tamasine?"

The girl looked blank. "Lavinia asked him what was funny. She shouted up."

Shouted up? Then the companion had been below them. At the bottom of the steps? Useless to expect Tamasine to clarify the point. It struck Ottilia suddenly that perhaps Sir Joslin had not in fact been laughing at all. Had he been in pain, he might have made sounds that were mistaken by his ward. And indeed by Miss Ingleby, who had asked him what was funny.

The boundary was within reach now, and Ottilia saw a gap in the hedgerow that Francis had used. It was plain that Tamasine had used it also for she headed directly towards it.

"Is this how you got in?"

The girl turned features aglow with delight towards her. "They can't make me stay where they put me."

Evidently. Unless they locked her in perhaps? Ottilia followed as Tamasine pushed through the gap and tripped lightly across the road. The snow here had already been trodden down, and tracks showed the passage of wheels. Then the roads were not impassable. Ottilia dared to hope her brother would be able to make it through after all.

A low stone wall separated the road from the property across the way, and Tamasine easily climbed over it, moving swiftly up the slight incline on the other side.

Ottilia called to her. "Wait for me, Tamasine! Remember, I do not know where your steps are."

The girl halted and turned, pointing uphill. "There."

"Very well, but let us go together."

To Ottilia's surprise, Tamasine waited for her to catch up. Her eyes were bright and it was evident these events were exciting her unduly. If she truly was deranged, nothing could be worse for her than to be party to a scene that must command the highest intensity of emotion.

Ottilia deliberately slowed her pace, which she was glad enough to do for even the little effort required to climb the incline was taking its toll. Aware that her pregnancy tired her more than usual, she was both impatient and dutiful in obedience to necessity.

"You have a deal of snow on your own account," she said, by way of distracting Tamasine from the present moment.

"Oh, yes, but I like to explore."

"So I gather."

"Simeon will let me go where I like."

Would he indeed? Then it augured little for his care of the child. Ottilia tried a throw in the dark. "Is Simeon your brother perhaps?"

Tamasine laughed out. "No, silly Lady Fan. I have no brother. Simeon is my cousin. He hid in the canes too."

Then this cousin Simeon had also been in Barbados. "Is Simeon in England?"

But this was beyond Tamasine, it appeared, for she changed tack. "Joslin won't stop him coming now."

Not if the poor man was dead. With a sensation of shock, Ottilia recalled the girl's earlier startling comment that Simeon would come when Joslin was dead. Surely she had not the wit to anticipate the fellow's death? If she had, the implication was unpleasant indeed. There was no point in questioning the girl further on the matter of this cousin. Better to wait for enlightenment from Miss Ingleby, assuming it was needed.

As they breasted the rise, a large white house surrounded by extensive gardens came into view below them. Some way ahead, Ottilia could just see Francis and another figure. He was bending over something on the snow which she took to be the afflicted guardian. Urgency engulfed her.

"We must hurry."

It did not take many minutes to traverse the ground that led to the next dip, but the figures ahead were lost to sight as they neared. Abruptly, Ottilia found herself at the top of a long flight of wide stone steps. The unexpectedness at once made her conscious how easy it would be to miss one's footing and fall. She paused to catch her breath, taking in the scene below.

Near a stone balustrade at the foot of the steps lay the crumpled body of a man. Sir Joslin was unlikely to have escaped serious injury in falling so far, if he had survived at all. Francis was crouched above the body, and Miss Ingleby stood over him. Even at this distance, Ottilia could see she was shaking.

Tamasine began running down the steps, causing Francis to look up. He raised a hand in salute and returned to whatever he was doing. The concentration of attention indicated there was something there to discover and Ottilia lifted her petticoats and held her cloak a little aloft with her elbows as she started her own descent, of necessity taking it slow. She stopped a couple of steps before the end, looking closely at what she could see of the guardian.

He was on his side, with one leg twisted awkwardly underneath him, the other set in a way that must be holding the body in position. One arm had fallen in front and stood at an acute angle over what was likely a broken wrist. The other was hardly visible, but half his face was open to the skies, the other hidden in the snow. His hat had come off and was nowhere to be seen.

The companion had shifted away, taking Tamasine with her and Francis stood up. Ottilia eyed his grave countenance. "He is dead?"

"I'm afraid so. But Miss Ingleby says he was alive when she sent Tamasine for help. You'd best take a look, my love."

He gave place and Ottilia came down the remaining steps and moved to examine Sir Joslin from in front. Dropping to her haunches, she looked first at what she could see of his face. Had it not been for the awkwardness of his position, the relaxedness of his features made him look as he might in sleep, in perfect repose. Yet his countenance was pale, with some lividity or bruising around the temple — from the fall, perhaps? Ottilia reached to pull up his closed eyelid.

"That is unexpected," she remarked, casting a glance across to Francis, who had moved behind the body and come down to her level again, watching her movements.

"What is?"

"The pupil is contracted. I was thinking of apoplexy, but then one would expect dilation."

Her hand brushed the man's cheek and found it damp. Recalling the sheen she had noticed on his brow and his damp palm, she wondered at it. Exertion? Or something more? Was the sweating profuse? In the periphery of her mind she took in having forgotten to put on her gloves and her hands were cold and possibly a trifle numb. She ran her fingers more firmly down Sir Joslin's still features. The dampness was strong and unmistakeable.

"He was sweating a great deal."

"What does that mean?"

"I had thought earlier he had exerted himself too much, but this signals some sort of illness." Ottilia had moved to slip her hand beneath the dead man's coat, looking for the condition of his shirt. It felt decidedly moist. "He is wet through, I think."

"But his body is still warm."

"Relatively. It will cool rapidly in this weather." She gestured to the slack face. "See, there is already a waxen tinge coming in, though he may have died mere minutes ago."

"How long since the girl came to us, do you think?"

Ottilia glanced across to where the companion was standing at a little distance, still clearly in shock, one hand firmly grasping Tamasine's wrist. Both females were watching them. Ottilia lowered her voice.

"Five or ten minutes? Perhaps a little more. There may have been some delay before she was sent for help. I daresay Miss Ingleby wasted a little time in trying to rouse him."

Francis frowned down at the body. "She said she had not moved him, for I asked her particularly."

"I doubt she would have the strength."

Her spouse was looking at Sir Joslin's bent arm. "Is that wrist broken?"

"It looks like it. There may well be other fractures from the fall. There is a contusion on his forehead which may have hastened his death."

"What, could he die from such a knock?"

"I suspect he was dying in any event. A blow to the temple would likely make him unconscious, so that any effort to rouse him must fail."

She saw Francis's eyes flick across to the two women. "Then you don't think it was the fall that killed him?"

Ottilia sighed a little. "For Tamasine's sake, I wish I might rule it out altogether, but it has undoubtedly contributed, although it does not look to have been entirely responsible."

"Then what did kill him?" came with a trifle of impatience from her husband.

"I wish I knew, Fan. It will take a post-mortem to be certain, but it looks very like an apoplectic seizure, apart from the sweating and the pupils. I cannot easily account for those, except to suppose he was suffering from an illness, which might have precipitated an apoplexy." Suddenly she recalled Sir Joslin leaning on the chair back in the dowager's parlour. Realisation struck. "He was supporting himself."

Her spouse frowned across at her. "What are you talking about?"

"I believe he was already feeling out of sorts when he came to the Dower House. He had difficulty remaining upright then, I think."

Francis rose to his feet. "There is nothing more to be done for him." He held out a hand and Ottilia allowed him to pull her up. "I had best see if there are men in the house who may carry him inside."

"The companion will know." Ottilia moved towards the woman, raising her voice. "Miss Ingleby!"

Thus addressed, the duenna started a little. "Yes?"

Francis took over. "Are there male servants in your house?"

"Why, yes. Joslin has —" Miss Ingleby broke off, threw a hand to her mouth, distress coming into her eyes.

Moved, Ottilia crossed quickly towards her. "Do not upset yourself, pray. My husband only wishes to have Sir Joslin conveyed into the house."

The companion nodded, and Ottilia noted that Tamasine, whose eyes were still trained upon the body, showed no sign of personal grief nor appeared to notice that of Miss Ingleby.

"There are two men who accompanied us from Barbados. Shall I —?"

"Stay where you are," Francis said. "I will find them."

He began walking towards the house, and abruptly Tamasine called after him. "Hemp and Cuffy."

Francis halted, turning back with a puzzled look in his face. "I beg your pardon?"

"She means their names," explained Miss Ingleby. "Hemp and Cuffy. Ask Mrs Whiting, the housekeeper — or the butler Lomax. Anyone will tell you."

Watching Tamasine, Ottilia wondered at her ability to follow conversations when she apparently had her attention elsewhere. Could one but persuade her to respond to a direct question, she might well have a deal to add to the picture. This being unlikely, however, Ottilia chose instead to tackle the companion.

"Miss Ingleby, are you up to giving me an account of what happened here?"

The woman looked surprised, but Ottilia did not trouble to explain her interest, certain Miss Ingleby was too shocked to dispute a stranger's right to ask. Ottilia smiled at her.

"You look exhausted. Why don't you sit down?"

She went to the low stone balustrade, thrust away the layer of snow that lay there, and then rubbed the damp and cold from her hands. With obvious relief, the woman sank down. She had not released Tamasine, who made no objection, but sat down beside her, looking expectantly up at Ottilia.

"That is more comfortable." Gentling her voice, Ottilia added persuasively, "Come, you will feel the better for unburdening what is in your mind."

A sigh escaped the woman. "Yes. I feel as if I can scarcely remember."

"I understand, but I have no doubt you will recollect everything once you begin."

Tamasine trained her eyes on her duenna's profile as the latter drew a deep breath. Again, Ottilia was moved to wonder at the child's ability to fix her attention.

Miss Ingleby averted her gaze from the body. "Tamasine chose to walk with Joslin and I had gone on a little ahead. I am not at all sure what happened. I was down here, and I heard Joslin laughing. I looked to see what amused him, and then he — he lost his balance and fell."

"How did he fall? Was it immediate? Did he pitch forward? Did he reel where he stood? Tamasine told me that he put his hands to his head."

49

The girl's gaze turned swiftly to Ottilia. "He fell over and over."

A faint frown creased Miss Ingleby's forehead. "I don't recall. I was so shocked to see it. He fell headlong, I think. And then he rolled." A sobbing gasp escaped her. "He landed at my feet, all in a heap."

"And you knelt to him at once, I imagine?"

She nodded. "Yes. I called him. He didn't answer." It came out in spasms, a staccato recital. "I felt for his pulse. But then I saw he was breathing. With difficulty. Dragging his breath as if it hurt. His eyes were closed. He looked — he looked asleep, but heavily."

"Did he seem to be in a stupor?"

Miss Ingleby looked up, a trifle wild-eyed with the recital of her recollection. "Yes, I think. I tried to wake him."

"How?"

"I shouted. I may have shaken his shoulder."

"But you did not try to move him."

"Onto his back? No, for I thought he might have broken a limb. I did not want to make bad worse."

"You did right," Ottilia soothed. "Then what happened?"

Miss Ingleby's cheeks were wet, unregarded tears seeping from her eyes. "I didn't know what to do. I sent Tamasine for help."

"I came for Lady Fan," piped up the girl, her bright smile lighting her face.

"That was well done of you," said Ottilia, but returned her attention immediately to the companion. "What happened after Tamasine left you?"

Miss Ingleby shook her head. "I hardly know. Joslin's breathing quietened, and I thought he was recovering. I called him again and again, but to no avail."

"His breathing grew less and less?"

A great sigh lifted the woman's shoulders and she sagged. "I could not judge. He looked so peaceful, as if he was merely asleep. If you would ask me just when he ceased to breathe, I cannot tell you. By the time your husband arrived, he had gone." She shuddered. "It was all so quick. It seems impossible he could be dead, and yet…"

Her eyes strayed to the body and she began softly to weep. Ottilia laid a hand on her shoulder, but her gaze was drawn to Tamasine. The girl was looking puzzled, as if this display of grief had no meaning for her. She watched in silence for a moment, and then turned her blue orbs on Ottilia.

"Why is she crying? She did not love Joslin. She is not his cousin."

Miss Ingleby's sobs redoubled and she withdrew her hand, which all this time had still been clutching Tamasine's wrist. Ottilia watched the girl closely, alert for any untoward motion.

"Your companion is in shock, Tamasine. And I am sure she was fond of Sir Joslin. One does not need to love someone to be shocked and grieved at their passing."

Tamasine blinked. "You are not crying."

"But I did not know your guardian."

The girl rose abruptly, moving to stand over the body. Ottilia followed closely, standing beside her, with one hand ready to seize the girl, should she make any attempt at leaving the area. The last thing needed at this moment was for Tamasine to go off exploring.

51

In a gesture that said more about her state of mind than any peculiarity of speech, the girl put out one foot and prodded at the inert body. "He is not pretending." The tone was matter-of-fact.

"I'm afraid not."

Leaning down, Tamasine cupped her hands to her mouth. "Joslin, are you dead?"

Ottilia grasped the girl's arm and pulled her gently back. "My dear child, he cannot hear you."

Tamasine turned to look at her and the china-blue eyes went suddenly dim. Then the girl opened her mouth wide and began to scream.

CHAPTER THREE

The wails reached Francis's ears as he stood in the wide hall, in rapid conversation with the housekeeper. She was a small woman, a trifle too stout for her height, giving her a dwarfish look. She had been staring up into Francis's face as he explained the situation, and it was evident the reality of events had not yet fully penetrated her mind for she seemed dazed and unable to do more than nod from time to time. Before he had an opportunity to request her to find the two servants, the screams from outside distracted them both.

"Miss Tam, that is." The woman put her hands to her ears in a gesture Francis took to be automatic. "I'd best make her room ready."

She bustled, turning towards the stairs, but Francis reached out to seize her arm.

"Wait, if you please!" The housekeeper looked at his hand, blinking confusedly. "I need the services of your two servants, Mrs Whiting. Cuffy and Hemp, I think it was. We cannot leave Sir Joslin lying out in the snow."

Her gaze widened and at last the expected shock leapt into it. She nodded several times. "Yes. Yes, I will get them. Or no, I will tell Lomax."

But even as she spoke, the green baize door at the back of the hall opened and a spare man of middle years came through. He stopped short at sight of Francis, a frown descending onto his brow.

"What's to do, Mrs Whiting? Shouldn't you go up?"

"It's the master, Lomax!" The housekeeper moved towards the newcomer with pudgy hands held out. "This gentleman says he's dead!"

The man's features blenched, although he accepted Mrs Whiting's hands and held them briefly, his eyes flying to Francis.

"I'm afraid it is true," Francis said, his tone suitably grave, if loud against the continued lamentations from outside. "Sir Joslin had the misfortune to fall down the garden steps."

Lomax put aside the housekeeper and came up to Francis. Eyes of an oddly light grey looked searchingly into his. 'He was killed by the fall, sir?"

Francis found himself in a quandary. The notion did not march with Tillie's analysis, but how much was it politic to reveal? He opted for caution. "We cannot be certain of anything until a doctor has seen him. For the present, I am anxious to have your master conveyed into the house. I gather a couple of fellows by the names of Hemp and Cuffy may be willing to assist."

For a moment the butler did not speak, but only eyed Francis in a considering way that he found decidedly disconcerting. Not to mention discourteous in a mere servant. Then the fellow seemed to make up his mind.

"I'll fetch them, sir."

Turning on his heel, he made all speed towards the green baize door and disappeared through it. Mrs Whiting had sunk into a cane chair placed by a large table to one side of the hall, upon which reposed a plethora of unrelated objects. His attention on the housekeeper, Francis vaguely took in a couple of candelabra still stuffed with last night's stubs, a collection of scattered papers, along with a whip, an odd man's glove, and several open containers spilling over with odds and ends.

It struck Francis as peculiarly masculine, besides arguing a lack of that sort of order usually obtaining in the houses of the English gentry. And with the death of the principal householder, the situation looked set to deteriorate. On impulse, he put a question.

"Who will take charge now that your master is dead?"

Mrs Whiting's glance flew up, dismay writ large upon her countenance. She drew a shaky breath. "I hardly know, sir. I suppose Miss Ingleby — or no, there is Miss Tam's aunt, I believe, but I have no acquaintance with her."

"She was not in the West Indies then?"

"No, sir."

"But you were?"

"All of us," said Mrs Whiting on another uncertain breath. She brushed a distracted hand across a plump forehead. "At least — not the maids or the cook."

"But yourself and Lomax?"

She nodded, looking a trifle puzzled at this line of questioning. Francis knew it was scarcely his business, but he had not learned a trick or two from his darling wife for nothing. Tillie would wish to know every tidbit of background detail, and he might as well glean what he could. He persisted.

"Miss Ingleby was also of the party who came from abroad, I gather?"

The woman's astonishment was plain, but she answered willingly enough. "Yes, sir. Miss Ingleby has been with Miss Tam since she was fourteen. None knows better than she how to do when Miss Tam…"

She faded out, rising with a little difficulty and moving towards the closed front door. Francis became aware that the cries of the young girl were growing louder. Before the women could enter, the party from the nether regions crowded through the green baize door: the butler, followed by two burly black men dressed in the livery of footmen. One glance instilled confidence these men were eminently capable of bearing the burden of the dead man's body.

"Ah, Cuffy and Hemp, I presume? Good day to you. Let us go and secure your poor master."

Upon which, Francis turned for the front door just in time to witness Miss Ingleby entering, dragging behind her the recalcitrant source of the unceasing racket. Tempted to cover his ears, he refrained, standing aside as the cavalcade swept into the hall.

"Oh, hush, Miss Tam, do," the housekeeper begged, having attached herself to Tamasine in a bid to assist by pushing from behind.

Miss Ingleby had the girl fast by one wrist. "Upstairs at once!"

Francis was tempted to protest at this treatment. Surely a more gentle approach would better serve? The girl had suffered a severe shock. Then it was borne in upon him that the squeals were rather those of protest than sorrow. At what point the quality of the girl's cries had changed, Francis could not say, his attention having been elsewhere. He recalled the oddity of her earlier behaviour and the discussion concerning her sanity.

He raised his voice. "My wife is still outside with Sir Joslin?"

Miss Ingleby checked briefly in her way to the stairs, throwing a glance over her shoulder. "Lady Francis said she would await your coming." Then the woman proceeded on her way, admonishing her charge as she went. "That is enough, Tamasine. Cease this nonsensical noise at once, or it will be the worse for you."

Again conscious of a sliver of sympathy for the child, Francis signalled to the waiting coterie of male servants and headed for the front door.

Ottilia watched the two footmen lay their burden down upon the coverlet of the four-poster in the apartment given over to Sir Joslin's use. It was of a fair size, but a cursory glance around showed it to be sparsely furnished. Besides the bed and bedside cabinet, there was only a large press and a long mirror, no doubt hired along with the house. Making a mental note to find opportunity to search the press, Ottilia returned her attention to the matter at hand.

Both the fellows Cuffy and Hemp, notwithstanding their great bulk, had dissolved into grief at sight of the wreck of their master. Neither one, to Ottilia's mingled sympathy and surprise, openly sobbed or ventured any remark. Instead, they obeyed Francis's terse instructions on the manner of lifting Sir Joslin's corpse, their tears falling freely throughout.

The care with which they handled him was marked, although they were panting with effort by the end. Ottilia read affection in the way the older of the two took time and trouble to dispose the limbs suitably despite the evident disarrangement of bone caused by his fall. As the men stepped back from the bed, Francis went forward.

"That was kindly done, and I must thank you."

He held out a hand to the nearest of the footmen, the younger of the two, whose colour was several degrees lighter than that of his colleague. Ottilia saw the fellow hesitate, glancing first at the hand and then at his fellow. The older man gave a brief nod — of permission? The other wiped his hand quickly down his costume and then reached to take the one proffered by Francis.

Francis shook the hand and smiled. "Are you Cuffy or Hemp?"

"Hemp, sir," said the fellow, his voice low and deep, in keeping with his large athletic frame.

"You were fond of your master, I think?"

Hemp put up a thumb and wiped at the residue of tears under his eyes. "Master Joslin was a good man."

The veriest trace of accent caught at Ottilia's attention and she wondered if Hemp had been especially educated for his sojourn in England. Francis nodded at the man and turned to the older fellow, again holding out his hand.

"You must be Cuffy then."

Was there a slight look of hostility in the dark eyes that raked Francis before the man ventured to take his hand? The older man was of beefier build than Hemp and not as tall. He had a bull-like head and there was a touch of grizzle in the tight black curls. His voice was even more a baritone than that of his colleague, and his accent was stronger.

"Master is dying how, sir? He is no flatfoot. Why is he falling?"

Francis released the man's hand. "I'm afraid we can't tell yet, Cuffy. We need a doctor's opinion before any conclusion can be made."

Ottilia saw her spouse hesitate, flicking a glance across at her. She gave an infinitesimal nod, and was startled to note that both Hemp and Cuffy evidently saw it. Each pair of eyes must have followed the direction of Francis's gaze.

"It is not certain that the fall killed him." Francis looked from one to the other. "It is possible your master was taken ill."

At that, Ottilia saw Hemp's glance shoot across to Cuffy's, and a look was exchanged. That these men knew something was evident. Before she could signal Francis to probe, however, the butler walked into the room. He had been briefly pointed out by her husband when the men had come out to collect Sir Joslin's body, but had elected not to accompany the corpse upstairs, murmuring an excuse of needing to console the rest of the staff, who were in a state of shock and upset.

He jerked his head towards the door, his eyes on the two footmen. "You two go down now."

Hemp and Cuffy made no attempt to argue, although Cuffy's steps lagged as he approached the door and he turned his head to look once more upon the sight of his master's body lying in the attitude of peace in which he and Hemp had laid him.

The moment they left the room, the butler looked towards Francis, hardly sparing a glance for Ottilia. "I am indebted to you, sir, but I think we need not trespass further upon your good nature."

Ottilia saw her spouse's lips tighten, and the clipped tone she knew well signalled his displeasure.

"We are only too pleased to be of service. You are perhaps unaware that Miss Roy came across to Lady Polbrook's abode to request our aid."

A frown descended onto the man's brow. "Indeed, sir? Then you are Lord Francis Fanshawe, I take it?"

"Perfectly correct, Lomax. And since I understand there is no one immediately in a position to take charge of matters here, I must feel it incumbent upon me to do what I may to assist the household in this unhappy affair."

It was all Ottilia could do not to burst out in astonishment. What in the world did Francis mean by it? He was far more apt to object to her thrusting herself into such matters than to wilfully declare an obligation.

The butler seemed to share her emotions, forgetful of his position as he burst out, "But it has nothing whatsoever to do with you!"

"For a start," said Francis, ignoring the remark, "it behoves me to lock this room until the doctor arrives."

"What doctor, my lord?"

"My mother sent for her own physician, Doctor Sutherland. I imagine he will arrive presently."

The butler looked chagrined and Ottilia regarded him with interest. Did he object to the doctor in particular, or was there a reason to reject outside help? Or was it that he did not want the door locked against him?

She butted in without ceremony. "Do you perhaps use a different physician in this house?"

Lomax seemed only now to take in her presence. He gave a brief little bow. "It has not yet proved necessary to call anyone in, madam."

"It will be more proper for you to address my wife as 'my lady'." There was an edge to Francis's voice that signalled to Ottilia his state of mind.

"As your lordship pleases." Ottilia thought the note of urbanity feigned as the man executed another neat little bow, and indicated the door. "After you, my lady."

She threw a glance at her husband and found a spark in the brown gaze. She felt it politic to comply with the butler's intention before Francis could vent his annoyance.

"Thank you, Lomax."

She nodded as she passed him, moving out into the gallery, which let onto the principal first floor rooms. There was a moment of hesitation before the butler followed her out, and she turned to watch Francis ostentatiously remove the key from the inside of the door and lock the room.

"I will keep this for the time being."

Lomax fairly glared. "Upon what right, my lord?"

Francis's lip curled in a smile of scant warmth. "I believe I have the advantage of you, Lomax, in having been through this procedure on my own account. Should it be necessary to call in the coroner, it is essential Sir Joslin's person remains untouched, as must also his possessions in this room."

The butler's eyes widened and Ottilia saw a tithe of horror — or was it fear? — fly into them before it was swiftly veiled. "What do you imply, sir?"

"I imply," said Francis with obvious deliberation, "that it is better for members of the household not to be in a position to be held accountable for anything that may go missing. Or indeed, for anything that might arrive."

"Arrive! What can your lordship mean by this?"

"Evidence, Lomax. I am speaking of potential evidence."

The butler's thin chest rose and fell sharply and a flush showed through the slight tan of his skin. There was positive venom in the look he cast upon Francis, but he did not hesitate to voice a protest, and with acrimony.

"You are suggesting foul play."

Francis slipped the key into his pocket. "I am suggesting nothing, Lomax. I am merely setting in train the usual precautions to be taken in the circumstance of an unexpected death. Your master was in the prime of life. The authorities may take the view that such a fall as he took ought not to have proved fatal."

For several seconds, the butler stared his defiance at Francis, who met his regard with one of his bland looks. Then, without a word, Lomax turned on his heel and marched away down the gallery.

Ottilia watched him run swiftly down the stairs. As soon as he became lost to sight, she turned to her spouse, unable to keep the mischief from her voice. "Dear me, Fan, have I to deem myself usurped in the role of investigator?"

An eyebrow quirked. "I am merely paving the way for you, my love. I could see the wretched fellow would balk if we did not take a high hand at the outset."

"We?"

He laughed. "A taste of your own medicine, Tillie. Let it be a lesson to you for the future."

She gave a gurgle. "Consider me thoroughly chastened."

"Yes, and pigs have wings," said her fond spouse. But he reached to take her hand and bring it to his lips. "And now what, if I may make so bold?"

Ottilia looked back to the bedroom door. "I should dearly love to make a preliminary search."

"I suggest you wait for the advent of the doctor. We will be hard put to it to explain ourselves should Lomax return to find us hunting through his master's things."

"After your refusal to allow anyone to tamper with the place? Yes, I imagine so."

"We had better go down." He eyed her narrowly as they started for the stairs. "Are you fatigued? You have been on your feet too long, I dare say."

Impatience riffled through Ottilia, but she bit back a retort. "I am perfectly well, Fan."

"Yes, but you ought to sit down after all this excitement."

"For heaven's sake, Fan, I am not made of china!"

"You are pregnant, and you know perfectly well you tire easily."

The tone was flat, all emotion withheld, and he insisted on supporting her as she began to descend the stairs. Ottilia reined in irritation with difficulty, perforce accepting his aid. To her chagrin, she did find herself a trifle fagged as they reached the hall again, and was not averse to sitting down when Francis led her inexorably to a cane chair to one side of the long table.

"If everyone would cease reminding me that I am over-exerting myself, I am sure I should not even notice any fatigue," she said aggrievedly, as she sank down.

"By everyone, I presume you refer to me," returned Francis, releasing her as she settled.

Ottilia read in his tone the elaborate affirmation of patience he had recently adopted, as if she were a recalcitrant child who must be humoured. She snapped.

"If you will persist in addressing me in that detestable fashion, Francis, I swear I shall scream!"

He did not speak, only regarding her in an enigmatic way that served to increase her ill temper, as if to outline the reason for it. For a moment her frustration intensified, but she managed to refrain from bursting out. And then the increasingly familiar sensation of guilt attacked her and her spirits dropped. She sighed aloud.

"Fan, I wish sometimes I didn't love you so deeply. It would make this a deal easier."

A rueful look crept into his eyes and his lips quirked in the way that never failed to soften her heart. The gentleness he was wont to use with her returned. "It will pass, my dearest one. It is not forever."

"Six more months," she groaned, putting out a hand and curling it into his fingers, which held hers tightly.

"Mama says you will come out of your megrims sooner than that."

"Megrims?" Ottilia threw up her eyes. "I might have guessed you would go to Sybilla for comfort."

"Advice, rather."

Ottilia grimaced. "Have I been hateful?"

"Horribly. But I am schooling myself to endure it."

She was obliged to laugh, but a sound from above recalled her attention to the matter at hand. She gestured. "Who is coming down?"

Francis shifted to the bottom of the stair and looked up. Instead of answering, he raised his voice to be heard from above. "Ah, Miss Ingleby. How does your charge?"

The companion did not answer this directly, Ottilia noted. Feeling at once energised with the freshness of interest, she rose from her chair and moved close enough to be able to see the woman.

"Mrs Whiting has her in hand." Arriving at the bottom of the stairs, she addressed herself to Francis. "Did you see Sir Joslin safely bestowed, sir?"

"Indeed. Hemp and Cuffy were assiduous in their care of him."

Miss Ingleby nodded, although there was a troubled look in her eyes, Ottilia thought. She sounded vague. "They were both devoted to Joslin. I cannot think what they will do without him."

Ottilia came up to her and took hold of one her hands, which was wafting ineffectually. "My dear Miss Ingleby, should you not see to your own needs? A nip of brandy perhaps? You have sustained a shock quite as severe as your charge."

The companion tugged her hand away, and her lip trembled. "I will survive it. Tamasine is another matter. I cannot think how we are to do."

"Mrs Whiting spoke of an aunt," Francis interjected, making Ottilia prick up her ears.

"Mrs Delabole, yes. She is the late Mr Roy's sister."

Ottilia made her presence felt again. "Is there no male relative who might take charge of Tamasine? She spoke of Simeon, I think."

Miss Ingleby jerked, as if the notion disturbed her. "Upon no account!"

"The aunt then?" suggested Francis.

"I must write," uttered the companion on a sharply indrawn breath.

Ottilia eyed her in no little growth of suspicion. There appeared to be much here to ponder. She tried again. "If Sir Joslin was her guardian, surely some provision was made in the event of his demise?"

Miss Ingleby's eyes flashed fire. "He was not expecting to die! Why should he make provision?"

Because, Ottilia might have said, he was dealing with a creature fit for an asylum. Such a remark could only have a negative effect. She attempted a soothing note. "My poor Miss Ingleby, I fear you are like to be much incommoded by this unfortunate affair. I beg you will allow us to assist you."

The companion stared, blankness in her gaze. "You? Why should you, pray? It has naught to do with you!"

Ottilia felt Francis bristle, and he spoke before she could intervene, his tone edged with anger. "My wife is merely trying to help, Miss Ingleby. I make every allowance for your present sorrow, but I suggest you mend your attitude."

The companion's gaze turned to encounter his and Ottilia readily noted her resentment. The creature's voice dropped, but she abated not one jot of ire. "I am glad of such assistance as you have both given, sir, but I can manage now. This matter need not trouble you further."

"Yes, so Lomax said also. But I tell you, as I told him, that I have no intention of removing from here, nor of unlocking Sir Joslin's door, until the doctor has seen him."

Miss Ingleby appeared stupefied, fixing Francis with an unblinking stare. When she spoke at last, her tone was vibrant with passion. "You locked his room? Upon what authority?"

"None," said Francis frankly. "I did so upon my own determination, and from a knowledge of what is necessary on occasions of this kind. I dare say the authorities will thank me."

"As I will not! It is not your place!"

"No, it is not. But I stand by it. If Sir Joslin's death proves to have been premeditated, you may well have cause to be glad of my actions."

Miss Ingleby went white. "No! No, do not say so. She did not mean to push him!"

"Tamasine?" cut in Ottilia quickly. "But we are not talking of that."

The woman's wild eyes came around to her. "What can you mean? What can you possibly mean?"

"As yet, nothing very much, Miss Ingleby. But it is evident Sir Joslin was taken ill before Tamasine pushed him."

"Ill? One of his turns?"

"What turns?" asked Francis swiftly, forestalling Ottilia.

Miss Ingleby caught a hand to her mouth, clenching the fingers. "An old condition. He suffered recurring bouts now and then."

Ottilia became brisk. "What was this condition?"

"His chest." The woman's hand came down and she joined it to the other, jerking her fingers. "I believe it was brought on by fever originally. Pleurisy, they thought. He was never strong afterwards."

Ottilia felt Francis's regard and glanced at him.

66

"That might explain everything," he said shortly.

"Possibly." She turned again to the companion. "What form did these bouts take?"

Miss Ingleby shrugged, shifting away a little across the hall to the table. "Joslin would not say much." She fiddled absently with one of the stubs of candle, pinching the blackened wick between unquiet fingers. "I observed that he became short of breath, and he would take to his bed for a few days. None but Cuffy was permitted to attend him."

Ottilia thought of the sweating and the hands put to the man's head before he fell. "Did he experience a recurrence of fever? Or headaches?"

The companion did not turn, her attention apparently centred upon the candle stub, which she had removed from its holder and now began playing it between her hands. "I don't know. He would not let me near him at such times." She threw a look over her shoulder. "You had better address these questions to Cuffy." A faintly acidic laugh came, and she added a rider. "Not that he will tell you."

This seemed only too likely, from what she had seen of the fellow Cuffy's evident regard for the dead man. In Ottilia's experience, devotion such as his inspired a stubborn sort of loyalty. Nevertheless, she resolved to secure an interview with him as soon as convenience allowed. She was just about to enquire further into the origins of Sir Joslin's illness when the green baize door opened at the back and a gentleman she knew well entered the hall, took a swift glance round and stopped short.

Giles, Lord Bennifield, heir to the Marquisate of Polbrook, was young, with light hair falling loosely to his shoulders above a striking countenance. His nose was straight, his lip prettily curved and a pair of green eyes held a startled expression as they travelled from Ottilia to her husband. The boy broke into speech.

"Good God! Uncle Francis, you here?"

Francis's brows had snapped together. "I might ask the same question, Giles. You must be very sure of your welcome to be entering the house through the back premises."

The young man flushed with evident discomfort as he moved further into the hall. "I was in the stables when I heard the news," he said by way of excuse. "I took the quickest route to find —"

He broke off, his colour deepening still more.

"Miss Roy?" came on a faintly ironic note from Francis. "You thought to administer comfort, I dare say."

"Well, yes," Giles admitted, his glance flicking to the other two occupants of the hall. He executed a small bow in Ottilia's direction. "I beg your pardon, Aunt. How do you do?"

Risking her spouse's wrath, Ottilia smiled at him. "Pray don't trouble with the formalities in such an extremity as this, Giles."

He turned to Miss Ingleby, but she forestalled him, speaking quick and low, her continuing upset obvious to Ottilia. "You should not be here, my lord. You need not suppose Sir Joslin's prohibition to have lapsed. His wishes are still paramount in this house."

To his credit, Giles did not flinch, and there was neither resentment nor hostility in his tone. "I came at Miss Roy's behest, ma'am. I had no notion Sir Joslin had met with an accident."

"Miss Roy's behest?" Francis's tone was sharp, and he threw a glance at Ottilia which she met with raised brows. "She sent to you? When?"

Giles had evidently not missed the exchange of looks for his glance went from his uncle to Ottilia and back again. "Early this morning."

"At what time precisely?" Ottilia's mind was running with conjecture.

Before Giles could answer, Miss Ingleby intervened, a vibrancy of wrath in her voice. "Who came to you, sir? Who in this house had the temerity to take such a message?"

Giles was frowning now. "One of the footmen. Hemp, is it? The younger of the two."

"That fellow!" The disparaging note was pronounced. "Oh, it was ever thus! The dratted girl can twist him any way she wills."

Ottilia caught Francis eyeing her again and dropped her voice to a mutter. "The time, Fan."

He nodded and turned instantly to his nephew. "It is imperative that you remember the precise time this fellow Hemp came to you, Giles."

The boy shrugged. "I don't know it precisely. I had not yet breakfasted."

"That's no use, for neither have we." Francis bent a direful frown upon his relative. "Do you tell me you waited upon breakfast after receiving an urgent request to come here?"

"For God's sake, Uncle Francis, she didn't say it was urgent!"

Giles threw up his hands as he spoke in a gesture abruptly similar to one Francis was apt to make and Ottilia stared at him. It had not before occurred to her that Lord Bennifield in any way resembled the menfolk on his father's side, for to her eyes he bore an uncanny likeness to the portrait of his mother Emily. Since the poor woman had been murdered upon the very day Ottilia made acquaintance with the Polbrook family, she had no live image with which to make a comparison.

Giles turned to Miss Ingleby. "Where is Tamasine? How has she taken it?"

"How do you think?" the woman flashed. "Her guardian is dead, sir. Did you expect her to dance on his grave?"

"Miss Ingleby, hush." Ottilia moved to the woman and grasped her hands. "You are overwrought."

The companion burst into sobs, dragging her hands away and throwing them over her face. Ottilia put an arm about her, murmuring soothingly, and glanced quickly about the hall, seeking for doors. "Is there somewhere we may escape to?"

She threw the question at Giles, who was looking both outraged and upset. As who could blame him? She heard Francis murmur to the boy.

"Do you know the house? Where can they go?"

Starting a little, Giles nodded and moved swiftly towards a door near the front of the house, throwing it open. "There's a parlour in here, Aunt Ottilia."

She thanked him and made to hustle the weeping companion towards the entrance. She encountered no opposition, but just as they reached the door, a peal of silvery laughter floated towards them from above and Tamasine Roy came running down the stairs. Her voice expressed unequivocal delight with no vestige of grief.

"Giles! You came! I knew you would." She pirouetted across the hall towards young Lord Bennifield, her bright blue gaze shining. "Isn't it wonderful? Joslin is dead and now we may be married!"

CHAPTER FOUR

For a moment no one moved or spoke. Francis was inordinately relieved to see his nephew looking as shocked as he felt. Despite forewarning of the girl's dubious mental state, the callous nature of her remarks could not but strike the normal mind. Tillie, he noted, looking across, was wearing that faint frown he knew betokened furious thought.

Before Francis could hazard a guess at the import of her cogitations, a roaring emanated from Miss Ingleby, shattering the silence. Breaking free of Tillie's hold, the woman advanced like an avenging fury.

"Ingrate! Is this how you repay his care of you? Foolish, idiot girl!"

A ringing slap landed on the child's cheek, and she instantly set up a screech.

"Miss Ingleby!" Horror was in Giles's voice.

But the woman had no ears for any word of protest or sense, and the resulting cacophony gave Francis the impression that it was the companion rather than Miss Tamasine Roy, who was deficient in wits.

"Upstairs! Upstairs with you this instant!"

"I hate you! I hate you!"

Tamasine flailed wildly as her duenna made to thrust her to the stairs. "Hate me if you will, but you will do as I say."

"I won't, I won't! Only wait until Simeon comes! He will avenge me!"

At this, Miss Ingleby's fury mounted. "As he did before? Simeon Roy will enter this house over my dead body!"

"Yes, and you will join Joslin in his coffin," shrieked Tamasine, clearly beside herself.

"What a commotion!"

Francis glanced round. His wife had not moved from the door to the parlour, where she stood watching the quick give and take of words. It was unlike her not to intervene and Francis wondered at it. The row was becoming incoherent and when he looked back, he found the companion appeared to be getting the better of it, having succeeded in manhandling the girl to the bottom of the stairs.

"Up with you! Move. Now!" Of a sudden, Miss Ingleby raised her voice and yelled. "Mrs Whiting! Mrs Whiting!"

"No, I won't, I won't!" screeched Tamasine, fighting desperately to prevent herself from being pushed up the stairs.

Giles had stood like a stock, his mouth agape. But when Francis saw him recover himself sufficiently to make a motion towards the two women, he marched swiftly across to seize his nephew by the arm.

"No, you don't, you young fool! Leave well alone."

Giles turned anguished eyes upon him, and tried to pull away. "But that woman is hurting her!"

"Stand! You will do no good by interfering."

A further hubbub behind them made him turn his head and he caught sight of both footmen, together with the butler Lomax, hurtling through the door from the servants' quarters. Francis drew Giles out of the way, allowing the men to pass, and found Tillie at his elbow, her eyes glued to the mêlée.

"Watch for attitudes, Fan. Who is with whom?"

He noted the fellow Hemp was ahead of Cuffy, while Lomax hung back. The younger man's deep tones were readily audible.

"I will take her, madame. Miss Tam!"

The girl's head turned, and to Francis's astonishment, she cried out and then threw herself headlong at Hemp, flinging her arms about his neck. He lifted her bodily off the stair and the girl's legs entwined about his hips.

Miss Ingleby, though still vocal, had ceased moving up the stairs, and it took a second or two for Francis to realise Cuffy had her by one wrist, impeding her progress. Above them all, at the head of the stairs, stood the dwarfish figure of Mrs Whiting, who called out.

"Bring her up, Hemp."

The footman went swiftly up the stairs, apparently not in the least incommoded by his burden. He and Mrs Whiting headed off along the gallery and were lost to sight.

Miss Ingleby's hoarse cries became muted, and she leaned against the balustrade, her free hand thrown across her eyes. At last entering the lists, Lomax went up to her.

"You should rest, Miss Ingleby. Let the others handle Miss Tamasine. I'll have Cook make tea and bring it up to you."

The companion was weeping quietly and allowed herself to be ushered up the stairs, the fellow Lomax talking soothingly the while as he accompanied her. The footman Cuffy lingered until the two had reached the gallery. Then he turned and came back down the stairs. Francis moved forward to accost him.

"We are awaiting the doctor, Cuffy. May we make use of the parlour, do you think, where my wife may sit down for a while?"

The fellow lifted his gaze and Francis met the dark eyes. They were shadowed with grief. "The doctor is for Master Jos? Why? Master Jos is gone. It is too late for the doctor."

Sympathy stirred in Francis at the hint of despair in the fellow's tones. "True, Cuffy. But in this country, there are formalities to be met. The coroner will expect to hear from the doctor before he can decide how to proceed."

Cuffy's gaze did not waver and a frown entered his features. "How is Master dying, sir?"

"That is for the doctor to say."

The footman continued to regard him for a moment and Francis found the back of his neck stiffening with the effort to keep his own gaze steady. At last Cuffy swung his eyes away and found Tillie. He made a slight bow and gestured towards the parlour door.

"You can sit there, madame. You would like a drink?"

Tillie's warm smile appeared and Cuffy visibly relaxed a trifle. "You are very kind. Coffee would be welcome, if it is not too much trouble."

"No trouble, madame."

The fellow went to the door and held it open while Tillie went through. Francis looked at his nephew. "Come, Giles."

The boy hesitated. "Should I stay, do you think?"

"I want a word with you."

Francis ignored the apprehensive gleam that appeared in his nephew's eyes.

Beset by anxiety, Giles watched his uncle close the parlour door. The last thing he needed was to answer tricky questions. He had no doubt they would prove awkward after Tamasine's outburst. He could wish she'd had the forethought to keep from speaking of the future in front of everyone, but then her eager innocence formed a great part of her charm. The dreadful event this morning must have overset her badly, and Giles half suspected Tamasine had not fully taken in the fact of her guardian's death. What else might explain that unfortunate slip of the tongue?

Yet he was the more exercised by Miss Ingleby's rough treatment of the poor girl. He was all too aware, for Tamasine had explained as much, how so many in the household were apt to surround her with shibboleths and restrictions. He must find a way to speak with her before he left the house, although he must first shake off his unwelcome relatives.

His uncle Francis was looking around the parlour, frowning question in his face. It was not new to Giles, but he recalled his own reaction at first sight of the place. It had an air of the exotic, although its furnishings were meagre, with none of the elegance that characterised the typical English gentleman's country home. There was a sofa and a couple of armchairs made up in some form of plaited reed, with flowered cushions of a bright hue and colourful fringed clothes thrown across their backs. A cane table was set to one side and a patterned rug decorated the floor instead of a carpet. The effect was incongruous against the striped wall-paper and the ornate fireplace and mantel with a fixed mirror above.

Giles saw his uncle glance across at his wife, who was standing near the sofa, angled to catch the heat from the fire, her gaze also wandering around the room.

"Well, Tillie?"

Their eyes met, and a little smile quivered on his aunt Ottilia's lips. "I suspect the effort is to make it as much like 'home' as possible."

"Barbados, you mean?"

"Just so. I dare say it was done for Tamasine's sake."

"To keep her in a calm frame of mind?"

Giles could not forbear interrupting. "Calm? How could she be calm in such circumstances?"

"My dear Giles," responded his aunt, "I am not referring to today's events."

A flash of annoyance raced through Giles and he did not trust himself to answer. He knew his uncle would take it in snuff if he addressed himself with acerbity towards Lady Francis. But his silence made his uncle testy.

"It is of no use to look mulish, Giles. Surely you must see what is obvious to the rest of us?"

Giles bit down on a sharp retort, affecting ignorance as the best defence. "I fail to understand you, Uncle Francis."

"I am talking of Tamasine's condition."

As if he had not known it! Why must the world and his wife presume to judge the poor girl amiss, merely because she was different? "What condition? She is a delightful girl." Recollecting the recent scene, Giles amended this. "At least, she is in the normal way."

To his consternation, his aunt Ottilia moved to him and set a hand upon his arm. With difficulty Giles refrained from throwing it rudely off.

"Dear Giles, it is very hard for you. She is a beautiful creature, is she not?"

At this, he could not forbear emitting a sigh, as ever haunted by the image of Tamasine as he had first seen her that day in the forest. "She is exquisite."

"And she has borne much this day." His aunt left him, and passed on to her husband. "I will leave you to explain everything to your nephew, my dearest."

Faintly relieved, for he would deal better with his uncle alone, Giles was a little surprised to hear a note of suspicion enter Francis's voice.

"Where are you going?"

"To see how matters stand now things have quietened down."

"I thought you were going to rest," his uncle protested. "And Cuffy is bringing coffee."

"I will not be gone long." She set a hand to his chest in a gesture that struck Giles as peculiarly intimate. "Besides, I am persuaded you and Giles will do better without me."

Francis covered the hand with his. "Be careful, my love. I don't want you running afoul of Miss Ingleby. She is in dangerous mood."

"She is grieving, Francis. Have you not realised that?"

Giles's mind leapt to the suspicion that had more than once attacked him, and he was not surprised to hear his uncle's question.

"You mean she was attached to the dead man?"

His aunt's eyes glinted mischief. "Very good, Fan. Much more and I shall find myself utterly redundant."

His uncle laughed and let her go, moving to open the door for her. As she went through, she paused to speak in a murmur. Straining, Giles yet could not hear what was said. The conviction his aunt was speaking about him threw him at once onto the defensive, and he hardly waited for Francis to close the door before bursting out.

"What was all that about? Had Aunt Ottilia something to say to my discredit?" He did not wait for a reply to this, but sped on, spurred by the rising emotions churning in his breast. "I need not ask why you are both against my interest in Tamasine. You are thinking of Phoebe, I'll be bound. But it is ridiculous to say I am promised."

"I don't say so," said his uncle unexpectedly as he moved back into the room. "Indeed I must be the last person to advocate an arranged marriage after the disaster…"

He petered out, and the familiar rise of anger and grief that burdened him yet gripped Giles. What peace of mind he had acquired in the year since his mother's tragic end had been shattered on his father's remarriage to that wretch of a Frenchwoman, saddling him with unwanted half-siblings and recalling last year's events to his mind with startling force. It had taken the advent of Tamasine to rouse him.

"You are talking of Mama and my father. But times have changed. And if I am to take my father's example for my model, I may consider myself free to do what the devil I wish."

Aware of the savagery in his tone, Giles turned swiftly away and crossed to the fireplace, drumming his unquiet fingers on the mantel. He did not look at his uncle, beset by the unpalatable remembrance that his own absence upon the continent had thrown the whole burden of the business onto Francis's shoulders.

His uncle's voice came quietly, but Giles, acutely sensitive in this connection, noted the suppressed irritation. "If you are able to perceive the unwisdom of your father's conduct, Giles, it makes even less sense for you to be following in his footsteps."

It was too much. Giles turned on him. "How am I doing so? Do you suggest I have used Tamasine as my father used Violette?"

"I am suggesting nothing of the kind."

"As if I would do so," he persisted, riding over the response. "She is the most innocent creature I have ever encountered. Only a monster would take advantage of her."

To his consternation, his uncle pounced on this, shifting to confront him. "That is precisely the point, Giles. She is as innocent as a child, for her mentality is not much above that state."

Giles stared at him, all his just resentment emptying from his chest and leaving it hollow. He thrust down on the snaking suspicions that had more than once attacked him. He would not doubt Tamasine. He trusted her, as he trusted his own judgement.

"You must have noticed the oddity of her behaviour, Giles. I don't say she is wholly deranged, but it cannot be gainsaid she is abnormal."

"Deranged? You have been listening to rumour, Uncle. Do you suggest Sir Joslin foisted a lunatic onto the county? If it were true, why is not Tamasine confined?"

"She may be at times, for all I know."

Agitation rode Giles and he broke away, shifting aimlessly about the parlour without seeing where he trod. Images chased one another through his head, and he tried in vain to thrust them away. Only half aware he spoke aloud, he sought blindly for those explanations that had previously occurred to him.

"She can be distracted, I know. Yes, she speaks often in a fashion you may regard as non sequitur, but what does that betoken? It is nothing more than a manifestation of the freedom of manners obtaining in that island. Tamasine cannot help it. They don't breed girls to be pattern-cards of virtue as they do here. They are not as strictly tutored in the West Indies, for Miss Ingleby told me so."

Giles was half-startled to hear his uncle respond, not having fully realised to whom his persuasions were addressed.

"No doubt she told you so in an effort to explain away those deficiencies of which you are fully aware."

"They are not deficiencies," Giles retorted, hot against his uncle for the word. "If she demonstrates a freedom we are unused to see here, why should that redound upon the state of her mind? I find it refreshing." To his consternation, his uncle Francis looked less annoyed than compassionate. "Why do you look at me like that? As if you pitied me!"

One of Francis's eyebrows went up in an expression Giles knew of old. "I pity any young man besotted enough to disregard what is right in front of his face."

"Besotted?" Giles gave a short laugh. "Useless, I suppose, to tell you how much in love with her I am."

"That's what I said."

Giles sighed. "You didn't, Uncle. You think I'm infatuated with a beautiful face." He crossed to the window and looked out across the wide lawns to the shadow of the forest beyond, and spoke again without turning round. "You might be forgiven for thinking so, I suppose. I admit I was dazzled by her loveliness at first. I took her for a village wench."

He remembered the oddity of her acceptance when he had kissed her. She had neither struggled nor reciprocated. He had laughingly told her to stand still, half expecting her to run from him. Tamasine had done just as he instructed. Then she had spoken of her guardian.

"Joslin will be cross when he knows you kissed me."

Giles had recognised the name at once, for he was present when Sir Joslin paid a courtesy call on his father at Polbrook. Shocked to realise he had taken a liberty with a girl of genteel origin, he apologised profusely. But Tamasine laughed.

"I don't mind. I hope you will come to visit me."

"At Willow Court? You may be sure I will." He then bethought him of her lone state. "But may I not escort you back there?"

Tamasine's tinkling laugh sounded again. "They don't know I am out. I escaped from Lavinia."

With which, she had turned and taken off through the trees before Giles had a chance to ask anything further.

His uncle's voice, speaking with urgency, recalled him to the present, and the heaviness of current events settled upon his chest once more.

"Giles, whatever your feelings for the girl, there is too much at stake here to be indulging in sentiment."

Turning, he eyed the seriousness of Francis's features with alarm. "What is at stake?"

His uncle disregarded the question. "Tell me, Giles, when Hemp came to find you, was it with a written or a verbal message?"

Thrown out of his stride, Giles answered without thought. "Verbal. I don't think Tamasine had time to write."

"What precisely did Hemp say to you?"

A sliver of foreboding raced through Giles. "Why do you ask?"

"Every detail is of import in these circumstances."

The feeling intensified. "What circumstances? Are you speaking of Sir Joslin's death?"

His uncle's dark eyes narrowed. "I'm speaking of his possible murder."

Shock ripped through Giles's chest. Aghast, he could only stare at Francis. Murder? The word was anathema, after what his family had undergone not so long since. Why in the world would anyone want to murder the man? And why, it occurred to him belatedly, was the detail of Hemp's message so important?

"I don't understand," he managed at length.

"You don't need to at this present. Just answer the question."

With difficulty, Giles brought his attention to bear on the moment the footman had come to him with Tamasine's message. "I'm not sure I remember precisely. He said, I think, that Miss Tam wanted me to come, and that her guardian would not mind."

"But you knew he did mind," came sharply back, "for Tamasine said as much to Tillie."

Discomfort surfaced out of the numbness invading his brain. "I hoped he might have changed towards me. I am not ineligible, after all."

"Far from it," agreed his uncle, "but that was not his reason for rejecting you."

Sudden rage hit Giles. "How can you know that? Did he tell you so?"

"There is no need to get up into the boughs, Giles." He made no response, struggling with his emotions. "Sir Joslin did not wish his ward to become entangled with anyone before her come-out."

The sentiment was not new to Giles. "Yes, so he said to me."

"Which prohibition, I presume, led you to meet with Tamasine clandestinely."

The sarcastic note was not lost on him. "You need not censure me, sir. I know it was wrong."

"But you could not help it."

Giles closed his lips on a violent retort. He was perfectly aware his conduct was unworthy, but he nevertheless resented the tone. Yet he would rather take that than open Tamasine's behaviour to inspection. Giles knew her pursuit of him sprang from innocence, but it was obvious his uncle would not agree with him.

"Was anything else said in the message?"

"Nothing more."

"Are you certain?"

He flushed with anger. "Quite certain, Uncle Francis."

Irritation showed in his uncle's eyes. "I trust you will refrain from showing that face to your grandmother, Giles. We have had fireworks enough at the Dower House."

So he knew. His grandmother's objections to his father's remarriage had been well aired, but he had no qualms on this point. "I can handle Grandmama."

"I envy you your insouciance." The dry note was pronounced, but Giles refused to rise to the bait. "Did you send any message back with Hemp?"

"I said only that I would wait upon Tamasine." Without thinking, he added, "And that I looked to hear more of the reckoning."

Too late he saw suspicion leap into Francis's face. "What reckoning?"

What in the world had possessed him to mention that? He could feel warmth rising and hoped his cheeks had not reddened. Tamasine had told him in confidence, and in the light of present events, it was scarcely felicitous to mention it. To his dismay, he found he had given himself away.

"You didn't mean to let that out, did you? Giles, this is serious."

His uncle's earlier words came back to Giles. "You surely didn't mean that about Sir Joslin having been murdered?"

"It is not out of count, Giles. For pity's sake, if you know something that may throw light on the business, you must speak out."

Writhing, Giles could not help the protest. "It was Tamasine's confidence. I can't betray her."

His uncle came up to him and gripped his arm. "This is not the moment for misplaced loyalty, my dear boy. I appreciate your feelings, but I promise you, you will do more harm by withholding the matter."

Torn, Giles gazed at him. "And if it is altogether damaging?"

Francis's dark gaze almost bored into him. "Randal's case was altogether damaging, Giles, but Ottilia found out the truth. You may trust in her." His uncle released him and fell back a step. "Come now, what of this reckoning?"

With a sigh, Giles capitulated. "Tamasine spoke of it in jest. She didn't mean anything by it, I'm convinced."

"Very well, but what did she say?"

Restless again, Giles went to the fire and resumed his drumming on the mantel, only half aware of what he did. "Sir Joslin would not allow her cousin Simeon to come and see her, Tamasine said. It seems they were playfellows in childhood, but there was a falling out. This fellow Simeon was sent home to England."

"And the reckoning?"

Giles turned to look at him, and he could not repress a rueful smile. "Tamasine says they swore vengeance together. They were little more than children. Only a madman would take the matter seriously." There was no sign of amusement in his uncle's face, and Giles heard the echo of his own voice with a sudden upsurge of shock. He spoke before he could weigh the wisdom of his words. "You think her mad, don't you? You think her capable of putting some such plan into action. But it's ridiculous, sir. Even I, when she asked for my aid in this, could not do other than laugh at it."

So far from laughing, Francis was staring at him in patent horror. "What aid? What did she ask of you?"

Tamasine's words rang in his head, all at once redolent not of innocence, but of sinister import, stilling his tongue. His uncle must have seen his reluctance.

"Giles, cut line!"

He tried for a nonchalance he was far from feeling. "Oh, it was nothing. A silly notion, not to be taken seriously."

"I'll be the judge of that, I thank you."

Giles let his breath go and capitulated. "Well, if you must have it, she asked if I could help to get her guardian out of the way so that this cousin Simeon of hers might come here. Don't look like that! She didn't mean she wished me to help him to his death!"

"Yet she pushed him down the stairs."

"Ridiculous! I'll not believe it."

"It's what she said herself. However, that is neither here nor there. How did you answer her?"

"How do you think? I made a jest of the matter, asking her should I call Sir Joslin out or waylay him on the road and shoot him outright."

"Are you serious?"

Giles gave a mirthless laugh. "Well, I said it, if that's what you mean. But of course I never intended it to be taken seriously."

Francis closed his eyes for a moment. "Give me strength! And when, if I dare ask, did this conversation take place?"

Before Giles could respond, a bell pealed through the house. His uncle started at it, turning his head towards the sound.

"If that is the front door, I dare say Sutherland has arrived." He was crossing the room swiftly, and turned at the door, throwing his finger out towards Giles. "Stay where you are! I'm not finished with you yet."

He flung open the door and disappeared into the hall. Giles followed, pausing at the door as he wondered whether to make good his escape. No servant had as yet appeared through the baize door at the back, and Francis was making for the front door. Giles stole noiselessly towards the back of the hall, and paused as he heard his uncle let out an exclamation of surprise. He could just see someone standing on the doorstep. His uncle grasped the fellow's hand and drew him into the house.

"In good time, Patrick. You are just the man we need!"

The man addressed, who bore a striking resemblance to his uncle's wife, pumped his hand with enthusiasm. "I suppose I need not ask if my sister is upon the premises? The day Ottilia refrains from poking her nose into such affairs I'll eat my hat."

Waiting for no more, Giles moved quietly to the green baize door and slipped out of the hall.

Tempted though she was to creep along the gallery, Ottilia knew it behoved her to hold to a pace that suggested she had every right to be wandering around the corridors of an alien household. Besides, she had her excuse ready. Since the start of her pregnancy, the needs of her bladder had become more frequent and pressing.

It was eerily quiet after the earlier rumpus, and she wondered where everyone had gone. Following in the direction she had seen Mrs Whiting and Hemp disappear, Ottilia listened for any betraying sound to suggest the rooms she passed were occupied. Arrived at the end of the corridor, she hesitated. Should she turn the corner and proceed towards the back of the house? Likely they accommodated Tamasine out of hearing of the principal rooms.

As she hesitated, looking along the passage, the sound of footsteps alerted her. On impulse, Ottilia retreated into the corridor from where she had come and opened the nearest door, slipping into the room. It proved to be an empty bedchamber, obviously unoccupied, the shutters closed, the bed-curtains tied neatly back and dark shapes indicating Holland covers laid over the furniture to keep out the dust.

Keeping the door slightly ajar, Ottilia peered through the crack and watched a squat figure pass in the direction of the gallery. The housekeeper? She was carrying a tray but Ottilia was unable to see what was on it.

Waiting only until the footsteps could be heard upon the wooden stairs, she slipped out of hiding, softly closed the door to the bedchamber, and set off along the passage that led down the side of the house. A sound of muttering presently rewarded her, growing in strength as she neared the next bend. Ottilia followed it to its source and halted before a door to a chamber situated at the back of the house. She stood listening for a moment and was able to make out words.

"...going too far, and I shall hate you for it... No, you shall not, do you hear? We are the princess, sir, our word is law... Come into the canes, Simeon, do, none will find us here... One, two, five, eight, three ... it is of no use to hide, for I will get you..."

A rush of warm sympathy, edged with a frisson of fear, rushed into Ottilia's bosom. She could not mistake the voice. Nor could the tenor of this inchoate speech do other than confirm the mental deficiency under which Tamasine Roy laboured. Poor child, to be thus afflicted! Was this typical, or brought on by the disasters of the day?

It occurred to Ottilia that the woman she had seen passing along the corridor had been here but a few moments since and her aspect had not appeared to be unduly dismayed, which suggested Tamasine's present manner was a regular occurrence. Was the door locked? Stealthily, Ottilia tried the handle. It turned, but the door did not budge, and she released the handle, trying to make no noise.

The muttering ceased. Curiosity overcame her and Ottilia put her eye to the crack in the door, trying to see into the room. A sliver of light gave her no proper view, but she thought a shadow wafted across. She put her ear to the woodwork and could hear nothing.

There was a key in the lock and Ottilia debated the wisdom of turning it and entering the room. Common sense prevailed. It was clear Tamasine had taken leave of what senses she had, if temporarily. It would be foolish of Ottilia to blunder in when she had scant knowledge of what to expect. Yet she could not resist the notion of removing the key and peering through the keyhole. Dropping down, she moved close and tried to see into the hole. There was light at first at the other end. Then it suddenly darkened and an eye became visible.

Ottilia jerked back. Tamasine had taken the self-same notion. The muttering started up again.

"Come in, my dear, do, and I will give you sugar drops... Do you not hear me?"

She waited a moment, and then once more put her eye to the keyhole. The other eye was still there and instantly the voice started up again.

"There you are! If you will open the door, I can come out to you."

Ottilia scurried upwards and back, away from the door, feeling ridiculously apprehensive. Merely because the creature sounded normal? Was it safe to open the door?

Becoming aware of the irregular beat in her pulses, Ottilia cursed herself for a fool. What was she about, to be interfering in this way? Francis would upbraid her, did he know what she was doing. Yet she could not make herself leave.

"Tamasine?" she ventured, pitching her voice low but loud enough to be heard through the wooden panels.

"Lady Fan!"

The voice was a high-pitched squeak, and Ottilia remained wary. Recognition did not necessarily mean lucidity.

"Lady Fan!" came again, on an excited note. "Have you the key?"

Ottilia was obliged to remind herself the creature had been anything but lucid a few minutes ago, but she thought it prudent to answer. "I am putting it back in the lock."

She did so, feeling absurdly like a traitor.

"Open the door, I pray you."

"I cannot, Tamasine, I am sorry."

The door shook and the handle shifted to and fro as the girl inside the room rattled at it. "Pray let me out, Lady Fan. I am better now, I promise."

Ottilia remained silent, her gaze riveted upon the handle, willing herself not to give in to the impulse to free the child.

"Lady Fan, Lady Fan, Lady Fan. Will you not open for me?" came in the same bright tone of gaiety the child had used before all the upset of her guardian's death.

Perhaps Giles was not so blameable, after all. With Tamasine's urgent pleas coming so prettily to her ears, it was hard indeed to hold on to remembrance of the peculiar mutterings she had heard not a few moments since.

Hasty footsteps coming along the corridor settled the matter. Ottilia looked to judge from which direction they came, intending to slip away by the other, but she was too late. A woman turned the corner of the passage down which Ottilia had come, and catching sight of her, stopped short.

Ottilia sighed and moved towards her, trying for a nonchalance that was far from the reality. "Are you feeling a little more the thing, Miss Ingleby?"

The companion's feet began to move again, but her features became pinched. "I suppose I need not ask what you are doing in this part of the house, Lady Francis. If you are determined upon interference, perhaps you would care to take my place? I'll warrant a single day would have you begging for release."

Ottilia immediately abandoned the excuse she had dreamed up, and opted for the truth. "I came to discover how things stood once calm had descended again."

"Indeed? Well, if you have any sense, you will stand away from this door when I open it."

The hazardous nature of this proceeding could not but strike Ottilia and she spoke without thinking. "Is that wise? I know little of Tamasine's condition, of course, but I have heard enough to realise she is in uncertain mood."

Miss Ingleby threw her a scorching glance. "Allow me to know my own business best, ma'am."

"I am sure you do. May I ask what you intend?"

"You may ask, but I see no reason why I should answer."

Ottilia bit down upon annoyance. "Miss Ingleby, if you think to drive me away by this means, let me assure you I am more resilient than you suppose."

For a moment the woman's defiant pose held, and then she sagged a little, sighing out a defeated breath. "Do as you wish. At least you had brain enough not to open the door yourself."

"I was sorely tempted," Ottilia confessed, feeling frankness would best serve her with this woman.

Miss Ingleby knocked on the door. "She can be persuasive."

No response was forthcoming to her knock, and Ottilia watched with interest as the companion did just what she had done, removing the key and putting an eye to the hole. Standing again, she lowered her tone.

"She will have heard me. I dare say she is already lying down on her bed, pretending to be asleep."

"I imagine all this excitement is the worst possible thing for her," Ottilia remarked, assuming the companion to have recognised they must be past all pretence.

"Oh, she thrives on it." Miss Ingleby's tone was decidedly offhand. "If there is nothing to stir her passions, she will invent something."

"You talk as if she were rational."

Miss Ingleby was turning the key in the lock, but at this she paused, looking round and meeting Ottilia's gaze, her expression set. "Make no mistake. She is perfectly rational — in her way."

Bemused and amazed, Ottilia watched her remove the key and pocket it. Then she turned the handle and opened the door, slipping quickly inside. Ottilia put out a determined hand to prevent the door from closing and followed suit.

"Shut it, if you please. And stay back."

Ottilia did as she was bid, setting her shoulders to the door and remaining there. Her eyes went directly to the four-poster, where Tamasine was indeed lying, her eyes closed. There was a bandage on one of her hands and Ottilia recalled her injuries from putting her hand through the glass. At least someone had found time to complete the task Ottilia had begun, if belatedly. Scarcely surprising, under the circumstances, that it had been forgotten.

There was little besides the bed in the room, bar a single press and a washstand. There were no mirrors, which must mean Tamasine relied upon another to assist at her toilette. Miss Ingleby? Or was there a maid willing to risk the girl's uncertain moods.

Troubled by the companion's last remark, Ottilia wondered briefly if the woman still sought to convince her of Tamasine's full command of her senses. Surely not, with everything that had passed? But then, what in the world could she mean by insisting Tamasine had a degree of rationality?

She watched Miss Ingleby approach the bed, which she did with some caution. But she had no truck with the pretence of sleep.

"Tamasine, did you drink your medicine?"

What medicine? Ottilia looked swiftly around, but there was nothing to support the notion any sort of medication was kept in the room. Then she noted a bedside cabinet, and wondered if it might be inside.

The girl opened one eye. A little smile escaped her and she sat up in a bang. "Did you think I was asleep?"

"No," returned the other, repeating, "Did you take your medicine? Did Mrs Whiting give you a dose?"

Tamasine stretched lazily. "Can't you see I'm better?"

"I must take that for my answer, I suppose. I desire you will remain here for the moment, for there is much work come upon me with your guardian's decease."

"What work? You are meant to take care of me."

"True, but I am not your guardian and there is a good deal to be settled."

"I don't need a guardian." The tone was petulant. "I am of age."

Miss Ingleby chose not to answer this, and Ottilia's mind roved the last few exchanges, astonished at the ability the girl had shown to take part in the give and take of conversation. She had not done so when they met earlier this morning. Perhaps the companion's charge of rationality had some substance.

"Someone must see to your affairs," Miss Ingleby said, "for I have no such authority. I will write to your Aunt Ruth."

Tamasine nodded, swinging her legs off the bed. "Oh, yes, and Simeon must be sent for."

Miss Ingleby's lips folded, but she did not argue and Ottilia surmised she had regained sufficient control of her grief to be able to choose her responses. It was clear her policy under normal circumstances was to avoid any confrontation. A wise precaution, blasted by her earlier shock.

The companion stood back from the bed, looking down at the girl. "Rest, Tamasine. I will come for you in an hour."

Ottilia noted a change in the blue gaze directed up at the duenna. Tamasine was wearing a faintly calculating look. "Will you lock me in?"

"Yes." No hesitation. "I cannot have you running off again today."

The girl's expression did not alter, but she essayed a slight smile. "Can I have Hemp to play with me?"

There was a brief pause. Ottilia could not see Miss Ingleby's face, but suspicion sounded in her voice. "What do you want to play?"

"Fox and Geese, if Hemp will bring the board."

"If you will promise not to try to persuade him to release you before I return, then I will send him up to you."

Ottilia heard this with both interest and amazement. For one thing, was Tamasine capable of playing a game demanding intelligent strategy? For another, were they in the habit of allowing the child to be alone in company with a male servant? And a girl of Tamasine's undoubted lack of discretion? Were they not fearful the fellow might forget himself and take advantage of her? She did not know Hemp, who was clearly well acquainted with the girl, but that he cherished an extraordinary regard for Tamasine she could not doubt.

The girl's quality ought to protect her, but Ottilia's naïve faith in the discretion of servants and mistresses had been severely shaken when she investigated the death of Francis's sister-in-law.

The companion headed for the door and Ottilia moved aside. She caught Tamasine's glance, receiving one of those blinding smiles.

"Farewell, Lady Fan," sang the girl.

"Au revoir." Ottilia moved into the corridor, where she waited for the companion to lock the door, lowering her tone. "What is the medication you use?"

"Laudanum."

"You know it is addictive."

To her surprise, a faint gasp emanated from the companion and she threw the back of her hand to her mouth in a gesture Ottilia remembered from earlier. Was it habitual, denoting agitation? She spoke from behind it, a gruff note in her voice.

"Yes, I know." Miss Ingleby gestured down the corridor. "I beg you will go back downstairs, Lady Francis. If you insist upon remaining, pray don't come up here again. I must fetch Hemp, and then I have letters to write."

Ushered without ceremony, Ottilia had perforce to retrace her steps along the corridor towards the front of the house. As she turned into the main passage that led to the gallery, she realised Miss Ingleby was no longer behind her. Halting, she looked back along the corridor, but there was no sign of the woman. Ottilia concluded she had taken another route, perhaps one set aside for the servants.

Ottilia continued on her way, a myriad questions running in her head. Sir Joslin Cadel's untimely death had seemingly unleashed a hive of hidden passions.

Never having seen his brother-in-law in action, Francis watched with interest, tempered by the anxiety instilled by what Giles had told him. He was missing his breakfast, and not even the spectre of his nephew's involvement in this affair had the power to distract his mind fully from the pangs of hunger. His hopes centred on Patrick Hathaway discovering the death to have been, if not natural, at least unconnected with any sinister intent.

Doctor Hathaway stood for a while at the foot of the bed and cast his eyes the length of the man's still body. Tillie was standing back from the bed, allowing him full access, and she caught Francis's glance.

"Patrick never touches until he has fully observed," she said, on a note of pride.

Hathaway did not glance up from his work. "The limbs are out of true."

"Yes, he was badly misshapen."

Tillie described the position in which Sir Joslin had been found at the bottom of the garden steps, while Patrick listened with concentrated attention.

Francis had taken to his brother-in-law at the outset, finding in him an echo of the common sense approach that characterised his sister. They were much alike, Patrick possessing the same clear grey gaze and well-defined cheekbones. Like Tillie, he was lean, though considerably taller, and loose-limbed with broad shoulders and a hearty handshake. He was much given to laughter and, so Francis thought, bore the burden of his ailing complainant of a wife with cheerful fortitude.

His advent at this bedevilled house was fortuitous, as he had explained to Francis as they waited in the parlour for Tillie to reappear, partaking of the coffee brought in by Cuffy a couple of minutes after Patrick's arrival.

"We lay not ten miles distant last night, Fan, having halted when the snow began to fall. When I found it to be clear this morning, I had the horses put to in short order so that we might arrive before any further fall could make the roads impassable."

Francis had wholeheartedly applauded this decision, only regretting the circumstance that had prevented his and Tillie's being at the Dower House to receive them. But Patrick waved this aside.

"You could hardly have done so. But no matter. Your mother gave us all the particulars, and as it seems this fellow Sutherland cannot be found, she desired me to come here directly."

For which Francis was heartily thankful. Particularly after his interview with Giles, who had seized opportunity and escaped, much to Francis's chagrin. The hideous prospect of his nephew falling under suspicion of murder had thrown him back into those dark days of his sister-in-law's death. Was he to go through it all again? Common sense told him nothing could be more unlikely, but he could not shake the apprehension. Should the conversation reported to him come to the ears of a coroner, there was no saying where it might end.

When Tillie arrived in the parlour, he had necessarily to wait for the brother and sister's effusive greeting before mentioning the matter to his wife. He supplied her with coffee, and was conscious of delaying the inevitable, taking opportunity instead to apprise his brother-in-law of the events of the day leading up to his arrival. But Tillie, with her usual astuteness, had divined his disquiet.

"What's to do, Fan? You look disturbed."

96

He tried to shrug it off. "It's nothing, my love, don't fret."

Tillie's clear gaze rested on him. "You spoke to Giles?"

Patrick looked interested. "Is that the young fellow I saw in the hall?"

"The wretch made good his escape while I was answering the door. After I had specifically told him to wait, mark you."

"What did he tell you to trouble you so, Fan?"

Francis turned back to his wife. "Tamasine spoke to him of a reckoning concerning her guardian."

Tillie's brows went up. "Did she indeed? How interesting."

"Interesting! The silly clunch was fool enough to make a joke of the girl's desire to be rid of her guardian in order to admit this cousin of hers into the house."

"Simeon?"

"Yes, but that fellow is of less importance than my nephew, who must needs put himself squarely in the firing line when you go ferreting for suspects."

"Good God!" exclaimed his brother-in-law. "Surely you don't imagine there has been foul play?"

"Until we know better, it is always a possibility." But to Francis's relief, Tillie gave him an understanding smile. "However, I cannot imagine we need waste any time on the proposition that Giles plotted with Tamasine to rid her of her guardian."

"That's what I've been trying to tell myself. But she did ask him to help her get the fellow out of the way."

"Dear me. A trifle too close to the bone, I agree." Tillie laid aside her cup. "In that case, the sooner we discover how Sir Joslin died, the better."

Francis headed for the door, gesturing as he went for his brother-in-law to accompany them. "My dependence is all upon you, Patrick."

But the sight of Sir Joslin's dead body so revived his anxiety that he could scarcely contain his impatience.

Tillie's recital of finding the body ended, Patrick's attention was once again on the corpse, and he proceeded in a methodical fashion, first checking the limbs. "This leg is broken, likely severely. He would have been permanently lamed had he lived."

"He already is lamed," Tillie said. "At least, Miss Ingleby spoke of a chest condition, brought on, she thinks, by pleurisy."

"That will come to light with the post-mortem." Patrick laid down the hand he had been checking. "This wrist is also broken."

"We thought so," Francis put in. "It was the only thing holding him in position."

Hathaway laid a hand to the man's face, and like Tillie before him, slipped it inside his coat. He glanced up towards Tillie. "Was he damp like this?"

"Yes, but still warm. He had only just died when we got to him."

Patrick made no reply to this, but lifted the dead man's eyelids one by one. He paused, a slight frown creasing his brow, and then lifted the lids again.

Francis knew an impulse to demand to know what he had seen, but he withheld it, watching in some puzzlement, and no little revulsion, as Hathaway leaned to the man's mouth, forced it open and sniffed. His nose wrinkled and he gave a slight shake of the head.

"What is it, Patrick?" Tillie demanded.

"I was hoping for a certain aroma, but it is unlikely to show so readily."

It occurred to Francis that the usual pungent odours of death were lacking. "That's odd." He moved from his post at the door where he was keeping lookout. "He doesn't smell of anything much."

Tillie cast him a sudden startled glance. "Heavens, Fan, how right you are! I knew there was something, but I could not put my finger on it."

It gave Francis an obscure kind of pleasure to have beaten her to the post, but he was too eager to hear what it denoted to make any teasing comment. He directed a questioning look at his brother-in-law. "Does it mean anything?"

"Assuredly. It is all of a piece with the sweating and the contracted pupils." He looked across at Tillie. "You thought he was in a stupor, you said?"

"Yes, and he looked just as peaceful in that position of discomfort as he does now. Miss Ingleby said he looked asleep and she could not tell when he stopped breathing."

"Yes." Patrick's tone was musing and he continued to regard the body, evidently deep in thought.

Impatient for more, Francis looked at Tillie and found her gaze fixed upon her brother. Unusually she refrained from question and Francis recollected that Hathaway had been her mentor. All she knew of medical matters she had learned from him. Francis was both touched and faintly amused, despite his disquiet, to discover in his forthright wife a tendency to defer to the judgement of one she clearly deemed her superior, at least in the medical field.

Patrick looked up at last. "You were thinking of apoplexy, I dare say?"

"Yes, but I could see it might not be so," said Tillie, eager now. "Surely the pupils should have been dilated? But Sir Joslin put his hands to his head and made sounds indicative of pain before he fell. I thought that might denote a cerebral inflammation. That contusion on his temple must be from the fall, so I have discounted it as a prior cause. I have been trying to discover if he was prone to headache, but to no avail."

"It may not have been pain, but giddiness," Patrick suggested. "Did he convulse?"

"Not that I know of, but I confess I did not think to ask."

"We can check that, but I suspect not. His countenance is not bloated, which I would expect with apoplexy. And, if my direction of thought is accurate, there will have been a promotion of perspiration, accompanied by a suspension of the excretion of urine and faeces, which would account for the lack of such odours."

Urgency prompted Francis. "What then, Patrick?"

"Only a post-mortem will tell us, but I am inclined to suspect an overdose."

"Overdose?"

"What, of some drug?" asked Tillie, an intent look in her features.

"Yes, a narcotic. Very likely opium."

CHAPTER FIVE

Her brother's suggestion took from Ottilia all power of speech as the implications jumped in her head. As at a distance, she heard Francis speak.

"Are you saying he was an opium-eater?"

"Not necessarily," said Patrick. "Ottilia spoke of a chest condition. He might have been merely in the habit of taking it against the pain."

"Laudanum." Ottilia glanced at her spouse. "Miss Ingleby feeds it to Tamasine."

"For pity's sake! What sort of household is this? They are all crazy, Patrick."

"No, only Tamasine is deranged." Ottilia became brisk. "Shut the door, Fan. We don't want to be observed."

He hesitated, a frown descending onto his brow. "Why shouldn't we be observed?"

"Because we must hunt for the laudanum."

Her brother snorted. "Oh, come, Ottilia, you are not seriously suggesting someone did away with the fellow?"

"She sees murder wherever she goes," rejoined Francis. "But now that we know the fellow may have been an addict, we can surely discount that theory."

Ottilia saw relief in his face and could not withhold a rueful smile. "I realise that is just the outcome you wish, my dearest, but I fear you are too sanguine."

"How so?" demanded her spouse, a rough note in his voice.

"Because there is nothing to say an overdose of opium could not have been administered by another," said Ottilia doggedly. "Indeed, it is the more likely explanation for anyone in the habit of taking it must know precisely how much would be safe. Addicts in particular."

At this, her brother entered the lists. "I cannot agree with you. It is far more likely to have been an accident. I have known of a number of cases where the accepted dose has been exceeded and resulted in death or near fatality."

"In opium-eaters?" asked Francis eagerly.

Patrick looked disconcerted. "No, you have me there. Still, I submit that over-indulgence in an addict would not be surprising. His judgement must be impaired."

"Nevertheless, it is well to be certain." Ottilia looked across at her spouse again. "Pray shut the door, Fan."

He did so, a world of discontent in his features as he crossed to the press standing to one side of the room. "I suppose I must concede that if Sir Joslin was in the habit of taking laudanum, he is certain to have a bottle of it handy."

He began looking along the top of the press which was crammed with bottles and jars and Ottilia headed for the bedside cabinet.

"Even if you find a bottle of laudanum, what will that prove?" asked Patrick, moving to join Francis, who was rapidly casting through the potions, glass clinking against glass in his haste. Ottilia noted that her brother did nothing to aid him, merely watching his motions with an air of scepticism. She had hardly taken hold of the handles of the small drawer in the cabinet when Francis uttered an exclamation.

"Here it is!"

She turned to find him holding up a small brown bottle. Patrick took it from him and crossed to the window, holding it up to the light. She moved to join him.

"Is there much left?"

"It is nearly three quarters empty. Not that it tells us anything other than that the fellow was apt to drink the stuff."

Ottilia took it from him and held it out to her husband. "Put it in your pocket, Francis."

He came to take it but did not immediately do her bidding. "You want me to impound it?"

She opened her eyes at him. "Of course."

His brows drew together. "What do you think it will tell you? You can't know how much has been drunk."

"It is a precaution, Fan. We don't want anyone removing the bottle."

"Except yourself," put in Patrick drily.

She ignored her brother. "Besides, there is no saying but that the bottle had been tampered with. Patrick may find the dosage well over what should be there."

"Oh, I am to test it, am I?"

Ottilia gazed at him. "Why should you not?"

"No reason beyond an utter disbelief in this ridiculous notion you have taken into your head."

"For my part," put in Francis with feeling, "I am ready to sanction any number of tests, if only to prove there has not been a murder."

"Yes, but I'm afraid there has been," Ottilia insisted. "Tamasine herself said she had killed her guardian."

"You will hardly believe anything that wretched girl says, when you've already suggested she is deranged."

"Which is just why she may have spoken the exact truth."

Patrick cast up his eyes. "She has the bit between her teeth, Fan. She will not rest now until she is satisfied of the facts."

"Don't I know it," said her husband, taking instant and, in Ottilia's view, unfair advantage of this support. "I wish to heaven that wretched girl had not set foot in the Dower House."

Ottilia dismissed this at once. "Even if she had not, our involvement was inevitable."

"Because of Giles, you mean. Damn the boy! Why must he choose to make a cake of himself over this of all females?"

"I shouldn't trouble your head about it, Fan. Ten to one, the whole idea of foul play proves void." Patrick glanced at his sister. "I think you are making a mountain out of a molehill, Ottilia, and with little to go on."

"You have not met the inmates of this house. I think I may be pardoned for being suspicious."

"How so?"

Francis was evidently unwilling to travel further upon this route, but she could not let it lie. "Have you not observed the cross-currents of secrets and passions in this house? I dare say every person in the place has something to hide."

"But that does not need to have led to murder," Patrick interjected.

"Precisely so," said Francis. "You must admit, Tillie, there is nothing to support such a supposition. You can have no real reason to be interfering further in their lives."

"You say so only because of Giles," Ottilia objected. She went to him, setting a hand on his chest. "Do you not think your apprehension will be better served by pursuing the matter, if only to make certain there is no reason for alarm?"

"But you have no real evidence of wrongdoing."

"As yet."

Francis eyed her in a frustrated way. "If you wish to know what I think, it is that you are so desperate for distraction, you will clutch at any straw."

This Ottilia could not deny. She gave him the smile reserved for him alone. "I admit it freely. But you will take the bottle? Indulge me in this, dearest Fan."

Before he could answer, Ottilia's brother irritatingly shoved his oar in again.

"You may as well give in at once, Fan. If you suppose you can stop Ottilia in full flight, you must have windmills in your head." He gave a short laugh. "Or else you're a more successful husband than I in managing your wife."

"For shame, Patrick. What sort of a wife do you take me for? I am perfectly biddable where my husband is concerned."

Francis fairly snorted. "If I did not know you better, my darling, I should be begging Patrick to take your pulse."

But he slipped the bottle into his pocket and Ottilia smiled her thanks.

"Lock the door again, Fan, won't you?" she said the moment they were all outside the room. "We don't want anyone touching the body until Patrick and Doctor Sutherland can conduct their post-mortem."

Patrick gave a shout of laughter. "What did I tell you? She's incorrigible!"

It had not been easy to persuade the fellow Cuffy into guiding Giles to the upper floor to Tamasine's bedchamber. He had been obliged to resort to bribery since his representations of his inamorata's urgent need to speak to him, as evidenced by Hemp's message that morning, failed of their intent.

"I know, sir, but now Master is dead," objected the man. "Miss Tam is resting now. Is not a good time."

Giles balked. "She has been left alone? At such a time?"

"No, sir. Hemp stays with Miss Tam now."

Shock rode him. "In her bedchamber?"

Cuffy merely stared, his features giving nothing away. Giles suppressed the urge to slam a fist into the fellow's jaw, but his determination to see Tamasine redoubled. The thought of that innocent in company with the burly footman, and without a vestige of a chaperon, made his blood boil. Had they no care for her reputation? He abandoned further argument and dug a hand into his fob pocket.

To his cynical satisfaction, Cuffy eyed the gold coin with the age-old look of avarice Giles recognised in those less fortunately placed than himself. He raised questioning brows at the man. "I will not keep Miss Tamasine above a moment."

A brief hesitation, and then Cuffy nodded, holding out his hand. Giles dropped the guinea into it. Without a word, the fellow took off, leading him up a back stair and through a collection of corridors, halting at last before a door upon which he knocked.

Giles waited, dismayed to feel less than joyful anticipation in his breast. His last sight of Tamasine being herded up the stairs returned to him, and as footsteps sounded within the room, he remembered Hemp was in there and recalled, with discontent, how she had leapt into the footman's embrace.

He heard the key turn in the lock and the door opened a crack. Cuffy murmured in a strange patois, in which Giles barely recognised the odd English word, and Hemp's dark gaze met his as the fellow pulled the door wider.

"You wish to see Miss Tam, sir?"

"I fully intend to see Miss Tamasine," corrected Giles, taking a high hand at the outset.

The man looked him over in a manner as irritating as it was disrespectful and Giles felt his fist itch again. For two pins, he'd knock the fellow into Kingdom come. Except that, even in his wrath, Giles was aware that if the man fought back, he was likely to get the worst of it.

Relief came in Tamasine's voice from within the room. "Is that you, Giles? Pray come in at once. Hemp, let him in!"

The fellow Hemp exchanged a glance with his colleague, who had stood back to allow Giles access. "Go in, sir. I will wait here."

Hemp held the door wide and Giles entered the room. His eye fell immediately upon Tamasine and he caught his breath. She was seated on the edge of a four-poster, and he felt warmth rush into his cheeks at the sight of her in such an intimate setting. Her smile was dazzling and she beckoned him to come closer, pointing to a little table on which a squared off board was set with little figures in various positions laid out upon it.

"See, Giles. We are playing at Fox and Geese." She held up a goose token.

A trifle nonplussed, he approached, taking in the board with its pattern of holed points and the plethora of geese stuck into holes around the unfortunate fox. Was this a ploy to take her mind off her grief? Or, as the treacherous thought entered his mind, was she truly untouched by her guardian's death? The late discussion with his uncle crept back, disturbing him at a deeper level he did not care to examine.

He shrugged the thoughts away and summoned a half-smile as he reached to take the hand she held out to him and clasp it warmly. "I was concerned about you, after the way your companion treated you. Are you all right?"

Her response was bright. "Lavinia is writing letters, so Hemp came to play with me. Would you like to watch?"

He was disconcerted. "Certainly. I mean, no. Tamasine —"
He glanced swiftly towards the door and was chagrined to see

the fellow Hemp standing before it. He lowered his voice, leaning down. "I wanted to talk with you privately, Tamasine."

She gave him her brilliant smile and patted the coverlet beside her. "Sit with me, Giles."

He was reluctant to do anything that might be wrongly construed, but the temptation proved stronger than his resistance, and he took his place to one side. His eyes strayed to the servant still standing stalwart at the door, but then Tamasine pointed an imperious finger.

"To the corner, Hemp."

For a moment Giles thought the fellow would object, his glance shifting from one to the other. Then he crossed to a corner at the further end and turned his back to the room. Giles's gaze returned to Tamasine, and he was about to speak when she put a finger to her lips, enjoining his silence.

Mystified, Giles nodded. Tamasine stood up, slipped out from behind the little table and tiptoed across to the door. Grasping the handle, she turned it. The door did not open.

A mewl of frustration escaped Tamasine, and the door handle was rattled with some violence. Giles leapt up and went towards her, but before he could reach her, she flew across the room and began beating at the footman's back, screaming.

"You stole the key! You stole the key!"

Stunned, Giles could not move. He watched the man stand and take the blows, neither turning nor flinching, but only bowing his head a little. Infuriated growls issued from Tamasine's lips and something in Giles could not endure it.

"Tamasine, stop! Tamasine, please don't do that!"

He was moving swiftly now, hardly aware of what he did. Reaching her, he tried to take hold of her, but the girl evaded him, escaping under his arm and running to the bed, where she overturned the little table with a furious kick, sending both board and figures flying. Then she flung herself down on the bed and burst into heart-rending sobs.

Giles glanced at the fellow Hemp, who had not shifted from his position. Distress swamped Giles. "Help her, can't you?"

Hemp looked briefly over his shoulder. "No, sir. It is better to leave her."

"In such distress?" The callousness of it struck Giles to the heart, and he went swiftly to the bed and reached down to the afflicted girl, hardly knowing what he said. "Tamasine, don't weep, pray. You have had a wretched time of it, my poor love."

To his combined discomfort and astonishment, Tamasine tumbled over and flung herself at him, throwing her arms around his neck and crying muffled pleas into his chest as he automatically held her to him.

"Take me away from here, Giles! Marry me and take me away! They are all against me. They hate me, Giles, they hate me! They are cruel and wicked and I will never be free if you don't take me away."

Appalled, Giles clasped the weeping bundle in his arms, perforce sinking down upon the bed and allowing Tamasine to cuddle wholly into his embrace in a fashion as indecorous as it was harrowing. Somewhere inside a bolt of strident common sense told him he was going to regret this, but the heady sensations that beset him in the present moment which seemed to promise him his heart's desire were overwhelming.

"Don't weep, my darling girl, don't weep! I will do anything you wish for, dearest, I promise you."

Tamasine stilled all at once, and then pulled away a little. Her lovely tear-stained face gazed up at him, woebegone and desperate. "Can we be married? Am I yours, Giles?"

For one breathless second, he hesitated. But Tamasine lifted her face to his, puckering her lips in mute invitation. It was too much.

Giles kissed her, wholly uncaring about the presence of the footman in the corner of the room. Drowning in the magic of her innocence and beauty, he groaned. Tamasine's lips left his and he opened his eyes. Her smile was radiant, all the erstwhile misery vanished.

"We are betrothed, Giles!"

A tiny voice inside his mind rose in violent disavowal, but Giles chose not to hear it. His honour, as much as his heart, was in play as he uttered fateful words.

"Yes, my darling Tamasine, we are betrothed."

She leapt from his embrace and began pirouetting about the room, throwing her hands in the air and twirling in a fashion that made Giles feel a trifle giddy. For his head was whirling as a plethora of difficulties leapt up, throwing him into disorder. For one thing, his suit had met with disapprobation in this household. For another, his father was going to explode.

Recalling his conversation with his uncle earlier, the infelicity of becoming engaged under these circumstances hit him abruptly. Urgency overcame him, and he got up, moving to catch Tamasine in mid-twirl and grasp her hands.

"Tamasine, listen to me!"

She gave him her bright smile, the china-blue eyes triumphant. "I will listen to you forever, Giles."

"But just at this moment, it is important to listen carefully." Why he emphasised the point of care, he did not wish to examine too closely, but apprehension was riding him. "We must keep this secret, Tamasine. Just for now."

To his surprise, she looked delighted. "A secret! And they will never know."

"Yes. Well, in due course we may tell them. But for now, with your guardian's death in question, we must be circumspect."

She crowed triumph. "They will never guess!"

Giles was conscious of impatience. Had she understood him? Had she taken in the difficulties? All at once, he recalled the presence of the footman. He shot the man a glance and found Hemp had turned at his place in the corner and was watching them with an expression Giles could not read. He turned to his newly betrothed.

"Tamasine!"

She opened her eyes at him. "Why are you whispering?"

"You must insist that Hemp tells no one."

Tamasine looked blank. "Hemp?"

"Yes! He must have heard everything. Can you persuade him not to tell anyone?"

She gave the bell-like tinkle of a laugh he loved so much. "Hemp will never betray me. Hemp is my best friend. Aren't you?" She left Giles and ran across to the footman, putting out her hands. "You won't tell them, will you? On pain of instant death."

The tone was gay and light, but the words sliced into Giles's mind like the cut of ice on skin. Giles shook the burn of it from his mind. She did not mean it. It was Tamasine's notion of a joke. In poor taste at such a time, perhaps, but she was too innocent to be troubled by shibboleths of that sort.

"I will not speak, Miss Tam," came Hemp's deep tones.

Giles breathed more easily. But the footman took hold of Tamasine's hand and, as if he led a child, brought her up to Giles.

"You should say goodbye now, sir. Miss Tam must rest."

Tamasine made no objection, rather to Giles's surprise, instead breaking into laughter and raising a hand to wave at him. "Goodbye, Giles. Come and see me again soon."

With which, she floated dreamily to the bed and lay down, closing her eyes with a sigh. Giles found Hemp waiting for him by the door, which the fellow was unlocking.

"Go now, sir."

Giles did not relish the semblance of an order, though the tone was polite enough. Bemused and not a little confused, Giles found himself obeying. In the doorway he looked back. Tamasine might as well have been asleep, for all the notice she took.

The door closed behind him and he heard the key turn in the lock. Cuffy was waiting. "You are ready, sir? We will go."

There did not seem to be much else he could do. Giles nodded and followed the man along the corridor, his mind beset with so many conflicting notions he scarcely knew what to think. Everything had happened so fast, his brain was afire with conjecture.

But one thought emerged from the maelstrom as he descended the stairs. He was betrothed to Tamasine Roy, and there was nothing he could do to change that. Not that he so wished. Yet a regretful thought snaked into his mind. As a man of honour, he was committed. He could not draw back.

Ottilia was guiltily relieved Patrick needed her husband's aid to hunt down the local doctor. Both men, accompanied by her eager young nephews, were to be off in Lord Polbrook's phaeton, borrowed for the duration of the Fanshawes' stay. Sophie Hathaway, always sickly, elected to retire to her room to lie down, attended by Teresa Mellis with a plethora of remedies on offer, leaving Ottilia with the welcome prospect of being alone for a while.

A belated and boisterous breakfast, attended by the whole party, had been enlivened with the tale of the doings at Willow Court, although Francis had the sense to refrain from mentioning Giles's involvement. Once or twice, his clipped tone drew a frowning glance from Lady Polbrook, but she made no remark. When the talk turned upon Ottilia's condition, her patience rapidly eroded. Between her sister-in-law's dismaying tales of her own pregnancies and Patrick's dire warnings, the distraction afforded by the events at Willow Court gave way to severe irritation.

She managed to contain her spleen while Francis guided her to the parlour and into a comfortable chair by the fire, but an insistence on her using a footstool nearly resulted in a quarrel.

"I am not an invalid, Fan."

"No, but Patrick says it is essential to put your feet up daily in order to avoid swollen ankles."

Ottilia consigned her brother to a place of great heat, a remark Francis pointedly ignored, instead fetching a cushion from the sofa to set at her back.

"I am perfectly comfortable without that."

Francis leaned down to press a kiss to her forehead. "Indulge me, my dear one." A teasing light came into his eye and he patted his pocket. "Tit for tat, Tillie. I need scarcely remind you of Sir Joslin's bottle of laudanum."

Effectually silenced, Ottilia endured the fussing until her spouse at last took himself off. Left alone, she removed the cushion and flung it across the room, at which precise moment her mother-in-law entered the parlour.

"An efficacious remedy for ill-temper, my dear Ottilia," said Sybilla, retrieving the cushion and seating herself on the sofa.

Ottilia cursed inwardly. She had left the dowager out of her calculations. But at least she need not mind her tongue. "I am wedded to a tyrant."

Sybilla laughed, leaning to warm her hands at the fire. "All men are the same with the first baby. Wait until you are on your third or fourth. He will not bat an eye."

"Allow me to get through one first, if you please."

An understanding smile came her way. "I gather Francis has been suborned by your brother."

"The wretch has put the fear of God into him."

"Upon what difficulty?"

Ottilia let out a sigh. "Oh, that in a woman of my age a first child may be dangerous."

Sybilla lifted her brows. "Loath as I am to draw your fire, Ottilia, that is generally regarded to be true."

"I know it, but it does not make it any easier to bear. I find the restrictions such a curse. I may not do this or that. I must take care of my health. And the worst of it is that Fan is perfectly correct. I am easily fatigued."

"It won't last. I'll wager in another month you will begin to bloom."

"Very likely." She was all too familiar with the probable pattern from her experiences assisting in her brother's surgery. "But it does not help me now, especially when I need all my strength with this excessively tricky business of Sir Joslin's demise."

Sybilla's eye gleamed. "Now we come to it. And you need not think I failed to notice my son's uncertain mood. May I enquire what is chafing him? All he would tell me is his fear you would be at it like a dog with a bone and I cannot imagine why that should trouble him, since such is your invariable practice."

Ottilia's irritation subsided, turned aside by the quandary of how she should answer. Little though she wished to introduce the subject, she could see no real advantage in concealment. Her mother-in-law was too astute to be long kept in ignorance of her grandson's potential danger.

"Well?" came from the dowager on a sharper note. "You need not dissemble, Ottilia, for I know that look. What is amiss?"

She capitulated. "I'm sorry to distress you, Sybilla, but we met Giles at Willow Court."

The dowager's features tightened and her black eyes snapped. "Did you indeed? Then he is dangling after the wench?"

Ottilia plunged in. "It is worse than that. Tamasine sent to him at an early hour this morning, requesting him to come to her there."

"Before Sir Joslin died? But she was here early this morning, breaking into my house!"

"I don't think Tamasine's movements have much bearing on the case. The point is —"

"I am perfectly aware of the point, I thank you," snapped Sybilla, cutting in without apology. "You would have me believe, I dare say, that Giles was in a plot with the girl to rid her of her guardian. Poppycock!"

"I have not suggested anything. Moreover, I should not for a moment believe your grandson capable of such an act. But —"

"I will tolerate no buts!"

Rising from her chair, the dowager moved restlessly to the door, glaring at the clear pane freshly inserted by the handyman Grig, who had found time to come over from Polbrook. Turning there, she fixed Ottilia with a stare from eyes vibrant with wrath.

"Do you think I can bear to go through all that again? You know, better than anyone, what I suffered to think that Randal —"

She broke off to draw a shuddering breath and Ottilia, her compassion stirred, remained silent, unwilling to pour coals on a flame she knew to be dangerous in its capacity for heat. The black gaze left her face, darting about the room as if it were unfamiliar. After a moment or two, Sybilla regained command and returned to resume her seat on the sofa. She looked across at Ottilia with eyes as bleak as they were before violent.

"Why should I suppose the son to be any more sensible than the father?"

Ottilia summoned a smile. "Yes, but I think Giles has more consideration. Although if as Fan thinks, he is besotted with the chit, one cannot hope to argue him out of it. Much less get him to acknowledge what is lacking in her."

Sybilla nodded, but returned to the heart of the matter. "Is there something in his conduct that must make him suspect?"

"Not in his conduct. It is her public assertion that they may now be married that damns him, if anything."

A snort escaped the dowager and she cast up her eyes. "As if any person of sense would believe a word the child utters."

"She is not a reliable witness, it is true. But I'm afraid there is a little more to it than that."

With no roundaboutation, she put her mother-in-law in possession of what Francis had told her of his conversation with his nephew. Sybilla did not speak for a moment, but the snap of her black eyes gave notice of her thoughts.

"The addlepated fool," she said at last, on a sighing breath that spoke her inner despair.

"Just so. But there is no need to fall into the dismals, ma'am. We are not yet at the point of determining anything more than the cause of death. If it was an overdose of opium, as Patrick suggests, there is yet the question of how it was administered."

"Not to mention who did the administering. I suppose I need not ask if you hold by your theory?"

"I don't yet have one. But if you mean to ask whether I remain suspicious, then I must say yes."

"But why, Ottilia?"

"Because Willow Court is a hotbed of passions, Sybilla. I should doubt whether any one of the inmates, bar the lower servants, may be eliminated as a possible murderer, Tamasine included."

"But, notwithstanding her abominable request of Giles, is she capable of planning to do away with her guardian?"

"Yes," Ottilia said baldly. "It is well to argue her mental state, but there is an uncanny streak of apparent rationality. I think she is eminently capable of ridding herself of the man she saw as standing in the way of her future plans."

The dowager balked. "What, to marry Giles?"

"I was thinking rather of this Simeon fellow. He is the one involved in her scheme of revenge, after all. Though whether Tamasine comprehends the intricacies of whatever plot was afoot between them, I strongly doubt."

The discussion was interrupted as the maid Biddy entered the parlour. "Lady Phoebe Graveney, my lady."

Ottilia all but started. Could there be a more inopportune moment for the arrival of Giles's prospective bride? Throwing a glance at Sybilla, she saw her thought echoed in the dowager's features before she schooled them to an enforced look of welcome.

The maid stood aside and a young woman came through the door. Curiosity overtook Ottilia and she regarded the visitor with interest. She was elegantly and expensively clad, as befitted the daughter of an earl, with a countenance pleasant rather than striking. The nose was neat, the cheeks tending to lean and the mouth well shaped, but the girl's best feature was a pair of speaking eyes, their colour indeterminate somewhere between blue and green.

Recalling Francis's inability to describe her, Ottilia could not altogether blame him. Her hair, under a pretty bonnet, was certainly on the dark side. But the melancholy thought struck that the poor child could not hold a candle to Tamasine Roy.

Lady Phoebe was greeting Sybilla with polite enquiries as to her health and the satisfactory nature of her Christmas festivities, but it was apparent the girl was labouring under strong emotion. Beneath the spurious air of calm, several wayward muscles in her face shifted, and deep in those giveaway eyes Ottilia detected a trace of anxiety. Or was it anguish?

"Phoebe, allow me to present to you my daughter-in-law, Lady Francis Fanshawe."

Ottilia concealed her too close scrutiny, producing a friendly smile. "You will forgive my not rising, I hope. I am increasing and thus obliged to take my ease."

The young lady commented suitably and was persuaded to take a seat next to the dowager, who proceeded through a fund of commonplace enquiries.

"Are your parents well?"

"Oh, yes, I thank you. Mama sends her compliments to you."

The girl's responses appeared to Ottilia as mechanical as the dowager's questions concerning Lord and Lady Hemington's sojourn with the latter's sister, and she began to wonder if this visit betokened more than mere courtesy. In a bid to test her theory, she waited a suitable moment to inject a dart designed to discover its validity.

"Have you seen Giles since your return, Lady Phoebe? I gather the two of you are well acquainted."

The visitor's cheeks grew pink and she fumbled with her fingers in her lap. "Oh. No, I have not. I mean, yes, we have known each other from childhood."

"But you have not yet seen him?" persisted Ottilia, ignoring a glare from her mother-in-law.

Lady Phoebe moistened her lips with her tongue, but her eyes gave her away. "I believe Giles has been excessively occupied."

"Yes, with the family. It has not been comfortable for him at home," cut in the dowager, black orbs snapping at Ottilia.

"No," agreed the girl in a hasty way, "although he has likely contrived to amuse himself elsewhere."

Sybilla stepped in quickly. "Oh, well, you know Giles. He hates wrangles. It is like him to escape if he can."

There was a silence, and Ottilia could not but feel for the girl. Was she wondering whether or not to ask the burning question no doubt hovering on her tongue? Ottilia took the bull by the horns.

"I was privileged to meet the extraordinary Miss Tamasine Roy this morning." The girl's eyes widened, revealing apprehension. Ottilia paid no heed to the dagger look she received from her mother-in-law. "Have you met her, Lady Phoebe?"

"No."

It was a breathy gasp. Ottilia held the girl's gaze and smiled sympathetically. "My poor child, you are dying to ask, are you not?"

"Ottilia!"

"Well, but is it not better for us to be open with Lady Phoebe? She will only imagine worse than the truth if she is not told, Sybilla."

A horrified look was the dowager's only answer, and Ottilia hastened to give her a reassuring glance. She had no intention of making free with the worst of what she knew to Giles's discredit.

The visitor glanced from one to the other of them. "Then he is dangling after her."

"No such thing," snapped the dowager, just as if she had not said exactly the same herself. "And he could get no good by it if he were. The girl is wanting in wits."

Lady Phoebe's dark brows snapped together. "The rumours are true?"

Ottilia chose to take this herself. "She is not in her right mind, if that is what you mean. But as yet I have no reason to believe she is fit for incarceration."

"You said you met her this morning, Lady Francis?"

Ottilia laughed. "With a vengeance."

A wistful look crept into Lady Phoebe's vulnerable eyes. "Is she very lovely?"

"Oh, a clap of thunder," said Ottilia frankly. "Even my husband was deprived of breath at first sight of the creature. You must not set any store by Giles having been bowled over."

"Ottilia, I wish you will be quiet." This from Sybilla, in severe irritation.

"Oh, no, ma'am, I had rather be given the truth."

Sybilla let out a sound of defeat. "In that case, you had best hear what has occurred this day. You are bound to get a garbled version otherwise. Ottilia?"

Obligingly, Ottilia gave a brief account of the day's events, dwelling on the oddities of Tamasine's visit and her guardian's subsequent death, and omitting all mention of Giles's presence in the house and the incriminating conversation.

"So you see must see, my dear Lady Phoebe," she finished, "that Giles will realise at last there is nothing to be gained by courting a girl who is not in her right mind."

"But is he courting her?"

Lord, but the girl was dogged! How to answer that? She prevaricated. "I hardly think it is serious."

Sybilla added her mite. "Certainly not. Giles has more sense."

This blatant falsehood appeared not to convince Lady Phoebe. "Has he? But Lady Francis said he had been bowled over."

"So must any man be upon first sight of the girl. Even I thought her like to a fairy princess."

Lady Phoebe's mouth took on a mulish look. "In that case, perhaps you will tell me why Giles should be haunting Willow Court, which I am reliably informed is the case."

Before Ottilia could respond to this, the little conference was brought to an end by the entrance of Sophie Hathaway, leaning heavily on Miss Mellis's arm.

Chagrin struck into Phoebe's bosom. Just when she had been getting somewhere! Indeed, she was persuaded both the dowager and Lady Francis were concealing something. She had not failed to note a couple of meaning looks that passed between them. But all attempts to garner the information she sought were now in vain, and Phoebe looked with scant approval on the newcomer.

She was a faded blonde, who must have had at one time more than a passing claim to beauty. It was marred by a discouraging aspect of debilitation, accompanied by a languid tone of complaint as she broke into instant lamentation.

"I could not get off at all, and I do so hate lying all alone." She sank into the armchair next to Lady Francis, but reached out to pat the hand of the woman who had assisted her into the room. "I could not keep poor dear Teresa hanging about me. That would have been most unfair."

"Poor dear Teresa has little else to occupy her," said the dowager, taking opportunity to present Phoebe.

Expressing herself suitably, Phoebe turned as soon as she could to the dowager's companion, for whom she always felt a little sorry. Her faded cheeks had pinked up a little, and Phoebe recalled the dismissive fashion in which Giles tended to treat the poor woman. A sliver cut at her heart at this remembrance of another black mark against him.

"How do you do, Miss Mellis? How is your leg? Do you feel it in this inclement weather?"

The companion coloured up even more. "Oh! Thank you. A little, Lady Phoebe, but it is of no moment." With which, she scurried to a straight chair in the corner, effacing herself as was her custom.

"What a pity you did not have Patrick to mend your leg, Teresa, for I'll warrant it would not trouble you so greatly," said Mrs Hathaway, taking up the conversation again. "Yet my poor husband's skill has proved unequal to my unfortunate ailment, though he does his best."

Phoebe listened with only half an ear, for she caught Lady Francis looking at her, an expression in her face for which Phoebe was unable to account. She had heard a deal about Giles's new aunt, and none of it false, if she was to judge by the manner in which Lady Francis had thrust her anxieties into the open.

"You can have no notion how I suffer," Mrs Hathaway was saying. "Oh, I don't complain. It is so tedious for everyone to be hearing about one's woes all the time. Only it is so melancholy to be permanently ill, though I make every effort to appear cheerful. One cannot be parading one's misfortune to one and all."

"What is your misfortune, Mrs Hathaway?" asked Phoebe, not with any desire to know, but merely in a bid to keep the woman talking so that she need not speak herself.

Nothing loath, the lady launched into a dismal catalogue which Phoebe would have found depressing had she been paying it the least attention. Instead her mind revolved around the lamentable intelligence that proved out all her suspicions and blasted the fond hopes in which she had basked these many years, secure in the conviction that her affections were returned, if not with ardour, at least in a measure sufficient to satisfy her.

She could almost wish Lady Francis had held her tongue, although it was better to know the worst. A pang smote her as remembrance struck. She had thought the worst had been and gone with the after effect of the scandal attending the death of the Marchioness of Polbrook. At the time, in the joyous anticipation of welcoming Giles home from his extended travels abroad, Phoebe's world had come crashing down when suspicion for his wife's death had fallen upon the marquis. The Earl of Hemington had all but forbidden the banns, repudiating the erstwhile arrangement and declaring that nothing would induce him to allow his daughter to ally herself with the Polbrook family.

Staunchly loyal, Phoebe had held out against Papa. The understanding between herself and Giles had been of long duration, although they had entered upon no formal engagement. Phoebe had been content to have it so, believing wholeheartedly in his constancy. Her breath shortened and all the discomforts that beset her bosom came tumbling to the fore. Her trust had been misplaced. Rumour did not lie, and the dear friend who had long captured her heart was in thrall to the beautiful Tamasine Roy.

Without thinking what she did, Phoebe rose abruptly from her seat, cutting into Mrs Hathaway's continuing monologue without ceremony. "Forgive me! I must go." Aware that her voice was husky, Phoebe struggled for calm.

"Good heavens, Phoebe, you have scarcely been here a moment."

Phoebe gave the dowager her attention, aware of a shake in her voice. "I came only to pay my respects, ma'am." She threw a tiny smile at Mrs Hathaway. "I must crave your indulgence. I hope you may feel better directly."

Then she hastened to the door and slipped out of the room. Alone in the hall, Phoebe halted a moment, catching at the newel post at the bottom of the stair in a bid to recover her equilibrium. Aware of having given herself away, she could only hope the visitor was too self-absorbed to notice. It was too late to expect as much from Giles's grandmother and aunt. Phoebe could only trust nothing would be said to Giles himself, for she knew Lady Polbrook for a fiery matriarch whose command over the whole family was absolute. But she doted on Giles.

This reflection served only to deepen the tumult under which Phoebe was labouring and she could not withstand letting out a groan.

"Dear me, that sounded perfectly despairing," said a voice behind her.

Phoebe turned quickly. "Lady Francis!"

The newcomer took her arm and drew her willy-nilly towards the dining-parlour situated off the hall near the front door. "Let us slip in here for a space. I dare say the fire has not died and it should be warm enough." Once inside, Lady Francis closed the door and drew Phoebe away from it towards the window. "There, now we may speak freely."

A pair of grey eyes surveyed Phoebe and she felt her face grow warm. Embarrassment threw her into speech. "I have nothing of import to say, Lady Francis."

"Call me Ottilia. Or Lady Fan, if you prefer," said the other with a smile that warmed Phoebe unexpectedly. "After all, we are going to be related, are we not?"

Phoebe tugged on an unsteady breath. "That is debatable."

"Has he offended beyond forgiveness?" The lady's gaze, disconcertingly clear, did not shift from Phoebe's face. "I beg you will set no great store by this little interlude."

"Little!"

"There can be no future in it, you know. Giles will realise that before long, and then you may be comfortable again."

Phoebe's gorge rose. "Comfortable? I shall never be comfortable again. Even if he recovers his senses, how could I trust him after this?"

Lady Francis did not speak for a moment, but a faint frown creased her brow. "I understood it was an arranged alliance between you?"

"And he may therefore spurn me for another with impunity?" She bit her lip on the fury rising in her bosom, noting the other woman's raised brows. Her tone became clipped. "I should not say so. There has been no formal offer."

"But you consider yourself promised, I take it?"

"As I thought he did. Evidently I had it wrong."

Lady Francis did not speak, but the sympathy in her features almost overset Phoebe. She turned and swept to the window, gazing out upon the drive without seeing it, struggling to regain her composure. The thought flitted across her mind that her father would never tolerate the match should he hear of this fresh disaster, with Giles's inamorata involved in the guardian's death.

Remembrance broke into her thoughts. There was something more, was there not? On impulse, she turned on Lady Francis. "I wish you will tell me the whole, Lady Fan."

"I beg your pardon?"

Impatience overtook Phoebe. "You need not look so startled. It is plain to me that you and Lady Polbrook are holding something back. What is it? What more is there to this business with Miss Roy? And pray don't try to fob me off!"

A little smile appeared. "Indeed, I should not dare attempt it."

Warmth crept up Phoebe's cheeks, and her voice became stiff despite every effort to maintain a cool tone. "You must excuse my bluntness, ma'am."

"I like it," said the other unexpectedly. "I must confess to a similar candour on occasion."

"Then exercise it now, I beg of you."

"Very well, if you insist. I am afraid Giles being in close association with Willow Court has put him in a little danger, should it prove out that Sir Joslin did not die a natural death."

Blankness invaded Phoebe's mind. "I don't understand you."

"Then let me be plain. I have a suspicion Sir Joslin was murdered, possibly by an overdose of opium. Giles was sent for to the house by Tamasine Roy this morning, and it appears that there was — when we do not yet know — some jest between them of the necessity to have Sir Joslin out of the way."

Shock clouded Phoebe's brain as she spoke her thought aloud. "You mean he may be suspected of making away with this man?" The memory leapt into her head of Giles's distress, when she had received his confidences on the subject of his mother's death. "It cannot be so! After what has passed? No, no, I dare not believe it to be possible."

But a seed of doubt rose. Lady Fan's next words fostered it.

"Not even if he were head over ears in love?"

A shaft sliced through Phoebe's bosom, and she felt the tremble at her lips. She suppressed it, meeting the other woman's steady regard. "I would wish not to think so. Yet one cannot truly know another's mind." She tried to bite back the words, but they would come. "If he was utterly dazzled, who can say? He might do a great deal for a woman if his heart was touched."

Lady Fan's gaze did not waver. "Have you reason to know as much?"

With difficulty, Phoebe spoke, unable to help the bitter note. "I thought I had, but it seems I was mistaken."

"You love him, don't you?"

The abruptness of the question pierced Phoebe to the heart, but she did not think of prevarication. "All my life."

"Yet you can still find it in you to fear his involvement in a possible murder."

Phoebe's eyes pricked. "Is it disloyal of me? I have never been blind to his faults. Indeed, this episode fills me with dismay as well as jealousy."

"How so?"

"It has long been my fear Giles might follow in those footsteps most dear to him, now sadly lost."

"His mother, you mean? I understand you, I believe."

Phoebe eyed her in some discontent. "I should not have spoken, I dare say. But I cannot suppose you ignorant of the truth, for I know you were instrumental in discovering who killed poor Lady Polbrook."

She dared not say more. Giles, she knew, had never acknowledged the truth of the rumours of his mother's frequent infidelities. Yet here he was, hell-bent on setting the countryside alight with his determined pursuit of Miss Tamasine Roy. And now he was potentially suspect in this death!

Her feelings threatened to overcome her. Summoning her courage, she prepared to take her leave. "I must go, ma'am. I should not have spoken with such candour. Pray do not betray me to anyone."

"You may be sure I shall not, my dear."

Phoebe thanked her, heading swiftly for the door. She turned there and looked back, beset by a nagging fear. "I beg you will send to me, Lady Fan, the moment you discover anything to the purpose."

She did not wait for an answer, but wrenched open the door and sped into the hall, grabbing up her thick pelisse, which she had left upon a convenient chair and shrugging it on without bothering to do up the buttons. Stepping out of the front door of the Dower House, Phoebe looked along the drive for the phaeton in which she had arrived and saw it a short distance away. The groom who had driven her was walking the horses. But the sight of her carriage paled into insignificance as a second vehicle turned into the driveway.

It was a curricle and pair, driven by none other than Giles, Earl of Bennifield.

Recognition threw an unwelcome surge of discomfort into Giles's chest. With reluctant acknowledgement, he realised he had been dreading this first meeting. It was not guilt, for there was no reason for him to feel it. But Phoebe was a dear friend, and he had hoped to confront her in his own time. With the knowledge of his present position with regard to Tamasine Roy, her advent just at this moment was little short of disastrous.

There was nothing for it now, however, for Phoebe had halted on the threshold of the Dower House and was clearly awaiting him.

Giles pulled up his pair as the vehicle approached the porticoed entrance, and waved his whip in salute. Waiting only for his groom to get down and go to the horses' heads, he leapt nimbly from the curricle and strode up to where Phoebe awaited him. He adopted as nonchalant a tone as he could command.

"When did you get back? I was not expecting you so quickly."

There was a deal of reserve in her usually frank gaze, he thought, but she answered coolly enough. "We returned a few days early. You know how Mama and my aunt cannot resist quarrelling if they are more than a week or two together."

Giles laughed. "Did Lady Hemington leave in a dudgeon again?"

To his relief, the sober look gave way a little and Phoebe smiled. "Not quite that. Papa made an excuse to come away early, especially, so he said, to prevent matters reaching that extreme."

"Shrewd of your father."

"He can't bear wrangles, as you know." Phoebe paused briefly. "Nor any hint of scandal."

Detecting a faint note of censure, Giles bridled. "I am hardly to be blamed for my father's follies."

"Not your father's."

The flash at her eyes made Giles poker up the more. "Someone has been busy."

Phoebe's gaze held his, and it came to Giles that of all things he had been dreading, the worst was her naked eyes. Even as a child, she had been incapable of hiding her feelings. It had the effect of throwing him on the defensive.

"You do blame me. I didn't think you would be so prejudiced, Phoebe."

Anger leapt into those orbs. "You didn't think of me at all!"

A truth that could not but add fuel to the flames, for Giles knew his only thoughts of Phoebe had been to negate the possibility of her standing as a bar to his pursuit of Tamasine Roy.

"Is that an accusation? If so, I should be glad to know how I have offended you."

Phoebe's tone became scornful. "Giles, that is unworthy. You know perfectly well that your chasing after some pretty petticoat is bound to reflect upon me."

"By which you refer, I collect, to Tamasine Roy?"

She eyed him frowningly for a moment, and when she spoke her tone had altered. "I hear she is a diamond of the first water."

The image of Tamasine's heavenly features, languid after his kiss, leapt into his head and his senses swam. He spoke without thought. "She is breathtaking. Such an innocent too." Only half conscious of putting out a hand, he dropped into the easy camaraderie they had always shared. "Phoebe, had you met her you must also have befriended the poor child. Her situation is pitiable. And now she has lost her guardian, her future is uncertain."

He broke off, recalling that his quixotic promise had now assured Tamasine's future. With relief, he remembered his insistence on secrecy, and realised he could say no more. "She is so very vulnerable," he ended, feeling how lame this sounded.

Phoebe looked at his hand but she did not take it. Baffled, and a little hurt, Giles withdrew it. When her glance rose to his, the violence of feeling in her eyes took him aback.

"Vulnerable? When she may well have engineered his death for her own advancement?"

Stunned, he stared at her. "Have you run mad?"

"Not I, Giles. I am perfectly in my senses, which is more than can be said for Tamasine Roy."

Resentment swamped him, the greater for the niggling doubt at the back of his own mind. "Are you at that? You, as well as everyone else? I would not have thought it of you, Phoebe."

"And I would not have thought you capable of scheming with your — your madwoman — to dispose of her guardian in order that you might take her to wife."

"What?"

Her voice rose to a pitch that physically hurt his eardrums. "Indeed I did not think it. I thought you a man of honour, of delicacy. But it seems I had it wrong."

"How dare you, Phoebe? I thought we were friends."

"Friends do not offer insults to each other."

His fury surged the higher with the recollection of his uncle's earlier disquiet regarding his jest with Tamasine. He hit back. "Then what am I to think of your accusing me of murder, for it is no less? Besides, what insult have I offered you?"

"If panting after a worthless doll is not an insult —"

"How in Hades could that insult you?" Giles thundered, riding over her. "You force me to remind you, Phoebe, that our friendship is all the relationship we have."

Her expressive eyes grew dark, and then flashed fire. "If indeed we have that!"

CHAPTER SIX

Pushing past Giles, Phoebe fairly ran towards the waiting phaeton, which had taken the place of his own vehicle, his groom having begun to walk the horses. Mortified, Giles knew an impulse to dash after her and retract his words. He ought at the least to go and hand her up into the carriage, but his feet remained rooted to the flags of the entrance portico. He did not move until the Graveney groom had assisted his mistress to mount and hopped up himself, taking the reins in hand and giving the horses the office to move off.

Phoebe did not look back, and her face remained firmly averted until the carriage had straightened into the drive and all Giles could see was the back of her bonnet.

Cursing, he went to ring the doorbell, reflecting that he could hardly do worse with his grandmother.

"Good day to you, Biddy," he said to the youthful maid who answered the door.

"Master Giles! Have you come to see her ladyship? We've visitors, my lord, for the doctor as is Lady Francis's brother is come with his family."

"I know all about that," Giles said, adopting a tone of insouciance that in no way reflected the slight rise of apprehension at the prospect of his interview with the dowager. Despite what he had said to his uncle, his grandmother could be formidable. Yet unless she was seriously displeased, he had hopes of succeeding in cajoling her, as he usually did. At this juncture, he desperately needed her support.

"Who is in the parlour at this moment, Biddy?"

"Her ladyship and Lady Francis," said the maidservant, counting off on her fingers. "Mrs Hathaway is there too. Oh, and Miss Mellis."

"Not my uncle?"

"He's gone off with the doctor and them two lads, my lord."

That was a relief. With luck, his uncle Francis had refrained from recounting their conversation at Willow Court. Nor spoken of Tamasine's embarrassing greeting. Still, he was in no mood to do the pretty.

"Do you think you could contrive to get my grandmother out of the parlour, Biddy? I'll wait in here."

As he spoke, he pushed open the door to his grandmother's study, as she chose to call the small library situated opposite the dining parlour. The maid assured him she would do as he wished, and hurried off. Giles took a turn or two up and down the room, pacing beside the glass-fronted bookcases along one wall and avoiding the knot of seating surrounding the fire. On edge, he flung himself into the chair before the escritoire in the bow window, fiddling with a pen from the inkstand and stabbing its point into the leather-bound blotter. His thoughts were not happy.

His grandmother was under the misconception he was all but betrothed to Phoebe. What would she say if she learned of this morning's unfortunate betrothal? It was not that he did not wish to marry Tamasine, but he was obliged to admit the moment was not propitious. He was rehearsing what he might say under his breath when the door opened to admit the dowager. She was unsmiling, and her greeting was not encouraging.

"Well, Giles?"

He got to his feet at once, essaying a smile. "I hope I see you in good health, Grandmama."

134

Her brows rose in a look that deepened his apprehension. "I trust you are not going to pretend you are come on that account."

He sighed out a breath. "No."

"Did you happen to meet Phoebe on her way out?"

Giles nodded, giving vent to a despairing sigh. "I didn't handle it well, Grandmama."

Her features softened and his spirits rose a little. She moved into the room. "I don't suppose you did. The men in our family seldom do know how to act in difficult situations."

Giles took his courage in his hands. "The thing is, ma'am, I don't consider myself promised to Phoebe."

To his discomfort, the black eyes sparked. "Not since you encountered Tamasine Roy at all events."

"Before that." He took a hasty turn about the open space between the desk and the chairs by the fire and faced her again. "The proposed match was not of my making, you know that. If Phoebe was led to expect it, you had better blame her father rather than me."

"Oh, I do," responded the old lady unexpectedly. "And yours."

"Then I wonder at your countenancing such a thing."

"It had nothing to do with me, boy. The notion came out of the heads of your father and Lord Hemington years ago."

Giles balked. "You need not try to fool me, Grandmama. Nothing happens in this family but it has your sanction."

An odd laugh escaped his grandmother, but Giles detected no humour in it. "I wish it was so, Giles. A number of events would not have taken place had that been true."

There was no mistaking the meaning of this. "You mean my father would not have been permitted to marry Violette."

"I could hardly prevent him." There was a snap in his grandmother's voice. "I don't object to his marriage per se, but only to the timing of it."

A growl of resentment burgeoned in Giles's bosom, and the whole vexed question of his mismanagement regarding Tamasine was relegated to second place. "Why didn't you stop my father? Why had he to sully Mama's memory?" Bitterness rose up to choke him. "And now, merely because I have met someone whom I could truly love, I am to be tarred with the same brush."

To his chagrin, his grandmother's lip curled. "Love? You are infatuated, Giles. And with a girl whose fitness for any sort of liaison must be in question."

"Tamasine is not deranged! I will not have her maligned."

The dowager's dark gaze raked him. "Either you are a blind fool or an obstinate one, but a fool you most certainly are, Giles."

He bit back the urge to respond in kind. "I thank you, ma'am."

"Don't be sarcastic, boy. It doesn't suit you."

With difficulty, Giles held his tongue. He whisked away again, refusing to meet his grandmother's eyes. Her voice came again, controlled but, to his ears, redolent with underlying rage.

"Foolishness I might forgive. What I cannot endure is that anyone should hold my grandson in suspicion of collusion to murder."

Giles whipped round, staring at his grandmother in blank horror. "You believe that?"

"Of course I don't believe it. Just as I would not believe it of your father, and with far more cause to do so. But I learned enough from that business to see how mud sticks. I have no wish for the world and his wife to point the finger in your direction, and therefore you will go no more to Willow Court. Nor seek that girl's company by any means at all."

Fury burned in his breast, and he forgot the real purpose of his visit. "You think Tamasine did it!"

She came up to him, looking him in the eye. "I don't know what to think, Giles. But I don't want you involved any further."

"I am involved." The truth of this hit home, and heat rose to his tongue. "I have done nothing ill-judged beyond what was said in jest. Yet I cannot and will not abandon Tamasine at such an hour. It touches my honour, ma'am."

The dowager's black gaze sharpened. "Your honour? How so?"

A flitter of apprehension shot through Giles. That came perilously close to giving the game away. He backtracked with haste. "I have done nothing dishonourable, I assure you. But if — if Tamasine is to be falsely accused, I must and will support her."

"For heavens' sake, boy, don't stand there like a martyr, spouting rodomontade fit for the stage! This is serious. If it is indeed found Sir Joslin was unlawfully killed —"

"If? It is not even proven, and poor Tamasine is thrown to the lions!"

His grandmother snorted, swinging away to perch on the arm of the nearest chair. "It was poor Tamasine herself who said she had killed her guardian when she ran to us for help."

Giles stared, shocked into silence for a moment. "She didn't mean it. I am persuaded she didn't mean it."

"No, for she scarcely knows what she is saying from one moment to the next."

The spark of his own doubts leapt up to goad him into defiance. "She is an innocent, I tell you! Why will you all persist in declaring her to be unstable? How can you judge, ma'am? You don't know her."

"I have met her once and that was enough. As it must be for anyone who is not blinded by a beautiful face. I would never have believed you could behave in a fashion as idiotic as it is unworthy. What in the world possessed you, Giles?"

Balked, he swept away to the desk, staring out of the window in silence. What in the world had possessed him indeed? Not that he did not care deeply for Tamasine, but how matters had proceeded to this extreme he was unable to fathom. Worse, his hopes of his grandmother's support were blasted. And that before she even knew of his betrothal. He dared not confess it.

He turned, trying for the note of cajolery that had never before failed him. "I did not think you would turn against me, Grandmama."

"How can I be held to have done so? I hold you in the strongest affection, Giles, as well you know, and I would not see you follow an example I must and will deprecate."

Touched on the raw, Giles threw up his hands. "I knew it! I will not endure a comparison with my father."

"I am not comparing you to him."

The implication hit and a shaft of pure agony sliced through Giles. All was forgotten but the recent blinding pain of loss. He fought it, struggling with the rising emotion.

"I will not hear ill against my — my mother. Do not speak of her in that vein to me."

His grandmother's face changed and she rose from her perch. "Giles…"

He threw up a hand. Pity was intolerable, and speech was beyond him. The rawness of his mother's murder had dulled, but it still had the power to reduce him to quivering grief. He swung towards the door.

138

"Giles, wait!"

He hardly heard the protest. All thought of his predicament vis-à-vis Tamasine Roy and her guardian's death was forgotten, the familiar pain roiling inside him. Once outside the front door, he hailed his groom with a wave and went swiftly to the curricle as it halted before the Dower house.

"You drive, Salton." He swung himself up into the seat. "Take me home."

Resting upon the daybed, which her husband had caused to be brought into their chamber upon their arrival at the Dower House, Ottilia had leisure to think. With the intention of ordering coffee, she rang for the maidservant before settling down to cast her mind over the happenings at Willow Court.

There was much to ponder. The extent of Tamasine Roy's mental incapacity was paramount, overlaid with the question mark set upon it by Miss Ingleby's insistence that the girl was rational. Of the companion herself, Ottilia had an impression of an attachment to the dead man. Was it ardent? Had they been lovers?

Then there was the unknown Simeon. Why was he forbidden the house? Was Tamasine in love with him, insofar as she could be? It was clear the girl did not reciprocate Giles's affection. If anything, she cared more for the manservant Hemp. There lay a tale worth uncovering.

The entrance of Biddy in answer to the bell interrupted her train of thought and she put in her request for coffee.

"If it will not give Cook too much trouble, Biddy."

The maid grinned. "She keeps the pot going for you, my lady, my lord Francis having told Agnes as you're partial to the brew."

This thought for her pleasure and comfort on her husband's part threw Ottilia into disorder. Francis was apt to tease her, claiming her liking for coffee as an addiction. But here had he paved the way for her to be served with it whenever she wished. And she had treated him to nothing but tantrums.

"Thank Cook for me, if you please, Biddy."

"It won't be above a moment, my lady." The girl dropped a curtsy and withdrew.

After this revelation, it took an effort for Ottilia, inclined to dwell upon a resurgence of her troubled conscience, to return to contemplation of the tangled affair of Sir Joslin Cadel's death. The tray arrived promptly, bearing the coffee pot, a jug of cream and an unnecessary bowl of sugar. A hardened drinker of the beverage, Ottilia preferred the taste without sweetening. A sip or two of the restorative had an efficacious effect and she was soon able to bend her mind back to the matter at hand.

Recalling her last thoughts of the fellow Hemp, she turned her attention to his colleague Cuffy. The older footman had been in a privileged position with Sir Joslin, besides holding him in high regard. Could she find an opportunity to question him? In spite of Miss Ingleby's expressed doubts, Ottilia's past successes gave her confidence in her ability to prise some detail out of the man, particularly in the aftermath of loss when people tended to open up more readily than otherwise.

She had just bethought her of the other two possible witnesses, the butler Lomax and the housekeeper Whiting, when the door opened and Francis entered the bedchamber.

Gratified by the sight of Tillie at rest upon the daybed, Francis yet forebore to comment upon it, remembering how she had become unreasonably irritated at his earlier insistence upon her putting her feet up. But the smile with which she greeted him put all recollection of that out of his head and he responded instantly to the welcoming hand she held out towards him, setting down her coffee cup.

"My dear and dearest love," she uttered in a tremulous tone that caught at the deeps of Francis's affection.

He did not speak, but took hold of her hand and allowed her to draw him down to perch on the edge of the daybed. Next instant, her arms were about his neck and he was gathering her close, though unable to help wondering at this sudden access of warmth. He murmured words appropriate to the moment and did not venture to question her until she at last sat back, one hand firmly tucked within his own.

Francis raised an eyebrow and she blushed prettily.

"Don't say it."

"Are you a mind reader all of a sudden?"

A quick little sigh escaped her. "Oh, you are astonished at my change of mood, you need not tell me."

Francis reached out his free hand to caress her cheek and tip up her face so that he might plant a kiss on her lips. "I'm well acquainted with your conscience, my dear one. Though I confess to curiosity as to what brought it on this time."

She broke into the gurgling laugh that never failed to warm his heart. "Fiend! If you must know, it was the intelligence, conveyed to me by Biddy, that Cook keeps the coffee boiling for me only because you told Agnes I am fond of drinking it."

"So it is Cook who has earned my thanks, is it?"

Her grasp tightened on his hand. "Don't be absurd. You know very well it was your thought for my comfort that reminded me how lucky I am to have you."

This was deserving of reward, and it was a little time before Francis released his wife and allowed her to resume her interrupted potations. She lifted the cup to her lips.

"Did you find Sutherland?"

Recalling his mission, Francis sat back. "We did, and he applauded our foresight in locking the door. He is going to arrange for the undertakers to remove the body this afternoon, and has invited Patrick to accompany him so they may confer upon his findings."

"That is excellent," Tillie said in a relieved tone. "I was afraid he might take it in snuff that Patrick usurped his authority."

"That is not in Sutherland's style. I know him of old and he is not one of these practitioners who insist upon their rights."

"Then he will let Patrick assist at the post-mortem?"

"I imagine so. But his first task, as we expected, is to call in the coroner to decide if an inquest is needed."

"Or failing him, the local Justice of the Peace, I presume?"

Francis's mind kicked. "My God, I hope not! The fellow is related to the Graveneys. We'll have him arraigning Giles or some such foolishness."

"Oh, he came here," Tillie exclaimed. "Did Sybilla tell you?"

"No, for I came straight up on hearing you had retired." A feeling of foreboding gripped him. "What happened? I know I could make no headway with the boy. He's as headstrong as Randal."

"And as misguided," put in Tillie drily. "He managed to quarrel both with Lady Phoebe and his grandmother."

Francis was conscious of a rise of annoyance. "Drat the boy! And I told him how things stood with Mama's temper."

"As to that, it was rather Sybilla who fell foul of her own tongue. She compared him to his mother, she told me, and Giles took a pet and ran off."

"Dear God," groaned Francis, and a longing to escape overcame him. "How soon can we leave this infernal hellhole, do you think?"

Tillie set down her cup without speaking, and Francis eyed her with suspicion. Had he not known it? She was set upon seeing this thing through. He was sorely tempted to burst out with a direct prohibition and insist upon leaving as soon as possible, but he hesitated to jeopardise the better relations between them due to her change of mood. Belatedly it occurred to him that they could hardly depart the moment her brother and his family arrived.

"I suppose we are doomed to remain for the duration of Patrick and Sophie's stay."

His wife's warm smile appeared. "And we can hardly leave poor Sybilla alone to deal with your nephew's love tangles. Not to mention his involvement in a possible murder."

"It's not our affair," Francis protested, feeling all the attendant annoyance at becoming involved himself. "Nor, I may add, is it Mama's role to settle Giles's future."

Tillie's brows rose. "Dear me, Fan. Do you suggest this business may safely be left to Randal to sort out? What in the world do you suppose he is going to do when he learns about Giles's possible inclusion in a list of suspects for murder? Besides, you know he is not to be trusted to act in anyone's best interests save his own."

This was too close to the truth to be borne and Francis jerked up from the daybed. "I'm damned if I take on the burden of my brother's son as well as everything else!" Turning, he read a retort in Tillie's eye and threw out a hand.

"Nor allow you to do so either. We have our own lives to lead."

For a moment his wife said nothing, only regarding him with that clear gaze as if she weighed up her response. Francis waited, gathering his forces to withstand any pleas she might make. Then she smiled.

"Very well, my darling Fan. We will do just as you wish."

Suspicion leapt into his breast and he frowned at her. "I don't believe you. You are merely trying to lull me so that you may cajole me at your leisure."

Her characteristic laugh escaped her. "I only wish I was, Fan." Then she sobered, her grey gaze contrite. "I have vexed you enough. It is your family and you must decide how to act. I own I had rather not leave matters thus unchallenged, but I will not wilfully add to your burdens. In my present uncertain mood, I am already a burden."

Francis was swept with a tide of emotion, not all of it felicitous. The protests would not be contained. "Ottilia, you unmitigated wretch, don't do that! You know perfectly well you could never be a burden to me, for one thing."

"No, I don't know it. A complaining wife is the very devil, for I have seen my poor brother driven near demented with it."

"That is beside the bridge. And don't compare yourself to Sophie, for pity's sake!" He shook a finger at her. "I know what you are trying to do. You think if you act the quiescent wife, I will turn the tables and allow you to do as you please. Well, it won't work."

To Francis's satisfaction, Tillie sat up in a bang, throwing her hands in the air.

"What do you want of me, Francis? If I insist upon staying, you will rail at me. And yet you refuse to have me give in to you. Do you want to battle it out? Or is it that it gives you pleasure to be proved right when I am unable to resist the temptation to interfere in matters you insist are none of my affair?"

Francis pounced on this. "Aha! You admit as much. You do want to involve yourself in the business."

"I have never denied it." The despairing note caught at him. "But I had rather give it up than vex you beyond all bearing. It may, after all, be a storm in a teacup, if the post-mortem proves void."

He frowned at this turn, recalling her vehemence last summer in the village of Witherley when she was in real personal danger, but a murderer was still at large. "You don't feel it touches your honour this time then?"

"Not in the least."

"But you would hate to leave it, wouldn't you?"

"Have I not just said so?"

Francis knew he was beaten. He had always admired Tillie's candour. And if he was honest, his own conscience would not allow him to walk away while a member of his family was in difficulties. Had it not been for Giles's involvement, he might well have stuck to his guns. Or would he? No, for the unpalatable truth was that Tillie's desires were paramount with him. But a few months married and already nothing would do for him but that his wife's every whim must be humoured.

He came to the daybed and sat down again, gathering her hands into his and holding them fast. His tone was rueful, for he noted the uncertain light in those clear orbs.

"Forgive me, sweetheart. I love you too much, that is the top and bottom of it, and I can't help rebelling against it. If I could, I would give you the moon. But it hurts to be so much at the mercy of my feelings for you."

Tillie's lip trembled and her eyes misted. "And I was foolish enough to be jealous for the moment when you admired Tamasine's beauty."

So that was it. He recalled the oddity of her look earlier, which subsequent events had driven from his mind. His fingers tightened on hers. "Foolish beyond permission, Tillie. A man may admire beauty without being touched by it. Especially when there is nothing in the world more vital to him than his own wife."

Tillie did not laugh, and a frown marred her clear gaze. "You fear for my life, don't you?"

He could not deny it. "More so now."

"Dearest, because you lost Julia does not mean you will lose me too."

The mention of his first wife gave Francis a familiar twinge, but he shrugged it away. "I know that."

"But it makes no difference." She nodded. "I understand just what you mean."

Francis brought one of her hands to his lips and kissed it. "You always do."

Her smile warmed him utterly. "Shall we see how matters work themselves out in the next day or two before deciding just what to do?"

"A compromise, Tillie?"

"Well, we can't leave yet in any event, and the post-mortem must certainly develop things in one direction or another."

Francis agreed to it and immediately found himself the target of one of Tillie's pertinent questions.

"What did you think of the butler and Mrs Whiting? I scarcely spoke to either. Were they of the West Indies party?"

"Both, yes," Francis said, recalling his conversation with the housekeeper. "She was certainly more forthcoming than

Lomax, but I suspect he may have more to contribute. He queried the reason for his master's death instantly, and his manner was evasive."

"Not to say downright insolent," stated Tillie, interest in her tone. "Now why, I wonder?"

Before Francis could think this over, there was a brief knock followed by the immediate opening of the door. A youthful blond head peered round.

"Auntilla? Can we come in?"

Ottilia threw an apologetic smile at her spouse and called out an invitation. "Of course, Ben."

The older of her two nephews swept in, his brother close behind. Until this visit, Ottilia had not seen them for the better part of a year except for a day or two upon the occasion of her marriage when they had been allowed home from school to attend. As she had previously been much in their company, she was struck by the change in them. Apart from their grey Hathaway eyes, both boys had always seemed to her to favour their mother, sporting her curly blond locks, tip-tilted nose and pretty bow mouth. But at nine and ten years of age respectively, the erstwhile childish plumpness of cheek that had graced Tom and Ben had grown lean, showing the high cheekbones on their father's side.

"Goodness, but you are beginning to look so like your papa," she exclaimed, regarding them both as they stood side by side before the daybed, Francis having risen to give place.

"Huh!" came scornfully from Tom. "I wish we looked utterly like him, then we'd not get such a ragging from the other boys."

"You wouldn't believe the insults we've had to endure, Auntilla," put in Ben, fisting his hands on his hips in a mannish way that brought an unaccountable lump to Ottilia's throat.

"Dear me," she managed, trying to keep her voice even. "I suppose I need not ask whether you have indulged in fisticuffs to punish the offenders."

"'Course we have," said Tom. "We soon sent them to the rightabout."

"Well, some of 'em at least," amended Ben conscientiously. "We took a drubbing from the bigger ones."

"Yes, we did," agreed his brother enthusiastically. "I was sporting a beautiful painted peeper for days, Auntilla."

"Great heavens, you must have been quite the hero," said Ottilia admiringly.

Both boys gave out loud guffaws at this, and a light laugh escaped her husband, who had retired to stand before the fire and was resting one arm along the mantel. "I wish my own nurses had taken such a novel view."

Ben looked round at him. "Auntilla ain't our nurse, Uncle Fan."

One of his eyebrows quirked. "Oh, I beg your pardon. I had understood she cared for you all these years."

"'Course she did, but she ain't a nurse, nor a guvnor," said Tom.

"That's governess, you donkey," corrected his elder brother. "At any rate, Auntilla weren't a governess or anything like that."

"No, she was just … just…" Tom frowned, struggling for a way to express his concept of his aunt's purpose in his life.

"She wasn't anything," Ben said firmly, to Ottilia's amusement. "She was just Auntilla."

"Yes, it was rather a mouthful for toddlers to manage." A mental image of the two little mites Ottilia had first taken in charge superimposed itself upon the grown features before her. "I dare say you consider yourselves too old now for a hug?"

For an instant neither boy spoke, and then as one, they threw themselves upon her in the old way, and Ottilia found herself both laughing and crying together as she hugged first one and then the other impartially.

"Now look what you've done, you horrid creatures," she complained, as at last they consented to release her. "You've turned me into a watering pot."

The boys shouted with laughter, Tom remaining seated on the edge of the daybed close by with one hand possessively grasping Ottilia's hip, while Ben took a stance on the other side of the bed, leaning over its back. The latter looked across to the fireplace, addressing himself to Francis.

"Uncle Fan, when are you and Papa going to get the body?"

It warmed Ottilia to see how the two boys had adopted their new uncle without question. But then they had ever been friendly souls, easy-going and comfortable with all. Just like Patrick, she reflected.

"We're not getting the body, Ben. That is a job for the undertakers. But I have the key to the room where it is laid, so I must accompany your father."

"Can we come?" asked Tom eagerly.

"Papa said no, Tom," his brother reminded him severely.

"But I want to see the corpse."

"You've seen hundreds of corpses."

"A slight exaggeration, Ben," Ottilia put in. She threw an apologetic look at her husband. "I hasten to point out, Fan, that they weren't actually permitted to attend post-mortems, but these two imps have a habit of finding ingenious ways to do what one would prefer they did not."

"Yes, but we never get to see the body before Papa starts cutting it up," complained Tom, disregarding this recital of his and his brother's misdeeds. "And we want to see where the murder happened."

"We don't know there has been a murder," Francis pointed out.

"Auntilla, has there been a murder?" demanded Ben, turning his interested gaze on Ottilia. "Was it the madwoman who killed the fellow?"

"How in the world should I know the answer to either question?" countered Ottilia.

"'Cause you always know answers, Auntilla," came scoffingly from Tom. "You just don't want to tell us."

Before Ottilia could think how to respond, Francis intervened. "I wish you will stop plaguing your aunt, boys. She is supposed to be resting."

Two disbelieving faces went from Francis to Ottilia and back again. Then the boys broke out with scorn.

"Auntilla never rests."

"She ain't like Mama, Uncle Fan."

"Anyway, she can't rest now," said Ben in a tone that clinched the matter, "because there's a black fellow at the kitchen door who's come with a message for her from the madwoman."

CHAPTER SEVEN

Ottilia had crossed the road and begun the ascent up the incline leading onto the gardens of Willow Court, the footman Hemp at her side ready with an arm to help her at need, before she realised they were accompanied. Turning, she beheld the creeping figures of her nephews a little way behind. Both boys froze on being spotted, their angelic looks belied by the almost identical expressions of guilt-ridden hope that leapt to their faces. Ottilia regarded them with a resurgence of the ancient exasperation that had so many times attacked her when she'd had them in charge.

"School does not appear to have changed either of you in the least."

Tom's face fell into a grin. "It has, for we've got even more chances for mischief."

His brother cuffed him. "Ape!" Then, turning to his aunt. "It ain't mischief, Auntilla. We want to help."

"Do you indeed? How silly of me to imagine you are motivated purely by curiosity."

Ben looked a degree sheepish and his own grin dawned. "Well, that too, of course."

"I suppose you realise that your father, not to mention your Uncle Fan, will both upbraid me unmercifully when they arrive with Doctor Sutherland?"

The boys were moving already, leaping nimbly up the incline towards her.

"They won't see us, Auntilla, never fear," promised Ben.

"No, we'll hide," said Tom on a note of excitement. "We're good at that."

"As if I didn't know it." Ottilia looked at the footman. "I make you my apologies, Hemp. Short of tying them to a tree, I don't see any means of preventing them from coming with us."

But the footman was looking amused. "I do not mind, milady. The boys will be no trouble."

Ottilia thanked him, refraining with difficulty from informing him that his confidence was misplaced. If one thing was more certain than another, it was that Ben and Tom would find some means of embarrassing her, unless she contrived to keep them occupied. An idea occurred.

"Well, if you mean to be of use, you had best do everything you can to find out about the sugar plantation and everything that happened there before the family came to England. I dare say Hemp will be able to tell you a great deal, if he is not too busy."

She cast a glance at the footman as she spoke, but was given no opportunity to make a formal request, for the boys immediately began bombarding him with questions.

"Was it huge, Hemp?"

"How did you get the sugar out of the canes?"

"Did you see any pirates on the ship?"

"Are all the fellows big like you?"

"I'll wager you've got a useful right, Hemp!"

A slow smile split the man's face, showing a fine set of white teeth. He shook his head slightly and tutted, but there was a laugh in his deep voice. "Eh, boys! You make my head go round."

"Beg pardon, sir." Ben dug his brother in the ribs. "Stow it, Tom!"

Tom had opened his mouth to ask another question, but he closed it again.

"First let me take milady to Miss Tam," said Hemp. "Then we will talk. You would like a lemon sugar drink?"

Both boys accepted this offer with alacrity and Ottilia thankfully resumed her progress towards the house. In a bid to inculcate her nephews with an idea of the seriousness of the matter, she related the circumstances of Sir Joslin's death as they descended the very stairs down which he had fallen.

Much of the snow had melted as the day warmed up, and it was therefore not as much of a shock as it might have been to discover Tamasine walking in the gardens, attended by Mrs Whiting. Or was it guarded?

Hemp went forward and Tom leaned close to whisper to Ottilia. "Is that the madwoman?"

"That is Tamasine," Ottilia responded sotto voce. "Pray don't keep calling her the madwoman."

"But is she mad?" pursued the boy. "She don't look it."

"Then why is she on a leash?" demanded his more percipient brother.

Startled, Ottilia looked more closely. Tamasine was indeed in some sort attached to the housekeeper, with a stout cord tied about the girl's waist, its other end looped around the woman's wrist. Ottilia could not judge the length of the lead that lay between them for they were close together as they moved.

Heavens, but was it truly needful to put the child in the sort of leading strings meant for a toddler? If Giles were to see this, might he be convinced or alarmed? For herself, Ottilia found it pathetic, underlining the dismaying plight of the fairy-like creature that was Tamasine Roy. Really, it was hard to believe her capable of conceiving of such a notion as to be rid of her guardian.

Hemp had by now reached the two females and both looked round at Ottilia. Tamasine waved. Enjoining the boys to wait where they were for Hemp, Ottilia went across. She had not seen Mrs Whiting other than briefly earlier, and was pleasantly surprised to find the woman's manner a deal more welcoming than Miss Ingleby's.

"Ah, you'll be this Lady Fan I'm hearing about, ma'am. I hope you'll forgive the shortcomings of the house on this occasion."

Ottilia smiled. "One could scarcely complain under the circumstances, Mrs Whiting."

The woman grunted, craning her neck a little from her stunted stature. "Good of you, ma'am, but I know you've been dealt short shrift."

Feeling it prudent to refrain from responding to an obvious reference to the companion's ill temper, Ottilia turned her attention instead to Tamasine, who was regarding her with the same look of intent interest she had displayed at the Dower House. Those first moments felt a far-off memory.

"I trust you are well rested, Tamasine," she ventured.

No reply was forthcoming, and the girl continued to regard her in silence.

A sigh escaped the housekeeper. "A trifle in the sulks we are, ma'am. She doesn't care to be attached, but it's good for her to be out in the air and I can't let her go off alone."

"Where is Miss Ingleby?" asked Ottilia, feeling certain it was in general no part of the housekeeper's duty to be minding the child.

"This business has brought much work on her," said Mrs Whiting excusingly and a shadow crept into her face. "No one else to see to things now that Sir Joslin is gone. It'll be different when Mrs Delabole gets here."

"Tamasine's aunt, I believe? Are you acquainted with her, Mrs Whiting?"

"No, for she never came out to Barbados. But the master kept up a correspondence with her."

"Tamasine's father, you mean?"

"That's right. I only hope she's willing to take charge of matters here, for otherwise I can't think how we are to do."

A fretful note sounded in the woman's voice and Ottilia noted Tamasine glance at her. Then she let loose with one of her silvery laughs.

"What are you talking about, Whitey? Simeon is coming. He will manage everything."

A rich colour overlaid the housekeeper's features. "Yes, you would think that, wouldn't you, young Tam?"

The girl's gaze came around to Ottilia and her dazzling smile appeared. "Simeon is the best person in the world."

A view evidently not shared by others in the house. "What can I do for you, Tamasine?"

The blue eyes widened. "For me?"

"You sent Hemp to fetch me."

Mrs Whiting's expression changed to annoyance. "That's where he was, is it? I'll warrant she's forgotten all about it by now."

Ottilia could not approve of the housekeeper speaking of Tamasine as if she were absent, but she held her tongue on the reproof hovering there and addressed herself to the girl. "Did you wish to tell me something perhaps?"

Tamasine laughed again. "I like you to be here. I wish you will come and live with us."

"I can't do that. My husband would be most disappointed to lose me, you know."

Tamasine pouted. "But I need you."

"How so? You have already a number of persons ready to serve you."

155

"But you will not lock me in."

So that was it. Ottilia could think of no satisfactory response to this remark. She changed the subject. "I wish you will tell me more about Simeon. He is your cousin, is he not?"

Tamasine frowned, her glance going to the housekeeper. "Whitey won't let me tell you." All at once, she thrust at the woman. "I don't want you, Whitey. Why don't you go away?"

Mrs Whiting stood stolid as a rock, setting her arms akimbo and meeting the girl's gaze without flinching. She did not speak and Ottilia had to admit to inadequate experience to judge how such tactics should be countered. She could not forbear making an effort.

"I don't suppose Mrs Whiting will mind, will you?"

She threw a meaning look at the housekeeper as she spoke.

The woman hesitated, and then shrugged. "Do as you will."

Ottilia smiled at the girl. "There now, Tamasine. You may speak freely."

But the child chose not to avail herself of this permission. "Lavinia does not like me to take cold. We will go inside."

Upon which, she started off towards the house at a great rate, almost pulling Mrs Whiting off her feet. Ottilia deftly caught the woman under one arm and supported her until she was stably moving at a swifter pace than her bulk warranted.

"Wretched child," she muttered under her breath. "Does it only to provoke me."

Ottilia made no comment, only keeping pace beside her, watching the swish of Tamasine's petticoats as she swept towards the entrance. She had found time to change out of the spangled confection into a double-layered seersucker gown with a green spencer atop, and she looked the picture of an English debutante.

The door opened as the party arrived at the house, revealing Lomax, who held the door, his expression discontented. "Back again, my lady?"

The tone had nothing of servitude in it and had the effect of hardening Ottilia's resolve. "Yes, Lomax, I am indeed back — at the request of Miss Roy."

He looked sceptical, but Mrs Whiting supported her. "She sent Hemp over. Lady Fan can't know enough to ignore such messages."

"Why should I ignore it?"

"I should have thought that was obvious," said the butler, not even troubling to add an appellation of courtesy.

"Not to me."

By this time, Tamasine had halted in the hall and was attempting to rid herself of the offending leash. At which moment, Miss Ingleby appeared from a room opposite the parlour.

"For heaven's sake! Must I do everything around here? Could you not keep her occupied for half an hour, Mrs Whiting?" Then she noticed Ottilia and her eyes blazed. "What is this? Have I not made it abundantly plain your assistance is not wanted?"

"Indeed you have." Ottilia could not help the snappy tone. "It appears Tamasine does not agree with you."

"She sent Hemp to fetch her over," Mrs Whiting repeated.

Tamasine broke into the argument without ceremony. "When Simeon comes, you will all be sorry."

"Oh, do be quiet, Tamasine," came irritably from Miss Ingleby. "You don't know what you're talking about."

The girl paid no attention. Having divested herself of her end of the lead, she threw it in her duenna's direction and sailed across the hall to the parlour. "Come, Lady Fan."

Ottilia was a little amused by the imperious tone, but she took advantage and followed. An infuriated discussion broke out behind them, conducted in lowered tones so that Ottilia was unable to make it out. She found Tamasine hopping about in a state of high glee.

"They cannot stop me. They think they have bested me but they are mistaken."

Her mind afire, Ottilia did not make the error of asking directly for enlightenment. "Well, that is excessively clever of you, Tamasine. But were you not going to tell me more of your cousin Simeon?"

Tamasine spun, throwing up her hands and smiling widely just as she had done in the snow in the early morning. Ottilia perforce waited until she should settle again. In a moment, the girl ceased turning and ran to the window, peering through the glass.

"Giles is not come."

"He was here earlier, Tamasine. Do you not remember?"

Tamasine turned, fixing Ottilia with a stony stare, the blue gaze suddenly unnerving in its intensity. "They think I mean to marry Simeon, but I will outfox them. You will see. There is a reckoning to be paid and I am not yet done."

A chill swept through Ottilia. Was this the voice of innocence? It seemed hardly credible the creature could conceive of some master plan and carry it through. And this sinister reckoning? Had it begun with the elimination of Sir Joslin Cadel?

Next instant, brightness re-entered the lovely visage and Tamasine danced across, seizing Ottilia's hands in a somewhat painful grip. "I am glad you came. Will you be my companion?"

158

Ottilia lost no time in quashing this notion, whether or no it might turn the girl against her. It was an effort to speak lightly and with assumed insouciance. Who knew what might set off the child's diseased mind to make her dangerous?

"Indeed, no, Tamasine, I am merely your guest. When one is married, you know, one's first duty is to one's husband. As you will find when you enter that state."

Tamasine released her hands, stepping back a pace, her smile vanishing. "I have no duty. Others have a duty to me."

"Assuredly," agreed Ottilia, and deftly changed the subject, moving to the sofa and touching the colourful shawl thrown across its back. "I do admire this style, Tamasine. Is this typical of houses in Barbados?"

For a moment it seemed the girl was not going to rise to the bait. She stared frowningly at the shawl, as if she did not understand the significance of Ottilia's words. Then she went behind the sofa and put out a hand to stroke it.

"Oh, I know them all. Blue, green, purple, red, yellow."

To Ottilia's interest and surprise, she pointed out each patch as she gave the colour. Was this how she had been taught? By demonstration only? It was not inconceivable she had grasped the letters of the alphabet in the same way, but whether she might have been induced to recognise the symbolism of letters grouped together remained a question.

Leaving the shawl, she shifted to the mantel, regarding herself in the mirror. Not, Ottilia noted, in the critical gaze other young ladies might use, seeking to discover errant curls or a defective mark. Instead Tamasine stared directly into her own eyes, almost as if they belonged to another to whom she spoke.

"Joslin does not want me to marry anyone for I have all the money." She turned suddenly, and Ottilia once more found herself the recipient of one of those fixed and chilling looks. "He died, you know. He cannot stop me if he is dead."

Startled, and not a little perturbed, Ottilia knew not what to reply. Her suspicions of the girl returned tenfold. Hard as it seemed to credit her with a murderous scheme, this freely confessed motive could not but raise spectres. Throwing caution to the winds, she risked all on a single throw.

"Is that why you pushed him, Tamasine?"

The blue gaze faltered and the girl looked abruptly vulnerable. A little gasp left her lips and her smooth skin wrinkled in a frown. "Did I? I don't remember."

"You told me you had killed him," Ottilia pursued doggedly, not without a qualm.

A whimper escaped the girl. "Where is Lavinia? Why does she not come?"

Ottilia's senses were alive with conjecture, but she could not feel it politic to employ her usual ruthless methods with this female. She adopted a tone carefully casual.

"Would you wish me to call Lavinia?"

Tamasine did not answer. She put her hands to her head and pulled at her hair, little quivers passing across her face meanwhile. Her eyes flicked this way and that.

Ottilia watched without speaking. What did this betoken? Was it real? It looked almost as if she were acting, for she had not before shown conduct comparable to this. She tried a gentle note.

"Tamasine?"

The girl glanced at her, but did not answer. Instead, she crossed the room and opened the door, where she stood for a moment, apparently surveying the hall. Then she threw a gleeful look over her shoulder. "They are all gone. I am free."

She vanished on the words, and Ottilia, though she hurried to the door, was too late to see where she went. But she could hear rapid footsteps on the wooden stairs and surmised the child had escaped to the floors above.

Ottilia could not reconcile it with her conscience to do nothing, although she was uncertain how to proceed. She crossed the hall and went to knock on the door through which Miss Ingleby had earlier emerged. There was no response. After a moment, Ottilia turned the handle and looked in, finding a book room which mirrored the parlour opposite in size. Casting a glance back into the hall, she seized opportunity and went inside.

A tambour desk stood near the window, its roll-top up. A collection of papers and ledgers spread out across the inner surface bore witness to Miss Ingleby's present industry. Two ledgers were open, one atop the other, and several documents, their seals already broken, had been piled in an untidy heap, as if a hasty hand had rummaged through them. A freshly sealed letter lay on the blotter and Ottilia read the direction.

It was addressed to Mrs Ruth Delabole at an address in the County of Berkshire. She hoped Miss Ingleby intended despatching the thing by fast courier. The sooner the woman got here the better, and no doubt she would waste no time if she knew how matters were left.

A glance at the ledgers showed them to refer to expenditures concerned with housekeeping and Ottilia turned her attention to the open documents. Without picking anything up, she scrutinised the one on top and a few lines told her she was looking at the instruction that gave Tamasine Roy into the guardianship of Sir Joslin Cadel. Was Miss Ingleby looking to discover if Tamasine's father had made provision in the event of Sir Joslin's demise? Ottilia recalled her defensive attitude when questioned upon this point.

Her fingers itched to sift through the pile for she could make out nothing of value from the few words visible in the items below the one on top. She had no right whatsoever to be examining anything and might with justice be criticised for doing as much as she had already done. Yet a streak of prescience insisted she look further.

Refraining from disturbing the papers, Ottilia examined the little compartments in the top, which proved to contain the usual assortment of seals, wax, pens and oddments. Turning to the drawers below, she opened the narrow central one and found a collection of clean parchments ready for use, which might argue a tidy mind if it were not for a scattering of odd slips of yellowed notes. The banked drawers either side she found to be stuffed with documents, some in tied bundles, others in disordered clumps.

Ottilia suffered a passing pang of sympathy for the unsuspecting Mrs Delabole, who must inherit this muddle, unless she proved willing to leave the bulk of it to a legal advisor. She was about to close the last drawer when a fragment in an unfolded letter caught her eye.

'...resembles too closely the conduct of my poor incarcerated Florine...'

Without thought, Ottilia twitched the letter out of the drawer and ran her eyes down the sheet. It was addressed to Sir Joslin, penned in a spidery uneven fashion, which suggested the hand that wrote it had been shaky or infirm. It was signed 'Matthew', and the burden of the man's plea was a request to use his daughter with gentleness.

'In you, my most beloved cousin and friend, I place my trust as I charge you with the care of my tortured little soul. She may not long burden you, cast as she is in her sad mother's mould. But while she lives, I conjure your mercy on her behalf. Let her be as free as it may be done without harm to any or to herself.'

There was more in similar vein, but the hints contained herein were enough to set Ottilia's mind ablaze. She stared at the paper, reading the words again as their inner meanings battered at her brain. Tamasine had taken the taint from the distaff side? Then she could be dangerous. What had the unfortunate Florine done to prove mad enough to be shut away from the world? What of this notion the girl might not live long? Ironic it was instead the guardian who had left this earth. Could the mother have died as the result of some act of insanity? Or might she have taken her own life?

These conjectures were interrupted by the sound of footsteps in the hall outside, apparently approaching the book room door. Ottilia stuffed the letter back in the drawer in haste and slid it shut. She looked about for a way of escape and headed for a second door that led away from the hall. Slipping through, she quickly closed it to behind her without fully shutting it. Then she put her eye to the crack in order to see who might enter the other room.

She heard the sound of the door opening, and footsteps crossed to the desk. By what she was able to make out, the intruder was male. Her eye ran down his legs and up again to his back and she caught the wig tied in a queue at his neck. The butler Lomax!

Ottilia held her breath, gripping the door for fear of it slipping from her grasp. From what she could hear, the fellow was sifting papers. Then he opened a drawer and rummaged within. A faint sound of exhaled breath reached her. Satisfaction? The drawer slammed shut and the man shifted out of her line of sight for an instant. Then he crossed it again and his footsteps told Ottilia he was heading for the door.

She hesitated, trying to decide whether she might safely re-enter the book room and aim by that way for the hall. But if Lomax was still within earshot, or hovering in the hall itself, she would give herself away. Thinking to look for another way out, Ottilia gently closed the book room door fully. Turning, she ran slap into Miss Ingleby.

CHAPTER EIGHT

The companion, standing a few paces away in the room Ottilia had entered, regarded her with a look compound of satisfaction and disdain.

"Spying again, Lady Francis?"

Ottilia opted for the bald truth. "Yes, I'm afraid I was." She gestured behind her. "I think Lomax has taken something from one of the drawers in there."

A swift frown swept away Miss Ingleby's former expression and she started forward, pushing past and wrenching open the book room door. Ottilia followed her in, watching as she went quickly to the desk and jerked one of the drawers open. She stared at its contents briefly and slammed it shut again. As she began a repetition of this action with the other drawers, Ottilia intervened.

"I cannot think you will possibly find out just what was taken, but I am fairly sure it was a specific drawer. He knew what he was looking for."

Miss Ingleby paused with her fingers on the handle of the middle drawer and glanced over her shoulder. "Just as you did?"

"I was merely browsing. I have no knowledge of the contents of that desk."

A scorching look was all the companion's answer and she turned her attention back to the drawers, continuing what she had started.

Ottilia moved to the other side of the desk, the better to watch the woman's face. She wore a look of pinched dissatisfaction.

"I believe Lomax sifted through those documents you have piled up there," she offered. "Before he opened the drawer."

Miss Ingleby cast a cursory look over the papers on the desk before her gaze came up. "Did you look at them?"

"I glanced at the one on top and I looked to note what the ledgers might contain, yes. But I stopped short of searching through the pile."

"You surprise me," came from the woman on a contemptuous note.

Ottilia thought a full confession would serve her best. If Miss Ingleby was persuaded of her candour, she might get further with the creature. "I did look in the drawers."

The companion was still opening and slamming drawers without making any real effort to look within. Ottilia believed she was principally engaged in an exercise to relieve her feelings for there was certainly no method to her actions.

"Did you find anything of interest?"

"Yes." Miss Ingleby stilled. Her eyes came back to meet Ottilia's. Was it alarm in them? She did not speak, but it was not difficult to divine her question. "I found a memorandum from, I think, Mr Roy to Sir Joslin. Written, I suspect, when he was debilitated, possibly close to death."

She allowed this to sink in, and could see from Miss Ingleby's sharpening expression that she knew the document referenced. Ottilia struck.

"Florine was deranged, was she not? Mr Roy's wife? She had to be locked up permanently. Why, Miss Ingleby? What had she done?"

The companion's features were taut, her gaze dark. With anger? Distress? Both perhaps. Her voice was icy, but even. "It was before my time."

"Yet I feel sure you know the story. How did she die?"

The woman's lips tightened. Looking down, she pushed the ledgers and the papers further into the inner recess of the desk and rolled the top into place, effectively concealing everything from Ottilia's view. Extracting a key from a pocket within her petticoats, she locked the desk with something of a flourish, and looked up again, throwing a look of triumph at Ottilia.

"I should have done that earlier, had it occurred to me that an uninvited guest might pry into matters outside her province."

The rebuke was just, but Ottilia felt no remorse. There was matter here demanding investigation, and she had rather be reviled and beforehand than hold back only to discover all vestige of evidence had been removed. Particularly in view of the butler's action and especially with regard to the possibility of Tamasine's having despatched her guardian to another plane of existence.

She was just wondering how best to respond when the pealing of the front door bell put her out of the necessity of doing so.

An impatient exclamation escaped Miss Ingleby and she turned for the door. Opening it, she looked pointedly at Ottilia and one hand invited her to leave the book room. She did so just as the footman Cuffy came through the servants' door at the back, heading for the front entrance. Was this Patrick, come with the local doctor and Francis to remove the body?

The difference in attitude toward the party headed by Doctor Sutherland was marked. Lomax treated him with the proper deference of a servant and Miss Ingleby assumed her best social manner, which the Fanshawes had seen in the early morning at the Dower House. Ottilia supposed the show of officialdom was responsible, although Sutherland had dispensed with the services of the coroner, who could not be reached.

"He will trust to the post-mortem to make his decision upon an inquest, in any event," explained the doctor, who proved to be a man of advanced age and well acquainted with the Polbrook family.

Ottilia was amused to learn he had seen her husband into the world and attended his childish ailments. "Dear me, sir, I feel I ought to question you closely to ensure I have not been hoodwinked."

Sutherland laughed out. "I cannot think Lord Francis would seek to conceal his youthful peccadilloes. Had it been his brother now..."

But here, Sutherland evidently felt he was overstepping the mark, for he harrumphed loudly and turned to the butler, asking to be conducted to Sir Joslin's remains.

Ottilia did not accompany the cavalcade, which numbered in addition to Patrick and Francis, two men from the undertakers armed with a stretcher, but contented herself with exchanging an eloquent look with her husband in hopes of warning him she had matter for discussion in plenty. Instead, when she saw Cuffy inclined to follow, she seized opportunity and hailed him in as low a tone as would serve to attract his attention without drawing Miss Ingleby's. The companion had followed up as far as the first flight and was standing looking after the men.

"Cuffy, a word, if you please?"

The footman paused on the first stair and looked back.

Ottilia smiled. "There is too much of a crowd up there already, do you not think?"

With evident reluctance, he abandoned his purpose, stepped off the staircase and came towards her, his features showing anew the grey drawn look that signalled his loss.

"Madame?"

Ottilia dropped her tone almost to a whisper. "Would you object to coming into the parlour, Cuffy?" A short line appeared between his brows and Ottilia surmised he was too wrapped in grief to divine her purpose. "I don't wish to be overheard."

At that, his eyes came a little alive and he glanced up at the still figure of Miss Ingleby.

"Just so," said Ottilia, and moved towards the parlour.

The footman slipped past to open the door for her and followed her in. The door shut with a soft click and Ottilia turned to find the man moving a little into the open space of the parlour.

"I hope my nephews have not been a trouble to you," she ventured, by way of an opener.

He echoed his colleague. "No trouble, madame. You want to talk of Master Jos's death?"

"Straight to the point, Cuffy," she said appreciatively. "Yes, I do want to talk of it. You were close to Sir Joslin, and I am hopeful you may be able to help me uncover the truth."

Cuffy's dark eyes burned. "Someone killed Master Jos?"

"I don't yet know," said Ottilia with truth, "but the suspicion cannot be avoided. Do you know anyone who might want to be rid of him?"

Slowly he shook his head. "He is a good man. Sick, but good."

Ottilia seized on this. "Sick how, Cuffy? What was amiss with him?"

One large hand came up to hit at the footman's chest. "Master has a bad lung. Fever catched him bad. His lung is no good after."

"How long ago did he suffer this bout of illness with his lungs?"

"Too many years. Ten, maybe fifteen. Master Jos is not working his plantation. He selled the place. He works only for Master Matt."

Ottilia hastened to unravel this. "You are saying Sir Joslin had his own lands but could not work them after his illness? But he had some capital of his own then? From the sale, I mean."

"He is not a rich man. He is trying to work the plantation, but it is no good. Overseer there cheated him. Master Jos lost money. He selled his plantation too cheap."

"Which is why he had to work for Mr Roy."

"He is not working too much. Master Jos keeps the books; also he looks to teach Mister Simeon how to make sugar, how to do distilling."

Ottilia's ears pricked up. Simeon again? "Was Simeon a good pupil?"

A scornful noise escaped Cuffy's lips. "He does not like to learn. He does not like to work. He is a lazy boy."

Filing this interesting tidbit away in her mind, Ottilia returned to the matter of Sir Joslin. "I gather your master suffered recurrences of his illness?" She saw puzzlement in the man's face and simplified her question. "He became ill again and again?"

A dark shadow seemed to cross the footman's face and he fetched a deep sigh. "He is bad too many times. He has too much pain." Again the fellow touched his own chest.

"Even here? In these last months?"

Cuffy's eyes gleamed his sorrow. "Here it is too cold, madame. It is not good for Master Jos's chest. He gets mighty sick."

Ottilia eyed the fellow. Should she dare so far without benefit of the post-mortem? Yet if she failed to strike now, who knew when another opportunity would present itself?

"He took laudanum for the pain, did he not, Cuffy?"

The man flinched as if he had received a blow. His eyes widened and his nostrils flared. Hoarsely, he spoke. "Why do you ask? Why is it you think this?"

"Because we found a bottle of laudanum on top of his press, Cuffy," Ottilia said coolly, her eyes never leaving his face.

The man turned his gaze away, one hand coming palm up towards her, as if he would signal a stop. He was plainly weighing what he should do, the dark eyes shifting here and there without intent. Then he backed a pace or two, and the hoarse note was again in his voice.

"I will go now, madame. I have too much work."

Ottilia watched him leave the room, wondering if Cuffy had any notion of how completely his over-reaction had convinced her Sir Joslin was indeed an opium-eater.

Sounds from upstairs betokened the removal of the dead man's corpse from the house and Ottilia went out into the hall, where she found Cuffy standing stock still, staring up at the men who, under Sutherland's direction, were stepping carefully down the stairs, burdened by the loaded stretcher, its sad cargo covered with a blanket.

Ottilia took in that Patrick and Francis were bringing up the rear, Lomax lagging a little behind. In the periphery of her vision, she noticed the parcel of servants crowding in through the green baize door at the back of the hall, Hemp among them. Remembering her nephews, Ottilia cast a rapid glance along the gathering row, and breathed a sigh of relief to note the absence of Tom and Ben.

The only sound in the place was the murmur of the doctor's voice as he kept a watchful eye on the proceedings, and the heavy footsteps of the men coming down the stairs. Just as they reached the bottom, the door to the book room was jerked open and Miss Ingleby appeared in the aperture. The woman took one look at the covered contents of the stretcher and the expression of irritation she had been wearing changed in an instant. A wail of anguish issued through her lips.

The world seemed to stop for a blinding instant of panic. The doctor turned in shock. The men carrying the stretcher halted, as did those on the stairs. Every eye turned to Miss Ingleby.

Then the creature moved with speed, throwing herself in the direction of the stretcher as her throat opened to give way to distraught sounds. As of instinct, Doctor Sutherland shifted to intercept her, holding her back as she struggled to reach the dead man.

Her heart wrung, Ottilia ran across the hall, catching at the woman's flailing hands. "No, Lavinia, no! Leave him be, my dear. Let him go."

Miss Ingleby either did not hear or paid no heed. Her cries redoubled and her eyes echoed her inner torment as Sutherland urged the stretcher-bearers to hasten across the hall and out through the door that someone was holding open.

Ottilia had all to do to keep the woman from bursting forth, and was thankful to see Francis and Patrick coming to her aid. The two gentlemen laid hold of the creature, leaving Ottilia free to try to bring her out of the ungovernable grief which had been seething all day. Drastic measures were called for and Ottilia raised her hand and dealt the woman a short sharp slap on the cheek.

"That is enough, do you hear me?"

The shock of it brought Miss Ingleby's lamentations to an abrupt halt. Her eyes rolled and then focused on Ottilia's face. Her breath caught once or twice, and then she began quietly to weep, sagging at the knees.

"Cuffy!" Francis called.

The footman shot forward, and Ottilia gave place as he caught the sinking woman and lifted her up into his strong arms. Ottilia was about to indicate the parlour when she was forestalled by the dwarfish figure of the housekeeper, whom she had not even noticed bustling up.

"This way, Cuffy."

There was a surge towards the parlour door. Ottilia watched the servants crowding round and turned to find her husband still there, but her brother moving swiftly to the front door.

"Patrick has gone to catch Sutherland," Francis told her, "so that he may be sure of joining with him in the post-mortem."

Ottilia seized his arm, and spoke in an urgent whisper. "Is the bedchamber unlocked?"

"Yes, and I've given Lomax the key. Why?"

Glancing quickly round, Ottilia discovered the butler haranguing the interested servants, presumably in a bid to send them about their business. There was no time to lose. She turned back to her spouse.

"Keep him from following me, Fan."

Without more ado, she slipped to the stairs and began lightly to mount them. As she approached Sir Joslin's bedchamber, she saw the door was open. Had Francis left it so? Slowing, Ottilia softened her footsteps, creeping on tiptoe to the doorway and sneaking a quick peek.

A rather short individual with a familiar blond head was standing at the press, engaged in inspecting the bottles ranged along its surface. Ottilia let her breath go and stepped into the room, only to catch sight of a pair of upturned breeches kneeling near the bed. She addressed this one of her nephews first.

"And just what do you expect to find under the bed, Tom?"

The boy straightened, turning so swiftly, he almost lost his balance. His impish grin appeared as he sprang to his feet. "Spiders and cockeroshes."

"Cockroaches," corrected his brother automatically. He had turned sharply at the sound of Ottilia's voice. His cheeks reddened a little. "Didn't expect to see you, Auntilla."

"Evidently." She wasted no words in expostulation. It would be useless in any event, adept as these imps were at inventing excuses. "Have you discovered anything of use?"

Ben's eyes began to sparkle. "I should say we have."

Tom leapt for his brother, putting a hand across his mouth, and hissing a warning. "Don't say anything about the —!" He broke off, throwing a look of consternation at Ottilia.

She thought swiftly. It never did to demand an answer. Glancing at the press, she noticed the drawers incompletely closed. "Secrets? Very well, I won't pry, but if you have taken anything from this room, allow me to warn you that it may well be evidence."

Two pairs of eyes exchanged anguished looks. Ottilia waited. Tom's shoulders sagged and his hand dived into his pocket. He brought out a handful of wrapped items and held them out.

"They're sweets, Auntilla. There are lots and lots in there. I didn't think they'd miss a couple."

Ottilia picked one up. It was thick and oblong, rather large for an individual confection, and there was an inscription in black lettering on the white packaging.

"Flora Sugars," she read. "Where did you find this exactly?"

Ben shifted away from the press and dragged the long top drawer open. He moved aside as Ottilia came to look, setting the package down.

"There's all sorts in here, Auntilla. It's not just sweets. Look!"

The drawer was a jumble of oddments of paper, packages of one sort and another, a couple of scrunched up gaily embroidered pocket-handkerchiefs, an odd brass buckle, a number of torn fob ribbons, several snuff boxes, silver and bone combs, and rings carelessly thrown among the rest.

Tom's hand sneaked in. Ottilia batted it away. "Don't touch!"

"But I'm only going to show you the packages of sweets," he said in an injured tone. "We never took those, Auntilla. See, there are humbugs and barley sugar drops."

"And sugared almonds," added Ben, reaching in to show her the appropriate package.

Ottilia's interest was aroused. Odd that these packages, also labelled 'Flora Sugars', gave notice of their contents. The humbug package was open and she held it up and looked inside. There were but a few sweetmeats left, fused together. But it was enough to point the difference.

"How many of the others have you got, Tom?" He set two down alongside the other, at the same time throwing a glance at his brother. Ben sighed and stuck his hand into his pocket, bringing out a single package. "That's all?"

Ben grinned. "I'm not as greedy as him." He set it with the rest.

Ottilia eyed the four oblong packets. Were they confections? They were inordinately large. An idea was floating at the back of her mind but she would need Patrick's more extensive knowledge. She ought to impound them, but having warned off the boys, she could scarcely pocket them herself. She compromised, taking one and slipping the remainder back into the drawer.

"I need your papa to look at one of these." She slipped it into her pocket.

"Why, Auntilla?"

"How can a sweet be evidence?"

"That remains to be seen," she said, rummaging in the drawer as the notion pricked at her. If she was right, there ought to be empty packets. Or would he have thrown them away? Sir Joslin was evidently a man of careless habits. He might well discard them in the drawer along with the half-empty package of humbugs.

"What are you looking for, Auntilla?"

"Empty packages. Can you see a wastepaper basket anywhere?"

As one, the boys swept the area, dipping here and there to find one. With a cry of triumph, Tom pounced, diving behind the press and coming up with a basket in his hands. Ben instantly rummaged within and Ottilia intervened.

"Take care! Let me look."

But her nephew brought his hand out, holding up a scrunched paper. "This, d'you mean?"

Ottilia took it and spread it out, looking for the label. 'Flora Sugars' was there, but no other writing. Before she could prevent him, Tom upended the basket, spilling its contents on the floor and both blond heads bent over them, hands scrabbling in the debris. Ottilia stood over them.

"Are there any more?"

There were five altogether. Her nephews spread them on the surface of the press and Ottilia eyed them with burgeoning excitement. This might explain everything. She directed the boys to clean up the mess and slipped the papers into the drawer, sliding them under the shambles within to keep them hidden. Knowing they would bombard her with unanswerable questions, she seized upon a distraction as her nephews completed their task.

"Where else have the two of you been roaming?"

"All over," said Ben, resuming his inspection of the bottles and jars on top of the press. "What's this stuff?" He pulled out a stopper and sniffed. Then he jerked back. "That's disgusting. What is it?"

Ottilia took it out of his hand. "Don't fiddle." Replacing the stopper, she laid the bottle down and was obliged to catch Tom's hand as he reached out for the bottle. "I said, don't fiddle." She then shifted both boys bodily away from the press. "I hope you haven't been spotted."

"'Course we ain't," scoffed Tom.

"We've been up and down and nobody saw us at all."

"You were supposed to be talking to Hemp, not running around the house."

"Hemp got busy, so we decided to explore."

"Yes, and you'll be glad we did, Auntilla, for guess what?"

"She'll never guess," said Tom with scorn. "You wait 'til you hear, Auntilla. You ain't going to believe it."

Without much expectation, Ottilia raised her brows. "Well, what?"

"It's right at the top of the house," said Tom.

"What is?"

Ben put a hand over his brother's mouth. "Stow it, Tom! Anybody might hear if you shout like that."

Tom looked contrite, but he pushed the hand away, lowering his voice to a whisper. "It's a room, Auntilla."

"A room? I see. I thought you were about to surprise me with a skeleton at least."

Ben gave her a reproving look. "This is serious, Auntilla." He lowered his voice and came closer. "You should see it. There's bars on the windows and mattresses all around the walls besides one on the floor."

"And there ain't nothing else at all," said Tom, his eyes sparkling with excitement. "You know what we think, Auntilla?"

But Ottilia, struck with a decidedly unpleasant crawling in her guts, had already guessed even as Ben spelled it out.

"When she gets dangerous, we think that's where they put the madwoman."

Following her nephew up the back stairs, Ottilia was relieved she was not again likely to run foul of Miss Ingleby, who was, she hoped, safely ensconced in the downstairs parlour. A better opportunity was unlikely to arise. She had sent Ben down to tell Francis what was afoot — a sop to her uneasy conscience.

A ripple of anticipation went through her, coupled with a feeling of satisfaction. There could now be no doubt of Tamasine's derangement. One did not confine a person in a room with mattresses around the walls unless there was a real danger of harm. To herself perhaps more than others? Was she prone to throw herself about in a frenzy?

Tom, sneaking up the narrow stairway, came to the top and paused. He turned with a whispered exclamation. "Somebody's up here, Auntilla!"

"Let me come there, Tom!"

She pushed her way past him and stopped, listening hard as she looked along the dim attic corridor, lit only from such light as came in from dusty windows under the eaves. A slight sound of swishing came to her ears. Yes, someone was certainly there.

"Is this where the servants are housed too?"

"No, they ain't, Auntilla. Hemp said they're on the floor below at the back of the house."

"Was the place deserted when you came up earlier?"

Tom nodded, leaning forward as if he sought to catch the sounds. "Is it the madwoman, do you think?"

Ottilia put a finger to her lips. Tamasine, if it was she, had hearing acute enough to catch their murmurs. She preferred to surprise the girl than to be surprised.

"Stay behind me, Tom."

She ought to make him remain where he was, but he was unlikely to obey such an injunction. Besides, she was all too conscious of an eerie feeling of apprehension. There was no saying what sort of condition one might find Tamasine in. But the urge to see for herself what the boys had described was too strong to be denied.

Once again lifting on tiptoe, Ottilia crept to the end of the corridor and paused there. The swishing had ceased. She drew a breath for courage and in one swift movement, swung out to take the turn.

The corridor was empty. She set a hand against the wall and sagged a trifle, looking along its length. A shadow moved at the far end. Her breath tightened and the heart froze within her chest. Peering into the dimness, she could just make out the pale oval of a face and the outline of a gown.

Ottilia swallowed her fright and called out. "Tamasine, is that you?"

There was no response. She could hear Tom breathing behind her and was reassured. At least she was not alone with the creature. She tried again.

"Tamasine? It's Lady Fan. I've come to see you."

For a long weightless moment there was nothing. Then the peal of silver bells echoed along the corridor. Tamasine's laughter. An instant later, she danced into the light, beaming.

"Lady Fan, Lady Fan, Lady Fan! Have you come to see my eyrie?"

Instinct prompted the truth. "Yes. May I see it?"

Tamasine halted halfway along and flung out a hand. It disappeared into an aperture. "Here! Come! Come and see!"

She vanished through the opening and Ottilia could hear her chattering within. She shivered slightly, reluctant now to follow.

"Are you going to go in, Auntilla?" Tom's whisper sounded overloud in the dimness.

"I think so. Wait here."

Cautious now, she moved quietly down the corridor. As she approached the opening, Tamasine jumped out, directly in her path. Before she could do or say anything, the girl slipped aside. A pair of hands, stronger than Ottilia would have believed possible, thrust into her shoulder blades and she pitched into the attic room. Losing balance, she fell to the wooden floor.

Disregarding the shock of pain, fearful of what the girl might do, Ottilia did not try to pick herself up, but pulled out of the ignominious position, turning to face the threat. But Tamasine had already moved into the room, running to the window and seizing hold of the bars.

"My eyrie, my eyrie," she sang.

Ottilia's common sense had not quite deserted her. Her nephew was in the corridor. She called out with urgency.

"Tom! Run and fetch Uncle Fan! Quickly!"

She heard his footsteps start off, but they were drowned by Tamasine's sudden mimicking yell.

"Run and fetch Uncle Fan! Run and fetch Uncle Fan! Run and fetch Uncle Fan!"

Ottilia watched the girl warily. Tamasine had turned, the bright blue eyes agleam with a manic light. Oh, dear Lord, why had she dared this alone? She tried a soft approach, trying to keep her voice light despite its shaking.

"Dear me, how silly I am to fall like this. Wait while I get up."

The girl made no move towards her, but merely stood, her back against the bars, the disquieting gleam trained upon her quarry. Ottilia felt like a rabbit under the eye of its predator. She pushed herself up from the ground, keeping her movements slow and steady, only half aware of an ache at her hip and hands that felt scraped and raw. She dared not look to assess the damage.

She tried for a normal note, affecting to look around while keeping the girl under constant observation. "So this is your eyrie, Tamasine?"

A tiny laugh escaped the girl. "My eyrie. They put me in here when I'm naughty, you see."

Or beyond the scope of management. But Ottilia did not say it. She took in the mattresses tied around the walls, the one on the floor covered in a mess of blankets. All were torn, shredded in places, straw escaping and wisping on the boards.

Ottilia took a step towards the door. "Well, I must thank you for showing it to me, Tamasine."

The girl's eyes rolled in an arc encompassing the beams above and the floorboards below. "Would you like to stay?"

A shudder ran through Ottilia despite all her effort to remain outwardly calm. To her consternation, her voice came out too high as she threw words out. Any words, enough to keep the creature's mind occupied.

"I can't. My husband is expecting me." She glided towards the door.

Tamasine darted across before her and stood in the opening, her hands going out to the jambs. "I said you must stay."

Ottilia hesitated. Tom must surely bring Francis at any moment. She had only to humour her, keep her sweet. The word threw question into her head and she spoke without thought, moving further into the room.

"Flora Sugars, is that the name?"

"Mine. They are mine, mine, mine."

The rising note itched at Ottilia's nerves, but she held her ground, infusing friendliness into her voice. "Did your guardian like confections, Tamasine? Sir Joslin?"

For a moment, the girl looked disconcerted. The gleam in the China blue eyes faded a little. When she spoke, she sounded altogether normal again.

"I eat the sugar out of the canes. Joslin likes sweetmeats. He makes them. Simeon makes them for me."

A memory jerked in Ottilia's mind. What had Cuffy said about distilling? Would Sir Joslin have combined that task with the making of sugar confections? And here once more was the fellow Simeon. How nearly had he been involved with the family in Barbados?

"Simeon makes them?"

"Yes, and Whitey gives me some."

Mrs Whiting was responsible for doling out sweetmeats? Then her suspicion had some foundation. She dared not say more. Tamasine was on the move again, tripping around the mattresses and thumping at them.

Lord in heaven, where was Francis? It seemed an age since Tom had run off, but in reality it could not be many minutes. She contemplated making another shift towards the door, but her heart misgave her. The creature was utterly unpredictable today.

As if in answer to the thought, Tamasine loomed up in front of her, the beaming smile in place, but the eyes perfectly glassy.

Ottilia remained still, holding her breath, meeting that peculiar gaze.

Hasty footsteps sounded on the wooden stairs. Tamasine turned her head, listening. Then, giggling, she sped to the open door, hiding in the space behind it, flat against the wall.

Breathing again, Ottilia stayed just where she was, waiting. The footsteps drove down the corridor and Francis appeared in the opening and halted, his eyes flying to her face. Ottilia spoke as pleasantly as she could manage.

"Ah, there you are, Fan. Tamasine has been showing me her eyrie, you must know."

She gave him a meaningful glance and flicked her eyes towards the door where the girl was standing. He nodded briefly, clearly catching her drift. He shifted into the room and deliberately leaned his weight against the open door, trapping the child behind. A grunt came, but Tamasine made no other protest. His voice was rough with concern and he sounded a trifle out of breath besides, but Ottilia thought it would pass for normal with the person for whom it was meant.

"That is excellent, my love, but I fear we must make haste. My mother expects us for dinner, as you know, and she will be wild with us if we are late."

"Very true," Ottilia said loudly and crossed with swift steps to the door, slipping through with a feeling of intense relief.

"Go! I'll follow."

The murmured command came in her ear as she passed. Ottilia needed no urging, relief coursing through her as she sped down that horrid corridor and made for the narrow stair. Within seconds, Francis was behind her. She glanced back.

"Is she following?"

"I don't think so. But don't stop. I've sent the boys home."

No further word was spoken until they reached the comparative safety of the gallery above the main stair. Francis caught Ottilia's arm to halt her and pulled her into his embrace. Ottilia snuggled, relieved not to have a peal rung over her immediately.

When he let her go, she gave him a deprecating look. "Are you livid with me?"

He cocked an eyebrow. "I ought to be, you wretch, but I'm too relieved you came to no harm."

Ottilia dropped her voice to a whisper. "She truly is out of her senses, Fan. There can be no doubt. I can readily believe she did indeed kill her guardian."

It was excessively late and Patrick had still not returned, but Francis had not been able to prevail upon either his wife or his mother to go to bed and wait to hear the doctor's news in the morning. Tillie's recalcitrance was no surprise, despite her obvious tiredness after the excitements of the day. He had anointed the slight grazes on her palms with a salve, ordered coffee and made her rest before dinner, with the result that she declared herself fully recovered from her ordeal and anxious for her brother's news.

Francis, using a stratagem as unscrupulous as any she had used as his fond wife later informed him, drew on their mother's sensibilities to get the boys ordered off to bed within minutes of the company entering the parlour.

"They have had a most exhausting day, Sophie. I imagine you will wish them to have an early night."

Sophie Hathaway at once swooped upon her reluctant sons, clasping first one and then the other to her bosom. "My darlings! Come up with me and I will tuck you in, for I don't mean to linger. I will be lucky if this terrible day has not brought on my spasms."

"But we want to wait for Papa," protested Ben, throwing a reproachful look at Francis.

"Yes, 'cause he's cutting up the body and —"

His mother's shriek smothered Tom's ghoulish glee, and she shuddered. "No, no, my darling boy, we have had quite enough of bodies for one day. Now make your bows, my loves, and thank her ladyship and we will go up directly."

It was plain Sophie's occasional cloying forays into motherhood were effective, for a couple of inexpert bows were made in the dowager's direction and the reluctant boys were ushered out, Miss Mellis following with offers of warm milk and hot bricks.

However, when Francis tried a like tactic with his own mother, he found her as adamant as Tillie.

"Do you imagine I could sleep without knowing whether or no there is matter for concern with Giles in question?"

"Will you sleep any better for hearing a murder has been committed?"

"Hush, Fan," admonished his wife. "At least there is a chance all of us may enjoy a good night's sleep if my suspicions prove to be unfounded."

"Ha! If I know anything of you, Tillie, you don't want them to be unfounded, sleep notwithstanding." She laughed, but there was a troubled look in her eyes. He abandoned his post by the mantel and went to join her on the sofa. "What is it, my love?"

He noted his mother glance across, her black gaze sombre. Inwardly cursing his nephew, he waited while Tillie seemed to gather her thoughts.

"Whether or not there is a murder, I am afraid we are in for a rough ride. What with that half-witted creature on the loose, and Giles infatuated, and poor Phoebe swearing she will have nothing to do with him, we are all going to have our hands full."

His mother groaned. "Yes, and ten to one that stupid child will involve us willy-nilly. She ought to be confined."

Since this point had been exhaustively discussed at dinner, Francis was relieved when the door opened to admit the maids, bearing the accoutrements for tea. The boys had talked without cease, their revelations causing Sophie to declare that she was unlikely to recover from the shocks of the day. Tillie showed no disposition to curb them, of course. Indeed, she had positively encouraged them to regale the company with all they had learned about 'the madwoman's attic' in their illicit adventures at Willow Court.

While the women busied themselves about the tea kettle, Francis found his mind dwelling on Tom and Ben's disclosures concerning the sugar plantation in Barbados. They had pumped the footman Hemp to some effect. Although the dowager had been sceptical, Hemp claimed the many slaves were well treated by 'Master Matt', although he was himself a free man.

"And so is Cuffy," said Ben, "though he was a slave before. He came from Africa when he was a boy."

The dowager exploded. "Stolen, I dare say!"

"Oh, do not say so!"

"I do not scruple to say so, Mrs Hathaway. I know all too much of that practice. An abominable humiliation, to be dragged from his rightful home by brigands calling themselves traders, hauled across the sea in stinking conditions and sold like a beast at auction. The whole proceeding disgusts me."

As Francis was well aware. His own views had been coloured by his mother's forthright opinions, which she never scrupled to air to anyone she suspected of profiting by the practice of human trafficking. Sophie was clucking with distress, but before he could frame an answer to placate the dowager's rising wrath, young Ben saved him the trouble.

"Hemp was never a slave though, ma'am, and he was born in Barbados. He says the plantation is home to him."

"He says they are family," added Tom, "even if they are black."

Tillie seized on this, fostering Francis's interest. "Does he mean they feel as if they belong to the Roy clan? Or have they been formally adopted?"

Both boys looked nonplussed, and Ben shrugged. "Don't know, Auntilla. Hemp just said he's a Roy too."

Tillie's quick frown told Francis this piece of information had piqued her interest. He made a stab in the dark. "Did Hemp say why he and Cuffy came with the family?"

"As if they had a choice!"

Francis frowned his mother down as Ben answered.

"Hemp only said they wanted to come, so p'raps they did choose."

"Oh, I do hope so," said Sophie. "How dreadful if they were forced to come away from all they knew."

"Hemp's a great gun," Tom cut in, disregarding this. "He showed me a boxer's trick and he told us about making sugar and everything."

"But I thought he was a footman," Francis objected.

"Hemp says you have to know all the special jobs," put in Ben, "just in case."

"Yes, 'cause if there's a peddyemic, the work goes on just the same."

"You mean epidemic, you noddy," corrected Ben, punching his junior in the shoulder. Ignoring his mother's deprecating protest, he added, "Barbados is a bad place for fevers, Hemp says."

This accorded with the long-term illness suffered by Sir Joslin, and Francis was about to direct the conversation into this avenue when he was forestalled by Tillie.

"What did Hemp tell you about making sugar?"

Tom brightened at this show of interest. "He and Cuffy used to help in making it. 'Specially when it got boiling, 'cause the dead man was a weakling and he couldn't stand it."

"Goodness, Tom, whatever do you mean?"

Ben gave an exasperated sigh. "He didn't say it right, Mama. He means boiling the sugar when the crop was ready. Everyone had to join in then because it had to be done fast. Hemp says boiling is a tricky job 'cause you have to wait for the sugar to crystallize and throw in the right amount of juice. Lime juice, he says, 'cause lemon would spoil it."

"Was Sir Joslin in charge of this procedure?" Tillie asked.

"Yes, because the other fellow was lazy," announced Tom.

"What other fellow?" Francis demanded.

"Simeon," supplied Ben. "He wouldn't do boiling work even though he was meant to supervise sugar-making. But he only liked working in the distillery and making rum and confections."

Tillie's startled look had intrigued Francis, but he knew better than to enquire into her thoughts in public. But as Toby and Agnes came in to serve dessert at this point, the discussion was abandoned. Recalling this now, Francis was about to enter upon the subject when his ear caught the sound of an arrival in the hall. Rising, he went to open the door.

"That must be Patrick at last."

So indeed it proved, and Francis ushered him in, as eager as he knew his wife would be to hear the results of the post-mortem. But he was mindful of the needs of a man's stomach.

"Have you dined, Patrick?"

"I had a bite of supper with Sutherland while we discussed our findings."

"Then let me get you a tot of something. Port? Or would you prefer Brandy?"

Patrick heaved an exhausted sigh as he dropped into a chair. "Good of you, Fan, but as I see I'm just in time for it, I'll take tea. I need to keep my wits about me to withstand Ottilia's cross-examination."

He threw a teasing glance at his sister as he spoke, and Tillie's look of keen anticipation could not but amuse Francis, despite his inevitable disquiet.

"Well, brother mine? What did you discover?"

Francis handed him a cup and saucer and offered sugar. Patrick took up the tongs, dropped two lumps into his tea, and stirred the liquid thoughtfully. "It is as I suspected."

Tillie jumped in at once. "Then Sir Joslin was poisoned with opium?"

Patrick took a meditative sip of tea, and Francis was obliged to suppress a riffle of irritation. "It is always difficult to be certain. The symptoms of narcotic poisoning are not conclusive."

Francis cast up his eyes. "Capital!"

His brother-in-law spared him a glance, but made no comment, merely resuming his remarks. "Taken together, however, Sutherland agrees that everything we found, along with your combined observations at the instant of death, points to opium as the most likely cause."

"Well, what did you find?" demanded his mother with pardonable impatience.

Patrick frowned. "Are you sure you wish to hear, ma'am? Such details are scarcely suitable for a gentlewoman's parlour."

The dowager snorted. "If your sister's candour has failed to dismay me, my dear Doctor Hathaway, I doubt I will swoon at anything you may have to say."

Patrick's amused eyes flickered to Tillie. "Ah, I should have known you must have been well and truly broken in."

"Yes, and it is not your practice to rein in either, Patrick," she retorted, "so pray don't keep us in suspense."

He grimaced. "The facts are not pretty."

"They never are," Francis cut in, "but I can vouch for it that my mother is almost as hardy as your sister. She will not flinch."

"I thank you, Fanfan." She waved a hand at Patrick in her characteristic gesture. "Proceed, sir."

A lurking smile remained, but Patrick inclined his head. "Very well, ma'am. The most telling evidence was in the blood clots, although the blood on the whole was fluid."

"Where were the clots?" asked Tillie. "In the brain?"

"Yes, and in the cavities of the heart too. The blood vessels in the brain were congested, but that you may get also with apoplexy so it is not conclusive. However, there was lividity of the skin, which was also showing signs of peeling. With narcotics, the body is apt to pass rapidly into putrefaction. Hair and cuticles were already separating on the slightest friction, and the stomach, intestines and large vessels were distended with air."

Francis could not forbear to comment. "How disgusting. How glad I am not to be a doctor."

Patrick laughed, but Tillie was clearly too interested to pay the slightest attention to this divagation. "What of the stomach's contents? Did you discover anything there?"

Patrick's eye brightened. "The odour of opium was obvious immediately upon opening the stomach. Sutherland concurred, fortunately, because it dissipates rapidly and is otherwise undetectable in the juices of the stomach without chemical analysis."

"How in the world can you smell opium?" asked the dowager frowningly.

"Oh, it has a very particular odour."

Despite his queasiness, Francis was interested. "Can you test the stomach's contents?"

"Fairly readily. A simple procedure is to use a frog. If it should go comatose and die, we could say with near certainty opium was present. But a better test is on urine, although it is a complex procedure. However, as we suspected, death had suspended natural functions so that the bladder was full. Sutherland is engaging an apothecary to carry out the necessary analysis."

His mother appeared to have been following closely. "And if opium is found, can you conclusively state it to be the cause of death?"

"Taken together with the incidence of perspiration and contraction of the pupils of the eyes, Sutherland and I are agreed on it without that," Patrick said. "But to prove a point, it is advisable to ask for the analysis."

Glancing at Tillie, Francis saw she could scarcely contain her excitement. "I suppose there is no way to tell how much opium had been consumed?"

"Only insofar as we know what level of ingestion is likely to kill a man."

"Which is?" Francis demanded.

"It much depends on circumstance."

Francis sighed with frustration. "I might have guessed as much."

"The problem is that it raises too many questions. Is the person accustomed to taking it? What time of day was it ingested? Was the stomach empty at the time?"

"Oh, good God!"

A smile came Francis's way, and it seemed to him his brother-in-law relished his catalogue of difficulties. "One must also take into account in which form the drug was taken. With grains, for example, thirty-six could procure death. But for a man the size of Sir Joslin, perhaps as many as sixty grains might be needed."

"For pity's sake! One would say there was nothing certain at all."

Tillie disregarded this. "And if he happens to be an opium-eater?"

"Sixty must still kill him, if taken all at once."

"But how does this translate into terms one may understand?" Thus his mother, echoing Francis's sentiments. "If it was taken as laudanum, for example, how much would it be?"

"Then we would measure it by drops or ounces. An ounce or two could readily prove fatal within a reasonable amount of time, but a dose on the order of six ounces might kill within a half hour."

The dowager threw up her hands. "Oh, this must be impossible to unravel!"

"I agree with you utterly, Mama."

Patrick grinned. "I'm afraid it nearly is impossible. And it also makes it difficult to judge at what time Sir Joslin took the dose. It might have been as many as five hours before the poison started to act or as little as three hours. Even then, the point of death may have been delayed by some hours."

Here the dowager entered a caveat. "But the fellow appeared perfectly well only minutes before, for we all saw him in this very room."

Tillie cut quickly in. "He was sweating, however, for I noted beads of perspiration upon his brow and his palm was damp. I thought it had been from his exertions in hunting for Tamasine."

"And he fell down the stairs," added the dowager. "Surely that must have hastened his death?"

"It will certainly have been a contributory factor," Patrick agreed. "Had he collapsed without that complication, and an emetic had been given, it is possible he could have survived. And death would have been delayed, even had he died in the end."

Ottilia was frowning, her fingers shifting in a way that suggested she was performing a rapid calculation in her head. "Then could we at least surmise he ingested the poison in the early hours of the morning? Around five or six o'clock? For it must have been nine or later when he died. Do you not think so, Fan?"

Thus appealed to, Francis frowned. "I never looked at my watch and you were up early."

"You may take the time from Teresa's being downstairs," his mother offered. "She is always up by eight and thirty."

"Half an hour or so to the time Sir Joslin arrived then."

"It does not matter, Ottilia," said Patrick. "You may be reasonably confident of having the time of death as precisely as one could hope, having come upon the scene within minutes. But that brings us no closer to the precise time at which Sir Joslin took the dose."

"But at least we can assume he had taken it on an empty stomach, do you not think? Even if he subsequently breakfasted."

Patrick gave her a rueful look. "I'm a man of science, Ottilia. I assume nothing without proper evidence. There are far too many factors to be taken into account."

Francis saw the look of disappointment sweep over his wife's face, and eyed her with concern. She caught the look and gave him a tentative smile.

"We must bow to Patrick's dictum, I fear, and let it go. What is more to the point is the question of whether the poison was self-inflicted or administered by the agency of another."

A sense of outrage began to overtake Francis. Was there to be no conclusion? What in the world was the point of doing a post-mortem if it told you precisely nothing? "Then we are no further forward."

Tillie got up abruptly from her chair. "Oh, yes we are, Fan. We know how Sir Joslin died. The details, the minutiae that will keep Patrick and Sutherland from careless speculation do not matter. Opium was the cause, and that is sufficient to tell me that someone in that house, whether the dead man or another, has been either careless or downright malicious."

Her beloved features took on that look of determination that Francis had come to dread. "And I mean to find out who."

CHAPTER NINE

There was a brooding sense of tension pervading Willow Court, although the place was quiet. Ottilia found it almost tangible. Lomax, upon opening the door, did not speak for a moment, instead passing a steady gaze, in which she read hostility, from Ottilia's features across to Francis and Patrick. Having agreed beforehand that her brother should take the lead, she was free to observe.

Informed the visitors wished to question Cuffy, the butler's gaze narrowed and his tone was nothing if not insolent. "Upon what occasion?"

Patrick raised his brows, preserving his usual mildness of voice. "That you may learn in due course."

Lomax did not shift to open the door, instead posing another question. "Upon what authority?"

"I am acting for Doctor Sutherland," Patrick said without hesitation. "We are as yet wanting certain information for his report to the coroner."

"Information?" The one word held a derisory note and a muscle flickered faintly in the butler's cheek.

"As to the apparent cause of death."

Lomax's eye grew suspicious and Ottilia was aware of Francis pokering up. His temper, already uncertain, was obviously chafing at the man's attitude. No clear evidence pointing as yet to murder, their situation was peculiarly sensitive and it was imperative, in Ottilia's view, to maintain stable relations with the staff. This could not be done by using the high-handed coercion Francis was apt to adopt when annoyed. And Ottilia knew too well how any form of disrespect, especially towards his wife, was like to drive him into fury. Especially now, when Giles's involvement was liable to make anything rouse him.

To her relief, Patrick's calm assurance carried the day and Lomax consented to allow them entry, showing them into the front parlour.

"I will send Cuffy in to you."

The moment the door closed, Francis broke out. "That fellow is riding for a fall. How dared he address you in that discourteous fashion, Patrick? I was within an ace of planting the wretch a facer!"

Patrick grinned. "Yes, I thought you were growing a trifle restive."

"Restive! I should like to have him under my command for a single day. I'll warrant that would mend him. If this is a sample of Barbadian manners, I thank God I was never tempted to adventure there."

"I doubt he is typical." Ottilia went up to her husband and laid a calming hand to his chest. "I wish you will not get up into the boughs, my dearest. We are treading difficult ground."

"Yes, well, if I have to endure much more of Lomax," said Francis, not in the least mollified, "I promise you I shall make it more difficult yet."

"That is just what I'm afraid of, Fan. Do pray calm yourself. After all, we are not intending to question Lomax —"

"As yet."

"— and Cuffy is perfectly courteous."

"He had better be, by God!"

At which point, the door opened to admit him and Ottilia turned with relief to greet him. "Ah, Cuffy, thank you for coming to talk to us." The footman's large frame was poised in the doorway, his dark glance going from one to the other.

196

Ottilia smiled at him. "Come in and shut the door, if you please."

While he did so, she threw a meaning glance at Francis, who threw up his eyes, but evidently understanding her, retired to the fireplace and rested his arm along the mantel. Patrick shifted out of the centre of the room, thankfully taking his cue from this manoeuvre.

Cuffy still looked apprehensive, but the menace of the two gentlemen being reduced, he ventured a step or two into the room. With the view of making him more comfortable still, Ottilia seated herself on a chair nearby before opening negotiations. She did not beat about the bush.

"Cuffy, it has been found that your master died from opium poisoning."

Consternation leapt into the fellow's eyes and his big face crumpled a little. His deep voice was hoarse with emotion. "Master never takes too much. He takes enough medicine to give him a good feeling. When he has much pain, he took it."

Ottilia seized on this. "But he took more 'medicine' than he needed for the pain, did he not, Cuffy? He was what we call an opium-eater, I think. An addict?"

Cuffy's eyes rolled and tears squeezed out, tracing down his cheeks. "He starts to take it for pain only. It makes him feel too good. He likes too much to take. I say to him many times, don't take this medicine. Master Jos tries to stop, but he cannot stop."

Ottilia felt for the man, his affection lacerated by his master's habit. "You were the only one he would allow to be with him at such times, am I right? He relied on you, Cuffy, to keep him from harm."

Cuffy nodded, lifting his thumbs to dash the tears away, though they kept coming. "Master Jos does not like anyone to see him bad with this medicine. I stay by him, I do not let anybody come. He is happy for a few hours before he goes to sleep."

"And you remained with him all the time, until he returned to his normal state?"

Cuffy nodded. "He gets too bad. He needs help. If I do not stay, he gets dirty, he forget to eat."

Ottilia could well imagine it. But there was a more urgent question to ask. "Did your master take opium the night before he died, Cuffy?"

Puzzlement crept into his features and he sniffed as at last his tears ceased to fall. "He did not call me."

At this Francis intervened. "Did he always call you? Is it not possible he took the stuff without calling you?"

Cuffy started, as if he had forgotten the presence of the gentlemen. His tone immediately became more subservient. "No, sir. He calls me every time."

Ottilia found her brother's eyes on her and looked a question.

"Are you supposing that he took the dose unknowingly?"

"Just so," she agreed, returning to the footman. "Cuffy, how did he take the medicine? Was it the laudanum?"

"He takes it from the bottle," Cuffy replied, and then put his fingers a couple of times to his mouth in a gesture of eating. "Sometimes he likes to take a sweet."

"A confection?" asked Ottilia. Excitement rode her as she recalled Ben's words about Simeon, who would only distil rum and make confections. The image of the wrapped sweets in Sir Joslin's drawer leapt into her mind. She threw a glance at her brother. "Can it be taken so?"

"Oh, yes. You may readily obtain opium in the form of a confection, for it is an easy way to get children to take it. But the dose in a sweetmeat would be minimal."

Which disposed of that theory. Unless — could someone with knowledge of the sugar trade make up a sweetmeat with sufficient opium to kill? She resolved to show Patrick the prize in her pocket and the empty papers. She opened a different line. "I notice your master was partial to tobacco, Cuffy. He took snuff, did he not?"

"Sometimes he takes tobacco," the footman admitted. "It is bad for his lung, it makes him cough. He does not take too much."

Francis entered a caveat. "You are surely not suggesting he could have ingested opium by that means?" He glanced to Patrick for an answer.

"Unlikely, I submit," returned her brother. "But possible."

"Well, by what other means might it be introduced?"

Ottilia noted Cuffy's puzzlement increasing, but she said nothing, only waiting for Patrick's response to her spouse's question.

"A number of ways, although one must remember opium has a bitter taste. And again, which form of opiate are we discussing? Some forms are stronger than others."

"Might one disguise the taste with sugar?" asked Ottilia.

"If enough was used. Or alcohol."

"What, wine?" suggested Francis, jumping on this. "Or, no. What did the boys say last night? Rum?"

Ottilia's mind leapt. The distillery! Did those who knew how to boil sugar also make alcohol? Could they mix opium with rum without it being detected? Who then? The fellow Simeon, and Sir Joslin himself. Though why should he trouble to make such a mix if he was in the habit of taking opium as laudanum? Who else? Hemp or Cuffy?

She turned swiftly to the footman. "Cuffy, did you used to make rum?"

A flare of anger lit the fellow's eyes. "You think I give Master Jos bad rum?"

Ottilia held his gaze, but did not answer directly. "Was Sir Joslin in a habit of drinking rum?"

For a moment she thought the man was going to refuse to answer, perhaps stalk out of the room. His eyes burned. "Master Jos does not drink rum too much."

"But he did drink it?"

Cuffy growled low in his throat. "I do not put medicine in the rum so I can cheat Master Jos, so I can make Master Jos more sick. Master Jos takes rum when he wish to take too much medicine. He puts a little medicine in the rum. Sometimes Miss Tam makes too much trouble for Master Jos, he get too angry. He takes rum to forget this anger with Miss Tam."

Then all Tamasine had to do was to ensure she infuriated her guardian more than usual. Assuming she knew enough to be aware of his habits. But then she must also have knowledge of distilling, must she not? Or did she simply have to tip a large measure of laudanum into a bottle of rum? Which presupposed she knew where it was kept — if indeed such existed. On impulse, Ottilia addressed something of this quandary to Cuffy.

"Was Miss Tam ever allowed in the distillery?"

This turn threw the man into evident confusion. He blinked, looking from Ottilia to the faces of the men in mute question. Both Francis and Patrick were frowning, and she realised neither had made the same mental jump.

"Bear with me, Cuffy," Ottilia said gently. "There is a reason for my asking. Could Miss Tam have ventured there?"

Cuffy seemed to sink a little. "Miss Tam goes all over the plantation. Master Roy says she can go where she want. She follows Mister Simeon sometimes."

"Which took her into the distillery?" pursued Ottilia relentlessly.

He nodded. "Yes, madame. Sometimes she goes there. But she likes more to go in the cane fields. All the slaves look out for her, to see she is all right. Sometimes the slaves chase her out from the field."

"Did anyone go with her? Was she constantly watched by one particular person perhaps?"

"When Miss Lavinia has come, yes. Before she comes, Miss Tam just goes all over."

"Alone?"

Cuffy shrugged. "Slaves are everywhere, they watch her good. She is never alone. Sometimes she goes along with Hemp. He looks out for Miss Tam."

"You mean he looked after her?"

"Yes, madame. I look out for Master Jos. Hemp looks out for Miss Tam."

Light clicked in Ottilia's brain. "Which is why the two of you were chosen to come to England with the family?"

A huge sigh wrenched out of Cuffy's throat. "It is not good to come here. It is too cold. Master Jos's chest was very bad."

"But not the night before he died," Ottilia pointed out drily.

Comprehension dawned in the dark gaze. "You think Master Jos is killed."

"If he did not take a dose of opium himself, Cuffy, it looks that way."

"He did not take it." Cuffy spoke slowly, his brows drawing together. "He calls me if he takes it." A pause as he eyed Ottilia. "Nobody hates Master Jos. Nobody here."

"Someone elsewhere then?" Ottilia demanded instantly. "Simeon perhaps?"

But here the footman balked. His mouth clamped shut and his gaze dropped from Ottilia's to the colourful rug on the floor. He shuffled a little and then edged towards the door.

"I have plenty of work. I will go now, madame."

Ottilia made no attempt to stop him, but watched as he crossed quickly to the door and left without a backward glance. Turning, she found her brother's questioning gaze on her, while Francis was staring at the now closed door, a frown between his brows.

"Are we to infer from this retreat that Simeon, whoever he is, did indeed hate Sir Joslin?" asked Patrick.

"Is it not plain enough? Though how the devil the fellow did the trick from a distance is beyond my imagining!"

"Oh, it is not impossible, Fan."

"Well, if he did, he must at least have had an accomplice," suggested Patrick.

Francis cocked an eyebrow. "Tamasine herself?"

"Scarcely a reliable partner in crime. It has given us food for thought, however." Ottilia made for the door. "Meanwhile, it behoves us to take another inspection of the bedchamber."

Her brother stared. "For what purpose?"

"The rum, Patrick. In case Sir Joslin has a bottle stashed away. Besides, I have something to show you there."

Sounds from within Sir Joslin's chamber alerted Ottilia before the trio entered the room. She glanced at her husband, raising her brows and then looked through the open doorway.

The press was open, one tray pulled out from which Mrs Whiting was in the act of removing an item of clothing. A trunk stood nearby and Miss Ingleby was standing above it, evidently engaged in folding and packing away items of clothing from a pile laid upon the bed.

Both women looked round as Ottilia entered and the companion uttered an impatient exclamation, throwing down the garment she held in her hands.

"Not again." She came towards the intruders, arms akimbo. "What does this mean, if you please? Why are you here?"

Ottilia stood back and gestured towards her brother. "Patrick."

He strode nonchalantly into the wider space. "Our purpose is sufficient, ma'am. I am acting for Doctor Sutherland in gathering evidence against a possible inquest."

The woman blanched. "Inquest?"

"Into Sir Joslin's death. Surely you must know that until the coroner has all the facts as to the cause of death, he cannot decide whether an inquest need be held."

Miss Ingleby hissed in a breath and shot a look of venom at Ottilia. "I need not ask from whence came the spur for such a move. Are you determined to discover evil, Lady Francis? Is it not enough that we are bereft?"

Francis swept past Ottilia. "Mind your tongue, ma'am! You will accord my wife a proper respect."

Miss Ingleby faced him without fear, much to Ottilia's admiration and interest. "Or what, sir? Will you see me in the stocks? Raise a hand against me?"

"I will face you down, ma'am," said Francis furiously, "before I allow you to address my wife in such terms."

The companion came back strongly. "Your wife, sir, has interfered here beyond what may be tolerated. We neither sought nor desired your assistance, and you will oblige me by removing her forthwith."

"I will do no such thing."

Patrick harrumphed loudly, drawing Francis's attention. "If I may, Fan."

To Ottilia's relief, the mild tone served to curb her spouse's ire a little and he stood back, though he nevertheless kept a choleric eye upon the companion.

"Miss Ingleby," Patrick said coolly, "I'm afraid it may come as a shock to you, but I am bound to inform you that the post-mortem carried out upon Sir Joslin's body revealed conclusively that he died from poisoning by opium."

A gasp escaped the woman and she stared at Patrick in the numbness of shock, looking much as if she had been struck in the face.

Glancing quickly at Mrs Whiting, up to now a helpless and bemused spectator of the proceedings, Ottilia saw apprehension leap into her features. Neither woman, it was evident, had been ignorant of Sir Joslin's habit.

"It is therefore incumbent upon me," Patrick pursued, taking advantage of the heavy silence, "to make a search of this room for any means by which a fatal dose of opium could have been administered to the victim."

Miss Ingleby found her voice, a strangled croak. "Victim? Administered?"

Ottilia cut in without compunction. "Just so. Either by himself, or by another."

The companion's hand lifted and the back of it hovered at her mouth in a gesture Ottilia recalled from the previous day.

"No," she whispered. "He would not have taken his own life. I will never believe that."

"Then we are left with the alternative," Ottilia said ruthlessly, pushing through to confront the creature. "There is of course a third possibility."

The woman's eyes dilated, and her tone was wretched. "Which is?"

"An accident, Miss Ingleby," Ottilia said, gentling her tone. "He may not have realised just how much he had taken."

It was the least likely solution, but it served to bring the woman out of shock. She visibly pulled herself together, her dazed eyes darting about the chamber as if she thought to find some evidence to support the latter notion. Ottilia took advantage of her state.

"Will you let Doctor Hathaway make his search, ma'am?"

The woman nodded, moving in a vague fashion towards the door. Mrs Whiting, looking anxious, made to follow her. Ottilia intercepted the housekeeper, speaking in a low tone.

"Pray keep her from re-entering this room until we have done, Mrs Whiting."

"I'll do my best."

She began to move, but Ottilia stayed her. "One moment, if you will. How is Tamasine today? Is she in her room?"

Mrs Whiting looked curiously at Ottilia, as if she did not understand her interest. "Hemp has taken her for a drive."

"Ah. You wanted her out of the way while you did what was needful in here."

"Yes, ma'am. Unpredictable, she is."

Decidedly. Feeling a trifle disappointed, Ottilia almost let the woman go. But a thought occurred. "Mrs Whiting, I believe there is much you might add to my —" Remembering her invidious position in this house, she checked what she had been about to say and resumed smoothly, "— Doctor

Hathaway's gathering of information on Doctor Sutherland's behalf. Would you object to talking with him in a little while?"

The woman cast a glance at Patrick, whose faintly questioning expression was bland enough to pass for one eager for new knowledge, Ottilia hoped. Then her gaze returned to Ottilia's face, her brows drawn together.

"Miss Ingleby says it's you who wants to know, ma'am," she said in a tone bordering on the accusatory.

Ottilia opted for frankness as she had done with the companion, and essayed a rueful smile. "True. I have in the past had a little success in this line, and in this case I am concerned particularly for Tamasine."

"Well, with Sir Joslin gone, so are we all," conceded Mrs Whiting. "But I don't see what it has to do with the manner of the master's death."

"It has a great deal to do with it," Ottilia returned, delivering a body blow without compunction. "How shocking if she were to be consigned to Bedlam for murdering her guardian." Taking instant advantage of the woman's evident horror, she threw in a clincher. "Or even hanged, should the justices decide she was wholly responsible for her actions."

Mrs Whiting's features matched her name for pallor and her eyes dilated as she stared at Ottilia, opening and shutting her mouth in an ineffectual fashion that screamed her agitation. Ottilia waited, holding the woman's eyes.

"No! No, I couldn't let them," she managed at length.

"You could hardly stop them."

Mrs Whiting looked away, her breath short and unsteady. She shivered, as if the images conjured up by Ottilia's words were too much to endure. "All right, I'll talk."

Ottilia ignored the gruff tone and the resentment that almost matched Miss Ingleby's. "Thank you. We will send for you to the downstairs parlour in due time."

Nodding dismissal, she watched the little creature waddle to the door with something less of her usual bustle.

Walking swiftly across, Francis shut the door, and Patrick let out a whistle. "Phew! What a tartar you are, my dear sister."

She was inclined to laugh, but her spouse chose to take up the comment. "That's nothing. She can be a deal more ruthless than that, I promise you."

Ottilia tutted. "Do you want to know the truth of it, or don't you?"

"I just want to know it wasn't Giles, as you are perfectly well aware," snapped Francis. "Can we get this over with, if you please? If we are going to search, for pity's sake, let's get started."

"Let me first show Patrick what I found." She moved to the press as she spoke, pulling open the long top drawer and searching therein. "There are packages of confections. These, you see. They have each an inscription: barley sugar, sugared almonds and the remains of humbugs." She took them out as she spoke. "The others, however —"

She broke off, abruptly aware that the three oblong packets purloined by the boys, which she had put back in the drawer, were missing. She rummaged, only half aware of Francis picking up the packages.

"Flora Sugars? Is this the trade name for Roy's business?"

"Associated with his wife, Florine," Ottilia said without ceasing her search.

Patrick was checking the bottles ranged along the top of the press. "Good God, look at this, Fan. Pomade and Jessamine butter. Perfumed mouth water too. A jar of Bergamot snuff? This is a nice little box though."

He was joined by Francis, who picked up the snuff box and examined it. "Ivory and jade. A trifle too pretty for my taste."

"But it argues another bad habit, equally bad for the fellow's lungs."

"Tobacco?" Francis was inspecting further items. "What in the world? Cold cream and almond paste? And this is orange-flower water, Patrick. Do you use such things?"

Her brother laughed. "Not I. This Cadel fellow seems to have had a fastidious attention to hygiene."

"Personal vanity more like. The man was clearly a fop."

"Or leaning towards femininity?"

"You think so?" Francis made a derisive sound. "That rather puts paid to your notion of Miss Ingleby fancying herself in love with the fellow, Tillie."

Ottilia was staring into the drawer, puzzling over the missing sweets, but at this she looked across at the two men, distracted. "You mean she had hoped in vain for his favours? They were not then lovers, I surmise," she said, thinking aloud. "She was distraught. She might have felt some affection. Or heavy disappointment perhaps. Did she seek only for the protection of a ring upon her finger?"

Her spouse threw up his eyes. "He was scarcely likely to marry her, was he, if Patrick's surmise is correct?"

"No, and it is scarcely germane at this moment. Where in heaven's name are those sweets?"

Both husband and brother stared. Patrick glanced at the discarded packets well labelled and containing humbugs or sugared almonds. "I presume you don't mean those?"

Ottilia slipped a hand into her pocket and brought out the single oblong confection she had taken the day before. She held it out. "There were four of them in here. I took only one to show you. Someone has taken the others."

All at once she recalled the empty packets retrieved from the wastepaper basket, and began to hunt again, only half aware of the two gentlemen studying the sweets.

"Flora Sugars," Francis announced, reading over Patrick's arm. "What is in that one?"

"It does not say."

"Just so." Ottilia was shifting items around in the drawer in haste. "Why should someone take those and not the others? It must be deliberate."

"You don't seriously suppose this confection is larded with an overdose?"

"You said it was possible, Patrick."

"Yes, but not enough to kill."

Francis grabbed the thing from his hand. "But why should anyone remove it, if it's innocent." His frowning gaze came around to Ottilia. "And who? Whom do you suspect?"

"Were not those two women packing in here when we entered?" asked Patrick, sounding interested, at least in this point.

"Yes, but they didn't empty the drawer," said Francis at once. "The ones she is talking about have been selected out from the rest. Are you still looking for them, Tillie?"

Ottilia abandoned her search as futile. She toyed with mentioning the empty packages she had stuffed into the drawer, but on balance decided to keep that close for the time being. Meanwhile, her brother's sceptical gaze shifted from Francis to herself.

"I suppose your so-called murderer crept in here in the dead of night and secreted the evidence?"

"You have no idea how cunning these murderers can be, Patrick," said Francis. "But if there is one thing more certain than another, it is that Giles cannot have taken the thing."

"No, I think we must confine our suspicions to someone in the house," Ottilia agreed.

"You are jumping to conclusions." Patrick sounded exasperated. "In the first place, it's highly unlikely that any confection could be used to poison a man."

Ottilia balked. "Why not? Such laudanum sweets may be given to children. You've prescribed them yourself."

"I grant you this looks just like that sort of laudanum lozenge. They are wrapped like this, and then packed in sets in boxes."

"There you are then," she returned, her mind still busy. How many to a box? Had Sir Joslin a box of them to hand?

Her brother sighed out an irritated breath. "Ottilia, you are fair and far out. Laudanum lozenge it might have been, but it could only have been used by the dead man to relieve some disorder as simple as a headache."

"Or his chest pain, perhaps?" Francis put in.

"Certainly. But to suggest one of these could be larded with enough opium to provide a lethal dose, absolutely not. Even were it possible, the sugar would be insufficient to disguise the taste."

Ottilia began to feel baffled. Instinct? Someone had definitely removed both the missing sweets and the packaging she had secreted into the drawer the day before. She threw out a fresh notion.

"What if he were to eat several at once?"

"No," said her brother with finality. "He would have to consume the whole box, and would likely fall asleep before he could do so."

Ottilia sighed, relieved she had kept the tale of the empty packages to herself. "Then I must take your ruling on it, Patrick. I suppose there is little future in analysing this then?"

"None at all."

"Oh, dear, I really thought we had something."

Patrick's eye gleamed. "In any event, I thought we were here to search for rum."

Ottilia's mind snapped in. "Yes, we were. Do you take the press and I will look around the bed."

Francis was standing over the half-packed trunk. "What about this?"

"A waste of time," said Patrick. "You can't suppose those women would pack up a bottle of rum."

"Check it, Fan," said Ottilia, heading for the bedside cabinet. She struck lucky at once, discovering a flat-shaped bottle concealed in a corner behind the chamber pot. But when she rose with it in her hand and would have opened it, her brother stayed her.

"Wait! Give it to me."

She handed it over at once. "Why? What are you going to do?"

He sniffed at the edges of the cork. "Definitely alcohol." He shook it. "Less than half full, I should think."

"Aren't you going to open it?" asked Francis with impatience.

"I am opening it."

Patrick moved the bottle a little away from him and eased the cork out with his fingertips. There was no instant aromatic scent to tickle Ottilia's nostrils. She was not surprised. The rum might or might not contain opium, but the niggle of the sweetmeats had superseded her interest.

"Why the excessive caution?" Francis demanded.

"Because I don't want to fall down in a dead faint." He shook the bottle, sniffed the air and then brought it to his nostrils. "Hm. It's not an obvious scent, but there is definitely a mix here."

"Then you will have it analysed?"

"I think we must, Fan. We are doing as much with the laudanum you found. Though there is no saying whether it is from this bottle that Sir Joslin drank the dose that killed him."

Ottilia eyed her brother. "If you are doing so much, you may as well add the sweetmeat, do you not think?"

"Humour her, Patrick. Her instinct is rarely at fault, you know."

He rolled his eyes. "I dare say I'll get no peace until I do. But I personally doubt any of this will lead you to Ottilia's alleged murderer."

She thanked him and threw her spouse a grateful look, but her disquiet was palpable. All the signs indicated her brother was right, but she could not rid herself of a conviction that the secrets of Willow Court hid a tapestry of evil.

Mrs Whiting had been persuaded to sit in one of the shawl-covered chairs, while Ottilia took the other. The woman thus could not easily see either Francis or Patrick without turning to locate them. Patrick had taken a cane-seated chair, while Francis chose to lean against the wall between the two sets of windows.

The housekeeper's discomfort was plain, augmented by the incongruity of her girth against her short legs, which only just reached the floor. Ottilia could see the toes of her black shoes awkwardly pressing down.

She began with a commonplace designed to set the creature more at her ease, for she would not disclose anything pertinent if she remained resentful. "I wish you will tell me more of Tamasine's life in Barbados, Mrs Whiting. She told me herself that she was used to hide among the sugar canes."

The housekeeper pursed her lips. "I don't see what that has to do with anything."

"Indulge me, if you please. I gather she is much attached to Hemp?"

The switch of topic put a frown between the woman's brows. "As much as she's attached to anyone. Hemp handles her best of all of us, which isn't surprising."

"Why?"

"Because Mr Roy put him in charge of her when she was just a toddler." Disapproval was writ large in the housekeeper's countenance. "Not that young Hemp was much more than a piccaninny at the time."

Ottilia's ears pricked up. "Indeed? How old was he?"

"Nine or ten, or thereabouts."

"Then he was her constant companion for some years?"

"In between his duties and his schooling."

"Ah, I thought he'd been educated."

Mrs Whiting sniffed. "They all were, after a fashion, the slaves. Mr Roy insisted on that. Employed a schoolmaster for the purpose. But he taught Hemp himself. Gave him what you might call extra-curricular lessons."

Evidently the black boy was a favourite. A random thought occurred to Ottilia, startling in its potential ramifications. So bizarre was the notion that she hesitated to give it voice.

"What happened when Miss Ingleby came?" she asked instead.

A derisive expression came into the woman's face. "She put a stop to it. Or tried to. Thought it was unseemly. But Miss Tam wouldn't have it. Too used to the fellow by then."

213

"She was fourteen, I understand?"

Mrs Whiting sighed faintly. "Can't blame Miss Ingleby, I suppose. She was fresh out from England and didn't understand colonial ways. Scared of the black workers. She thought it was downright dangerous letting a brawny young black fellow make free with a girl of Miss Tam's years."

Ottilia could not but acknowledge she had thought the same, but she did not say so. If her sudden suspicion was correct, the child must have been quite safe.

"But you say Tamasine would not be parted from him."

"Oh, she didn't have much to do with him, except when she managed to escape from Miss Ingleby. Hemp was working all hours by then, both in the house and out. But Miss Tam would follow him all over when she got the chance. And seeing Hemp was the only one who could quiet her when she got into one of her rages, Miss Ingleby was obliged to call him in time and again."

Ottilia pounced on this. "But Tamasine was not permitted to fly into rages, was she, Mrs Whiting? She is kept sedated with laudanum, is she not?"

The housekeeper visibly started at the mention of the drug, her eyes flying to meet Ottilia's, her lip faintly trembling.

"And you, Mrs Whiting," Ottilia pursued doggedly, "are in charge of giving her the drug. Where do you keep it? Is it under lock and key?"

For several minutes the woman could only stare, a myriad collection of thoughts evident in the changing reflections within her eyes. In the periphery of her vision, Ottilia noted that Francis had shifted away from the wall and her brother was leaning forward, both men in tense attitudes of concentrated attention. She kept her gaze trained upon the housekeeper, maintaining the pressure.

At length Mrs Whiting spoke, her voice hoarse and protesting. "It's strictly controlled. I know exactly how much to give her. I've been doing it for years. I've never made a mistake."

"Did I suggest you had?"

The woman's hands gripped together and belligerence entered her tone. "I don't know what you're suggesting. You said the master died of opium poisoning, that's all I know. Do you mean to accuse me, is that it?"

Ottilia gentled her voice. "My dear Mrs Whiting, I am merely trying to discover where in the world your master came by an overdose of the drug massive enough to kill him. If you assure me that Tamasine's laudanum was secured where no one could have taken it, then —"

"Who'd take it from my housekeeping cupboard?" interrupted the other. "It's locked and I keep the key on my belt." She felt for the chatelaine that hung from her waist and rattled the keys hanging from it with some violence. "I'd have noticed if anyone had tried to get it off me, wouldn't I?"

"Do you sleep with it under your pillow?"

Mrs Whiting gaped. "Sleep with it under my pillow? No, of course I don't."

"Then is it possible someone could have sneaked into your housekeeper's room at night and abstracted it?"

A disbelieving laugh escaped the woman. "What, and sneaked back in afterwards to return it? Rubbish! It couldn't have gone. I'd have noticed it missing. Moreover, I'd have noticed if the level in the bottle of laudanum had gone down. I told you, I keep it strictly controlled. I can show you, if you like. I write it all down in my book."

She stopped, breathing hard. Ottilia smiled. "Thank you, Mrs Whiting, I would like to see it."

It was clear from the expression that swept across the housekeeper's face that she was outraged. She glared at Ottilia and shoved herself forward so she could place her feet flat on the floor and push herself up from the chair.

"You better come with me."

Nothing loath, Ottilia threw a conspiratorial glance at the two men and followed her from the room.

Francis had barely managed to exchange a brief word with his brother-in-law when the door opened again and the butler came into the room. He eyed them both with undisguised irritation.

"Still here then, sirs?"

Francis's hackles rose. "As you see."

Lomax's lip curled in an insolent fashion. "Found your murderer, have you, my lord?"

With difficulty Francis kept a rein on his temper, and fired a broadside. "Not yet. But then we haven't questioned you, Lomax."

The man's brows snapped together. "I didn't kill him!"

"No?"

"No! Nor, I may add, did anyone else in this house."

"That remains to be seen."

"So he took opium, so what?" A sneer crossed the man's face. "Did you think Miss Ingleby wouldn't tell me? Not that we didn't know that already."

"Then it rather leaps to the eye that one of you might have helped him to his overdose."

Lomax closed his lips tight. He was plainly unnerved, for his gaze swivelled from Francis to Patrick and back again, a faint twitch attacking his cheek, which was certainly a degree paler than it had been.

Taking a leaf out of his wife's book, Francis pressed his advantage, his mind flitting over the various bits of information Tillie had so far garnered. He seized one at random.

"Tell me about Flora Sugars, Lomax."

"The master's manufactory?"

To see the man so rattled could not but give Francis a feeling of satisfaction. His annoyance settled and he began to enjoy himself. "By master, you mean Mr Roy, I take it? We took it for a trade name for his products. Was that correct?"

Lomax's frown spoke his growing puzzlement. "Yes, but I fail to see what that has to do with —"

"Did he name the place after his wife?" Francis interrupted, keeping the pressure on. "Florine, was it not?"

"It wasn't Mr Roy who called it that. It was Mrs Roy's father. She inherited the place."

"And it became Mr Roy's property when they married?"

Lomax nodded, looking more and more perplexed by this line of questioning.

"Sounds like a handsome dowry," commented Patrick, drawing the butler's glance.

A derisory look overspread the man's features. "A handsome bribe, sir."

Francis could not repress a gasp of shock. "You mean he knew Florine was deranged when he married her?"

"The master thought it a worthwhile bargain." The cynical note was pronounced and Francis watched him closely. "Had an eye to the main chance, had Mr Roy. And the mistress was easy-tempered to begin with."

"You were there?"

"I came with the property. I was a footman then."

So his loyalties were rather with the wife's family than with Roy. Less likely to be loyal to his master then?

"It would appear Miss Ingleby is the most recent addition to the family circle."

Lomax blinked in a baffled way, as if the change of subject confused him.

"I believe she joined you only when Miss Tamasine was fourteen," Francis pursued. "A relative newcomer then?"

"You won't find anyone ready to include her in the family circle." The old derisory look was back. "She wouldn't have been, if Mr Martin hadn't died."

"Who was Mr Martin?"

"Overseer. Miss Ingleby came out to marry him. One of these arranged marriages. Martin perished of fever before she arrived and she'd no money to go back to England."

"So your Mr Roy gave her a post as governess to his daughter," put in Patrick, a note of approval in his voice. "He sounds a most considerate fellow."

Lomax had nothing to say to this, and it was plain to Francis that his opinion of his former master's character left something to be desired. He shifted ground.

"We understand that all the black fellows had to work in the sugar manufactory from time to time. Was that true of all those in Mr Roy's service?"

"You wish to know if I had a hand in distilling," stated the butler flatly, his cynicism once again rife. "It wasn't part of my duties, but I was interested enough to learn a bit. Some of it had its uses."

"Such as the making of rum?"

Lomax shrugged. "Make of it what you will, sir. But if you're trying to discover whether I laced his rum with opium to poison Sir Joslin, I fear you'll be disappointed. I doubt there's anyone in the house who doesn't know he kept a bottle hidden in the stupidest place you could think of. Who empties chamber pots but the servants?"

"I should have thought of that," Ottilia said fretfully, when Francis relayed this tidbit over a luncheon back at the Dower House.

The meal was attended only by the three of them, the dowager having roused herself to take Sophie Hathaway to visit one of their neighbours. There was no sign of the boys, who were doubtless off on some adventure of their own.

"Is it still worth taking an analysis of the bottle, Patrick?" asked her husband.

"We must be thorough. If we should find a fatal dose, you may at least console yourself with the reflection that your nephew is not the perpetrator. He cannot have known about the hiding-place."

"Unless Tamasine told him," put in Ottilia, earning herself a black look from Francis.

"I thank you. Just when I was beginning to feel a trifle relieved."

Ottilia sighed. "Yes, and it is not of the least use to be sanguine, for I am obliged to concede that Tamasine's laudanum is strictly controlled, just as Mrs Whiting claims. I would defy anyone to get into her cupboard, and her records are impeccable. Only she could have used that particular source."

"If she did," Patrick said, a faint frown wrinkling his brow, "it would be easy enough for her to cook her books, would it not? *Quis custodiet ipsos custodes*, eh?"

"Miss Ingleby," said Francis, "if it concerns the girl Tamasine."

But Ottilia regarded her brother with interest. "Detection, Patrick? Am I to understand the man of science is shifting his ground?"

Patrick grinned. "You are very persuasive, sister mine."

"Isn't she just?" put in her spouse.

"Not that I'm convinced, but the flaw in Mrs Whiting's testimony rankles."

"Yes, I do not think we can rule her out," Ottilia agreed.

"Or anyone, come to that," Francis said on a note of irritation. "If you ask me, the lot of them are capable of murder."

"I'm afraid you are right, Fan. And that is not all, for we have still this fellow Simeon to take into account."

"Yes, but he wasn't even here," objected her spouse.

"That doesn't mean he is not culpable. I doubt some of Tamasine's more bizarre notions came out of her own head."

"But how would he instruct her from a distance, if the wretched girl cannot read or write?"

"An accomplice?" suggested Patrick.

Francis jumped on this. "Someone on the spot, yes. But who?"

Ottilia ran a mental eye across the inmates of the house. "Not Miss Ingleby, I think. Mrs Whiting perhaps. Or Lomax."

Francis was drumming his fingers on the table. "That fellow Hemp seems to be as thick as thieves with the chit."

The idea startled Ottilia, throwing doubt into her mind. She had thought to have conveniently pigeon-holed the footman into the Willow Court scenario, but had she overlooked this possibility? If she was right about Hemp, would he knowingly aid and abet the fellow Simeon in whatever scheme he had dreamed up? His grief had been real. He would not have connived in a plot to murder his master. The same applied to

Cuffy. The fellow would have to be a supremely gifted actor to be as convincing as he had been. And had not Hemp told the boys Simeon was a lazy fellow? Did such an opinion preclude helping Tamasine to correspond with the man? For if one of them was writing on Tamasine's behalf, it must surely be the educated Hemp.

The silence at the table impinged upon her consciousness and Ottilia came to herself to find that both gentlemen were staring at her intently. "What?"

"You were deep in thought. If I've learned nothing else in these months with you, my love, I've learned when to let you be."

Ottilia smiled as she put out her hand across the table. Francis took it and kissed her fingers, holding them lightly as he quirked one eyebrow. "Well?"

"I don't think either Hemp or Cuffy killed Sir Joslin," she offered, giving a brief summary of her reasoning.

"Then that leaves Mrs Whiting, Lomax, the Ingleby woman and Tamasine herself," Francis recited, ticking them off on his fingers.

"And Simeon, I infer," put in Patrick, "if only by proxy."

A flurry of footsteps in the hall interrupted the conference as Ben and Tom erupted into the dining-parlour, both out of breath and bursting with excitement.

"And where, may I ask, have you been?" demanded their father, with an assumption of severity. "Absent without leave, and no message to explain —"

"We did leave a message!" broke in Tom. "At least, we would have left one, if we'd thought of it."

Noting Patrick's twitching lip and Francis's faintly raised eyebrow, Ottilia quickly intervened. "You look as if you are big with news, the two of you. What is afoot?"

As one, the boys dashed past their father and crowded about Ottilia's chair, almost falling over their words in their hurry to get them out.

"We've been talking to Hemp and Cuffy, Auntilla," disclosed Ben.

"Yes, and you'll never believe what they told us!"

"It's about the madwoman."

"Tamasine?" asked Ottilia.

"Not that madwoman, the other one," came scornfully from Tom, as if she should have known.

His brother cuffed him. "Let me tell it, you're not making sense." Ignoring Tom's loud-voiced protest, Ben turned back to Ottilia. "It's the madwoman's mother, Auntilla. You know, the one they call Florine."

"She was mad too," put in Tom irrepressibly.

"What about her?" asked Ottilia, trying to stem the tide.

"I'll wager you don't know how she died," said Ben, blue eyes fairly blazing with excitement.

Ottilia's heart missed a beat as her mind took a leap and she eyed Ben's angelic features with concentrated attention. "Tell me."

Tom elbowed his brother in the ribs, glee in his face. "Go on, Ben."

"She got poisoned too. With opium."

CHAPTER TEN

The drive from Polbrook to Willow Court was relatively short, but Giles took it at an easy pace, having a care for his horses. His conscience pricked him, for while his black mood held, he had driven the greys into a lather, careering about the countryside in a vain attempt to throw off the memories invoked by his grandmother's words.

Failing to find relief, he sought it instead in the brandy bottle and the effects of his potations kept him at home while his father and the Frenchwoman he was obliged to acknowledge as stepmother showed themselves in church for Sunday Service, accompanied by his two half-siblings. He could wish his sister had not retired to stay with their Aunt Harriet the moment the festivities had concluded. He might have confided in Candia, for she was never critical. They had besides grown closer through the adversity of recent events. If the worst came to the worst, he could follow her to the Dalesford's estate.

His distresses subsiding, the reflection struck him he had failed to attend upon Tamasine for too many days, which scarcely accorded with the conduct of an affianced husband.

Honesty compelled Giles to admit a faint reluctance to present himself at Willow Court. Not that he was in any way regretting his hasty proposal. He wanted nothing more in life than to marry Tamasine, yet unworthy doubts plagued him of her mental capacities.

The blame lay with his relatives, and with Phoebe's forthright condemnation. Giles would not have thought it of her, and was inclined to resent her attitude. Anyone might suppose her all but jilted, which certainly was not the case. He had never given her reason to think he would fall in with the scheme concocted by their respective fathers. Nor had she shown any disposition to encourage such a match.

His sense of ill-usage grew. By heaven, but apart from his sister, he was unlucky in his association with females! Not only did the girl he had hitherto considered his greatest friend condemn him, but the chit with whom he'd fallen in love had jockeyed him into making a declaration before he'd had time to consider his position.

The infelicity of this thought jabbed into his mind and he tried to quash it. Had Tamasine not been such an innocent, he might with justice make the complaint. But her charm lay in the natural insouciance that paid little heed to the dictates of convention. He admired that in her. If there was a sneaking traitorous thought that such a wayward character did not augur well for a future marchioness, Giles was resolute in crushing it out of existence.

But he could not avoid the lessening of enthusiasm with which he directed his cattle towards the dwelling of his inamorata. He must set that down to the slight headache that still afflicted him from his depredations upon the brandy bottle.

Pulling himself together, he turned the equipage into the drive and trotted the greys around behind the house to the stable block. His groom jumped down and went to the horses' heads, steadying them even as one of the stable lads came out to his assistance, and Giles was able to alight.

"Giles!"

The cry came from behind, and he turned to find Tamasine coming towards him from the vegetable garden situated at a little distance from the stables. The brightness of her welcoming smile in the matchless countenance set his doubts to rest, and Giles strode forward to meet her.

"You must forgive my tardiness." He hunted for a plausible excuse. "I was detained on business and I would not disturb you on a Sunday."

Tamasine did not appear in the least put out. She smiled sunnily upon him as she came up, putting out her hands. "They are all gone and you can know the secret first."

Giles took her hands and raised first one and then the other to his lips. "You are as lovely as ever."

Her delighted laughter smote his ears. Belatedly he took in the import of her words. He looked down into her innocent orbs and sighed anew at the sheer impact of her beauty.

"But it is our secret, my dearest, is it not? I already know it."

Tamasine did not respond to this sally, but pulled her hands away and turned. Her wave drew attention to a figure a few paces behind, which Giles had not noticed until this instant.

"Simeon, come!"

He stared blankly at the gentleman addressed, his hackles instinctively rising as he took in the bland good looks and easy carriage. As the man approached, he noted dark locks falling from under a beaver hat, a tall and well-formed figure and features that placed the fellow's age at a few years his senior.

"Lord Bennifield, I infer?"

The newcomer sketched a slight bow with a careless grace that made Giles set his jaw.

"You have the advantage of me, sir."

"Simeon Roy, my lord. I am Tamasine's cousin, you must know."

The implication struck Giles like a blow. This was the fellow concerned in Tamasine's "reckoning". They had sworn vengeance together, she'd said. He wondered uneasily if he had been too sanguine in supposing it had been a joke between them.

"Simeon has come," Tamasine announced unnecessarily. "I knew he would. I told them all. And he will avenge me." She turned a glowing face towards the man. "Won't you, Simeon?"

The fellow Roy gave an indulgent laugh that grated on Giles's ear, and his tone was positively avuncular. "I am your obedient servant to command, my dear Tam."

"Yes, and they will be sorry." Gleeful, she turned back to Giles. "Simeon won't let them put me in my eyrie, and I can wander as much as I like."

"As long as you don't set the countryside by the ears, my pet."

A form of address that could not but revolt. As if the girl was a dog. To Giles's satisfaction, Tamasine ignored the remark, addressing herself to him instead.

"Joslin wouldn't let him come, but now he's dead and he can't stop Simeon any more."

A twinge of something like disgust attacked Giles, but he brushed it aside, and tried to capture her hand, speaking in a low tone meant for her ears alone. "Can we talk, Tamasine? Where is Miss Ingleby?"

To his chagrin, Roy chose to answer this. "I gather that Lavinia, along with Lomax and Mrs Whiting, has gone to attend the inquest. I found little Tam here in the charge of Hemp."

Shock jerked at Giles. "Inquest? So soon?"

Why had no one mentioned it to him? Not that he had been next or nigh the Dower House since Grandmama chose to ally herself in the enemy camp. But his uncle Francis might have sent him word. Especially as there had been this ridiculous notion that he could be involved in Sir Joslin's death, merely

because of his association with Tamasine. His chagr increased when Roy answered on Tamasine's behalf.

"I dare say there was urgent need for it. My cousin Joslin death was wholly unexpected, I understand."

Giles gazed at him, reflecting that the fellow did not ye know the half of it. He could not speak of his aunt Ottilia' suspicions before Tamasine, however. "I thought Tamasine was your cousin."

"Joslin too, though a trifle more distant. Matthew, Tamasine's father, you must know, was my first cousin through our fathers. Joslin hailed from the distaff side."

"Giles, you didn't kiss me," chimed in Tamasine with impatience.

Feeling warmth rising in his cheeks, Giles withdrew a pace. "Not in public, Tamasine."

Her laughter tinkled. "It's only Simeon, silly. He won't mind."

"Well, I do."

Giles with difficulty held back a glare as his glance swept the look of cynical amusement in the other man's face. Tamasine paid no heed, but reached up to catch at Giles's shoulders, raising her face to his. He dipped his head and gave her a quick peck on the lips, unable to help his gaze from shifting to Simeon Roy, who was openly grinning.

Laughing again, Tamasine turned her radiant smile on her cousin. "We are betrothed, Simeon. Giles is going to marry me."

Horrified, Giles shot a look at the fellow's face. Roy appeared entirely unmoved, merely raising a pair of dark brows.

"Indeed? I must congratulate you, my dear Tam. An excellent catch."

Giles cut in swiftly. "It is not generally known. I must beg you to keep silent on this subject, if you will."

The brows rose higher. "Oh? Did not my cousin Joslin approve your suit? Now, how improvident of him. I must confess myself astonished he did not jump at the chance to offload — I mean, to see young Tam so suitably established."

The slip had not escaped Giles and a sliver of apprehension shot through him. There was no visible change in Tamasine's expression. With luck, she had not understood the implication. He felt compelled to defend.

"Sir Joslin was unwilling to see Tamasine betrothed to anyone before her come-out, but I had felt hopeful of persuading him to change his mind before long."

Simeon Roy openly laughed. "Come-out? You are jesting?"

Giles frowned, as another of those uncomfortable shards attacked him. "Why should you think so?"

But at this, the fellow raised a deprecating hand and fell back a little. "My dear Lord Bennifield, if you don't know, far be it from me to enlighten you. I would not care to do my little cousin such a disservice."

Undecided between demanding an immediate explanation or planting the fellow a facer, Giles hesitated too long.

"And now I fear I must leave you, my dear Tam," said Roy with another flourishing bow. "I trust my valet will have unpacked by now and I may hope to remove the travel stains from my person and freshen up in general."

Tamasine had watched the give and take of words without, to Giles's relief, apparent alarm, but at this she entered a protest. "You are going? But Simeon, I want you to stay with me."

The fellow smiled and chucked her under the chin. "But you have your betrothed to amuse you."

A daunting scowl marred Tamasine's exquisite features for a moment. "But I want you!"

"Now, now," said Roy on a chiding note. "No tantrums, my child, or I shall be sorry for having come all this way to see you."

Tamasine stamped her foot. "I hate you, Simeon!"

To Giles's faint and reluctant admiration, Roy refused to rise to the bait. He laughed instead, seizing his cousin's hand and lifting it to rest against his cheek for a moment, in a gesture peculiarly intimate. It was also distinctly possessive and made Giles's hackles rise all over again.

"No, you don't. You love me really. And I shall be with you again in a trice, never fear."

With which, he released her hand and walked quickly away towards the rear of the house.

Giles looked at Tamasine, half fearful of an explosion, but found her once again wreathed in smiles as she turned to him.

"Simeon is going to save me."

Save her from what? But he did not ask. Instead, he offered his arm. "Would you like to walk a little, Tamasine?"

With a cry of delight, she tucked her hand into his arm and set out beside him, walking as sedately as any debutante as he led her around the drive towards the lawns at the front of the house. His doubts faded.

"I am sorry we cannot announce our betrothal just yet, my dearest."

Tamasine flashed him a frowning look. "Why can't we?"

"I fear it would be thought a trifle callous, with your guardian but just dead."

"But if he is dead, how can Joslin object?"

"I don't mean that. Besides, I'm afraid Miss Ingleby will not countenance my suit."

229

"Lavinia is not my guardian."

"No, but in the circumstances, you are in some sort in her charge."

Tamasine blinked, as if the idea puzzled her. "But Simeon is here now."

The thought of his inamorata being in the charge of Simeon Roy did nothing to allay Giles's disquiet, but instinct bade him hold his tongue on that score. It was plain Tamasine held the fellow in high regard, and it would be impolitic to criticise him in her presence. Giles dismissed the fleeting notion that the resulting tantrum would be both embarrassing and distressful.

"I'm sorry to say my family are not sympathetic to our union. I fear it may take a little time to accustom them to the idea."

Tamasine had nothing to say to this, although she gave him a narrow glance in which he thought he detected a faint echo of malignance. But that could not be. Tamasine was nothing if not pure in heart. He was persuaded she could not wish harm to anyone.

"I dare say it will be best for me to await the coming of your aunt, my dearest, and apply to her formally for permission to marry you."

To his astonishment, Tamasine let out a trill of her characteristic laughter, making him wince. "I haven't got any aunts, silly Giles."

He halted in the middle of the drive and turned to stare at her. "But I understood that your aunt is your nearest living relative. Mrs Delabole, is it not? Your Aunt Ruth?"

She met his gaze with blank incomprehension in her own. "I don't have any Aunt Ruth."

"Have I misunderstood then? Your father's sister?" It was clear from her expression that this meant nothing to Tamasine. Belatedly it occurred to him that she might never have met the woman. And she was so very young. "Perhaps she did not visit Barbados. Or you were too young to remember. But your father must have mentioned her."

Tamasine's countenance broke into the radiant smile. "We shall get married quickly. Now, before they come back. Then no one can stop us."

So innocent! "I'm afraid it isn't as simple as that, my dearest. Not in this country. I must first procure a licence. Besides, I would not wish to put your reputation in jeopardy with an elopement. We must be married in form and with the consent of your guardians, whoever they prove to be. You deserve no less."

To his dismay, her brows began to lower and a scowl twisted her lovely features. She pulled away from him. "Don't you want to marry me, Giles?"

"Of course I do. You know I do."

He tried to capture her hands but she evaded him.

"You will have to catch me first!"

Laughing, she scampered towards the lawns where pockets of snow in the hollows bore witness to the recent poor weather. Giles went after her, as one in honour bound, but without any real sense of enthusiasm. Tamasine's peculiar upbringing was promising to create no end of difficulties. She was ignorant of the many rules of conduct and decorum which to him were second nature. How could he explain the obstacles in their path?

He caught up with her in a trice and caught at her shoulders. "Tamasine, we must arrange a meeting. We cannot talk like this, where we may be interrupted at any moment."

Her laughter tinkled. "I shall find you in the forest."

It did not suit Giles's sense of propriety to continue to meet her clandestinely, especially with his grandmother's prohibitions nagging in his head. Nor could he approve the notion of her wandering into the forest on her own. But as things stood, he could see no other way of ensuring their privacy for long enough to enable him to clarify everything satisfactorily. Without troubling to enquire into his suddenly urgent need to treat the secret betrothal with as much circumspection as he possibly could, Giles reluctantly agreed to the scheme.

"Very well, if you wish. Let us meet tomorrow early."

"I can't escape before breakfast. Lavinia locks me in at night."

Shocked at this news, Giles was nevertheless conscious of a sliver of relief somewhere inside him. At least she could not get into mischief as she had done on the day of her guardian's death.

"At ten then? I'll seek you in the hollow where I saw you first. You remember the place?"

She tinkled at him, the blue eyes sparkling. "Giles, Giles, Giles. I remember where you kissed me."

He winced. "Don't remind me. I am ashamed. It was shocking conduct."

Tamasine's eyes became abruptly glassy. "I liked it. You liked it too."

"I liked it excessively, but the fact remains —" He broke off, feeling all the futility of continuing to argue the point. He smiled instead. "Then we are agreed? Ten o'clock in the hollow?"

"Ten o'clock in the hollow," Tamasine repeated, like an echo, her bright eyes still holding that disturbing look.

Giles hesitated, warily watching her. It struck him that he was anxious, as if he confronted a snake and did not know what it might do. The random thought streaked across his mind, leaving him with a hollow feeling inside and the first stirrings of a whisper of panic. To what had he committed himself?

Then Tamasine's expression altered completely, and a melting look of adoration overspread her lovely countenance. "You are my hero, Giles. A hero for the sugar princess."

She came up to him and threw her arms around his neck, clinging so tightly that he almost choked. The gesture was over before he could protest, and Tamasine stepped back.

"Now I am going to find Simeon," she stated in a voice so matter of fact that Giles was startled at the change.

Before he could do or say anything more, Tamasine was off, running like a hare towards the far corner of the house. Reaching it, she ducked down the side and disappeared from sight. She had not looked back.

Ottilia had allowed herself to be dissuaded from attending the inquest, which was to be held before Justice Delaney. Her capitulation was ostensibly in response to Francis's suggestion that those inmates called to give evidence might reveal more in her absence than if confronted with someone they knew to be somewhat biased. She had been chastened at the thought.

"Am I biased?"

"They think so, which is the important point."

Ottilia eyed him. "Do you think so?"

To her surprise, her spouse grinned. "I think you want to be, my dear one, but your innate honesty will not permit you."

She was obliged to laugh. "Wretch! How dare you read me so well?"

They were in the privacy of their bedchamber and Francis kissed her. "Have you not yet realised that I am a keen student of Ottilia?"

"You are a cozening rogue rather."

"A deserved scold," he conceded, his unruly eyebrow quirking, but he grasped her hand loosely. "Will you take my advice?"

"This is not yet another attempt to ensure I don't exert myself unduly?"

His mouth twitched on a smile. "That too, of course."

Ottilia was tempted to give in at once, merely because he asked it of her. But if truth be told, she did not believe any new evidence was likely to arise at the inquest, and she had not been called, despite having been the first person with any medical knowledge to examine the body. She had no authority and with two doctors on the case, her testimony must be superfluous.

"Well then, I shall keep Sybilla company." She added with a mischievous look, "As long as you promise faithfully to regale me with the whole."

"Would I do otherwise? This is the advantage of an elephantine memory. I shall bring you a word for word account."

Ottilia bubbled over. "A summary will do. Unless there is something new, of course."

Not that she had any such expectation, since the coroner had ordered the inquest on completion of the investigations of Sunderland's apothecary. To Ottilia's disappointment, the confection proved to have insufficient opium content to account for Sir Joslin's death, although the apothecary conceded that it was a strong dose. She had taken it up at once with Patrick.

"Stronger than that prescribed for children?"

"To a degree. But, as I told you at the outset, not strong enough to kill."

Ottilia did not again pursue the idea of the effect of several of the sweets in one go. Her brother was bound to pooh-pooh it again. But she filed the notion in the back of her mind, unwilling to abandon the confections altogether.

The news from the bottle of laudanum was no better. It contained the expected amount. And the mysterious bottle from behind the chamber pot proved to contain a mixture of rum, sugar and again opium, but nowhere near enough to kill Sir Joslin. Had he downed a combination of these items? Some answer there must be, for the testing of the contents of his stomach suggested the man had indeed ingested a severe overdose of the drug.

"I would not be in the justice's shoes for a fortune," she observed to her mother-in-law when the two of them were alone in the parlour.

Sophie Hathaway was enjoying a rare period of release from her own ailments and was intent upon taking advantage of it. The dowager having made it abundantly clear that a couple of excursions in Mrs Hathaway's company were more than enough, it had fallen to Miss Mellis's lot to escort her, along with her protesting offspring, upon an expedition of pleasure to take in a little of the surrounding country while the weather held.

"If you cannot unravel it, Ottilia, I dare say Robert Delaney will find it an impossible task. He is a severe sort of man and painstaking, but I have never thought highly of his powers of observation. "

"You must at least be relieved Giles's involvement is unlikely to be entered into it."

"Yes, if those wretches from Willow Court do not make it their business to point the finger at him."

"I doubt the question will arise at all as things stand."

Sybilla drew an obviously taut breath. "It is to be hoped it does not. Delaney makes a point of directing his juries and, since my idiot son must needs make a scandal throughout the county, the fellow is not above putting Giles in the frame merely upon principle."

Ottilia clicked her tongue. "Come, Sybilla. If he is as painstaking as you say, surely he will not act with such prejudice?"

"I wonder if Phoebe thinks so. She is a favourite with him, I know, and if he feels she has been slighted, which one can scarcely deny she has —"

"I am persuaded you need have no fears on that score," said Ottilia, and made haste to change the tenor of the conversation. "What is certain is that Delaney will not be given any of the information we have already unearthed. He and the jury will be obliged to go on what Patrick and Sutherland have been able to supply."

The dowager stared. "Then why in the world should he call the companion and the rest of them?"

"Miss Ingleby was with Sir Joslin when he died, and Mrs Whiting and Lomax are the senior occupants of the house. I imagine they will only be called upon to corroborate times and circumstances prior to the death. No one is going to label Sir Joslin an opium-eater, and all three can testify to the poor condition of his health."

Aware that Sybilla was eyeing her with her usual sharpness, Ottilia raised her brows in enquiry. The dowager let out an irritated breath.

"You think he is not going to bring in a verdict of unlawful killing."

A laugh escaped Ottilia. "I don't see how he can. The best I can hope for is an open verdict, though it is more likely to be accidental death."

"For which I will be thanking my maker, even if it disappoints you, my dear Ottilia."

"I won't be disappointed precisely."

"What then?"

She sighed. "It will make it a lot more difficult to pursue my enquiries, for the wretched creatures will be quick to reject any further effort to uncover the truth."

"Undoubtedly." Then Sybilla sat up with sudden energy. "But they won't stop me from doing all in my power to extract my grandson from the toils of that dreadful girl."

Ottilia cocked her head to one side. "You think it will be necessary? For my part, I suspect he will find out his own folly soon enough."

It was evident her mother-in-law was not so sanguine. "I wish I might agree with you, but my experience of young men argues the contrary. For all I know, he is planning to elope with the chit."

"If he does, I doubt they will get beyond the first stage before he realises his error. Make yourself easy, Sybilla. Difficult as I find Miss Ingleby, I cannot accuse her of neglecting her charge. She might give them the slip now and then, but as a rule, I doubt Tamasine is permitted to leave the house at all without an escort."

No sooner were the words out of her mouth than a tapping at the glass of the French window was heard. Looking across, Ottilia perceived the child Tamasine herself. And she was not alone.

The dowager had also seen the visitor, for she groaned aloud. "Why cannot the wretch use the front door?"

"You had as well ask why she threw a stone through the glass the last time," Ottilia pointed out, rising from her chair and crossing towards the windows.

"Who in the world has she brought with her?" demanded Sybilla.

As Ottilia reached the French window, she attracted Tamasine's wide smile and the child gestured with excitement to the man standing a little behind her, who looked to be young and personable. A wild presentiment shot into Ottilia's brain as to his identity and she hastened to unlatch the door and pull it open.

"I have brought Simeon to see you," said Tamasine without the slightest preamble. "I said he would come."

"You did indeed." Ottilia was pleased to find her surmise had been correct as she took in the fellow's dark good looks. "Mr Roy, I think? Do come inside, both of you."

Moving aside to allow the two access, Ottilia took stock of this Simeon about whom she had heard so much. He entered, moving with a natural grace and ease that was reflected in his smile.

"How do you do, Lady Fan?"

His drawling voice was as rich as the molasses he had no doubt had occasion to make in Barbados, and his confident figure held something of a swagger. He wore his dark hair loose, in the shaggy cut currently in vogue among young men. His lips were full, his nose straight and his eyes, in which a gleam of calculation was immediately apparent, were a liquid brown. Ottilia wrote him down as a charming rogue.

His use of her nickname gave rise to a slight feeling of antipathy, but since he must have had it from Tamasine, she did not trouble to correct him. She took time with an introduction to the dowager, over whose hand Simeon Roy bowed with exaggerated courtesy.

"Tamasine has given me an account of your kindness to her, ma'am, upon the occasion of her accident."

Sybilla's reception was frosty. "Indeed? I had not thought Miss Roy recalled the occasion."

Mr Roy's smile would have melted butter. "Oh, she tells me everything, ma'am. We are avid correspondents."

The blatant untruth of this assertion struck Ottilia at once. Even could Tamasine write, which was in serious doubt, any such intimacy must have been clandestine, considering Sir Joslin's views. And if Ottilia was any judge, Tamasine was incapable of the needed secrecy.

She urged the visitors to sit down, and was not surprised to see Simeon dispose himself upon the sofa in an attitude of careless languor. Tamasine immediately took up a position beside him, her blue eyes fixed upon his handsome face.

"Tamasine tells me, Lady Fan, that you have been of invaluable assistance in this tragic hour."

Unlikely as it was that the child could have expressed herself in such a fashion, Ottilia took it as if at face value. "I am happy to have been of service, but I believe Miss Ingleby is more than capable of dealing with any matters which may arise."

A faint look of scorn crossed the young man's features. "Oh, Lavinia is efficiency itself. Yet she will be relieved of her responsibilities soon enough."

Sybilla cut in without ceremony. "By whom? Yourself, for instance, Mr Roy?"

Simeon Roy threw up hands of mock horror. "I? Heaven forbid! The last thing in the world I could wish is to be saddled with settling affairs at Willow Court."

"Yet you are here."

He fetched an elaborate sigh. "I could hardly absent myself at such a moment. With my cousin in need of my support? No, no, ma'am, it would be cruel in me to refuse her plea."

Ottilia raised her brows. "Tamasine asked you to come?"

Simeon was smiling into the girl's adoring eyes. "Her entreaties could not be ignored, could they, my dear little Tam?"

Tamasine's blue gaze roved his features. "I knew you would come."

Which was scarcely a straightforward affirmation, and Tamasine had said as much to Ottilia days since. She watched the young man raise a hand to lift the girl's chin a little, a teasing note entering his liquid voice.

"How could I resist you? You know well I am as wax in your hands."

A delighted ripple of Tamasine's bell-like laugh emerged and she caught his fingers in both hands, clutching them tightly. "Simeon, Simeon, Simeon. If they don't like it, we will hide from them, and Hemp will tell them we have run away."

"Ah, now, that is an excellent plan, Tam," said her cousin in an indulgent fashion, but he withdrew his fingers from her grasp and wagged a finger in her face. "But I have a better one."

Tamasine's eagerness was child-like. "What is it?"

"That you shall know presently."

Ottilia thought this air of mystery must be deliberate. She could not but acknowledge that Simeon appeared to be adept at handling Tamasine's wayward manner. She sought a way to prick through his self-satisfaction.

"Am I right in thinking that it is some time since the two of you have met, Mr Roy?"

He was not in the least disconcerted, merely fetching another sigh. "Alas, yes. But we have contrived nevertheless to remain the best of friends as well as cousins, have we not, my pet?"

Thus appealed to, Tamasine added her mite, turning to look at Ottilia. "Simeon writes to me all the time."

"And do you write back?" asked Sybilla shrewdly, sending a glance of question in Ottilia's direction.

Tamasine did not trouble to answer, her attention once more taken up by the young man at her side. But Simeon Roy's expressive countenance turned to the dowager, comprehension in his gaze.

"Oh, she can write, ma'am. After a fashion. Can you not, my pet?" His glance caressed the child before returning to Sybilla. "Tamasine uses pictures rather than letters. She is quite an artist, and her illustrations are perfectly to be understood, by those who best know her mind."

Secretly impressed by the young man's swift understanding and his open acknowledgement of Tamasine's difficulties, Ottilia was yet unable to count him other than a rascal. She might be tempted to discount Miss Ingleby's intense disapprobation, had she not also Cuffy's testimony. She probed gently.

"Was it Tamasine who told you of Sir Joslin's death then, Mr Roy?"

"Not at all, ma'am. I have lately been staying with my cousin Ruth, and I was there when Lavinia's express arrived."

"You mean Mrs Delabole?"

"Precisely, ma'am. I confess my natural grief at the news was tempered by the thought of being able to see Tamasine again. But Ruth's shock was so severe, I felt it a mercy I happened to be there."

Ottilia threw her immediate suspicions into the open. "Are you in the habit of visiting Mrs Delabole?"

The young man spread his hands, looking rueful. "Sadly, no. And I will admit that poor Ruth was by no means delighted, but she took pity on me nevertheless."

"You were not welcome? Now why, I wonder, Mr Roy?"

His brows rose. "Why, I should have thought that was obvious. Ruth was a fond sister and she knew of my falling out with Cousin Matt. Still I hoped to persuade Ruth to intercede with Joslin on my behalf."

"Joslin would not let Simeon come," put in Tamasine. "I wanted him to come."

Simeon spread his hands again. "You see? The moment I knew Tamasine was in England, I wrote to Joslin for permission to visit her."

"Which he refused?" queried the dowager.

The young man turned to Sybilla, his smile wry. "Old prejudices are hard to break, ma'am. I was but a youth when I left Barbados, you must know. Yet I failed to persuade Joslin of my change of heart."

"Dear me, Mr Roy," said Ottilia lightly, "you assume knowledge on our part which we do not have. We had heard from Tamasine that you were forbidden the house by Sir Joslin, but we are ignorant of the reason."

Simeon gave vent to a laugh in which surprise and ruefulness were neatly blended. "Oh, dear, and I had so nearly confessed my sins. You must forgive me. The peccadilloes of one's youth are apt to haunt, and it is hard to remember anyone involved with the family could be ignorant of them."

"Well, we are wholly ignorant," said Sybilla flatly. "And I daresay it will suit us all better if we were to remain so."

"Oh, believe me, ma'am, I had far rather nothing of the matter was spoken of outside the family. Only my little Tam here is nothing if not confiding, and since you, Lady Fan, have befriended her, it did not seem to me possible that she had not acquainted you with all."

Tamasine had been all the while an interested spectator of the discussion, but at this, she turned her blinding smile upon Ottilia. "I should like you to know all my secrets."

"Well, that is extremely generous of you, Tamasine, but I think we must allow your cousin his privacy." Without giving either a chance to reply, she turned the subject. "Is Mrs Delabole then with you? Did you escort her here?"

For the first time, she noted a faint look of chagrin creep into the fellow's eyes. Had he wanted the conversation to continue upon the topic of his misdeeds? He recovered himself swiftly, throwing in another one of those deprecating smiles.

"I offered to do so, but Ruth would not hear of it. Realising she might be here some time, she had perforce to make arrangements for her absence at home. She has a numerous family, you must know, and it is not a simple matter for her to drop everything at a moment's notice."

"So you came on ahead?" Sybilla surmised.

Once again, Simeon Roy cast an eye verging almost on the avuncular upon the young girl at his side. "I rushed to the rescue in the shortest possible order."

It occurred to Ottilia to wonder whether Mrs Delabole's rejection of his escort had rather concerned itself with Sir Joslin's prohibition of Simeon's presence at Willow Court. Had the young man come here against her wishes? Had he seized his chance, knowing she was preoccupied, and made haste to plant himself in the place ahead of her arrival?

Before she could think how to introduce a question of this nature, the front door bell was heard to peal and Tamasine jumped up, running to the French windows.

"Simeon, come quick! Before Lavinia catches us."

But he remained just where he was. "If you suppose I am afraid of Lavinia, my dear little Tam, you much mistake the matter. Come back and sit down."

Tamasine did no such thing, instead thrusting open the door and looking out into the garden, as if she thought to see her duenna approaching the house by that way.

Simeon gestured in her direction, casting a deprecating glance at the two ladies and lowering his voice. "Lord knows what fears have been inculcated in the child's diseased mind."

This was the first time any member of the Willow Court household had spoken overtly of Tamasine's derangement. Miss Ingleby had ceased pretence, but such remarks as she let fall were veiled. Ottilia, who had been scathing of the pretence, found herself subject to a bewildering change of face when confronted by this blatant admission. She was spared having to answer by Sybilla's testy demand.

"Pray will you at least induce the child to close the door, sir, before we all freeze to death?"

Uttering an apology as spurious, Ottilia suspected, as his earlier sincerity, Mr Roy leapt to his feet and went after his cousin. He had just succeeded in persuading her to re-enter the room and close the door when Biddy entered to announce the visitor.

"Miss Ingleby."

The companion swept into the room, her eyes flashing at the couple by the French windows. She did not even trouble to utter a word of greeting or apology to the inmates of the

Dower House, but scarcely waited for the door to close behind the maid before discharging her spleen.

"So, you are come, are you? How dare you flout Joslin's expressed wish? Lord knows I did not expect to return from the inquest only to find you encouraging the child to disobedience. I told you to stay in your room, Tamasine."

"I won't," retorted the child wildly. "You can't make me."

"We'll see about that."

Miss Ingleby started towards her, but Simeon Roy stepped forward to intercept her.

"Let her alone, Lavinia. She wanted to introduce me to her friend, Lady Fan, that is all. She has come to no harm."

"I don't need you to tell me that, Simeon Roy," began Miss Ingleby furiously.

She was interrupted. Sybilla rose with a swish of her skirts, her tone biting. "That will do!" All three countenances, redolent with surprise, turned towards her. "I have no knowledge of the manners obtaining in Barbados, I am happy to say," continued the dowager on an acid note, "but in England, it is not the custom to indulge in a quarrel in your neighbour's parlour." Her irate gaze turned upon the hapless duenna. "In particular, before you have even had the grace to acknowledge the presence of your hostess."

Miss Ingleby flushed, but her tone remained belligerent. "In that case, ma'am, perhaps you might with advantage teach your daughter-in-law to refrain from unwarranted interference in your neighbour's lives."

Sybilla drew herself up. "Are you telling me how to run my family?"

"Why not? Lady Francis makes no bones about telling me how to run mine."

Simeon Roy threw up his hands. "Ladies! Ladies! Pray do not come to blows, for I will take the fault to myself."

The dowager left off glaring at the duenna and swept the young man a scorching glance. But before she could unleash her fury, he had stepped up to Miss Ingleby, catching at her unquiet hands.

"Lavinia, I confess myself wholly at fault. Forgive me!"

The woman snatched her fingers from his grasp. "Don't touch me! You need not think to cozen me, Simeon. Those days are long gone."

"But not forgotten, my dear."

He had the temerity to laugh — a foolhardy proceeding, in Ottilia's opinion. So indeed it proved, for Miss Ingleby's eyes narrowed to slits of rage and her voice came low and vibrant.

"Would you taunt me thus? After what you attempted? Oh, for all your protestations, you have changed not one iota, Simeon Roy. You will not win this prize, I promise you."

With which, she stormed past him, seized Tamasine's wrist and dragged her to the French windows, utterly ignoring the girl's shrieking protests. Being all too well acquainted with Miss Ingleby's moods, Ottilia refrained from interfering as the woman turned the handle and wrenched open the door. But she was surprised that Simeon Roy did nothing, merely watching the two women, a look on his face of complete unconcern, even amusement.

The door closed behind them, cutting down the noise. As it faded, Sybilla turned her irate glance on the young man. "Well, sir?"

Simeon swung round, his features instantly taking on that deprecating look at which he appeared to be well practised. "My dear ma'am, I must beg to offer you my abject apologies. On behalf of Lavinia, more nearly than my poor little cousin.

She cannot help herself. But Lavinia, I fear, is sorely beset. She was over-fond of Joslin."

"How do you know that, Mr Roy?" demanded Ottilia at once, at last rising from where she had remained an interested spectator of this revealing scene. "You have not been in Barbados for some little time, I gather."

Simeon's confidence did not falter. "My dear Lady Fan, I thought I had made it abundantly clear that Tamasine had kept me informed of all that went on within the family."

"And you believed her without question? Despite knowing that her view of events must necessarily be wholly subjective?"

He sighed. "You are right, of course. Tamasine sees everything in life as it concerns herself. But we were so very close, you see. I have learned to read between the lines."

"However that may be, sir," said Sybilla, once more entering the lists and by no means mollified, "I must request you not to bring the girl here again. I will not be subjected to rudeness a second time."

Mr Roy bowed. "Your objection is perfectly understandable, ma'am. I will endeavour to keep Tamasine from disturbing you."

"If she should wish for me, Mr Roy," Ottilia put in quickly, having no desire to be excluded, "be so kind as to send to me, and I will come over to Willow Court."

He raised his brows. "My dear ma'am, do you think that advisable? With Lavinia in her present humour, there is no saying what may happen. I am in dread of the moment when she discovers that our little Tam has engaged herself to your grandson, Lady Polbrook."

CHAPTER ELEVEN

Sybilla's features whitened. "What? It's a lie!"

Ottilia was in no less shock than her mother-in-law, but she took this up at once. "Do you know this for a fact, Mr Roy?"

"Since Lord Bennifield himself confirmed it to me a little before we came across, I have no reason to doubt it."

With which, he bowed in a perfunctory fashion and took himself off through the door to the garden, so swiftly that Ottilia at once decided he had made the announcement deliberately in order to throw the cat among the pigeons. The match was evidently not to Simeon Roy's liking. It did not take much imagination to work out why.

She moved to ensure the door was latched, hearing Sybilla break out behind her.

"Is there no end to the foolishness of the men in my family? Like father, like son! What in heaven's name should take the boy to engage himself to that lunatic? He is plainly besotted!"

"Yes, but I doubt that was his reason," Ottilia cut in before the dowager could get into her stride.

"Reason? I am minded to think him as mad as the girl!"

Ottilia came back into the room. "Calm yourself, ma'am, I beg of you. I shall count myself astonished if anything comes of this betrothal."

"It most certainly will not, if I have anything to say to it."

"I don't doubt you have everything to say to it," said Ottilia with a flash of merriment. Her mother-in-law's irate gaze turned upon her and she quickly held up her hands in a gesture of peace. "No, don't rip up at me, Sybilla. Well as I understand your feelings, we will achieve nothing by your flying into a fury."

The black eyes caught fire and for a moment Ottilia thought she had gone too far. Then the dowager let out a sigh and sank back among the cushions, momentarily closing her eyes. Ottilia waited in silence. At length, her mother-in-law spoke again, her tone grudging, if more moderate.

"You are right as usual. I must strive, I suppose, not to visit my dissatisfaction with Randal upon his son."

"No, indeed, tempting though it may be," Ottilia agreed with a twinkle.

Sybilla sighed again, and noting the taut curl of her own fingers, fastidiously straightened them. Then she looked across at Ottilia. "Why do you think Giles did it, if not because he is in love with the wench?"

"I don't think he did it at all. I imagine it was all Tamasine's doing."

"Well, I can believe her capable of any impropriety, but do you suppose she asked him to marry her?"

"Not at all. I expect she merely stated that they were to be married. It's what she did the morning of her guardian's death. And, given Giles's refusal to recognise her shortcomings, I dare say he was motivated by chivalry."

"To accept her, you mean?"

"Or merely to accept a fait accompli."

The dowager gave her a derisive look. "And nothing at all to do with the fact that he has fooled himself into thinking he is head over ears in love, I dare say."

"That too, of course." Ottilia perched on the arm of her mother-in-law's chair and took her hand. "Don't look so distressed, ma'am. If Giles is not already regretting the event, I give you leave to call me a dunderhead. Oh, he won't admit it," she added, seeing a hopeful look creeping into Sybilla's features. "I'm sure he feels bound by whatever foolish promise he may have made and will not readily be encouraged to relinquish it. And if you value my advice —"

"Do you think me such a simpleton that I would make the attempt? It would be useless."

"Besides setting up his back. Not," Ottilia added hastily, "that you care for that."

Sybilla let out a groan. "Yes, but I do. One should not play favourites, but the boy was ever the delight of my life. And he knows it. I hate being at outs with him."

"Well, you need not be."

"How can I help it?" She released her fingers from Ottilia's grasp and sat up with sudden energy. "Ring the bell, Ottilia. I'm going to send for Giles and demand the truth."

Ottilia rose and went across to the bell-pull as requested, but nonetheless entered a mild protest. "Do you think that's wise?"

Her mother-in-law's eyes were snapping again. "I will not take that young man's word for it. I know the type. A mischief-maker if ever I saw one."

"Even so, would he say Giles had confirmed it, if he had not?"

"I intend to find out," declared Sybilla, as the door opened. "If my grandson has indeed become engaged to Tamasine Roy, he will not dare deny it to me."

About to speak, Ottilia hesitated as a shocked look came into the dowager's face. She was staring at the door. Ottilia turned quickly and her veins turned to ice. Lady Phoebe Graveney was standing in the doorway, and it was evident from her expression that she had heard the fatal words.

Numbness settled over Phoebe's mind. She ought to feel shocked, betrayed, but the single thought repeating through her head was that she had lost. Only half aware, she allowed herself to be ushered to the sofa, her fingers caught in Lady Polbrook's fierce clutch.

"Ring the bell, Ottilia. She needs a drop of something to revive her."

In a daze, Phoebe watched Lady Francis — or no, Lady Fan was her preference, was it not? — move to the bell-pull and tug upon it. She caught the woman's eye as she returned towards the sofa and uttered the first words that came into her head.

"I only came to see if you had news from the inquest. Even though Robert was presiding, Papa would not permit me to attend."

Lady Polbrook let out a snort. "So I should hope."

Phoebe shifted her gaze to the elderly lady's face. "But I wanted to. I need to know."

"As do we all."

"I shall be obliged to ask Robert myself," Phoebe said, thinking aloud.

"Mr Delaney, you mean? I doubt that will prove necessary, my dear."

Lady Fan's calm tones were balm to Phoebe's ears. She seemed to have a knack of maintaining just the right manner to forestall any form of hysteria. Phoebe drew a painful breath and let it out again.

"I would very much like to scream."

"Pray don't," said the dowager. "We have had tantrums enough this day."

"I won't. I have been brought up to think badly of any such public display."

Lady Fan let out a peculiarly musical laugh. "The perfect marchioness."

"Oh, pray don't." A twinge at her heart caused Phoebe to throw her hands over her face.

"Ottilia, have you no tact?"

"My dear Sybilla, this is hardly the moment for tact."

"How can you say so, you dreadful girl? Here is poor Phoebe —" She broke off as the younger maid entered the room.

"My lady?"

"Brandy, Biddy. Lady Phoebe has sustained a shock."

This penetrated Phoebe's foggy mind. "Oh, no, pray. I so much dislike it."

"Port, then. Biddy, bring the port and three glasses."

Phoebe made no further demur, feeling unequal to the task of repudiating Lady Polbrook's attempt to revive her. The moment the door shut behind the maid, the dowager broke out again.

"You must not take it to heart, my child. If my fool of a grandson has indeed engaged himself to that mad creature, you may be sure I will speedily put a stop to such nonsense."

Phoebe looked at her. "If he has pledged his word, he cannot draw back."

At this, Lady Fan put her oar in again. "But she can, and I am sure she will before long. If there is a betrothal, I imagine it is nothing more than a game to Tamasine. Besides, if she marries anyone, which I feel to be unlikely, it will be Simeon."

"Simeon?"

"Her cousin, Simeon Roy. She said he would come and he arrived today. I have no doubt at all there is a concerted plan in place, on his side at least."

"What, Ottilia, you think he means to marry her?"

"Let us not forget she is the sugar princess, Sybilla, and heir, I don't doubt, to her father's wealth."

Bewildered and heart-sore, Phoebe could only stare at the woman. She was treated to a warm smile.

"Don't look so oppressed, my dear child. For my part, this engagement is the best thing that can have happened."

"Ottilia!"

Phoebe blinked at her. "How so?"

"From Giles's perspective, I mean. Or from ours on his behalf."

A faint ache began in Phoebe's head as she tried to follow Lady Fan's train of thought. She was about to put a question, but Lady Polbrook was before her.

"It is just like you to talk in riddles, Ottilia. For heaven's sake, say what you mean!"

"Pardon me, Sybilla. To my mind, Giles cannot have been expecting to find himself betrothed, at least at this juncture."

"Yes, you said you thought it was Tamasine's doing."

Phoebe was conscious of a rise of hope, but she entered a caveat. "She could not be so lost to all sense of propriety as to ask a man to marry her."

"She is just so lost. Indeed, she has no notion of propriety at all."

"That at least is true," said Lady Polbrook on an acid note.

"But if Giles loves her, that will not weigh with him," Phoebe objected.

"I dare say he will try to ignore it," Lady Fan returned. "But it cannot be long before he recognises that a girl of her stamp could not possibly be an asset to him, do you not think?"

About to repudiate this in no uncertain terms, Phoebe hesitated. The Giles she knew and loved — or thought she knew — would never have countenanced impropriety in a female. He was such a high stickler, he refused to believe his own mother could have exceeded the bounds of polite behaviour. Phoebe had heard several ranting speeches on the subject, to which she had listened with sympathy and held her tongue on the gossip that had been rife about the neighbourhood for years. Indeed, her attachment to Giles would have been frowned on by her own father had the young man not demonstrated a rectitude completely opposite to his mother's conduct. Yet Tamasine Roy had succeeded in wrenching him from the path of virtue.

"Even if he does realise it, which I take leave to doubt, his involvement must preclude any thought of a future with —" Phoebe broke off, startled to find herself speaking so freely.

"With you," finished Lady Fan, her tone dry. "Well, that is as you determine, my dear Phoebe, but I am sure he will be available should you change your mind."

"Change her mind? What in the world do you mean, Ottilia?"

The question was destined to remain unanswered. The door opened to admit the maid, bearing a tray, and, close upon her heels, Lord Francis and a gentleman unknown to Phoebe. The former addressed himself at once to his wife.

"Your powers are still needed, Tillie. The jury brought in an open verdict."

The young footman was outwardly compliant, yet Ottilia's best confiding manner failed to pierce a subtle defiance. She had managed to corner him in the parlour by dint of shielding behind Patrick's intent. While her brother went to the deceased's bedroom to conduct a new and ostensibly authorised search, accompanied by Francis, Ottilia waylaid Hemp, who had answered the door. Fortuitously, since her principal object in coming to Willow Court this morning had been to question him.

She had viewed the open verdict as a boon, all her suspicions revived by the jury's inability to accept that an unexplained overdose of opium could be accidental. It seemed that the Honourable Robert Delaney had given a thorough summation of the case to the twelve men serving, his statements directing them clearly in the line of an accident. The foreman, however, polite and diffident, had painstakingly explained the jury's findings to the presiding judge, apologising for the inconvenience.

The jury understood, Francis reported, that it was going to cause difficulties, but insisted upon their conviction that, as the doctors were adamant about the cause of death, the deceased could not have ingested the opium without knowing he was taking it. With no evidence to prove he did have knowledge of it, the jury could not rule out the possibility that someone else introduced the opium into him by some means or other. Therefore the only recourse open to them was to return an open verdict.

Robert Delaney, in his turn, had no alternative but to set the local constable to enquire more particularly into the case. Without naming names, he had declared an interest and said he would pass the whole affair on to one of his fellow justices.

"Which, I might say, is just as well," said Francis. "The wretched fellow is far too fond of Phoebe to suit me. Thank the Lord he is conscientious enough to realise he cannot act in the matter under the circumstances."

"Does that mean some other man will enter the fray?"

"Not immediately. Justice Lovell is presently away, so you only have to deal with the constable, if indeed he comes in your way."

Ottilia had regarded him with lurking mischief. "Does this mean I have your blessing, Fan?"

He had all but snorted. "With my idiot nephew actually engaged to that crazy girl? I should think so. The sooner you solve the thing, the better pleased I shall be."

Ottilia lost no time in resuming the pursuit, lighting upon Hemp as the likeliest source of further information. But the footman was not proving to be as malleable as she had hoped.

"On the day Sir Joslin died, you carried a message to Lord Bennifield, did you not?"

"I did, milady."

"Are you in the habit of taking Miss Tamasine's messages, Hemp?"

A faint frown marred the smooth coffee-coloured features. "Why, milady?"

Ottilia raised her brows. "You sound suspicious."

"I do not understand the purpose of your question."

The tone was deferent but she was quick to note the hint of steel beneath it. She tried for a mild approach. "Oh, I merely wish to ascertain how much Miss Tamasine relies on you. I gather you are a favourite with her."

Hemp made no comment, but his eyes were wary.

Ottilia changed tack. "Tell me, can Miss Tamasine write?"

The dark eyes narrowed. "Milady must have realised her education is limited."

Which was no answer at all. She would have to be more direct. "I wondered if you wrote her letters for her, Hemp?" Surprise flickered in his face and was swiftly veiled. She pushed. "You are not going to ask me to believe your own education is limited."

His chin lifted a fraction and his jaw tightened. His tone was stiff. "Master Matt wanted me to learn."

"Was that usual?"

He hesitated. Ottilia saw the decision form before he spoke.

"Not usual. I was privileged."

Indeed. And for a good reason, if her instinct proved true. But she refrained from expressing such thoughts aloud. Time to strike hard.

"Did you write for Tamasine to Mr Simeon Roy?"

"Ha! Write to him? Not if she paid me!"

There was no mistaking the disgust. Was there anger too? He recollected himself immediately, his mien returning to subservience, his eyes flicking away.

Ottilia took instant advantage. "Then who did, Hemp? Mr Roy claims to have carried on a regular correspondence with her, but you and I both know she could not have written to him herself."

Hemp's gaze came back to her. "If Miss Tam had help, she did not tell me."

"Pardon me, but I find that surprising. I can't imagine there is much she would not confide to you. And I doubt she is good at keeping secrets."

Once again he took refuge in silence. Ottilia wanted to press him, but it was obvious she would get nowhere by so doing. Surprise, in Hemp's case, might prove the best path to success. She gave it to him, in full measure.

"There's a reckoning, Hemp." She saw the word strike home as his brows drew together. Time to attack. "What do you know about it?"

"It is only a game." The words were blurted out. "She plays these games."

"I've no doubt. But what is it all about, Hemp? I am persuaded you know."

He took in breath and let it out in a bang. His look became fierce. "You want to make her guilty. You want to say she did this thing."

"She told me she did."

"She does not know what she says. If she thought of killing, she did not understand what it meant. It is not a real thing for her, this death of Master Jos."

Ottilia smiled. "I believe you are right. But Mr Simeon Roy is not similarly handicapped. If he were to instruct Tamasine to do a thing, she would carry out his wishes, do you not think?"

Sudden understanding lit the dark eyes and they flared. "That is what you thought, milady? You believe I would be party to letters between Miss Tam and this Simeon Roy, with a plot to kill Master Jos?"

Ottilia took it head on. "I had to consider the possibility."

Hemp's anger held for a moment. Then he sighed out a breath. Against all protocol, he turned his back on Ottilia and crossed to stare out of the window.

She waited, not unhopeful. Her opinion of his intelligence and character was rising by the second. She could not help but feel sympathy with his situation, born to a life that gave him no real prospects, nor outlet for his obvious talents.

Without turning around, he spoke, his voice rough with emotion. "Miss Tam is too innocent. She did not understand why Master Matt sent Simeon Roy away from the plantation. He is a villain, that one. He tried —" Hemp broke off, hesitated, and began again. "What he did Master Matt could not forgive. Nor I. But for Miss Tam, it was another game spoiled. She does not like us to spoil her games." He looked round, despair in his face. "I swore to Master Matt that I will look after her. I swore on my life. But with Miss Tam it is not easy."

"So I should imagine." Ottilia moved a few paces towards him, schooling her tongue to persuasion. "Was that the source of this reckoning, Hemp?"

"So I think. Miss Tam tells me only there is a reckoning, that someone must pay."

"You don't know who?"

He shook his head.

"Nor why, for certain," she suggested. "You suppose it to concern Simeon. Indeed, Tamasine told my nephew that she and he swore vengeance. But although her guardian is dead, she told me she was not yet done. That gives me to think, Hemp, that perhaps this reckoning may be something quite other."

He turned to face her, puzzlement in his tone. "What else? There is no other reason for vengeance."

"Yet how is one to fathom the workings of a mind like Tamasine's?"

She spoke almost to herself, but Hemp's reaction startled her.

"It is not her fault! She was born from that crazy one. Master Matt did great wrong to make a child with her. He knew so, for he confessed it to me. He believed it was his sin, and Miss Tam suffers because of it."

There was so much despair and pain in the man's words that Ottilia was touched. But the mention of Florine was too good an opportunity to miss. "Did Tamasine have much contact with her mother?"

Hemp shifted with evident discomfort. "When she was small, before the mistress had to be locked up."

"How small?"

"Until four or five."

Ottilia hesitated, wondering how to put the question she was burning to ask. These were sensitive issues and the footman's involvement made him cagey. But the matter could be pertinent.

"What happened, Hemp?" Puzzlement overlaid the distress in his face. Ottilia hastened to elucidate. "Why was the mistress locked up? What had she done?"

For a moment she thought he was not going to answer. He looked away, and back again. Again, he took the wary route. "It is ancient history."

She opted for truth. "It may help to unravel the present maze."

The dark eyes met hers, a glint in them that spoke of an old rage, long felt and burning slow. "The mistress could not be trusted with the slaves. One day she went too far."

"How?"

"She interfered with a boy."

The words were grated. The meaning penetrated and an odd notion flicked in Ottilia's mind. Was Hemp the boy? If so, why was the incident particularly bad? Bad enough to precipitate Mr Roy's decision to have his wife put away permanently, it appeared. But this she could not ask. She changed tack.

"But I take it this was not all. Was she violent?"

"She became more so as the years went by." His jaw tightened. "The worst was when she hurt Master Jos."

"Badly?"

He nodded, and brought it out flat and hard. "She said he raped her. She was defending herself."

"But Mr Roy did not believe it?"

His lip curled. "Rape a woman? Master Jos?"

"Yes, I see." She wondered briefly if there was something in the air of Barbados, to breed passions that led to violence.

"Tell me, did Tamasine ever visit her mother once she was incarcerated?"

"Mrs Whiting took her regularly, but she never left her alone with the mistress. I waited outside."

"In case she became dangerous and you had to intervene?" Ottilia guessed.

"Miss Florine was strong. Miss Tam also, when she is angry."

"When she is thwarted?"

He looked disheartened. "She does not mean it. She can be gentle. She can be loving."

Was she capable of true loving? Ottilia doubted it, but it would be cruel to disabuse Hemp, whose affections towards the child could not be in doubt. But it was far other than the sort of feeling to which Giles was in thrall. Hemp's feelings, she was persuaded, were of quite another sort.

She was toying with the advisability of putting her suspicion into words when a sudden cacophony broke out beyond the parlour door.

The shouting below attracted Francis's attention. He left off his search through the drawers in the press where, at Tillie's request, he was hunting for the missing sugar sweets, and glanced across at his brother-in-law, who was seated upon the bed, engaged in mathematical calculation.

"What's to do?"

Patrick tucked away his notebook and pencil and stood up. "We'd best go and see."

Francis led the way into the hall, and the voices raised in anger were immediately audible.

"You come here, trying to cozen your way in, as if the lot of us were not perfectly aware of your intent."

"That's Miss Ingleby," Francis said, leaning over the gallery rail.

He could see the companion over by the door to Sir Joslin's erstwhile study, which was open. It was evident the argument had been going on for some moments, and had spilled out into the hall. The other party was standing at the foot of the stairs, his great-coat on his back, hat in hand, evidently in the intention of leaving the house. Was this the fellow Tillie had spoken of? The Roy cousin?

"And what of your intent, my dear Lavinia," came from the man in a drawling tone. "Well and truly are your fond hopes smashed, are they not?"

Miss Ingleby's cheeks became stained with red. "You know nothing of the matter. Joslin was fond enough."

"Fond? You had less chance of attaching him than I, had my tastes run in that direction."

Aha, so their suspicions of the fellow Cadel's preferences had foundation. The comment had an inflaming effect on Miss Ingleby.

"Be quiet, you hellion! I hate and loathe you!"

"That's not the opinion you held of me at one time, my dear," sneered her tormentor.

She uttered a shriek. "Don't dare begin upon that subject, Simeon Roy!"

"You ought to know by now there is nothing I would not dare. Indeed, if anyone in this household may claim intimate knowledge of me —"

The woman threw herself back against the doorjamb, one hand rising to her throat. "You would taunt me thus? With an episode in the past which filled me — which still fills me — with disgust and shame?"

The fellow Roy's arrogant stance did not alter. He leaned a little more at his ease, the sneering note pronounced. "To my recollection, Lavinia, you welcomed my advances with far other than disgust. And as for shame, you had none. There, that is cutting up a character indeed."

Miss Ingleby ran towards him, her hand flying up as if she would slap his cheek, but Roy stepped forward and caught her wrist, holding her off.

"Ah, would you, my sweet? Too ambitious. I am not the youth I once was, to be caught unawares by the claws of a jealous strumpet."

A strangled sound, much like the snarl of an infuriated cat, escaped Miss Ingleby's lips. She wrenched herself free and fisted her hands before his face. "If ever I deserved that name, it was all your doing. You made of me what I became, just as you tried to do with that unsuspecting demented child."

"Tamasine adores me," returned Roy in a superior tone, "which is why you could not endure to see us together."

Miss Ingleby's features became the more enraged and the fists were raised to either cheek, stabbing at her own face as if she sought to punish it for ever catching the fellow's attention.

"You fiend! You don't love her, you never did. You eloped with her only for the sake of her fortune."

Roy launched his upper body towards her, losing some of his assurance in a display of temperament almost equal to her own. "Much you know about it! You were so jealous you could not see beyond the end of your nose."

"I saw through you right enough, Simeon Roy! And if you think to find an ally here, you are mightily mistaken. None in this house will support your schemes, and Tamasine is too well guarded to be spirited away this time."

The combatants suffered an interruption. A voice was heard crying out for the companion, and Mrs Whiting came waddling down the corridor behind Francis and Patrick.

"Miss Ingleby! Miss Ingleby!" She did not appear to notice the gentlemen standing to the side of the staircase as she hurried down. "Miss Ingleby, have you seen Tamasine? She is not in her room."

Simeon Roy let out a gust of crude laughter, as he shifted further into the hall. "Slipped her leash again? So much for your strict guardianship. The chit is more than a match for you, Lavinia."

The taunt went unregarded. Miss Ingleby met the housekeeper at the foot of the stairs. "Have you looked in the attics?"

Mrs Whiting was puffing, one hand at her ample bosom. "I've not the strength to go up there. I searched all the rooms on the first floor."

Ignoring the fellow Roy, Miss Ingleby sailed down the hall, out of Francis's line of vision and he heard her calling for the footmen.

"Hemp! Cuffy!"

The lighter voice answered at once. "I am here, madame."

"Hemp, thank heavens! Run up to the attics and check for Miss Tam."

Francis stepped forward to meet the fellow as he reached the top of the stairs. "Can we help?"

Hemp paused. "No, sir, I thank you. I know all the places where Miss Tam hides."

With which, he was gone, his steps pounding along the corridor. A deep voice sounded below, and within a moment, Cuffy came charging up the stairs and disappeared in Hemp's wake.

"Come on, Patrick."

Francis led the way downstairs. Simeon Roy had disappeared, and Miss Ingleby was in urgent conference with Lomax by the green baize door at the back of the hall.

Spying his wife standing just inside the parlour door, Francis crossed quickly to her and slipped inside. He waited only for Patrick to join them before closing the door softly behind them.

"And what did you make of all that, Tillie?"

A sneaking regret for the situation into which he had precipitated himself plagued Giles as he waited in the woods. He was chilled, anxious and irritable, feeling as much guilt at appointing this clandestine meeting as he felt apprehension at its object.

Word of the open verdict had reached him the previous evening, his uncle having sent Toby with a note. All Francis's arguments intruded upon his peace of mind, cutting it to shreds. Not that he truly believed a charge of murder could implicate him. He had not been next or nigh Willow Court until after the fellow's death. The niggling worry that had seeped unwanted in his mind was far more pertinent.

Could Tamasine have had a hand in her guardian's death? Though he steadfastly believed in her artlessness, that trusting nature might prove her undoing. Could she be worked upon by another to do what she did not understand to be wrong?

His encounter with that cousin of hers rankled. He had not liked the fellow. Roy had been altogether too free with Tamasine, and it was plain she was disposed to be fond of him. Had she not indicated she was relying on his services to right her wrongs? He remembered his uncle asking about the reckoning. Was this the vengeance she and Simeon Roy had sworn? Could it have a bearing on this unexplained death?

And all this added to the necessity to arrange an elopement. Common sense told him it was the only possible course, were he to meet his obligation to marry Tamasine.

When had he started thinking of it as an obligation? Not a day since, he would have sworn he could like nothing better than to make her his own. Today, in light of the verdict, everything his relatives had said to the disparagement of his inamorata's mental capacities had come swirling into his brain and refused to be dislodged.

The light running footsteps coming through the trees startled him, even though he was expecting to hear the sound. Schooling his features to a welcome he was far from feeling, he strained for a sight of Tamasine. His heart jerked as he caught a glimpse of her. She was flitting from tree to tree, hiding at each point as if she feared pursuit.

"Tamasine!"

She reappeared, looked directly at him, waved and broke into laughter as she hid herself behind another tree.

Giles struggled to overcome a rise of exasperation. Was this a moment to be playing silly games? "Tamasine, come here!"

She slipped into sight again, laughed delightedly, and came towards him at a run, her arms held out. He received her perforce into his embrace, almost falling at the impact.

"Steady! You nearly had me over."

She allowed him to set her on her feet, but her arms twined around his neck and she gazed up at him with those shining blue eyes and her wide smile. "Giles, Giles, Giles! Will you kiss me? You must kiss me."

Her beauty was breathtaking, and for a moment a revitalised wash of pleasurable sensation swept over him. He lowered his lips to hers and kissed her with a fervency he had not previously dared. To his combined shock and amazement, Tamasine pressed herself closely against him, sinuous in her motions, although her mouth remained closed to him, unmoving under his.

The oddity of the womanly body and the child's kiss struck him forcibly and he tugged himself free, holding her off, as he hastily sought for excuses.

"We must not. It is bad enough that I am meeting you in secret. I must not compound the fault with such liberties as this."

A flash of something vengeful showed for an instant in her eyes. Cold and alien. Then it vanished and she was laughing again.

"Silly! You can kiss me as much as you like. They can't see. They can't stop us here."

Giles did not know how to answer this. Her naivety had been endearing, but could only irritate in his present mood. He strove for patience.

"Not now, Tamasine. I need to ask you something."

"Giles, Giles, Giles," she sang, and there stopped, smiling up at him.

Disconcerted, he stared at her. Was she not the least bit interested to know he must question her? Any ordinary girl would be agog. Eager, anxious, or both. With an inward sigh, he took her hand and led her to a fallen tree trunk, obliging her to sit. Nothing loath, she planted herself where he put her and sat, looking up at him, apparently awaiting his pleasure.

How to begin? He meant to lead up to it gently, but it occurred to him that subtlety was not Tamasine's forte. There was nothing for it but to be direct.

"Tamasine, you remember you told me there was a reckoning?"

Her expression altered at once. He could not with justice call the look in her eyes now anything but malevolent.

"They will pay."

They? Instinct prompted Giles. "Who?"

She looked surprised. "Joslin, of course."

"But he is already dead." Who else?

She frowned, puzzlement flitting across her face. Then her brow cleared and the tinkling laugh sounded. "Yes. There, Giles, you see. The reckoning came to him after all."

He wanted to ask, by whose hand? But he was afraid of the answer. Then he remembered his earlier thoughts of Simeon Roy.

"Why did he have to pay a reckoning, Tamasine? What did Joslin do to you?"

The wide-eyed look was bent upon him. "Not me, silly. Mamma. She died. He had to die too. I pushed him down the steps. Joslin hurt Mamma, didn't you know?"

CHAPTER TWELVE

The day was clement, and Phoebe knew herself well enough recognised in the immediate environment for a lone walk to be perfectly safe. Willow Court was across the way from the Polbrook Dower House at Barnwells, which was only a matter of a mile from her own home at Hemington Court. She had no intention of burdening herself with either a groom or her maid upon this particular mission. To dispense with the services of either was not wholly unprecedented. To dispense with both might well attract notice.

Phoebe did not care. Let the world make of it what they would, she had every right to this foray. Lady Polbrook meant to send for Giles to discover the truth, but what was the use of that? If he was promised, then so be it. But what better way to discover for herself than by going directly to the horse's mouth? The conviction Giles would heartily disapprove of her action served only to make her the more determined. He had forfeited all right to be the arbiter of her conduct. But that did not mean she was prepared to give him up without a fight.

She reached her objective without incident, and was just walking up the drive to approach the front door when she was accosted by a voice.

"Who are you?"

The bright tone of interest came from a little distance and Phoebe turned, casting her eyes about the sun-dappled lawns.

A figure was poised at the head of a set of stone steps, half silhouetted against the brightness behind. It was female, Phoebe realised, taking in the shadowed gown beneath a dark pelisse. A pulse fluttered in her throat as she lifted a hand to shade her eyes the better to see who had hailed her, suspicion at once burgeoning as to the figure's identity.

As she did so, the female ran lightly down the steps and started towards her. Phoebe moved closer, her gaze hunting the features as they became momently more visible. There could be no doubt of the female's youth, and since she wore no hat, the golden hair clouding around her head was clearly visible. Within feet of the girl Phoebe halted abruptly, her heart plummeting.

Oh, but the creature was exquisite! Such clear blue eyes, such a rosebud of a mouth and a little tip-tilted nose. Small wonder Giles had fallen head over heels for the wench.

"You must be Tamasine."

A huge smile broke across the girl's lovely face, mirroring the day's unexpected sunshine. Phoebe's heart sank to the soles of the sturdy boots she had donned for walking, and for the first time in her life she regretted her own lack of beauty.

"Who are you?" repeated the girl, without troubling to answer Phoebe's supposition.

Phoebe grabbed at the remnants of her dignity. "I am Lady Phoebe Graveney." She began upon the excuse she had prepared. "I came only to offer my condolences on your sad loss."

The girl Tamasine appeared unmoved by these words. She did not respond at once, but merely stood, her china blue gaze drinking Phoebe in from her head to her heels. Then she opened her mouth in that dazzling smile again.

"You are not beautiful."

"Alas, no," said Phoebe before she could stop herself.

"Your boots are muddy."

Phoebe was disconcerted, but she answered readily enough. "The day looked so fine, I forgot about the recent snow. I'm afraid it has left the roads in a quagmire in places."

"I like to walk in the woods. But they won't let me if they catch me first."

Dear heaven, but could not Giles tell at once that this girl was abnormal? A burning sense of injustice invaded her breast. How could Giles prefer such a creature to their settled companionship?

The girl's confidences were not yet at an end. "They don't know I have got out. Lavinia will scold me dreadfully, but I have Simeon to protect me now."

At a loss how to answer, Phoebe felt her brain in a whirl. Her mind caught on the name of Simeon, and a half-formed spurt of hope prompted her into intemperate speech.

"Who is Simeon? Are you betrothed? Then you no longer favour Giles!"

Tamasine's blue eyes darkened and a faint frown creased that perfect brow. "Giles met me in the woods. He comes when I send to him."

A sliver of hurt raced through Phoebe's bosom and turned swiftly to rage. "Does he indeed? I would not set too much store by that, if I were you, Miss Roy. Giles has shown himself fickle once, and I dare say he may do so again."

Too late Phoebe realised the foolhardy nature of this speech. A malignant look entered the other girl's eyes and her head turned on one side in a manner that was distinctly unnerving.

"Giles is mine, for he kisses me. He is not yours."

Despite every evidence of the need for caution, Phoebe could not prevent the protest from leaving her lips. "He was! Until you came here, he was completely mine."

The only warning was a low mewl, like a kitten with its tail vibrating as it readied to attack. Then Tamasine pounced.

Phoebe caught two blows to the head before she took in that she was under siege. Reeling, she tried automatically to defend herself, throwing up her hands against the onslaught. Tamasine batted them out of the way and leaped for Phoebe's throat. The grip deprived Phoebe of breath and she staggered backwards, losing balance and crashing heavily to the turf. The punishing fingers were ripped away by the fall, but her adversary landed almost on top of her.

Instinct made Phoebe roll onto her front even as she fought to drag breath into her lungs. She felt the monster grab at her shoulders and curled inwards, hugging her own head for protection. Blows pummelled at her back. She concentrated on controlling her breath and enduring the pain, keeping her body as balled a target as she could.

The creature was shrieking incoherently and somewhere in the periphery of her mind Phoebe thought she must be overheard and dared to hope for succour. It came sooner than she could have expected. Above the sounds of Tamasine's raucous screeching and the hammering blows, Phoebe made out running footsteps. Then voices sounded.

"I'll grab the madwoman off, Tom, while you help the lady."

"Get her round the breadbasket, Ben," came another eager voice.

Only half recognizing both voices were youthful, Phoebe's hopes soared. Next moment, the shrieking intensified, but the blows ceased and she was released from the weight of the body against her back.

"Quick, ma'am, get up!"

Daring to open her eyes, Phoebe found a young face, flushed with excitement, upside down near her own, blonde hair falling about it.

"Thank you," she gasped, and with the boy's help, scrambled to her feet as speedily as she could manage for the discomforts of her maltreated body.

"Get her away, Tom, quick!" shrieked the other boy and Phoebe turned to find the youngster tight against Tamasine Roy's back, his arms clamped about her middle as he was being flung this way and that while the girl heaved herself around in an attempt to throw him off.

Her shrieking protests were unintelligible, but Phoebe had no time to take in more for her youthful rescuer grabbed her hand and started to drag her towards the set of stone steps where she had first seen the girl Tamasine standing.

"Come away, ma'am, quick, while Ben has her fast."

Phoebe hurried to obey, allowing the boy to pull her rapidly towards the steps, although she could not resist looking back to where the other was still hanging on grimly as he and Tamasine Roy shunted about the lawn.

"Someone's coming!" said her companion, halting abruptly at the foot of the steps.

Thundering footsteps could be heard and Phoebe looked towards them and found several running figures, a tall black man in livery taking the lead.

"Miss Tam! Miss Tam!" Reaching the struggling pair, he seized the girl bodily, pulling her against himself and holding her forcibly in place. "Stop, Miss Tam! You have Hemp now, Miss Tam. Stop it now, you hear me?"

Released, the other boy came belting across to where Phoebe and her escort stood transfixed, yelling out, "Don't stand there! Run!"

Thus adjured, the boy holding Phoebe's hand set off up the steps. "Come on, ma'am! No time to lose."

Phoebe nearly stumbled as she climbed the stairs, and quickly found herself supported on her other side by the second boy.

"Steady, ma'am. Tom, slow down a bit."

Finding herself at the top of the flight, Phoebe paused, catching her breath. Unable to resist looking back, she saw the girl Tamasine Roy was now held by the footman and another man, who were bearing her, still screaming, towards the house, accompanied by two women, the whole cavalcade creating a cacophony fit to be heard all over the county.

With all danger past and safe in the care of Lady Polbrook and her daughter-in-law, Phoebe found herself gripped by the shock of her experience. She felt battered and bruised, and her head was swimming a trifle as if she must surely swoon. She could not stop shaking, and the glass thrust into her hand by Lord Francis threatened to spill its liquid into her lap.

"Give it to me, my child," came the dowager's crisp tones and Phoebe was glad to relinquish the glass into the fingers that grasped it and held it to her lips. "Now take a sip."

"Is it brandy?"

"After what you told us yesterday? It is port, child. Drink it."

"She would do better to drink a tisane and lie down for an hour," suggested a voice Phoebe did not know.

"Presently, Doctor Hathaway. There, that is better. Gently, my child."

Obedient to the pressure and the voice of command, Phoebe did as she was bid and the dreadful sensations began to leave her. In due course she found herself able to follow the gist of the conversation being carried on in lowered tones.

"Lucky we were there," one of the boys was saying, "or the madwoman might have killed the lady."

"Lady Phoebe, Ben, and what in the world can you mean?" came from Lady Fan.

"The madwoman had her by the throat," said the other boy.

"And Lady Phoebe went down, and the madwoman kept on beating her until I grabbed her away."

"If we weren't there, she would have beat her to death," said the boy Tom, a ghoulish note in his voice that caused Phoebe to shudder.

"Do be quiet, boys!" This was an authoritative tone from the man Lady Polbrook had called Doctor Hathaway. "What I wish to know is why the two of you were there at all."

There was a silence and Phoebe felt a change in the atmosphere. She pushed aside the glass once more at her lips and looked across to where the two blond boys stood, confronted by a tall man who bore a striking resemblance to Lady Fan. She had to speak.

"Oh, pray don't scold them, sir. I dread to think how I would have fared without their intervention."

Doctor Hathaway glanced at her, and she was relieved to note the good humour in his countenance. "My dear ma'am, if my sons were able to be of service to you, I am only too happy. But their presence at Willow Court still calls for explanation."

"We were following the madwoman," said the boy she recalled as Ben.

"Upon what occasion?"

"Well, we saw her escaping."

"And we followed her into the woods," disclosed Tom, who had led Phoebe from the grounds.

Here Lady Fan intervened, and Phoebe was relieved to see merriment in her eyes. "It did not occur to either of you to raise the alarm, I collect?"

Evidently not, from the anguished glance exchanged. The boy Ben frowned in furious thought for a moment, and then looked relieved as this exercise evidently rewarded him.

"Well, if we'd wasted time going for help and hadn't followed her, she might have got lost."

"Ah, I see. So you kept her in sight."

Ben brightened at this show of acceptance. "Yes, and when she came out again, that's why we followed her to Willow Court, 'cause we were going to tell them where she'd been."

"Ingenious," commented Lord Francis.

Doctor Hathaway laughed out, and Phoebe felt acutely relieved. She could not bear to think the boys might be punished after what they had done for her.

"Have another sip, child," said the dowager, presenting the glass to Phoebe's lips again.

Phoebe shook her head. "I am feeling a deal recovered, if a little sore."

"I should think she is sore," burst out Tom, looking round at his elders. "The madwoman beat her dreadfully, Auntilla."

"Yes, so you said." Lady Fan crossed to the sofa, and Phoebe looked up into her concerned countenance. "Are you much hurt, my dear?"

Phoebe let out a shaky breath. "I scarcely know. I feel a degree bruised."

"You will feel it more as the day wears on," said Doctor Hathaway, coming to flank Lady Fan. "I can give you a salve, ma'am. I'm sure my sister will be happy to anoint your hurts."

"I should not dream of troubling you, ma'am."

Lady Fan smiled. "Then take the salve with you. I dare say your maid can do the business as well as I."

Scarcely had Phoebe agreed to this when the dowager's maid appeared in the doorway. "Lord Bennifield, my lady."

Phoebe jumped violently, her eyes flying to Giles's striking presence as he strode into the room and stopped short, blinking at the roomful of people.

"Good God, I had not expected such a crowd!"

His gaze swept the faces, settled for an instant on Lady Polbrook, and jerked back to Phoebe seated beside the dowager. Discomfort gathered in his handsome features and Phoebe's pulse hammered furiously in her chest.

"You are opportune, Giles," said the dowager on the edge of a snap. "Poor Phoebe here has been so unfortunate as to be the target of an attack."

Shock swept across his face. "What? An attack? How in the world —?"

"Tamasine Roy tried to strangle her," continued his grandmother, and Phoebe could not acquit her of relishing the pronouncement. "When that failed, she took to beating Phoebe nearly senseless."

There was a moment of silence, and then Giles sank into a chair, kneading his brow with a fist. "Oh, my god!"

Before anyone could say anything, the boy Tom suddenly spoke up, in a tone of bright innocence. "You're the fellow who was meeting the madwoman in the woods."

For a moment Giles was tempted to repudiate the charge. But in the face of what had happened to Phoebe, denial was useless. The thing was blown. Willingly could he have thrown the lad through the window.

"Well, Giles?"

His grandmother's tone was arctic and he winced. He dropped his hand and looked across at her. "Well, what, ma'am? Which accusation do you wish me to answer first?"

"No one has yet accused you of anything. But since you ask, let us at once be clear. Are you, or are you not, betrothed to Tamasine Roy?"

Shock swept over him. "How did you find out?"

"Then it is true! Oh, Giles, how could you be so idiotic?"

This was no answer, but to his relief, his aunt Ottilia stepped in. "I'm afraid it was Simeon Roy who betrayed you, Giles."

Fury lit in Giles's chest. "That fellow! He has a deal to answer for."

His uncle cut in. "I dare say, but that does not explain your conduct."

"Which particular conduct are you citing, sir? It seems as if everything is my fault!"

Relief came from an unexpected quarter.

"Not everything, Giles. You cannot be held accountable for what the creature did to me."

Phoebe was actually smiling at him. He regarded her with wariness, belatedly hearing the brittle note underneath her words. The smile did not reach her eyes.

He sighed, feeling suddenly weary. "Perhaps I am. I led her to believe in my sincerity, despite the realisation..."

He broke off, recollecting his company. He had been within an ace of taking Phoebe into his confidence in the old way. He glanced about the room, discovering the presence of a stranger standing alongside two boys, one the tell-tale who had given him away. Sudden irritation erupted.

"How in the world did you know I had been in the woods with Tamasine? Were you watching us?"

"You may be thankful they were," came snappily from Phoebe. "If they had not followed that creature, I would not have been rescued."

Had he not seen behind that spurious smile? The tone touched a raw nerve within him, a hurt he was unable to place. Restless, he stood up again.

"Why in the world did you go there? What possessed you?"

"Well, if you don't know that, you are a bigger fool than I supposed."

"Children, children!" chided his aunt Ottilia.

Giles paid no heed. "You had no right, Phoebe! What should take you to interfere?"

Phoebe shot to her feet, and at the back of his mind Giles noted how unsteady she was. Her words overbore the thought. "If we are to talk of rights! What right had you to spurn me for a bedlamite? As for mine, I went to meet my rival, to fight for you, if you must know, being an even bigger fool than you! Little did I suppose I should meet her returning straight out of your arms."

"No such thing. I have more conduct than to take advantage of an innocent girl."

"Oh, indeed? Then I must have imagined it when Tamasine boasted of your kissing her."

"She did not. You are making it up."

Phoebe flung out a hand towards the two boys. "Ask them if I am making it up. And I daresay, if we were to put them on oath, they could readily bear witness to even worse conduct on your part."

Infuriated, and all too conscious of being in the wrong, Giles erupted. "That's what you think of me, is it? Well, let me tell you —"

"Oh, for heaven's sake, be silent, the pair of you!"

279

His grandmother's snapping tone had the effect of cutting him off mid-sentence, and Giles retreated to the mantelpiece, drumming his fingers on the wooden surface there and keeping his gaze firmly away from the rest of the party. He heard the dowager speak again.

"Phoebe, sit down, child. Don't allow yourself to be goaded. It is undignified and unnecessary besides." She paused briefly, and her tone altered. "I make you my apologies, Doctor Hathaway. This is a poor return for your assistance, and you are supposed to be on holiday."

A laugh from the guest drew Giles's attention.

"Make yourself easy, ma'am. Like my sister, I am inclined to enjoy a trifle of liveliness. Besides, I must hope our relationship may allow you to count us into the family and therefore no apology is called for."

"You must be off your head, Patrick," said his uncle Francis. "Though that alone may qualify you, for the place is rapidly turning into as frantic a bedlam as Willow Court."

The words had hardly left his mouth when a sudden hammering sounded on the French windows. Startled, Giles looked across the room and, to his utter disgust and sorrow, saw Tamasine Roy outside, her fists beating the glass. Her pearly teeth were bared and the wild look at her lovely eyes had indeed a stamp of insanity.

Pandemonium broke out in the parlour, and as one in a dream, Giles heard the reactions as he stared at the girl with whom he had believed himself in love, to whom he had pledged his life, his future.

"Dear God, the wretch is back again!"

"Pray don't let her come near me!"

"Whatever you do, Francis, don't open the door!"

"Uncle Fan, she's going to break the window!"

"For pity's sake! Patrick, quick! We'll go out the back way and seize her from there."

"We'll come with you, Papa."

"No, stay here with Auntilla."

Giles watched bemused as his uncle and Doctor Hathaway hurried from the room, while the boys raced back to the French windows, swiftly followed by their aunt.

"Ben! Tom! Come away at once! You'll only make her worse."

Ottilia drew the two youths away from the window, where Tamasine had given over beating at the windows in favour of rattling the doors, incoherent sounds issuing from her mouth. Aghast, Giles remained riveted until his grandmother's irate tones grated on his ear.

"This only was needed! To be besieged in my own home by a lunatic."

A yearning for relief swept through Giles and he grasped at a random thought, catching at straws. "She is distraught."

"Distraught? The girl is demented! Can you still doubt it, Giles?"

"I must, Grandmama, I have no choice." He turned to his aunt. "You know about these things. Is it the grief? She is bereaved. The loss has driven her to this. I was near losing my mind when my mother died."

His aunt Ottilia laid a hand on his arm. "I wish I might agree with you, dear boy, but I cannot."

As of instinct, his eyes went next to Phoebe. Her gaze was fixed upon Tamasine, but as if she felt his regard, she turned. Giles received a shaft of something from those tell-tale eyes that bordered perilously on agony.

"Your sufferings, Giles, were real. Tamasine Roy feels nothing for her guardian, nor for anyone, including you."

Wild with despair, he flung a hand towards the French windows. "What then do you call this?"

A little gasping sigh escaped her. "I call it pitiful, Giles."

He was silenced, baffled by her abrupt change of face. Where was the righteous anger, the accusation? Her words crept back into his mind, and their meaning could not be gainsaid.

A sudden flurry of activity outside the window attracted his attention. The two black servants had arrived on the scene just as his uncle Francis and Doctor Hathaway appeared. In seconds, Tamasine was captured, the two footmen catching her between them so that she was lifted right off her feet, where she began to kick. There was a brief discussion and then Tamasine was borne away, still shrieking imprecations, her legs flailing.

As the noise retreated, silence permeated the parlour so completely that Giles felt as if an aeon of time were passing. Into his head floated the words Tamasine had spoken, and the hideous truth of them made him utter aloud.

"She did do it. She killed him. She pushed him down the stairs. The reckoning in revenge for her mother."

Despair gripped him, and the age-old cry of his childhood rose up as he turned to the one person who had always been able to offer him succour.

"Grandmama, what am I to do?"□

CHAPTER THIRTEEN

"I knew there was more to be learned about this reckoning."

Ottilia moved restlessly to the window in the bedchamber. The sight of the remains of the snow, criss-crossed now with the footprints of many birds, reminded her of the first time she had seen Tamasine Roy. She sighed.

"Poor little sugar princess."

Her brother's measured tones reached her. "Compassion, Ottilia? For a murderess?"

Ottilia looked across to where he was sitting at his ease upon the daybed, but Francis interrupted before she could speak.

"We have yet to be certain the girl is indeed a murderess, Patrick. Believe me, if Tillie had been convinced by Giles's words, she would have said so by this."

He was leaning against the mantel, as was his wont. The three of them had retired to the Fanshawe's chamber as the only place likely to afford privacy, Sophie and Miss Mellis having returned from an outing to the shops in nearby Thrapston before the explosive events of the morning could be thoroughly thrashed out.

Sybilla had despatched Phoebe on her way in her own carriage with her maid Venner in attendance to see the girl safely home, and was now closeted with Giles in her study. The boys, on pain of expulsion from any further involvement in the investigations, had been excluded from the conference. Ottilia did not doubt they would be up to some mischief, and guessed they were likely at Willow Court at this moment, trying to find out what had happened to the madwoman, as they insisted on calling Tamasine. She was guiltily aware that she had not drawn their father's attention to this likelihood, in hopes something materially useful might be discovered from their explorations.

Her husband shifted his back from the mantelpiece and came across to her. "I wish you will take a rest, Tillie. If you are not exhausted by all this hullaballoo, I assure you I am."

She allowed him to usher her to the daybed, which her brother obligingly vacated, instead drawing up a straight chair to the fire. She took up a comfortable position, moving her legs to make room for Francis to perch beside her.

Patrick caught her eye. "Well, Ottilia?"

"It is not well at all, I fear. This but complicates matters, without bringing us any further forward."

"But if it shifts suspicion away from the young fellow Roy?"

"Does it, though?" put in Francis. "We know he tried to obtain the hand of this sugar heiress years ago."

"And was exiled for his pains," Patrick agreed, crossing one leg over the other. "But even if he aspires to gain her fortune that is not to say he must needs eliminate the guardian. If he could worm his way in, he could as easily elope with the girl."

Ottilia put up a finger. "That is the crux of the matter."

"An elopement?"

"No, Fan. Worming his way in. He has an accomplice in Willow Court. Someone kept him informed."

"How do you know?" demanded her brother.

"He makes no secret of the fact that he kept up a correspondence with Tamasine. But Tamasine cannot write. I have no faith whatsoever in Simeon's assertion about the girl making herself understood in pictures. Nor is she capable of sifting the necessary information to pass on."

"No, she is no plotter." Francis laid his hand over hers where it lay in her lap. "Who, then? You believed Hemp when he told you he was not party to it. And Cuffy's attachment to his master was evident that first day."

"Ah, and the Ingleby female was clearly in love with the fellow," put in Patrick with interest. "Who does that leave?"

Ottilia could not resist. "Well, you are both so knowledgeable on the subject, why don't you tell me?"

"Whiting and Lomax," said Francis at once.

"Just so, Fan. However, I cannot imagine why Mrs Whiting should be in cahoots with Simeon Roy."

Francis removed his hand and sat back, the furrow lifting from his brow. "Lomax, then. I'll believe it of him. The fellow is both surly and insolent. What is more, I recollect that he was not of Matthew Roy's party and need not be considered loyal to him. He came with the original sugar heiress, Florine, and had been in her father's employ."

"Yes, that must stand against him." Ottilia recalled another instance that pointed to the butler. "He also filched a piece of paper from the desk on the morning of Sir Joslin's death."

Patrick's lips twitched. "I hardly dare ask how you know that?"

"I saw him. What is more, he knew just what he was looking for. I marked it particularly, for he gave an audible sigh when he found it."

"What in the world could it have been?"

"As to that, Fan, I have a suspicion, but as there really is no evidence to support it, I will keep my own counsel on that for the moment."

Her brother snorted. "How very unfair."

"Ha! This is typical, Patrick. She will never disclose something of which she is uncertain."

"Then for heaven's sake, sister mine, at least share with us your views about this business of the mother's death."

Ottilia frowned. "That is puzzling. I am inclined to believe Tamasine is confused. She may have heard something and added up two and two to make five."

"That I can well believe," he said, his voice returning to its habitual even tone. "These mental derangements do not allow for logic. I have read a number of papers by practitioners in the field. The subjects tend to be completely literal in their thinking. They will take a statement at face value. If someone told Tamasine her guardian was in some way responsible for her mother's death, she would likely make the assumption he had actually killed her."

"But did not Giles say she told him Sir Joslin had hurt her mother? She did not say he killed her," objected Francis.

"True. But Tamasine said her mother died and Sir Joslin therefore had to die too. The mother was also deranged. Suppose she attacked Joslin. If he then was obliged to use force to overpower her, his actions might be taken by Tamasine as having caused her death."

Ottilia stared at him. "Patrick, that is genius."

Her brother laughed and Francis gave him a mock slow handclap. "Bravo, old fellow! You have joined the ranks of the Fanshawe detection team."

Ottilia interrupted the ensuing exchange of banter. "Florine attacked Joslin and hurt him badly, for I got it from Hemp. That may account for this reckoning of Tamasine's."

"That's why she pushed Joslin?"

"Just so, Fan. But my problem is not solved by that."

"How so?" Patrick leaned forward, setting his elbows on his knees.

Ottilia was amused to see his interest fully aroused. "Tamasine told me she is not yet done. And that was after Joslin was killed."

"But when she told Giles, she was clearly speaking of Joslin."

Ottilia looked at her spouse and put up an admonitory finger. "Do not be misled by the child's changing her tale to suit her convenience, Fan. There is rationality there. As far as someone in her condition can be rational. We must take note of Patrick's dictum. If she is literal, we must take her literally. If she says she is not yet done, then there is more here than we have yet discovered."

"Once you know it, will you have solved it, do you think, Tillie?"

"Perhaps, Fan." She sighed. "If only we can also ascertain the whereabouts of those wretched missing sweets."

Sybilla's descent upon Willow Court upon the following morning proved untimely. Escorted by her son, with Ottilia in attendance, she entered into a scene of chaos.

Bandboxes and portmanteaux littered the hall where several persons were assembled. Cuffy, who had opened the door to the visitors, no sooner closed it behind them than he hefted a couple of the bags and followed Hemp, already climbing the stairs, similarly burdened.

A matronly figure, enveloped in a thick travelling cloak, was engaged in discussion with Miss Ingleby and Lomax. All three looked towards the new arrivals and Ottilia noted exasperation entering the companion's face. She moved towards them, but before she could speak, Mrs Whiting came bustling through the green baize door, accompanied by a chambermaid carrying a quantity of fresh linen.

Miss Ingleby was obliged to give place to allow the cavalcade to reach the stairs, a trifling delay which allowed Ottilia to get in first.

"Lady Polbrook wished to speak with your charge, Miss Ingleby, but I see we are inopportune."

"Extremely so." The woman's glance swept the party, and came to rest on the dowager's face. "Tamasine is not at liberty today, ma'am."

Sybilla's black eyes snapped. "Then I will content myself with you, Miss Ingleby. Shall we step into the parlour?"

"I am much occupied, as you see. Mrs Delabole has just arrived, and —"

"Ah, you must be Tamasine's aunt," cut in Ottilia, sailing across the hall towards the matron, who was staring in frowning silence.

She was a faded creature who must once have been beautiful. A few strands of flaxen locks escaped a pretty cap under a serviceable bonnet, which framed a face with skin softened by the years, whose plumpness disguised its creases. Her eyes were blue like Tamasine's, but paler in hue, and just now showed their owner to be flustered.

An uncertain smile formed on her lips as she took the hand Ottilia held out. "How do you do? I'm afraid I…"

Her voice was soft, a little breathy and she spoke with hesitance, question in her face.

Ottilia smiled. "Pray don't be dismayed. You do not know us, but we are neighbours. I am Lady Francis Fanshawe. Allow me to present my mother-in-law, the Dowager Marchioness of Polbrook, who lives across the road. My husband and I are staying with her. Oh, this is my husband."

Looking bemused, Mrs Delabole shook hands. "Forgive me, Lady Polbrook, I am but just arrived, I'm afraid, and I know nothing of the neighbourhood."

Sybilla inclined her head. "I was a little acquainted with Sir Joslin. Allow me to condole with you on your loss."

"Oh, thank you. Though I hardly knew the man, you know. I mean, we met a great many years ago, before Matt — my brother, I mean — went off to Barbados."

"Then your situation is unenviable, if you are obliged to take all in charge."

"Indeed, and I have left everything at sixes and sevens at home. I do not know how we are to do." She seemed to recollect herself and tried for a measure of calm. "But I must not run on. Miss Ingleby, perhaps…?"

As the woman turned to the companion, Francis saved the day, moving to open the parlour door. "Shall we await your pleasure in here, ma'am? No doubt you will require a little time to yourself after your journey."

"Ah, how thoughtful, yes. Miss Ingleby will arrange everything, I am sure, if someone will only direct me to my chamber."

A prudent retreat seemed in order and Ottilia followed her mother-in-law into the familiar parlour. She detained Francis as he closed the door.

"I'm going to run upstairs in a few moments, Fan, while you remain with Sybilla."

"Do you think that's wise, with everyone running hither and yon?"

"That is just why. No one will pay me the least attention."

"Pray, what are you about, Ottilia?" demanded the dowager, who had taken a seat near the fire. "Our mission here is set."

"Yours, Sybilla, yes. Mine is to discover what has happened to Tamasine."

The intelligence that the girl was incarcerated had been carried to the Dower House by her nephews on the previous evening. Just as she had guessed, they had raced back to Willow Court the moment they escaped their father's eye.

"Locked up in the attic she is, Auntilla."

"Bouncing off those mattresses like a jack-in-the-box!"

"And screaming and screaming!"

The image conjured up in Ottilia's mind had harrowed her, engaging her sympathies for the poor child's unenviable condition. Whether she was still in the attic remained moot, but Ottilia meant to brave the place again if necessary.

Tamasine's room was quiet. Ottilia put her ear to the door, but no muttering rewarded her. The key was in the lock and she tried the handle. It turned and squeaked a trifle as, with care, she pushed inward. The girl was evidently not in her bedchamber. Just to be sure, Ottilia peeped around the edge of the door.

No erring daughter of the house was visible, either wandering or lying on the bed. The place was empty, which suggested she was still in her attic room. If so, she had been held there for hours. Could it be good for her?

Then Ottilia bethought her of Simeon Roy who had not been of the party downstairs. Suggestive perhaps? She could not suppose he had been permitted to remove Tamasine from the premises. The companion regarded him with too much distrust.

Leaving the child's bedchamber as she had found it, Ottilia sneaked along the passage towards the back of the house, seeking for the stair she had used before when Tom led her to Tamasine's eyrie. Unlikely anyone would be coming up. They were too much occupied below. She found the narrow stair and, not without a flurry of trepidation, hurried up to the floor situated under the eaves.

The sound of voices caught at her ears, but muffled. Was the door to Tamasine's eyrie then locked? She turned the corner and crept along the passage, glad to think there was someone with the creature, if it was indeed her voice she had heard.

The door was open, but when Ottilia looked around the jamb, she could see no one. She went into the room proper and found it empty. Moreover, the voices still sounded muffled. Heavens, were they coming from above?

Standing still, she listened, cocking her head and gazing at the slanted ceiling.

A high-pitched laugh sounded. That must be Tamasine. But there was a second voice. Deeper? A sense of intrigue gripped Ottilia. Now, how in the world was she to find a way onto the roof? Convinced the voices were above her, she sped out of the room, heading for the stairwell.

No access there. She took the stairs to the landing below, moving rapidly along one side and then the other, hunting for another stair to no avail. At last she found herself back in an upper storey of the main gallery. At once Ottilia saw that the stairs continued on up and she followed them. The turn brought a door in sight, open to the elements. A patch of dull sky showed through.

As she reached it, she could again hear the voices. Some sort of recitation seemed to be in progress, more than one voice sounding together. Ottilia stepped through the aperture and onto the roof. It looked to be extensive, but the immediate pathway led between two elevations and opened out onto a flat surface surrounded by low walls either side, then continuing into another pathway beyond.

Simeon Roy was leaning against the inner wall under a tiled elevation while Tamasine was sitting cross-legged on the flat surface nearby, evidently undisturbed by the biting wind that was already making Ottilia shiver.

Some sound must have betrayed her for Simeon turned his head. Consternation leapt into his face, but he recovered swiftly and the habitual languor succeeded it. He pulled away from the wall, dropping into one of his nonchalant poses.

"If it is not Lady Fan come to seek you out, my little Tam. What a lucky girl you are today."

A shriek of delight emanated from Tamasine and she sang out. "Lady Fan, Lady Fan, Lady Fan."

Ottilia walked up to the man, uttering a pleasant greeting. "How do you do, Mr Roy? I trust you are well today, Tamasine?"

"Welcome to my eyrie," said the girl in the most ordinary of tones.

Startled, Ottilia could not think how to answer for a moment. Was this then the place she regarded as her eyrie, rather than her prison attic room? Or did she not descry a difference?

"Why, thank you, Tamasine, I am very glad to be allowed to come."

"You won't be for long."

The mutter came from behind her and Ottilia threw an admonitory glance over her shoulder. Simeon Roy responded with a quirked eyebrow and an amused look.

Ottilia ignored him. "What are doing up here in your eyrie?"

Tamasine turned her hands, setting her knuckles together, and wiggled her fingers. "See? I can make people in the steeple. Simeon showed me."

"In the church, Tam. The people are in the church, not the steeple." Simeon played the nursery game on his fingers. "Here's the church and here's the steeple. Look inside and see all the little people."

"The preacher, the preacher," called Tamasine.

But even as Simeon began upon the rest with the preacher going upstairs and saying his prayers, the girl sprang up from her position on the floor, interrupting him with a demand for Lady Fan to look at her picture. She ran to the low wall and Ottilia was astonished to see an old mattress had been set against it. She began scrabbling inside, pulling out straw and flinging it this way and that.

Ottilia turned to Simeon Roy, keeping her voice low. "Is it safe?"

His brows lifted. "For you or for Tam? She won't attack you if that is what you fear."

Ottilia refrained from informing him of the earlier occasion when she very nearly had been a victim of Tamasine's demented state.

"I meant her being on the roof? Why does she come up here?"

His lip curled. "I can no more fathom the intricacies of Tam's mind than you, Lady Francis. I did suggest she might prefer to come in. She says she likes it here."

Ottilia shivered and rubbed her arms. "I can't think why anyone would put a mattress up here. She cannot lie in this cold surely?"

"I imagine she brought it up here herself. Or persuaded Hemp to do so. I doubt she wants it for its proper purpose."

"For what then?"

But the question answered itself, for with a cry of triumph, Tamasine brought forth a crumpled collection of papers, scattering them as she hunted through them, chucking them in a disorderly way to join the wisps of straw.

What in the world would she be at now? But Ottilia was not going to enquire of the wretched Simeon. She would get no satisfactory answer.

"Does she know Mrs Delabole has arrived?"

"That's what I came up to tell her. She is not interested."

"Lady Fan! See? I found it!" The cry came from Tamasine, who was now holding up a scrunched ball of paper. "I made a princess picture."

Ottilia moved to join her and took the balled paper the child held out. "May I open it?"

"It's me," said Tamasine gleefully. "I am the sugar princess."

Taking this for tacit permission, Ottilia gently prised the paper apart and spread the creased sheet open. A jumble of unrelated lines and curves rambled across the paper, drawn with what looked to be charcoal. There was no impression to be made of it in any real sense, but Ottilia produced an admiring look.

"Why, this is indeed the sugar princess, Tamasine."

For a moment the girl said nothing, eyeing Ottilia with the disconcerting stare of vacancy. Then she snatched the paper and tore it across and across, throwing it into the air. The wind caught fragments and they fluttered away, scattering across the roof.

"Wrong answer," murmured Simeon Roy from behind her.

"A little late to be telling me that," Ottilia snapped.

Tamasine ran to the mattress by the low wall and threw herself down upon it, lying perfectly still with her face buried. Was she feigning sleep the way she had on the first day with Miss Ingleby? Seizing her chance, Ottilia turned to confront Simeon.

"I thought you told me she could communicate in pictures."

"Oh, she can when she chooses. If you were to inspect some of these creations she buries in her mattresses, I don't doubt you would find plausible drawings, even recognizable in some instances."

"It does not sound much like a communication to me, if she does not know what she draws."

"One has to catch her in the right mood."

Ottilia could have slapped him. "This is nonsense, Mr Roy, and you know it. I wish you will stop trying to pull the wool over my eyes. You have not engaged in correspondence with the child, unless by the medium of some intermediary."

An enigmatic smile creased the fellow's mouth. "It is not I who believes there has been a murder at Willow Court, Lady Francis. I think you will find it difficult to convince my cousin Ruth of anything of the kind."

Her exasperation was interrupted by the sound of dragging. She turned from him to see Tamasine pulling the mattress across the roof floor. She started forward just as the girl, without apparent effort, heaved the thing over the parapet, squealing with laughter. Then she jumped up onto the wall, stepping hazardously along it and singing out in a gleeful fashion.

"I'm walking on water, walking on water, walking on water."

"Tamasine, no!"

Simeon caught her arm as Ottilia made to rush to pull her down. "Quiet, ma'am! She's as lithe as a cat. She won't fall."

Ottilia watched in an agony of apprehension. "How can you be sure?"

"She was used to climb trees and she could rope dance as a child. She has no fear at all. She is safe, as long as no one startles her."

The admonitory note cut at Ottilia's nerves. She could not take her eyes off the girl and stood as if frozen to the spot, willing her to come down. It seemed an age while she pranced along the wall, utterly oblivious until a flapping of wings produced a bird taking off from a nearby chimney. Tamasine halted and pointed.

"There is the witch! Look, it's a black crow like Lavinia!"

A manic explosion of laughter escaped her while Ottilia, unable to bear the suspense, took a step towards her. Then Tamasine jumped down and spun on the spot, crying out that Lavinia was a black crow. Reaching her, Ottilia slung an arm about her shoulders and hustled her back to a safe position in the middle of the roof.

"Come now, my dear, should you not think of coming inside? We will all take cold if we stay here."

Aware her voice shook she looked to Simeon and found him utterly unmoved by the child putting herself at risk. Infuriated, she forced him into the fray.

"Simeon will take you down, will you not, Mr Roy? I am sure our sugar princess will be happy to go with you."

She danced away from Ottilia. "Simeon, Simeon, Simeon, will you rescue me?"

"With the greatest pleasure on earth, my dear little Tam. Come, let us satisfy Lady Fan and return you to your eyrie."

With which, he threw Ottilia a mocking glance and guided the chattering girl into the pathway between the roof elevations. Feeling quite sick with the aftermath of dread, the fate of the luckless mattress loud in her mind, Ottilia trailed behind, wishing she had not come up at all. The horrible access to an easy death, for Tamasine or another, was too dismaying to contemplate.

The discussion was growing heated and Francis longed for his wife's return. Mrs Delabole was looking perfectly bewildered, and who could blame the woman? His mother's snapping black eyes and icy tone warned of her rising temper, and Miss

Ingleby's point-blank refusal to believe in the so-called betrothal was enough to set flinders to the flames.

"You must be dreaming, ma'am. Or else your grandson is deceiving you."

"The news," returned his mother in the clipped voice he knew all too well, "came not from my grandson, but from Mr Roy."

Mrs Delabole looked startled. "Simeon? But how would he know any such thing? He cannot have been here much longer than I."

"Long enough to cause trouble, as he always does," said the companion on a derisive note. "The child has been unmanageable since he arrived."

The dowager once again made herself heard. "The point, Miss Ingleby, is that there can be no question of this betrothal going forward. Giles's father will never permit him to marry a female of an unsuitable rank, even setting aside the sad condition from which this girl of yours suffers."

"She is not my girl, I thank God. You had much better address yourself to Mrs Delabole, ma'am. Tamasine is her responsibility now."

The newly arrived matron appeared horrified by this. "Oh, no, no, I cannot. My dear Miss Ingleby, it is quite impossible for me to take charge of the child. I am sorry for her, of course, but you will have to remain with her, indeed you will."

"And if I don't choose to? You cannot make me, you know. I am minded to live a better life than to be forever at the beck and call of a creature with no consideration for anyone save her own insane desires. Lord Bennifield is welcome to her, for all of me."

Mrs Delabole stared at her, open-mouthed. Francis caught his mother's gaze and was subjected to a violent rolling of the eyes. He supposed he must take a hand.

"You must be aware, Miss Ingleby, that a marriage with my nephew is ineligible. Neither would it suit Tamasine, when all is said. She is scarcely equipped to take on the role of a future marchioness. That being so, and I submit it is none of our affair, but I would advise you to keep her close before you lose her to this young fellow Roy."

The companion rose in one swift movement, her eyes blazing. "Never! He shall not have her, be sure! I will lock her up and throw away the key before I permit him to pursue his vile schemes."

"Then you do intend to remain in charge of the girl?" The dowager rose to confront her. "What I wish, Miss Ingleby, is that you will make it clear to Tamasine that her so-called engagement to my nephew is at an end."

The woman gazed at her aghast. "Tell her? Tell Tamasine? Are you mad too? I should not dare to for my life! You can have no notion what she is like when she is thwarted."

"Can I not indeed? After she came beating at my doors yesterday?"

Miss Ingleby flung up a hand. "That! A mere nothing, Lady Polbrook. You have not seen her in full flood. If you had — any of you — you would never enter this house again." She turned on the unfortunate Mrs Delabole. "Find another companion for her, ma'am, for I have done. I am minded to pack my bags at once, but I have more compassion than to leave you in so perilous a state. I will remain until you employ another, but I advise you to begin advertising at once."

With which, she stalked from the parlour, slamming the door behind her with a force that shook the windows. Francis exchanged an exasperated glance with his mother, but his attention was drawn to Tamasine's aunt, who gave a whimper.

"Heavens, what in the world am I to do? Where does she think I may find a replacement at such short notice? I do not even have any notion what sort of person might be suitable. Nor where the girl is to go, if she cannot remain here." She seemed to recollect herself, casting a deprecating glance at the dowager. "I beg your pardon, but it is really too distressing for words."

"You need not apologise," said his mother, reseating herself and flapping a dismissive hand. "I quite understand and I am very sorry for you, Mrs Delabole."

Francis, feeling equally sorry for the creature, was moved to utter such comfort as occurred to him. "I should not take it too much to heart, ma'am. Miss Ingleby is of that ilk of female who says one thing one day and changes her mind the next. I doubt she means to leave you in the lurch."

"Well, she said as much, but how can I be certain she will not walk out of the house tomorrow? Then what should I do?"

"Rely upon the fellow Hemp and Mrs Whiting, ma'am. The latter administers the doses that keep Tamasine quiet, I believe, and Hemp appears to be the one person capable of controlling the girl."

"A black footman? One of my brother's slaves?"

"He is a free man."

He glanced as he spoke at his mother, fearful of her breaking out against slavery in general. Much to his relief, the dowager, although her mouth became pinched and her eyes aglitter, chose not to take up the point.

"Most odd," commented Mrs Delabole. "Highly irregular, too, but that was Matt all over. Why he must needs ally himself with that —" She broke off in haste, colouring.

His mother batted it out into the open. "You did not approve of your brother's marriage?"

She sighed. "How should I? There is no denying he came by his fortune through it, but the female was scarcely of a class with his deserts. Moreover, he knew of the fatal taint from the outset, for he wrote as much to me when the poor woman had to be incarcerated. You may imagine how I took such news."

"Just as I took the news that my grandson proposed to marry her daughter," said the dowager on a snap. "I trust I may rely upon you to scotch any such belief among your people here?"

"Oh," said the creature, looking helpless. "Yes, I suppose you may. At least, surely they must know? I mean, if the entire household is aware... And if Miss Ingleby feels it will not do to speak of it to Tamasine, I am sure they must fall in with the notion of secrecy."

"The point is, ma'am, my grandson will not be visiting here any more. I could wish her guardians might prevent Tamasine from coming to seek him at my house, but that, I fear, is a vain hope. It has been made abundantly clear that the girl escapes with ease."

Mrs Delabole appeared horrified. "She does?"

"I'm afraid so, ma'am," Francis cut in. "As I understand it, she is locked up in her room when no one can escort her, but she seems to have the proverbial cunning of the insane in her ability to evade those who mind her."

The door opened and he looked across to find his wife in the aperture. Relief swept through him and he went across at once, lowering his voice. "You found her?"

"To some purpose. She was cavorting about on the roof, to my horror. Simeon is with her. Is all well here?"

"Well? You jest! The Ingleby woman went off in a huff and refuses to have anything to do with the business of Giles's alleged betrothal. What is more, she told Mrs Delabole to find a replacement for her. Not that I believe she will walk away, for where would she go? Without means or another position, it seems foolhardy, even for her."

"Just so. Nor do I think she would leave while Simeon Roy is upon the premises." She moved into the room as she spoke, addressing herself to the matron, who seemed to have been engaged in a low-voiced conversation with his mother. "I understand Mr Roy has told Tamasine of your arrival, ma'am. I found him with her — er — upstairs."

No mention of the roof then. Not much to Francis's surprise, Mrs Delabole looked decidedly ill-at-ease at this news.

"Do you mean she is planning to come down?"

"Apparently not at the moment, though there is no saying what she may take it into her head to do."

"So I apprehend."

Tillie gave her a warm smile. "It must be hard for you to be thrust into this difficult situation, ma'am. If there is anything I can do to help, pray do not hesitate to call upon me."

The woman gave her a surprised look. "Oh. Well, thank you, Lady Francis. As yet I have no notion myself what I must do, beyond sending for the lawyers, which I have already done. I hope someone may arrive in short order to take charge of all the papers and so forth."

"Have you any notion how Sir Joslin's affairs are left, ma'am?"

Mrs Delabole spread her hands. "None whatsoever. He was not in correspondence with me. Miss Ingleby wrote to tell me of his death and requested my presence since I am Tamasine's next of kin and Sir Joslin was her guardian. I hope and trust this duty will not in fact devolve upon me, for I cannot imagine how in the world I could look after the girl."

"Well, let us hope some other provision has been made. I cannot think your brother, who appears to have anticipated every eventuality, will have neglected to foresee this possibility."

"Oh, do you think so indeed?"

"Well, I have it on the authority of Cuffy, who looked after Sir Joslin, that he has been unwell for some years."

"Yes, I believe that is true." She smiled, a trifle tremulously, Francis thought. "Perhaps I am anxious without cause."

At which point, the dowager unwisely chose to intervene. "There is cause enough if Sir Joslin was indeed poisoned."

Shock leapt into the woman's face. "Poisoned! Good heavens almighty! Poisoned by whom?"

"That is just what my daughter-in-law is trying to discover, Mrs Delabole."

Francis could have cursed aloud. Just when Tillie had managed to settle the woman. He bent an admonishing eye upon his mother, who met it blandly. The Delabole female was staring at Tillie as if she confronted a freak at a fair.

"You, Lady Francis?"

Tillie took a chair next to the wretched woman and reached for her hand, patting it in a soothing fashion. "It is by no means certain, ma'am. Sir Joslin died of opium poisoning, yes, but whether it was an accidental dose or administered by another has yet to be determined."

"But — but who —? I mean, why would anyone wish to poison him?"

"Your niece, for one," stated the dowager. "And she is demented enough to attempt it."

"Sybilla, pray don't frighten Mrs Delabole more than you need."

"She may as well face the truth. Where is the sense in beating about the bush?" Turning on the unfortunate aunt, she added with relish, "You will find, Mrs Delabole, this entire household partakes of your niece's dubious conduct. Miss Ingleby is bad enough. Young Roy is worse, for he couches his barbs under a smooth tongue. As for the rest, ask my daughter-in-law if they are not as peculiar as they can stare."

"Ma'am, that is enough," Francis said, taken with sympathy for her victim's evident dismay.

"More than enough," echoed Tillie.

The Delabole female herself came hard on her heels. "I beg you will say no more, Lady Polbrook, or I shall not sleep a wink in this house."

"I shouldn't think you would," rejoined his mother. "It is difficult enough for me and I am merely a neighbour."

"Come, come, ma'am, it is not as bad as that." Tillie, pouring balm on troubled waters as usual. "My dear Mrs Delabole, pray do not be unduly alarmed. Although perhaps it is as well you know what is going forward, for I will be glad of your permission to pursue the matter with questions as it becomes necessary."

"My permission? But I know nothing about it!"

"You are, if you will forgive me, the senior inhabitant of the household at this moment."

Mrs Delabole uttered a fretful cry. "You mean they will look to me for guidance? Heavens above, I wish I had not come!"

"Nothing of the sort," said Tillie soothingly. "The household runs perfectly well since they all know how to do. But neither Miss Ingleby nor Lomax — the butler, that is — can gainsay me if I am able to say you have requested me to continue my investigations."

CHAPTER FOURTEEN

Phoebe could have done without the presence of the Honourable Mr Robert Delaney when Giles showed up in the parlour, despite the fact she had requested her cousin to call upon her at an hour when she knew her parents would be from home. She had questions she preferred to put to him without the listening ears of the Earl of Hemington and his lady, though she had been obliged to allay his alarm and disapproval.

"I should not be here, Phoebe, with your parents absent. This is most irregular."

"I know, Robert, but my need is urgent. And I cannot have Papa hearing what I may ask you. You must promise me you will not tell him."

Her cousin lowered his head and bent a frown upon her over his spectacles. "This is not like you, my dear Phoebe, to be having secrets from Hemington and your dear mama."

Phoebe sighed and sank into her favourite chair by the fire. The little parlour was peculiarly her own and had been the scene of many a lively discussion with Giles in happier times. Situated on a corner of the mansion on the second floor, it boasted a couple of ancient sofas, her own comfy chair, her escritoire and several bookcases filled with her favourite volumes.

"Nothing feels very much like me at the moment, Robert."

Her cousin, whom she knew had ever a soft spot for her, pulled across the straight chair from in front of her desk and brought it to the fire, taking his seat and peering closely at her.

"My dear child, are you taking this business to heart?" She looked up, startled, and he pursed his lips. "Did you suppose me ignorant of what has been going forward? Do you not understand why I felt obliged to relinquish the Willow Court matter into Lovell's hands?"

Phoebe blinked at him. "I did not know you had."

"Well, it was so. Your father also cautioned me and he was right. I had hoped the matter might be settled with a verdict of accidental death, but once an open verdict was brought, I really had no choice but to declare an interest."

Dismay swept through Phoebe. "An interest? In what respect?"

Robert tutted. "Come, come, child. Because your parents have not spoken, do not suppose young Bennifield's antics have passed unremarked."

A tide of warmth rushed into Phoebe's cheeks. "I hoped they had not heard of it. I know Papa will be furious."

"He was, yes, but your mama persuaded him to refrain from speaking to you upon the matter. She is a good deal more observant than you suppose, my dear Phoebe."

Phoebe shrank into herself. "So it would seem."

She glanced across at Robert's unusually mellow countenance. He was younger than her father, although he was himself a family man with a hopeful brood of his own. But she knew he had been indebted to Papa for many an introduction to pave his way in the world and his stiff moral rectitude had won for him the respect of his peers and election to the House of Commons. It had been only a matter of time before he became a Justice of the Peace as well. He had assumed the role a few years earlier and had proven a just, if stern, dispenser of the law. She could not own herself surprised he should elect himself out of further investigation into Sir Joslin's death.

"Come, child, why did you send for me? What is the matter?"

Gathering her courage, Phoebe looked him in the eye. "I believe Giles is cured of his tendre for — for the girl. But…"

"But?"

She swallowed. "It is this open verdict, Robert. I had not realised you were no longer involved in the investigation."

"And if I were?"

"Well … well, even if you are not, I felt I could not do better than to consult you."

His brows rose. "What has this to do with your young gentleman, my dear?"

"Well, that is just it, Robert." Her anxiety surfaced and she swept on. "Has it anything to do with him? He cannot be supposed to have plotted with Tamasine, can he? I know Sir Joslin did not approve his suit, but surely you cannot suppose Giles would go so far as to help her dispose of her guardian?"

Robert's expression altered, and a measure of his customary disdain entered in. "This is because of that business with his father, I take it? You are afraid of history repeating itself?"

Phoebe gripped her fingers together in her lap, and nodded.

"As I understand it, my dear, there was a cogent reason for Polbrook to be suspected of making away with his wife. It is manifest, now that he has married the creature."

"Yes, I know, but he did not do it, did he? Nor, I venture to say, would Giles dream of any such undertaking."

A faint smile curved Robert's mouth. "My dear girl, there is no evidence to suggest Bennifield had anything to do with Sir Joslin's death. Moreover, I could not find, from sifting the details of the inquest when I prepared the report for Lovell, that Miss Roy, despite her unfortunate condition, could have been instrumental in her guardian's death."

"But Lady Francis believes he was murdered."

Robert's tone became sceptical. "Yes, I have heard of the lady's apparent prowess in that line, but I take leave to doubt of anything useful coming from her poking her nose into what does not concern her."

"It concerned her because Giles was involved," Phoebe said, unable to help a resentful note. She had taken to Lady Francis Fanshawe and formed a good opinion of her common sense. "Her husband is his uncle, after all."

"I am perfectly well acquainted with Lord Francis, I thank you, Phoebe. I have known the family for some years. And I may say, I am in agreement with your father that if it were not for Polbrook's rank and fortune, an alliance with them would be out of count."

"Well, it does not now look as if there will be an alliance, so Papa may rest easy," Phoebe flashed.

"Oho, so that is it, is it?" Robert's look became indulgent. "My dear Phoebe, I trust you will think well before you throw away such an advantageous opportunity, merely upon a whim."

"A whim? When I have been insulted and degraded? Thrown aside as of no account?"

At which inopportune moment, one of the footmen entered upon his knock and announced Lord Bennifield.

Giles halted upon the threshold, his gaze going at once to Delaney, who rose to his feet. Phoebe felt a flush rising in her cheeks, her embarrassment in no way mitigated by what Robert chose to say.

"Ah, Bennifield, there you are, my dear boy. I believe Lady Phoebe has something she wishes to say to you."

Phoebe kept her eyes lowered, a riot in her bosom as she heard Giles's response and recognised an unwonted humility in his tone.

"How do you do, sir? Am I intruding?"

"I will be leaving directly. Phoebe desired my — er — advice." A pause and then, "Phoebe, my dear?"

She looked up. "Yes, Robert?"

"Send for your maid, my child. Unless you would wish me to remain?"

"No!" Realising this was scarcely polite, she amended it. "No, indeed, there is no necessity for either. We are accustomed to leave the door open whenever we —"

She broke off, conscious all over again, and was unable to help shooting a look at Giles. He appeared pale, but his expression was determined. Lord help her! What did this visit betoken? What would she say if he meant to proffer an apology? She did not feel in the least little bit forgiving.

Delaney looked from her to Giles and back again. Then he walked over to the door, pointedly setting it wide. He looked back to where Phoebe remained, still in her chair, her clenched hands on its arms.

"Remember what I said, Phoebe."

She kept her eyes on him, refusing to look again at Giles. "Yes." It was non-committal, but she did not feel like giving the assurance he sought. She was by no means certain she wished any longer to marry Giles, even should he offer for her, which she doubted was his present intention.

Robert nodded at Giles and passed out of the room. Phoebe kept her gaze steadfastly on her lap. In the periphery of her vision she saw Giles approach. He did not sit, although Robert had left the chair conveniently placed. The silence lengthened.

"Phoebe!"

It was tensely said, a wealth of feeling in the one statement of her name.

She could not prevent her eyes from rising to meet his. The green orbs were shadowed with fatigue. Or was it emotion? A pang smote her bosom.

"You look dreadful."

He grimaced. "I feel it."

"You had best sit down before you fall down."

Aware her tone was grudging, Phoebe watched him drop into the chair, heavily, as if he were burdened with the weight of the world. A flash of memory struck her. Thus had he looked when first he had come to her after the death of his mother. Her heart ached. Had he truly loved Tamasine after all?

"You are hurting, are you not, Giles?"

It was not at all what she had meant to say. Nor had she dreamt of softening her tone towards him. He nodded dumbly, and Phoebe experienced a shaft of hatred for the mad girl. She wanted to rake her nails down that china doll of a face. The realisation brought her up short. Where was her dignity? It had lain in the dust long enough, had it not? She hardened her heart.

"I dare say you will get over it in due course."

A flare at his eyes brought the old Giles back for an instant. Then it faded. He lifted his hands in a hopeless gesture and Phoebe was shocked to see a tremor in his fingers.

"I deserved that perhaps." He drew in a breath. "No, not perhaps. I did deserve it."

"It was not meant to flay you, Giles."

He bit his lip. "Then it should have been."

Another silence fell. Phoebe felt as if her heart cracked aloud and she had all to do to remain quiescent in her chair. She did not know whether she wanted to slap him or throw herself into his embrace. Both probably. How dared he come to her in such a guise? Bemoaning his lost love and abasing himself in a fashion as lamentable as it was unnerving. Never before had she seen him lose his assurance so completely. Phoebe could not endure it.

"Don't do this, Giles!"

His brow furrowed. "Do what?"

"Scourge yourself as if you have broken the Ten Commandments. For heaven's sake, stand proud!"

A mirthless laugh escaped him. "Proud? After what has passed? I've been fifty kinds of a fool."

"You have indeed, but that is no reason to bow your head and beg for my sympathy."

His eyes flared again at that. "I'm not begging for sympathy!"

"Then what are you doing, may I ask?"

He flung up off the chair. "Begging for forgiveness, you impossible female! Or I would do, if you would not take up such an intransigent attitude."

Phoebe was likewise on her feet. "What attitude did you expect? I've been humiliated, assaulted and cast aside like an old glove. By rights I ought to beat you about the head with a footstool!"

"Well, do it then! I don't care what you do to me, if you will only cease behaving like a tragedy queen!"

"Tragedy queen? How dare you!"

All control gone, Phoebe swung her arm, her hand flying towards his face. Giles caught her wrist and held her off, glaring with a violence to match her own.

"No, you don't, you little shrew?"

"Let me go, you brute!"

"Never in this life!"

She let out a strangled scream of rage, trying to wrench her arm away. For an eon the issue hung in the balance as she struggled against his iron grip. Then a tide of colour overspread his features.

"What in hell's name am I doing?"

He let her go so suddenly that she almost fell. Giles stepped forward and caught her. Phoebe froze in his clutch, her heart leaping like a scalded cat.

"Phoebe..."

It was guttural. Instinct told her what it meant, but the fleeting thought was overborne as Giles jerked her hard against him and set his lips to hers and the world exploded.

Sensation was all she knew for a while and she came adrift at last with her heart singing and her eyes opened to a wild look in Giles's eyes as they seemed to devour her face.

"Phoebe, I didn't know. I swear I didn't know."

Did not know his own heart? But she did not ask, a hushed expectancy warning her that words alone would never serve the moment. She brought up one hand and brushed his lip with her finger. Then she smiled at him.

"You know now."

Leaving her spouse and Patrick in the front parlour, Ottilia penetrated to the nether regions of the establishment, following Cuffy, who had let them in, and walking boldly through the green baize door and into the usual rabbit warren of corridors that comprised the servants' quarters.

Discovering her on his tail, the footman turned, exhibiting some degree of astonishment. "You wish for something, madame?"

Ottilia smiled. "Indeed I do. Pray be good enough to conduct me to Mrs Whiting's room."

Cuffy hesitated, but she stared him out and at length he nodded without comment and turned to take the lead. Ottilia recalled the stillroom as she passed from the last time when she had inspected Mrs Whiting's books, although she could not remember the precise route. Noise and chatter from the kitchen reached her, along with the aroma of spices, coffee and the inevitable smell of half-cooked vegetables.

The housekeeper was at her desk, writing in a ledger and looked none too pleased at Ottilia's invasion. Forestalling criticism, she got in first.

"I trust you will not object to my calling upon you here, Mrs Whiting. I have been requested by Mrs Delabole to discover anything I can to shed light upon the mystery of Sir Joslin's death."

The housekeeper humphed and set down her quill in its receptacle on a china ink stand. "I don't recollect as you needed anyone's permission at the off, my lady."

Touché! But Ottilia let it pass, calmly taking possession of a chair set by the wall and bringing it close enough to converse. The place was cramped, the inevitable locked cupboard taking up the bulk of the available space. The desk was little more than an aged writing bureau and a comfortable cushioned armchair took prominence near the door, a footstool before it and an occasional table to one side.

Ottilia set her chair between the footstool and the desk, beginning without further preamble. "Would you object to telling me more of your erstwhile mistress? I mean Tamasine's mother Florine."

She was quick to note the tell-tale flutter of a couple of fingers where Mrs Whiting's hands now rested in her lap, the moistening tip of a tongue catching at her lower lip.

"What did you wish to know?"

A good question. One could hardly give utterance to the uppermost thought. Ottilia tried an oblique approach, albeit touching on the meat of the matter. "I gather she was eventually found to be too prone to mischief to be permitted to roam abroad."

A snorting laugh escaped Mrs Whiting. "Mischief? You could call it so. Yes, we had to shut her away. For her own good as much as anyone else's."

"As you did Tamasine the other night?"

The woman flinched. "How do you know that?"

"Come, Mrs Whiting, let us be frank. The girl is deteriorating, is she not? Is it the transition to this country, do you think? Or the unsettling events that have occurred? I cannot imagine it has been anything but deleterious to have her in such an excitable state."

The housekeeper let out her breath in a whoosh. "You have no idea! If only the Master hadn't died and we'd not to bring her to England, I could've kept her calm in the places she knew. We had to put her back in the attic last night and all, for she went off into one of her fits when Mrs Delabole tried to reason with her."

Ottilia could not but feel sympathy for the aunt, thrust into a situation of which she was fairly ignorant. "What happened?"

"I scarcely know. It were all chaos by the time I got into the dining parlour, which is where it all started. There was Master Roy, who had grabbed hold of young Tam, and what with her screaming the way she does and Miss Ingleby screeching at Master Roy, and poor Mrs Delabole with her hands over her ears and looking bewildered, I can tell you, ma'am, it was a right do."

"It sounds so indeed. Did you not at once call for Hemp? He seems to be eminently capable of controlling Tamasine."

"Yes, but Hemp wasn't there, for now Master Jos has gone he's the only one who can drive the carriage and Lomax sent him for supplies, what with the company augmented beyond our expectations and Cook threatening to give notice. I tell you, it took Simeon Roy and Cuffy both to get Miss Tam up to the attic and I had the devil's own job to get a dose into her too."

The housekeeper's unusual garrulity spoke her anxiety more than the creases of concern in her face. Ottilia knew not what to say to mitigate the horrors of an evidently painful scene. But she need not have been concerned for Mrs Whiting sighed with a sound of defeat.

"It's a nightmare, ma'am, the whole thing. God knows what'll happen now! With Master Jos gone, and this Mrs Delabole with a numerous family of her own and vowing she can't have Tamasine in the house upsetting her own brood. Not that I blame her after last night, for she's a mother and she's to think for her chicks. But what's to become of the poor child, that's what I'd like to know?"

"Indeed." Relieved at the woman's access of sudden confidences, Ottilia took immediate advantage. "How would you have managed her in Barbados?"

"Put her in the same house we kitted out for the mistress. She'd the run of the place, and as long as I kept the dosage up, she weren't too much trouble."

"You had charge of her?"

"She'd a couple of slave minders in there with her, but I supervised it all, yes."

The moment seemed propitious. Could she probe now? "Mrs Whiting, is it true that Florine attacked Sir Joslin?"

There was no mistaking the sudden fury in the woman's eyes. "Who told you?"

314

Ottilia ignored this. "You see, Tamasine seems to be under the illusion that the position was reversed. She seems to believe Sir Joslin had a hand in her mother's death."

She had expected a scornful rebuttal. It did not come. The housekeeper eyed her, chewing her lip the while. Ottilia waited, and was rewarded.

"The child's confused. Likely she's been fed such lies."

Ottilia's mind took a leap. "By Simeon Roy?"

Now the scorn came, evident in a curled lip and a cold stare. "He'd say anything to gain a point. Foolish boy! To think he could make a wife of the girl. Did he suppose Master Matt had not tried it before him? Aye, and failed miserably. I could have told him, for I've seen her worsen as the years have gone by, just like her ma."

"You were with Florine before she married Matthew Roy?"

"Me and Lomax both. We come with the property. I knew the mistress from a child."

"That's why you were detailed to care for her needs?"

"I knew how to do. Been doing it for years."

The woman was well softened up now. Ottilia dared to probe the mystery at the forefront of her mind. "Mrs Whiting, there is one other thing I meant to ask you." She paused, letting the tension grow as the housekeeper's expression became wary. "It is about the Flora Sugar confections."

"Confections?"

Was that a flash of fear? Ottilia dug in. "I found them in Sir Joslin's drawer."

"Ah, yes." A faint breath. Relief? "He was fond of those. We brought packets and packets with us."

"And you feed them to Tamasine?"

"Why shouldn't she have them? Little enough pleasure she has as it is."

315

Ottilia pounced. "What about those large ones? The laudanum sweets?"

Was it a faint look of alarm in the woman's eyes? To Ottilia's chagrin, a commotion in the corridor beyond cut off the interview. Voices were raised, and the door swung open in a bang. Hemp looked into the room, his face grim.

"Miss Tam has escaped, Mrs Whiting."

"Oh, mercy me, here we go again!"

Mrs Whiting leapt up with alacrity, waddling purposefully into the corridor as Hemp vanished from sight. Ottilia followed more slowly, cursing the ill timing of this interruption. Hemp was ahead, pounding towards the hall, Cuffy in pursuit and the housekeeper steaming along behind. None paid the least heed to Ottilia in the rear.

She reached the hall behind the rest and caught sight of Francis looking towards the green baize door, his gaze anxious. She waved and he pushed through to her side.

"Thank the lord you've come back! The place is in uproar."

Her spouse did not exaggerate. Mrs Delabole was standing just in front of the bookroom door, looking bewildered. Hemp and Cuffy were deep in discussion, but Miss Ingleby overbore the male voices as she rounded on the housekeeper.

"I told you not to let her out too soon. Did you not give her the laudanum last night?"

"Of course I gave it to her," snapped Mrs Whiting, defending herself with vigour. "She was half asleep by the time I took her to her chamber."

"Then she ought to be sleeping still."

"What did you want me to do, give her enough to send her into oblivion like the master?"

The companion lifted a hand and dealt the woman a violent blow across the face. Mrs Whiting cried out, backing off and throwing a hand to her cheek. Mrs Delabole uttered an outraged gasp and started forward, as did Ottilia, but both were forestalled by Hemp, who strode up to the companion and shifted her bodily away from the target.

"That is enough, madame. You know well Miss Tam can get out if she wants."

"Not from the attic, she can't."

Hemp was not deterred by the irritation in the woman's voice. "She cannot be left all night in the attic, madame. I will not allow such cruelty."

"You will not allow? Who made you master here?"

"I am master of what happens to Miss Tam, madame. You know well she is left in my care. It is a sacred trust. I made a promise to my master."

Hemp did not raise his voice, but the determination was steel strong.

Miss Ingleby tossed her head. "Your promise! I can't think what Mr Matt was about to entrust the girl to a slave."

"Entrust the girl to a slave?" came an echo from Mrs Delabole, her eyes round.

Hemp's tone became charged with fury. "I am no slave, madame. I am a free man. I am here by my own will. None but Miss Tam has a claim on me."

"Hemp!" The warning came from Cuffy, interposing his bulk between the companion and his fellow. "You keep your temper, boy. More important we find Miss Tam now."

The young footman was breathing heavily, his gaze fixed on Miss Ingleby. Ottilia watched with interest as he visibly reined himself in, the fire dying out of his eyes. He turned to his colleague.

"Mister Simeon?"

Cuffy shook a grizzled head. "He is not here. He took his carriage."

Hemp came swiftly alert. "The curricle?"

"Maybe he took Miss Tam for drive?"

Miss Ingleby re-entered the lists, turning on the hapless housekeeper once more. "There! That is where your inefficiency has led us. Taken her for a drive? I wish it may be so innocent. That fiend means mischief, I'll be bound."

The unfortunate Mrs Delabole's voice cut in, high and quavering. "What sort of mischief?"

Miss Ingleby turned on her, her tone vicious. "With Simeon Roy, you may be sure it is the worst possible mischief."

Ottilia was attacked with a rise of sympathy for Tamasine's aunt. She looked both confused and distraught, and no wonder. She put up her fingers to her cheeks, her tone one of complaint.

"I don't understand any of this. Is he not fond of his cousin?"

"Too fond, that's the trouble," snapped the companion. "At least, he pretends to be. You don't know the worst of that creature, ma'am. If you did —"

The front doorbell clanged.

Mrs Delabole threw up her hands. "Is this him now perhaps? Oh, dear, I wish I had not come."

No one moved for an instant, every pair of eyes turning to the door. The bell clanged again.

"Is no one going to answer it?" Francis demanded in an exasperated tone.

For the first time, Ottilia noticed her brother, who crossed to the front door as the bell sounded once more. As he threw the door open, two figures appeared in the aperture, all too well known to Ottilia. She made for the door but Patrick got in first.

"Boys? Good grief, what have you done now?"

"Not us, Papa! It's them!"

This was Tom, but the elder of her nephews pushed past his father and plunged into the mêlée in the hall, closely followed by his brother. Both were red in the face and panting. Ben sought Ottilia's gaze.

"We came for Auntilla!"

"We ran all the way!" gasped Tom.

"From the Dower House?"

"No, Auntilla. The church ... in the village."

"He's got her! The fellow she likes!" Ben managed.

Silence swept through the hall as the implication hit. Ottilia broke it. "Are you talking of Tamasine?"

"The madwoman, yes. He's got her!"

"Simeon Roy?"

Patrick came from behind and seized his elder son by the shoulder. "Ben, talk sense. What's the fellow doing with Tamasine?"

The boy gulped in a steadying breath. "We heard the man say he's got a licence," he produced. "They're going to be married."

CHAPTER FIFTEEN

By the time Francis fetched up at the village church, the ceremony was already under way. Putting a finger to his lips, he stole quietly into the dark interior, Patrick at his heels. Miss Ingleby had wanted the footmen to go, but he had scotched that plan at birth.

"Let us waste no time in argument. Hemp and Cuffy are worthy fellows enough, but you will scarcely deny that my presence on the scene is likely to have more impact with the parson."

"Then they will go with you."

"The fewer the better, and the less noise made abroad."

"Let Lord Francis go, Miss Ingleby," said Mrs Delabole, taking a hand. "The clergyman will pay no heed to footmen."

The companion had remained dissatisfied. "But neither of them know how to control Tamasine. If she should fly into one of her tantrums…"

At which, Patrick had intervened. "I am a doctor, ma'am. I will do whatever may be found necessary."

Wasting no further words, Francis chose expedience and left the house, followed by his brother-in-law. They made all speed towards the church on foot. There was little to be gained by wasting time on a return to the Dower House to commandeer one of the carriages and order the horses to be put to.

The rector, an elderly man well known to Francis from his childhood, was enunciating in his feathery voice the opening sequences of the marriage ceremony. In the dimness of the interior, Francis could make out three figures standing at the altar before the cleric. The identities of the two men could not be determined in the shadows enveloping them, but the female's cloak glinted red in a shaft of light from one of the narrow windows to one side.

A vivid image of Tamasine upon the day she had first burst into their lives came into Francis's mind. The spangled gown, covered by a billowing red cloak.

"It is she," he murmured. "The deed is not yet done, thank the Lord."

He would have started forward, but Patrick stayed him. "Wait for the impediment bit."

In his heightened state of anxiety, it seemed to Francis to take forever for the parson to reach the relevant point, although it must have been barely moments.

"If any man can show just cause, why they may not lawfully be joined together, let him now speak, or else hereafter forever hold his peace."

Taking a breath, Francis strode towards the altar, raising his voice. "The marriage cannot go forward."

The two men jerked about. As Francis neared, he saw the second was the Willow Court butler. So he had indeed colluded in the young man's plots. Tillie was right. There could be no doubt of the fellow Roy's identity, though Francis had not previously met him.

The man flung himself towards the intruders, throwing out an accusing finger. "Who the devil are you to interfere? What do you mean by it?"

"I am Lord Francis Fanshawe, and my purpose is to stop this farce before it goes any further."

He cast a glance as he spoke at Tamasine, who had turned to watch. She was, for a wonder, smiling her beatific smile and she let out a high-pitched laugh.

"Simeon is going to marry me."

Francis knew better than to argue with the wench. He concentrated on Roy, but was forestalled by Lomax.

"This is intolerable! Even here you dare to stick your nose into what does not concern you?"

Roy turned to him. "You know this man?"

"It is Lady Francis's husband, and a worse busybody you could never meet."

Francis exploded. "Your insolence is only equalled by your temerity, Lomax. You had best consider your position in this, since you have chosen to aid and abet Roy in his wrongdoing."

"Wrongdoing?" Simeon Roy dove a hand into his pocket and brought it out, flourishing a leaf of paper. "I have the necessary licence. If Mr Dewberry here is satisfied, what have you to say in the matter?"

"I have this to say. You do not have the permission of the lady's guardians."

Roy uttered a scornful laugh. "Tamasine is of age. She is free to choose whom she would marry. It happens that she prefers me."

"Except that she is already betrothed to my nephew," countered Francis with relish.

He had not intended to bring Giles into it, but if that was what it took to do what his wife had enjoined him to do, then so be it. Before he had offered his services — or rather, imposed them on the assembled company, he reflected ruefully — Tillie had grasped his arm and whispered a frantic message in his ear.

"Fan, please go yourself. You must stop this! I cannot think Tamasine's life is worth a penny if that fellow manages to make her his wife."

The announcement had an immediate effect on the Reverend Mr Dewberry, who had been gazing stupefied upon the scene. He at once entered the fray. "My lord, do you tell me there is a prior engagement?"

"Indeed I do, Mr Dewberry, though it has not been publicly announced. But I am assured that Mr Roy knew of it."

Simeon Roy at once began upon a protest. "Nothing of the kind, sir. That betrothal was dissolved only the other day, by Lord Bennifield's grandmother herself."

"Lady Polbrook? Are you certain, sir?"

The fellow Roy continued to argue his case with the cleric, and Francis found his brother-in-law at his elbow.

"Lomax has made himself scarce." Francis glanced about the church. There was no sign of the butler. Had his words borne fruit? He could well believe the fellow would never endanger his own interests in support of the man Roy. "Draw off the boy, Fan, and I'll put the rector in possession of the facts."

Francis thanked Patrick in a low tone, and went instead to the girl's side. Best not to enjoin her to come away. Subterfuge was more likely to work, and no doubt distract Roy from his argument with the parson.

"Tamasine, do you not wish to marry Giles?"

Her eyes were feverish with excitement, and laughter trilled out of her. "Of course, silly. But first I am going to marry Simeon."

Francis thought fast. Recalling how his wife was apt to deal with the girl, he kept his tone mild. "Ah, but I'm afraid you can't marry both. The law does not allow it, you know. You must choose."

His voice must have carried for Roy turned sharply from his conference with the rector. Leaving the fellow without ceremony, he pounced.

"What are you telling her? Tam, my pet, don't you listen to him."

Francis ignored him, concentrating on the girl. Devoutly hoping that any falsehoods in the house of God might be forgiven, since his purpose was sufficient, Francis infused his voice with regret.

"Giles will be most unhappy."

"Be quiet! Enough of your lies, sir!" This from Simeon Roy in a savage under-voice. And to the girl in a tone of unctuous flattery, "Tam, you love me best, don't you? You are my little china doll."

Tamasine gave a delighted squeal. "Yes, I am, I am!"

"Giles is waiting for you," Francis said, with difficulty suppressing a spurt of anger. How dared the boy work upon the child's mind in this unscrupulous fashion?

"Giles, Giles, Giles," sang Tamasine, clapping her hands. "He wants to kiss me."

"Of course he does. Come with me, and I will take you to him."

Roy threw an arm around Tamasine's shoulder, holding her fast to his side. His tone became brittle. "You are staying with me. You are my little sweetheart, my little darling, my little pet. Are you not, my lovely?"

Tamasine beamed up at him. "Yes, and Lavinia won't let me marry you because she wants you for herself."

"Exactly so, my sweet. And therefore we have made our plans in secret and we are going to be married this moment."

"Oh, no, you are not," Francis murmured in a voice only loud enough for Roy to hear. "I'm afraid the cleric will no longer be persuaded to perform the ceremony."

Simeon Roy's confounded look was almost ludicrous. Releasing the girl, he turned quickly, hissing in a breath as he saw Patrick had drawn the rector some feet away towards the entrance to the vestry. He swung back on Francis, his handsome visage contorted with a snarl.

"Damn you both! Don't think I'm beaten. There are more ways to skin a cat."

Triumph rose up in Francis. "But not for you, I think, Mr Roy. You've lost this round." With an oath, the man lifted his balled fists, the threat implicit in his eyes. Francis adopted the soft tone of command that had served him so well in his soldiering days. "Don't even think of it. Your henchman has gone, and we are two. You will get the worst of it, my friend."

For a moment, the issue hung in the balance, and Francis braced himself to withstand an attack. Then Simeon Roy let his breath go and sank back. His tone turned as smooth as oil, his voice a drawl that Francis surmised was habitual, a deliberate pose of nonchalance.

"Well, I have no mind for a bloodied nose. I retire from the lists for the nonce, defeated." He gave his arm to Tamasine, who was watching the give and take of words with no diminution in her gleeful expression. She was evidently thoroughly enjoying the contretemps. "Come, my pet. It seems we are doomed to save our nuptials for another day."

The rector's fluttery tones came from behind him. "Sir, I must beg you not to repeat this endeavour elsewhere."

Roy turned on him. "I fail to see how it concerns you, sir."

"It concerns me, sir," said Dewberry, his tone grave, "because you have attempted to perpetrate a fraud upon the blessed sanctity of matrimony."

"As I told you, sir, it is untrue. Lord Bennifield's betrothal does not stand."

"That, sir, is immaterial. Even had that weighed with me, I should certainly not perform the ceremony without first consulting with Lady Polbrook. Also, I might add, Mrs

Delabole, whom I understand to be this lady's guardian since the demise of — er — well, since her former guardian's demise."

The curling lip that characterised Roy's smile appeared. "Oh, Ruth will put no bar in my way, I am persuaded."

"That, sir, remains to be seen." The cleric lowered his voice, clearly attempting to escape Tamasine's wide-eyed gaze which went from him to Simeon as if she followed the conversation, which Francis was persuaded could not be the case. "You are in God's house, Mr Roy. Dare you seriously expect me to marry you to a lady who clearly has little or no understanding of the vows she is expected to make?"

Simeon Roy cast a fulminating glance at Patrick's impassive countenance. "So that is your game, Doctor Hathaway? Below the belt, sir, very much below the belt." Turning his back on the cleric, he smiled down into the girl's face. "Come, my pet. We shall go home and confound Lavinia. She will be very angry with us, and that will afford us a deal of amusement."

Tamasine's squealing laughter painfully smote Francis's ears, and he hung back to wait for Patrick, who was bidding the rector farewell. Francis added his thanks to the man, with an apology for putting him to such trouble.

"Indeed, my lord, you have earned my gratitude. I am thankful to have been spared the ignominy of being the cause of that poor creature's future unhappiness, if the gentleman in the case is truly only concerned with her fortune, as the doctor here informs me. I had heard rumours, of course. It is sad to understand them to be true."

Francis replied suitably and made good his escape. "We must hurry, Patrick. There is no saying but that Roy may not try another throw if we are not close behind him."

"He's rogue enough, I grant you."

"Yes, but I can't help but admire his insouciance," Francis admitted. "He seems to have boldness enough for any fate."

With what patience she could muster, Ottilia was engaged in attempting to calm Mrs Delabole's multiple distresses. The woman was clearly out of her depth, saying over and over that she could not undertake to care for 'that creature', as she referred to Tamasine, and expressing the forlorn wish that Ottilia had not sent her spouse and brother to interfere.

"You cannot wish your niece to be placed under the care of a man who is clearly bent upon using her for his own ends."

Mrs Delabole struck her hands together. "But you don't know that. Perhaps he is genuinely fond of the girl."

"He may well be, though I take leave to doubt it since he is perfectly aware of the ramifications of her condition."

"Yes, but if she remains single, what is to be done with her? I don't want to be saddled with her, Lady Francis, though I am of course sorry for the wench. I don't mean to be unkind, but —"

"I am sure you don't, ma'am, and no one could accuse you of it. It must be hard indeed to be thrust into this situation."

"Well, it is," insisted the matron, almost tearfully. "I have a numerous family of my own, you must know, and it is difficult enough to manage my own children. Really, my brother should have made better provision. I cannot think what he was about, arranging for her to be sent over here. He ought to have kept her in the West Indies where she might be safely watched, instead of unleashing her upon an unsuspecting public."

"That, I fear, is past praying for, ma'am."

"True." Mrs Delabole sighed, her features crumpling. "She is quite deranged, you know. My brother made no secret of it to me. Indeed, I believe he found relief in writing of it without restraint. He knew I should make no undue judgement."

Ottilia's ears pricked up. "I should be most interested to hear what he told you, Mrs Delabole, if you don't object to speaking of it."

"How should I at this juncture? There is no concealing it from you, I am certain."

"No, for I have seen her at full cry. But go on, Mrs Delabole."

"Matt saw the signs when she was an infant. Tamasine had, he said, the same distrait manner he first noticed in his wife. Her attention could not be focused for more than a minute."

"That is well seen. I've wondered how they managed to teach her anything at all."

Mrs Delabole threw up a hand. "Heavens, nothing! She had lessons, but she was apt to abandon them in an instant. They were put to creating games to instil anything at all into her wayward mind. She was forever playing tricks, vanishing into the sugar canes and causing everyone the maximum amount of trouble. A terrible charge upon my poor brother! And she had cunning, he said." Compassion showed in her features, but it proved not to be towards Tamasine. "What upset poor Matt the most, I think, was the little streak of cruelty that ran through the child. She delighted in inflicting pain. They could not permit her to keep pets, for she was not to be trusted with them."

Ottilia's heart grew cold at the thought. "My brother says it is a symptom of the inability to see the world from another's shoes."

"Exactly so. Matt was convinced that, like his wife, Tamasine occupies a world of her own. Everyone else is incidental."

Ottilia could not let this pass. "Not all persons, I believe. She does genuinely care for Hemp, I am sure."

"Hemp? The black slave?"

The touch of revulsion in her voice caused Ottilia to become tart. "I am informed he is a free man, ma'am. At all events, Hemp is the one person who can control your niece."

Mrs Delabole shuddered. "My niece! How in the world could I take her in charge? I should never know a moment's peace. Mr Roy is welcome to her, for all of me!"

Revolted by the woman's wholly unsympathetic attitude, Ottilia abandoned all effort to be tactful. "I hate to say this, ma'am, but I fear young Roy has no proper interest in Tamasine beyond acquiring access to her fortune, which I believe is considerable. Once he had it, I fear he would find means to rid himself of a singularly poor bargain of a wife."

The matron stared at her, evidently unable to make the leap. "I cannot think what you mean, Lady Francis. How should he be rid of her? Not divorce, surely?"

"A surer means than that, I think."

"Surer? What in the world are you implying?"

Dawning dismay was in the woman's eyes. Before Ottilia could say more, the sound of the front door slamming penetrated to the parlour. With a muttered expletive, she jumped up and raced out, with every expectation of finding a cavalcade returning from the village church.

She found only the butler Lomax. She eyed him, trying to calm the jangle of her nerves. She managed as close an approximation to her normal tones as she could summon up.

"You are back then, Lomax. Can it be that you were not a party to this secret marriage after all?" The fellow's angry glare told her otherwise, but he did not speak. Footsteps could be heard above stairs and Ottilia hastened to seize the moment.

"But it was you who kept Simeon Roy informed of events here at Willow Court, was it not?"

From behind her, Mrs Delabole gave a gasp. "Gracious, Lady Francis, what in the world do you mean?"

She had not expected the woman to follow her out of the parlour and could have done without her intervention. Although perhaps it was as well she knew what Ottilia suspected. She opted for clarification.

"I mean, ma'am, that Mr Roy is remarkably well informed about matters here for a man who has not been next or nigh the Barbados party since it came to this place."

Lomax produced a sneer almost worthy of Roy himself. "You'll believe what you wish to, I don't doubt."

"It rather leaps to the eye, Lomax. How long have you been in correspondence with him? Ever since he left Barbados? Or did you only seek him out when you arrived in England? Or no, more likely when you knew you must come here. Insurance, Lomax? You had a future to think of, had you not?"

She watched the effect of her words in the shift of muscles in his face, the tightening at his jaw, aware of Mrs Delabole's open-mouthed astonishment at her elbow. The footsteps were now on the stairs and Ottilia looked up to see Miss Ingleby, who paused, her accusing eyes on the butler.

"Where are they?"

He removed his taut gaze from Ottilia and it narrowed as he turned it on the companion. "Why ask me? I'm not the girl's keeper."

"But I am, Mr Lomax." The deep voice came from the back of the hall. Ottilia turned as one with Mrs Delabole as Hemp walked through to confront the butler. "Is it true, sir? What this lady says? You made a plan with Mister Simeon. You

brought him here so he can run away with Miss Tam —
again?"

"What?" Mrs Delabole's eyes were round. "Great heavens,
has he done this before?"

"He has, madame," responded Hemp. "Did not Master Roy
write to you of it?"

The woman's eyes fairly popped. "The attempted elopement!
I had forgot all about it."

Hemp turned back to Lomax. "Sir, you have not answered
me?"

His tone was respectful, but Ottilia detected steel beneath
which was not lost on Lomax. His chin went up and he
adopted a lofty manner.

"Don't think you can go accusing me, boy. I'm still your
superior."

"No, sir, you are not."

The front doorbell pealed through the house and Mrs
Delabole flinched. Lomax went to answer, no doubt relieved
to be spared having to deal with the footman's intimidating
hostility. The thought was overborne in Ottilia's mind as
Tamasine tripped into the house, evidently in high gig. Her
heartbeat quickened. Had Francis been too late?

The girl danced up to her companion. "You didn't catch us,
Lavinia. We were too clever for you."

Miss Ingleby looked aghast, as well she might, her gaze flying
to search Simeon Roy's face. He had entered behind Tamasine
and his manner was as urbane and drawling as ever.

"Don't look so appalled, my dear Lavinia. Surely you know
little Tam wishes for nothing more in life than to be my wife?"

"No!"

Lavinia's cry was strangled and she backed, her features
distorted. Ottilia felt Mrs Delabole's fingers clutch her arm and

turned to find the woman's cheeks drained of colour. Had she taken the jump? Did she now realise of what Simeon Roy might be capable?

Then Tamasine burst into her high-pitched giggling laugh, jumping up and down. "We fooled you, we fooled you, we fooled you! Lavinia couldn't catch us."

"Miss Tam!"

The deep voice claimed her instant attention. She turned to Hemp, shrieked and flung herself upon him, calling out his name several times in that singsong way she had. Watching Hemp receive her into his embrace, the thought struck Ottilia that here was the only genuine affection the girl exhibited.

Hemp released himself and, talking low into her ear, ushered her up the stairs.

Belatedly, it occurred to Ottilia that Mrs Whiting had made no appearance. Was she busy in the nether regions, or merely steering clear of the contretemps? A quick glance round showed her that Lomax had seized the chance to slip away.

Mrs Delabole was still gripping her arm and Ottilia turned, wondering what she could possibly say to offer comfort. Yet another peal at the front doorbell brought Cuffy to the fore. Ottilia had not even realised the elder footman was upon the scene. He opened the door to Francis and Ottilia started forward. She had no chance to speak for Miss Ingleby forestalled her, throwing out an accusing finger.

"How could you let this happen? So much for your unwarranted interference! You were supposed to stop it!"

Her husband's calm tones brought instant balm. "Your reproaches are misplaced, Miss Ingleby. The marriage did not take place."

The companion stared at him, her gaze painful in its intensity. "You were in time?"

"Just."

"Oh, thank heaven!"

She put a hand to her bosom and fell back a little, reaching out to grasp the newel post at the bottom of the stairs. Simeon Roy moved up close, pushing past Ottilia and Mrs Delabole without ceremony, venom in both tongue and eyes.

"Relief, Lavinia? It will be short-lived, I promise you. This is but a minor setback. I haven't waited this long to be bested now. Do your worst. Lock her up, drug her until she's stupid with the stuff. You won't stop me. I mean to marry the wench and I will, whatever it takes."

With which, he turned sharply and cast a mocking glance across the audience of visitors, sweeping over Mrs Delabole too. His voice jeered.

"You're all deluded. You most of all, Ruth, but you are less blameworthy than these interfering busybodies." He eyed the visitors with disdain. "You see what you think you see. There's more here than meets the eye."

He made for the front door, but Ottilia moved to intercept him.

"Assuredly, Mr Roy. Much more. Let me see if I have gauged it aright."

His lip curled. "I have no interest in your musings, Lady Francis."

In one movement, Francis was before him. "You'll keep a civil tongue in your head when you talk to my wife, Roy, or you'll answer to me."

Simeon fell back, opening his arms. "But I am perfectly courteous, sir. What did I say that you could possibly take amiss?"

"I misliked your tone."

Roy threw up his hands and his smile became unctuous, his voice a mockery of obsequiousness. "My dear sir, you behold me abject." He bowed towards Ottilia. "I meant no offence towards your good lady. I am merely desirous of removing from this intolerable gathering forthwith."

"Not so fast, my lad."

Ottilia heard her brother's voice with surprise. She had not seen him enter the house.

"Ah, the good doctor," said Roy, flourishing a hand in his direction, seemingly unaffected by the manner of Patrick's interruption. "To whom I am indebted for traitorous murmurings to the rector. Your solicitude is remarkable, sir, in matters that don't concern you. Did I not hear that you are responsible for discovering the cause of my poor cousin's untimely demise? Though anyone who knew him could have told you his habit at the outset."

"If you mean that I assisted at a post-mortem after an untimely and unexpected death, you are correct, sir." Patrick moved to flank Francis. "But at this present, I wish to caution you, Mr Roy."

"Caution? Against what?"

"Your actions this morning could readily put you, along with the butler, under a charge of kidnapping. I would advise you to think carefully before you attempt another such escapade."

"I hardly think such a charge would stand. Tamasine is my cousin, after all."

"But a court of law would not consider her fit to consent to the scheme you propose. As a medical man, I am qualified to bear witness to her state of mind."

The struggle in Roy to maintain his pose of nonchalance was visible. Until Miss Ingleby intervened.

"There now, Simeon. That is all your scheming has led to, you villain!"

He turned on her, rage twisting his features. "Vixen!"

"Oh, not again!" came on a pleading note from Mrs Delabole. She was ignored, hastening out of the way as Simeon closed in to the companion.

"You've always stood in my way. You turned Joslin against me as well as Matt. You couldn't have me, so you made sure Tamasine would not either."

"To be sure I did," she snarled back. "What sort of life would she have with you, selfish brute that you are?"

"Better than she has with you. I can offer her frolicking and freedom, a chance to enjoy life for a change."

Ottilia pounced, taking a couple of steps towards him. "For how long, Mr Roy?" He turned to confront her, his brows snapping together. Aware of Francis at her back, stiffly protective, Ottilia did not hesitate. "How long could you keep a wife you could not present to your acquaintance? How indeed could you enjoy the riches she brought you when you might not show her abroad? Or did you mean to keep her confined as your cousin Matthew did Florine, with a couple of servants to see she came to no harm?"

A gasp escaped Mrs Delabole. Had she at last understood the alternative?

Miss Ingleby dived straight back in, scorn in her tone. "Ha! Answer that if you can, fiend!"

The woman might be for once on Ottilia's side, but she could do without the companion's doubtful assistance. She kept her eyes on Simeon Roy, determined to push through. "Did you suppose Hemp could be persuaded to join your household? He is the only one here truly capable of controlling Tamasine."

"Balderdash!" The sneer was back on the man's face. "He's no more to her than any other slave."

"You are either blind or stupid, Mr Roy, if that is what you believe. But I don't think you do. You know quite well what value Hemp holds in Tamasine's life. But it would be a deal too much to expect of him, to come to your aid in this, after you and Lomax had cheated him out of his inheritance."

Shock held Francis speechless, and he at once saw his stupefaction echoed in the faces of Mrs Delabole, Miss Ingleby and Patrick. Roy, on the other hand, appeared unmoved. He raised pained brows.

"Forgive me, Lady Francis, but I have not the remotest conjecture as to your meaning. Inheritance? Hemp? A black servant?"

As Francis might have expected, Tillie was not in the least disconcerted.

"Oh, come, Mr Roy, he is a deal more than that, and you know it."

From the gallery above, Hemp himself spoke. "Say no more, milady."

Miss Ingleby turned sharply, and started up the stairs. "Where is she? Have you left her alone? Is she locked in?"

"Mrs Whiting is with her, madame."

"Is she calm? Does she need a dose?"

"She is happy. She is quiet."

Simeon Roy gave out another of his sneering laughs. "Of course she is. Even if we failed in our objective, Tam is always delighted to outwit her duenna."

"Because you encourage her," Miss Ingleby slammed back, turning to descend the stairs again.

"Naturally I encourage her. Nothing delights me more than to goad you, Lavinia." The companion raised a hand to strike him, but he caught her wrist. "Ah, would you, vixen?"

To Francis's amazement, she did not fight to release herself, but drew close, spitting her words into his face.

"I would use my nails to wipe that smug look off your face! You were arrogant as a boy, and you haven't changed. Lord knows what I ever saw in you!"

The man seized her other wrist, holding her close against him, the sardonic look on his face matching his voice. "Whatever you saw, Lavinia, you wanted it more than your own virtue. And you haven't changed."

With a squeal of rage, Miss Ingleby exerted her strength to free herself. With a mocking laugh, he released her. She backed away.

"Devil! Ingrate! I hate you! I hate you more than life!"

Turning, she flew for the study door. Roy plunged after her. "You lying witch!"

She disappeared into the room, the man on her tail. The door slammed behind them both and the raised voices became indecipherable, and then muted as the row was carried away to another part of the mansion.

CHAPTER SIXTEEN

"Lord above, what a pair!" Francis turned to catch Tillie's reaction.

She was looking at Mrs Delabole, whose expression gave every indication of horror, while Patrick was openly grinning. He would have given much to enquire into his wife's thoughts, but they were still encumbered with the aunt. He remembered the presence of the footman and glanced up the stairs.

"Is this a sample of what went on in Barbados, Hemp?"

The footman was watching the door, but he turned his head at that and came on down to the hall. "It is not for me to speak of it, milord."

Mrs Delabole let her breath go and threw up her hands. "Well, I wish to heaven someone would speak of it! I have never seen such a display. Never! My poor brother must be turning in his grave, I should think."

Tillie took the woman's hand and chafed it. "I am sorry for you, Mrs Delabole. It must be uncomfortable indeed to be thrust into this maelstrom."

The poor lady's eyes filled. "I wish I was at home again. I can't bear all this uproar."

"It will pass, ma'am," Tillie soothed. "Why do you not go into the parlour, Mrs Delabole. I am sure you would be the better for a cup of coffee. Hemp will arrange it, I am persuaded."

Francis watched with some dissatisfaction as his wife ushered the afflicted female into the parlour and disappeared from sight, leaving the door open. He turned back to Hemp. "Before you go, pray tell me this. You at least may say you cannot wish for such a man as this Simeon Roy to have charge of Miss Tamasine."

"I do not wish for it, sir. I mistrust him and I do not believe he truly cares for Miss Tam."

He gave a brief bow and started in the direction of the servants' quarters. But Tillie, darting out of the parlour, caught up with him.

"One moment, Hemp. Do you think I might have a word with Miss Tamasine? Is she locked in?"

A frown creased the man's features as he turned. "Mrs Whiting is there."

Which was no answer. Impatience gnawed at Francis, but he saw Tillie's special smile appear and held his peace.

"If you were to accompany me? There is nothing Tamasine might say that I would not wish you to hear." The fellow hesitated. Francis was not surprised to find his wife pursuing her advantage. "In any event, I would appreciate a few moments of your time, Hemp. There is something with which I think you may be able to help me." Her warm smile appeared. "Would you meet me at Tamasine's door once you have alerted the kitchens about this coffee? Perhaps Cuffy will bring it. I won't be above a moment."

The dismissal was plain and the footman appeared to acquiesce. A slight bow and he went off through the baize door at the back of the hall.

"Tillie, what in the world are you about? Why should you speak to Tamasine? You will get nothing sensible out of the girl. And while we are about it, what did you mean about that fellow Hemp and an inheritance? Why did he stop you from saying any more?"

She raised her brows. "Dear me, Fan, which question would you wish me to answer first?"

Before he could respond, his brother-in-law intervened, stepping up to catch his sister's arm. "Hold hard! What I want to know is what you make of those two." He jerked his head towards the study door. "For my money, there is a deal to be learned from that little contretemps."

Diverted, Francis stared at him. "What do you mean?"

Patrick released Tillie's arm. "Isn't it possible we have it altogether wrong? What if Miss Ingleby and the Roy fellow are in cahoots, rather than he with Lomax?"

"In cahoots? After that display? You must be all about in your head, Patrick."

"Think about it, Fan. Could they not have played this little comedy for our benefit? We are not supposed to imagine anything but enmity between them. Then the boy marries the child, apparently in the teeth of her companion. As her husband, he becomes her banker with access to her fortune. In due time, as Ottilia suggests, he rids himself of the encumbrance."

"And takes up with Miss Ingleby so that they both may live on the proceeds," Francis finished with enthusiasm. "Ingenious. What is more, if there is a better motive to be rid of the guardian, I have not heard one."

As of instinct, he turned to see how his wife regarded this development. But Patrick was before him.

"Well, sister mine? Possible, do you think?"

Tillie's brows rose. "Oh, possible indeed, brother mine."

Francis knew that tone. "But wrong? Go on, Tillie, why?"

"I grant you the farcical elements in their behaviour, Patrick, but I think the spark and fire is genuine. What is more, it would surprise me if they are not at this moment engaged in a passionate embrace."

Bewildered, Francis threw up his hands. "But you are painting the very picture to support Patrick's theory."

"Ah, but not, I fear, a premeditated plot." She touched a hand to his chest in the intimate gesture she was wont to use. "Have you not remarked that creature's volatile nature? She is no more capable of duplicity on the scale needed to carry out such a scheme than she can help responding to the urgency of attraction she feels towards young Simeon."

"But he is more than capable of it," Patrick insisted.

Tillie turned to him. "Undoubtedly. Yet his suave front disintegrates every time he comes in contact with Miss Ingleby. Had you not noticed?"

"I don't believe it," declared Francis. "The woman was clearly head over heels for Sir Joslin."

"Sir Joslin represented security, a future. Oh, I dare say she was fond of him, but she cannot have been ignorant of his preferences."

Patrick entered a caveat. "That does not preclude her loving the fellow."

"Between that sort of cool affection and the intensity of passion we have just witnessed, there is a chasm. Successful relationships depend upon a bridge between the two."

Francis was silenced. Tillie had just described the exact phenomenon to explain their union. It had not before occurred to him how rare it was. He knew his brother-in-law did not enjoy a like felicity. Nor, with a rapid scan across his relatives, could he point to another within his own family.

"She's right," he told Patrick, and grinned at his wife. "As usual."

Her warm smile appeared. "But I must give Patrick credit for his ingenuity."

"I thank you. But I bow to your superior intellect."

The ironic tone only made Tillie laugh. "When I have learned so much from you? Yes, I can see you allowing me so far. Fie, Patrick!"

His laughter rang round the hall, and Francis dealt him a buffet on the arm. "Do be quiet, wretch! You'll have us expelled."

"Yes, if Miss Ingleby were not otherwise engaged," said Patrick, but he suppressed his mirth.

"Well, Mrs Delabole will undoubtedly hear you. I must say I am sorry for that woman. She has an impossible task."

"Indeed she has, Fan, and therefore I will be grateful if the two of you will wait for me in the parlour with her. You may do what you can to calm her fears, which I may say are many and decidedly upsetting to her."

Francis groaned. "I thank you, that is all that was wanting to secure my total pleasure in this delightful day."

Ottilia twinkled. "Well, let Patrick do the work then."

"Ah, just the fellow," said Francis with a grin at his indignant brother-in-law. "You are a medical man after all, Patrick, you may as well make yourself useful."

"Any more and I shall leave you to bear the whole."

Ottilia left them bantering and headed for the stairs. She was relieved to find Hemp awaiting her by Tamasine's door as arranged. She kept her voice low.

"Is she alone?"

He nodded. "Mrs Whiting has gone."

"Did you arrange that?"

His gaze remained steady on her face. "It is what you wish, milady, no?"

"Just so. I admire your foresight." He did not answer, but turned to unlock the door. Ottilia put a hand on his arm to detain him. "One moment, Hemp, if you please?"

He paused, looking a question. She smiled. "When we are done here, would you object to coming out with me for a few minutes?"

His gaze narrowed. "More questions, milady?"

"A couple of matters you might help me with."

He said nothing for a moment, eyeing her as if he debated within himself. Not unhopeful, Ottilia waited. Abruptly, he nodded, dropped his gaze to the door handle and turned it, gesturing for her to go in ahead of him.

Tamasine was lying on the four-poster, her feet dangling over the end, twitching as she watched them, counting aloud. "One, two, buckle my shoe. Six, ten, a big fat hen. Eighteen, fourteen, maids a-courting." Her head turned, and the beatific smile appeared. "That's me. Maids a-courting."

"That is certainly true," said Ottilia, moving towards the bed.

She noted Hemp shifting to a corner. He had locked the door behind them. It occurred to her he must be long practised at effacing himself since the girl did not trouble to acknowledge his presence. Tamasine sat up in a bang, clapping her hands as the sing-song chant began.

"Lady Fan, Lady Fan, Lady Fan."

"Tamasine, Tamasine, Tamasine," echoed Ottilia, and was pleased to note how the game sent the child into an explosion of giggles.

She dared to sit beside the girl. Tamasine grabbed her near hand and squeezed it so hard that Ottilia winced.

"Not so tight, my dear, if you please."

Tamasine's bright eyes gleamed and the pressure increased. Ottilia bit her lip to stop herself crying out.

"Miss Tam!"

The girl's fingers opened abruptly as she jerked round. Released, Ottilia cradled her hand, unable to withstand a hiss of pain. Tamasine leapt up and ran to the footman, lifting her fists and beating at his chest, squealing the while. He neither spoke nor moved, making no attempt to stop the assault. It was over in a moment. Tamasine desisted, laughed and flung her arms about his neck. She rose on tiptoe and kissed his cheek.

"See, Hemp, I do love you."

"I know, Miss Tam. You be good now, huh?"

Like a child, Tamasine slipped her fingers from his shoulders to cradle his cheeks. "I'll be good. Don't be cross."

"Never with you, Miss Tam."

Watching, Ottilia experienced a little jolt of sadness. The poignancy of the moment caught at her. Here was this creature, lost in a maze of unreality, unable to control her every impulse of behaviour. Yet there was an instinct of genuine affection for the footman. She remembered Hemp protesting she could be loving.

Her thoughts faded as the girl came running back to the bed. "Let's play a game."

Ottilia seized on this. "Yes, let us. I am going to ask you something, and you see if you can answer."

Excitement shone in the blue orbs. "Yes, and then I shall ask."

She understood turn and turn about? So much the better. A game must disguise Ottilia's purpose. "I shall start." Ottilia pretended to think. "I know. What colour is your hair?"

"Sunshine."

"What an excellent answer."

A shriek of glee escaped the girl. She clapped her hands. "My turn!"

"I am ready."

"Lady Fan, Lady Fan, Lady Fan."

Ottilia was thrown for a second. Best to take it as a question. "Yes, I am Lady Fan."

Another shriek. "You are, you are!"

Ottilia held to innocuous questions for a few more turns, noting Tamasine's rising excitement at each answer, whether or not it was appropriate. When she felt the girl was sufficiently involved not to note the change, she dared the question she had in mind all along.

"If the reckoning is not yet done, what is still to do?"

The child quieted on the instant. A hushed feeling entered Ottilia's breast. Had she miscalculated? The stare was intense, but there was no trace of malevolence on this occasion. She waited.

The answer came on a whisper of breath. "Mamma."

Ottilia knew not how to proceed. She dared not speak, for fear of saying the wrong thing. She regarded the girl without, she hoped, showing any reaction, hoping for more.

Nothing came. A veil appeared to descend and Tamasine's eyes went blank. They closed and she sank slowly to the bed.

Alarmed, Ottilia looked across at Hemp. "Is she...?"

She hardly knew what she wanted to say. Was it a swoon? Had the child lapsed into coma? The footman walked swiftly to the bed and leaned a little to look at the girl's face. His eyes lifted to Ottilia's. He moved away from the bed and beckoned Ottilia to join him.

"She is unconscious," he murmured low. "It will pass in a moment."

She matched his level. "Does she do this often?"

"You touched something, milady. She cannot face reality. There are moments when she is lucid, but they are few and have this effect."

"Then she does have vengeance in her mind."

Hemp shrugged. "I do not think she understands the concept. If so, it is twisted."

That, certainly. But Ottilia was not convinced of Tamasine's ignorance. At her core, she knew, even if she was incapable of vocalising the notion to make sense of it.

"Lady Fan, Lady Fan, Lady Fan."

Ottilia turned. The child was up again, as bright and apparently carefree as before. She scrambled along the bed to her pillows and dug underneath the mound. Grabbing at an object, she tugged it out. Then she was off the bed, dancing to Ottilia's side. She was clutching a flat wooden box of Tunbridge ware, with a pretty inlaid design on the lid, of stars and crescents. A child's toy. Tamasine opened it up and held it out to Ottilia.

"You may have one, if you like."

A rush of heat cascaded into Ottilia's chest and her mind buzzed. Within the box lay a quantity of thick paper-wrapped rolls, each about three inches long, and emblazoned with the Flora Sugars emblem — the missing sweets.

Her mind afire, Ottilia waited for Hemp to close and lock the door behind him. She was just going to speak when he set a finger to his lips. A whisper reached her.

"Not here, milady. Miss Tam's hearing is acute."

He led her into the main corridor, taking a path towards the back of the house. Within a moment or two, he stopped, opening a door to one side. An anteroom was revealed, furnished with a set of inlaid commodes and a long mirror with an open door leading off through which Ottilia glimpsed the edge of a four-poster. An unused dressing room? A musty smell pervaded the place and the shutters were closed.

Hemp went across and opened them, revealing the back view from the Court. He remained standing by the window, half silhouetted against the light. He was so still Ottilia began to wonder what he was thinking. Was he apprehensive about her questions? He surprised her, coming to life and turning suddenly to survey her.

"You have worked it all out, I think."

Ottilia eyed him. "All but a few details, I believe, with which I am hoping you may be able to help."

He was looking in her direction but his position made it impossible to see his expression. Ottilia moved to the other side of the window. He watched her gravely, but did not speak. It struck her she was more nervous than him. She drew a steadying breath.

"You told me Florine Roy attacked Sir Joslin, but you did not tell me why?"

Was that a faint sigh? "It is not a pretty tale, milady."

"That much I had deduced from the hint you gave me last time."

He was silent for a space. Then he seemed to relax, leaning against the edge of the shutter and folding his arms across his chest. "With Madame Florine's malady there was a need not shared by Miss Tam. She is too innocent. Madame Florine was not innocent. She tried with Master Jos what she had tried with black slaves, to no avail. None would dare take this chance. A black man would be hanged for taking advantage of a white woman."

Ottilia was conscious of a sensation of kinship with her mother-in-law's abolitionist views. She refrained from any word of sympathy, judging that Hemp would take it amiss.

"I did wonder, when you said her story was that he had raped her. Sir Joslin was unresponsive, I take it?"

He nodded, and Ottilia noted the careful restraint in his face. Was this one aspect of the dead man's character he did not regard with sympathy?

"Madame Florine seized up a knife —"

"A knife! How is it possible she was allowed near any such implement?"

The black brows pulled together. "She escaped."

"Like Tamasine. The similarities do rather leap to the eye."

His frown deepened, a trifle of confusion coming in. Ottilia did not enlighten him as to her full meaning.

"What happened?"

"Madame Florine chased Master Jos into the sugar factory where they make the loaves. There are many sharp implements for trimming the sugar."

"Chased him? From where?"

"He found her in the canes and was seeking to return her to her house. She tried to — to interest him. When he refused, she seized a cut cane and began to beat at him. Master Jos was never strong. He ran, looking to seek refuge in the factory. The mistress cut him badly before slaves came at the noise and pulled her off."

His story ended, Hemp dropped his gaze to his folded arms, avoiding Ottilia's eye. She studied him, the burgeoning of conviction seeping into her mind.

"How long was it after this event that Florine died?"

Comprehension came into Hemp's eyes. Had he made the same leap?

"It was a matter of days, milady. We all thought it was connected, but nothing could be learned to prove anything at all. And the master was too distressed to pursue the matter."

"Yes, I suppose that was inevitable."

"May I ask what is in your mind, milady?"

Ottilia smiled, prevaricating. "I'm not sure. But on another matter, how old was Tamasine when Simeon Roy first attempted an abduction?"

The flash of rage startled her and he straightened, his arms dropping, his fists clenched. "She was a child! Barely sixteen. I wanted to kill him."

His voice was raw with pain. The urge to offer words of comfort was strong, but Ottilia could not afford to waste time. Besides, she was by no means sure she had any comfort to offer. The ideas revolving in her head were unlikely to alleviate Hemp's distress.

"How was the plot foiled?"

"Miss Lavinia realised what was afoot. She went to the master directly."

"Nor hell a fury like a woman scorned," Ottilia quoted.

Hemp's mouth twisted. "That is not for me to say, milady. There was much argument between Master Jos and my master, who wanted to send her packing."

"He thought she had neglected her charge?"

"Everyone on the plantation knew of the liaison between her and Mister Simeon. They were not discreet, and the slaves see everything. Besides, they quarrelled loud enough to wake the ghosts."

"Did Tamasine know of it?"

A harsh laugh escaped the man. "He told her, milady. He has no shame, that one. He encouraged her to think she might cut out her companion if they ran away together."

"She confessed all this to you?"

"Miss Tam has no understanding of secrecy. Besides, she has always spoken her mind in my presence."

Ottilia could not refrain from offering a crumb of comfort. "I must own I believe she is sincerely attached to you, if to anyone."

Hemp's complexion deepened in colour and his voice became gruff. "As I am to her."

"Yes, I have no doubt of it." Could she press for the truth now? Did he trust her enough? "Why did you stop me earlier in the hall, Hemp? Why did you not wish me to speak of that matter?"

Hemp's head came up, pride in every line, and the harsh note returned. "It is not for Mr Simeon Roy to know how matters stand."

"Yet he had Lomax hunt for some paper that might prove your claim. Lomax found it, and perhaps destroyed it, for all I know. I am sorry if this ruins your hopes, Hemp."

A faint smile surprised her as his pose relaxed a little. "It does not matter at all, milady."

"Doesn't it?"

"I am not dependent on proof. Mr Lomax does not know of it, but Master Matt made his dispositions before he died. He took care of me."

Ottilia sighed out a breath. "You cannot imagine how relieved I am to hear that."

"Master Matt knew that above all things I craved independence. I have presented my credentials to his lawyer here in England. I can leave here at any time, milady."

"Then you stay only for Tamasine."

Hemp's jaw clenched. "I gave my word."

Ottilia watched his face, a shaft twisting in her breast for the agony she detected there. She spoke softly. "What will happen to her, Hemp?"

At that, a choked breath escaped the footman's throat and his shoulders sagged. "That is the question which is killing me, milady. I don't know what to do for the best."

"You believe the day is coming when she will have to be wholly confined like her mother?"

He did not hesitate. "Yes, milady. It is what I dread. Sometimes, even I have difficulty in controlling her. I know how to keep her sweet, but if she is enraged…"

It was troubling Ottilia also. But not for the same reason. The dread she had hardly dared acknowledge rose up. She would dearly like to confide in Hemp, but until she had tangible proof of what she now believed to be the real explanation for events at Willow Court, she preferred to keep her own counsel. Yet she might relieve the fellow in one small way.

"I cannot help but sympathise with your plight, Hemp, but allow me to say that I wholly admire your unswerving loyalty to your little sister."

CHAPTER SEVENTEEN

"Simeon knew, of course," Ottilia told her audience from her stance by the mantel. "As did Lomax. Indeed, I imagine the only person who is ignorant of the relationship is Miss Ingleby."

Sybilla, comfortably ensconced in her corner of the sofa nearest the fire, was looking stunned and Francis shocked. Patrick, not much to her surprise, took it in his stride, his profession giving him insights into human frailties alien to those living in the exalted world of the aristocracy.

He leaned a little forward in his chair opposite the dowager and addressed her in a voice of calm reason. "I understand that colonial life is a good deal freer than our own, ma'am."

Sybilla snorted. "Don't you believe it. Raising a bastard son is common enough in our society."

"But not permitted to grow up alongside his legitimate sister," put in Francis, who had taken a seat next to his mother.

"These are especial circumstances, Fan," Ottilia cut in. "Though I think it unfair of Matthew Roy to saddle the poor man with the burden of Tamasine for the lord knows how many years. She is only two and twenty, after all."

"And her future is bleak."

"True, Patrick. Mrs Delabole's determination to avoid responsibility notwithstanding, I believe the whole lot of them will be involved for some time to come. I can't blame Hemp for being at his wit's end. Not to mention Miss Ingleby and Mrs Whiting."

"Well, if Roy succeeds in eloping with the wench, they may count themselves well out of it."

Ottilia eyed her spouse. "You think that would serve, Fan?"

"Oh, I know you believe the fellow capable of making away with her once he has secured her inheritance, but it strikes me as fanciful. Why her and not Sir Joslin?"

"I did not say he was not capable of wishing ill upon Sir Joslin."

"But you don't think he killed him, nor arranged for it."

Guilt caught at Ottilia and she was tempted to confess the ramifications now settled in her mind. Before she could decide, Sybilla cut in.

"We all know the child could not have carried out her cousin's bidding. The only thing she understood was the promise of marriage."

"Who said anything about the child? If Lomax was in cahoots with Simeon Roy throughout, as Tillie suggests —"

"I don't believe Lomax would or could carry out a cold-blooded murder. Truly, Fan, can you see such a weaselly fellow putting his own life in jeopardy?"

Francis looked struck. "I had not thought of that." He slapped a hand on his knee. "You mean to tell me after all this we are no further forward in the matter of who administered the opium to Cadel?"

Ottilia hesitated. The gradual change of heart had crept upon her these last days and she had said nothing as yet. Was this the moment to speak? Was she ready to face Fan's inevitable fury? She waited too long.

"Tillie, I know that face. What the devil are you concealing now? Come, out with it."

Suppressing a sigh, Ottilia capitulated. "I'm afraid I have altered my mind. It was not murder."

"What?"

Francis's brow grew black and the dowager visibly jumped.

"Have you run mad, Ottilia?"

Only Patrick refrained from comment, though he looked rather hard at his sister.

She returned her gaze to the thundercloud on her spouse's face. "I believe it was an accident." He was speechless, but his eyes expressed his thoughts. Ottilia hurried to explain. "I say that, but I do not mean a murder was not committed. One was, a long time ago. Sir Joslin was a victim of the residue of that murder."

The thundercloud was superseded by confusion. "What do you mean, Tillie, for pity's sake? You are talking in riddles."

"We ought to be used to that," came in acid tones from Sybilla. "After all this, you now tell us the fellow was not done away with?"

"He was done away with, but it was not meant."

"Tillie!"

She gave him a deprecating smile. "I sound as cryptic as Tamasine, I dare say."

"Worse, if anything."

"Pardon me, pray. I hesitated to speak of it, and perhaps that was wrong."

Francis let out a breath in which his wife read exasperation. "Will you be so good as to tell me what in the world we have been doing all this while, if we have not been investigating Sir Joslin's murder?"

"We have been." Restless, she trod the carpet between sofa and chairs, not looking at them. "If one wanted to make out a case against the person responsible, then a charge of manslaughter might hit upon the truth. But I strongly suspect the actual blame lies elsewhere."

"Now I am thoroughly at a loss," stated the dowager, throwing up her hands. "This becomes more and more nonsensical, and it is not like you, Ottilia."

Before she could respond to this, Patrick intervened, a laugh in his voice. "Blame her condition, Lady Polbrook. Pregnancy often has this effect. Something to do with chemical imbalances in the brain, or so certain of my brethren will have us believe."

For once, Ottilia was not irritated by her brother's wit, for it might offer a convenient deflection from the uproar she had caused. But it failed to appease Francis. He rose and came to her, taking her shoulders and turning her to face him.

"Tillie, I won't have this. You speak of manslaughter. Who did it then?"

Ottilia gave in. "Tamasine."

Francis's hands dropped and he blinked at her. Ottilia looked at the other two to find both staring.

Sybilla found her voice first. "You stated positively, I don't know how many times, that the child was incapable of carrying out the scheme concocted by her cousin."

"She did not carry out any scheme," Ottilia said. "Nor was there one. At least not one to kill Sir Joslin. That was never intended, but when it occurred, Lomax was not slow to apprise Simeon, so that he might take instant advantage."

Francis fell back a little, folding his arms as his brows drew together. "But if Sir Joslin had not died, how could they succeed?"

"That I don't know. Perhaps Lomax planned to abduct the girl into Simeon's keeping. I dare say there are many ways in which they might have managed to get her away. The only thing certain is they were in communication throughout and

Lomax was likely feeding messages from Simeon to Tamasine. She knew he would come, for she told me so."

"But only when Sir Joslin was dead, didn't you say?" Sybilla objected.

"Who knows what odd notion they may have concocted," Ottilia said with an uncomfortable shrug, perching on the sofa arm. "They might even have hoped or suggested she push him down the stairs, for all we know. But neither was of a mind to do away with him personally."

"Yet you say Tamasine committed manslaughter," her brother reminded her.

"No. What I am saying is that Tamasine was the conduit for the manslaughter." She did not expect anything other than the uncomprehending stares that came her way. She gave a deprecating smile. "I have not run mad, I assure you. You have not forgotten my preoccupation with those sweets, I dare swear?"

"Lord, not that again! I told you that lozenge would be found to contain insufficient opium to kill a man and the analysis proved as much."

Ottilia slipped a hand into her pocket and withdrew the confection the child had given her. "Tamasine has a whole box of these. What if Sir Joslin ate a quantity of them? She offered me one. She might well offer them to her guardian. You know there were some in his drawer. What I did not tell you, for which —" turning regretfully to her spouse "— I must beg your pardon, Fan, is that the boys and I found five empty packets in the wastepaper basket. I left them in the drawer."

Francis pounced on this. "You mean those vanished from there along with the sweets?"

"Just so. If Joslin consumed so many in addition to his opium-eater's dose, would not the level of opium be ramped up enough to kill him, Patrick?"

Her brother still looked dubious. "Possible. I can't commit myself on the point without further testing, however."

"But would not Sir Joslin know enough to refrain from eating these sweets?" objected the dowager.

"Not if the purpose of using them was kept secret from everyone."

"Tillie, what are you saying? Someone is deliberately giving the girl these confections to increase her laudanum dosage? And without anyone in the house being aware of it?"

All three of her relatives were now frowning at her. Ottilia stuck doggedly to her guns. "That is just what I am saying, Fan. Why else were they taken from the drawer when it was known we were investigating Sir Joslin's death? Moreover, remember what the boys found out? All at the plantation knew how to boil sugar."

Francis brightened. "Ha! That fellow Roy was adept at making confections."

"He was not the only one."

"Who, then, Tillie? Don't pretend you have not already worked it out."

"I think I have." Ottilia let her breath go. On the point of revealing her conclusion, she hesitated. She was sure she had it right. But could she prove it? The plan in her head might afford the necessary proof. Yet there was the danger it might equally precipitate an outcome she had begun to dread. Whether it was imminent she could not judge. But the escalating crises at Willow Court suggested it might well be.

"Ottilia?"

She flicked a glance at the dowager. Sybilla's delicate brows were raised in question. Ottilia looked from her to her husband and then turned to her brother, holding up the confection.

"Another analysis is urgent, Patrick. We must know if this one of Tamasine's is the same as those I found in Sir Joslin's drawer. Tomorrow, if you please. Then we will multiply the dose inside by five at least. I must go to Willow Court again and tackle the person I believe to be responsible." She held up a finger towards her husband. "And before you ask, yes, I will give you a name."

Having discussed how to proceed extensively with Francis in the privacy of their bedchamber, Ottilia was dismayed to have all her plans thrown out of kilter by the sudden arrival of Giles just as she, her spouse and her mother-in-law were rising from the morning meal. He came impetuously into the breakfast parlour, demanding his uncle.

"I need your assistance, sir, or my father is like to ruin all!"

Fortunately they were alone, the servants having just left with loaded trays. Miss Mellis had gone to brew a posset for Sophie Hathaway, who had not yet risen and sent down to say she could not fancy a morsel. Patrick had eaten and gone upon his errand to Doctor Summerton and the apothecary. And her nephews were long gone upon adventures of their own. Ottilia only hoped they would not make a nuisance of themselves at Willow Court.

The dowager let out an explosive sound. "For heaven's sake! What is my wretched son about now?"

Francis moved to his nephew. "What's to do, Giles? We are busy this morning."

The boy grabbed his arm. "This cannot wait, Uncle Francis. My father has taken one of his pets and nothing I say will appease him. But I know you have influence with him. He will listen to you."

Sybilla pushed in. "What have you been doing, boy, to put him in a rage?"

"Nothing, ma'am, upon my honour! He has taken a maggot into his head because Phoebe's papa cut up stiff about — about this business over at Willow Court."

"Well, one can scarcely blame him for that. But I thought all was agreed between you."

"Between Phoebe and myself, Grandmama, yes, but when I asked Lord Hemington for his permission, he read me a homily and said he was inclined to refuse it." Giles threw up his hands. "I know what you will say and it's true. I deserved a scold and I said so. Only Hemington sent a note to my father indicating his reluctance to allow his daughter to ally himself with our family, and —"

Not much to Ottilia's surprise, her spouse exploded.

"For pity's sake! He said so to Randal? Like a rag to a bull!"

"Yes, and now Papa says he will not permit me to marry Phoebe because he has no wish to be obliged to be civil to Lord Hemington for the rest of his days. Also that the thought of any daughter of Hemington's becoming Marchioness of Polbrook would choke him and that I must look elsewhere, and a good deal more besides. He won't listen to a word I say!"

"If he's in a rage, he won't listen to me either," said Francis. "And before you ask your grandmother to go to Polbrook, let me remind you that she and your father are barely upon speaking terms."

"I know that, sir. That's why I'm begging you to come back with me."

Francis groaned, but his mother intervened, setting a hand on Giles's sleeve.

"My dear boy, you have only to wait until your father comes down off his high ropes. I know Randal. His temper is quite as bad as mine, but he will look at the matter in a more sensible light when he is calm again."

Giles released himself and swept away, his agitation increasing. "He won't, Grandmama! I left him upon the point of sitting down to write a blistering response to Lord Hemington. All I could think of was to tell Gatcombe on no account to send anyone with the letter until I got back and come hotfoot to find you, Uncle Francis."

"Is there no end to my son's folly? Francis, you will have to go. Giles is quite right. If he will listen to anyone, he will listen to you. I had best come with you."

It was plain to Ottilia that neither Francis nor Giles wished for the dowager's interference. If one thing was more certain than another it was that her presence could only inflame the situation. Seeing neither gentleman dared gainsay her mother-in-law, she took a hand herself.

"Forgive me, Sybilla, but do you think that wise?" She smiled at the dowager's instant frown. "You said yourself you and Randal are too much alike in temperament. Should you not leave Francis to try what he may do first? And then, if Randal proves obdurate, you will do your part to bring him to reason — in your inimitable style."

A crack of laughter escaped the dowager. "You had as well say my intervention will make it worse and be done with it. Very well, I shall remain here. But you had best postpone your schemes for Willow Court until Francis returns."

"Yes, indeed. I dare say it will make no difference if we go later in the day, Fan."

Clearly reluctant, Francis prepared to depart with his nephew, but paused to admonish Ottilia. "Don't you take it into your head to go hunting this proof of yours without me, Tillie."

She smiled and touched his chest in the intimate way she used with him. "Only the direst necessity will take me to Willow Court until you return. All was quiet after yesterday's fracas, so I don't think we need anticipate trouble from that quarter today."

Within a half hour of the gentlemen leaving, however, Biddy entered to announce Mrs Delabole, who arrived in a state of high agitation. She hardly waited to hear her name before throwing herself into the parlour, looking wildly round and fastening upon Ottilia, who was just rising from the sofa.

"Lady Francis, thank heavens! I cannot bear it another instant! That dreadful woman has set the house by the ears and I know not what to do! I had to come or I should find myself quite as insane as that demented niece of mine."

Ottilia, having caught her flailing hands, attempted to apply a judicious damper even as the dowager was heard to mutter an explosive curse.

"Softly, Mrs Delabole, softly. I cannot help you unless you tell me calmly what has occurred."

"Calm? I feel as though I shall never be calm again!"

"Come, sit here, ma'am, and try to compose yourself." Pushing the woman into the sofa, she turned to the open-mouthed maid. "Tea, Biddy, if you please. And bring a glass of water immediately."

Dropping a curtsy, Biddy left the room, casting a curious glance over her shoulder at the afflicted matron. Ottilia paid no heed, sitting down beside the woman and chafing one of her hands. It availed her nothing. Mrs Delabole burst into noisy sobs. Patting her on the back, Ottilia exchanged an apologetic look with her exasperated mother-in-law and found her own pocket-handkerchief.

"If it is not one thing, it is another," snapped the dowager, but in a lowered tone. "What in the world can have happened now?"

"That we shall discover in due course, ma'am. Let us first make Mrs Delabole comfortable again."

This proved an unfortunate choice of words, for the distraught creature broke out again in hysterical style.

"Comfortable? In that m-madhouse? Oh, I w-wish I were at h-home again! It is too bad of my brother. If I had ever s-supposed I sh-should be ob-bliged to deal with his h-household, I sh-should have t-told him not to d-depend upon me. I hate the place! I hate the inmates! And now the wretched woman has upped and left and much as I loathe her, how in heaven's name do they expect me to do without her?"

At this juncture, much to Ottilia's relief, Biddy rushed into the room with a glass of water, but before this could be administered the company was augmented by Miss Mellis with Sophie Hathaway close behind her, both talking at once and adding to the cacophony of lamentations and tears.

"What is amiss? What is amiss?"

"Ottilia, what has happened?"

"Who is crying? Oh!"

"Gracious me, who in the world is this?"

"Be quiet, both of you!" cried the dowager, topping them. "We have enough on our hands as it is!" She rose from her chair and towered over Ottilia. "If you do not give this creature a salutary slap, Ottilia, I shall do so myself!"

Ottilia did not even look up, intent upon urging the sufferer to sip from the glass in her hand. "Hush, ma'am, she is beginning to recover. Come now, Mrs Delabole, you are looking better already. A little more, if you please. Very good. There now, lie back and rest for a moment."

The matron sank into the sofa, letting her head fall back against the cushions and moaning softly. To Ottilia's relief, Sybilla returned to her own chair, signing to the newcomers to sit down. Sophie took a seat next to the dowager while Miss Mellis effaced herself into her corner as usual, but both sat staring in mingled curiosity and revulsion as Mrs Delabole, one clutching hand at her bosom, began to breathe a little more easily in the ensuing silence.

Presently her eyes opened and she gazed in a bewildered fashion at the assembled females. Ottilia performed the introductions, hoping the normality of the proceeding might serve to soothe. It could not be said that Mrs Delabole played much part in these, nor was she likely to remember the names, but she nodded in a vague way and begged everyone's pardon, addressing herself in particular to the dowager.

"I am sorry to have barged in like this, ma'am. Only Lady Francis was kind enough to offer her assistance and I did not know where else to turn."

"It makes no matter," said Sybilla, gracious now that order had been restored. "You will be the better for tea, I dare say. It will be here in short order."

The matron, still clearly distrait, nodded again. "Yes. Thank you."

Ottilia judged it time to attempt to discover the cause of her distress. She knew better than to ask directly, however, couching her question in a loose fashion.

"I am guessing you were referring to Miss Ingleby when you spoke of her leaving, ma'am. Is that right?"

Mrs Delabole shuddered. "If it were not for Tamasine, I should be glad of it, the abandoned hussy! How dared she behave in such a fashion? And in a house where she is meant to set an example!"

An inkling of the trouble crept into Ottilia's mind. She had not forgotten the aftermath of young Simeon's attempt at wedding the heiress. Had passion overtaken the couple? Speculation was useless. She would have to ask.

"What did she do, Mrs Delabole, for you to call her so?"

Colour swept into the matron's cheeks and she darted a look across at the other women, ending up at Sybilla. "I wish I did not have to relate such a thing before you, my lady, but Lady Francis was there yesterday." She turned to Ottilia, an imploring look in her plump countenance. "You saw how it was with those two."

"Indeed I did." She took the bull by the horns. "Am I to take it that Miss Ingleby and Simeon Roy resumed their — er — earlier liaison?"

Shocked gasps emanated from two throats and the dowager snorted.

"Just as I thought. It could not be long before some such immorality erupted. I for one do not blame you in the least, Mrs Delabole, for wishing to wash your hands of the entire contingent."

This attitude, while it did not assist Ottilia, had the virtue of settling Mrs Delabole's alarms about relating the events that had driven her to the Dower House.

"Thank you, my lady, you comfort me."

Ottilia leapt in. "Do you feel up to telling us just what occurred, ma'am? Pray don't be apprehensive of speaking as you found. We are all strong-minded enough to hear it."

Thus adjured, the matron set a hand to her bosom again. "I was not present at the outset, I thank the Lord, but young Tamasine went into her companion's bedchamber and — and found them. The first I knew of it was the screaming and shouting just as I was taking my morning chocolate."

"How very disconcerting!"

This from Miss Mellis, prompting Sophie to respond. "Disconcerting? Good heavens, I should think it must have startled you to death, ma'am!"

Mrs Delabole drew a quick breath. "Well, not immediately. I am bound to state that with my niece in the house, such outbreaks are not infrequent. Naturally, I got up and hastened to find out what had set her off this time. By the time I reached the scene, there was such an appalling mêlée in progress I did not dare enter the room. My chamber is just along the corridor, you see, so I was the first to arrive, although the servants were not slow to come to the rescue, thank goodness."

Impatient of these details, Ottilia urged for more data. "Did Tamasine attack her companion?"

"Attack her? They were fighting like wildcats! At least, I dare say Miss Ingleby was trying to protect herself, but she rained as many blows as the girl did, for all of me. And that stupid looby was actually laughing!"

"Simeon Roy?"

"Yes. He was in the bed with them, rolling around as if he sought to evade getting hit himself. I screamed at him to intervene, but indeed he did come under attack for Tamasine leapt upon him and scratched his face."

"Not so amusing, I surmise," put in the dowager dryly.

"No, for he began bellowing too and if the black fellows had not thundered in, I don't know what would have happened. It took both of them, and Lomax too, to haul Tamasine off, by which time all three were making enough noise to wake the dead."

Ottilia's imagination was rioting, but her mind fastened upon the one important factor. "Where was Mrs Whiting while all this was going forward?"

"Oh, she came and hopped about, shouting to footmen to bring Tamasine to the attic so she might get a dose inside her, and she went off again. I imagine she met the others up in the attic where of course they had to take the child. I could hear her screaming for an age, but my attention was captured by Miss Ingleby."

The matron stopped, breathless from her tale, although it was plain the coming upshot was almost more painful to her than the cacophony of the fight. Anxious to hear the rest Ottilia might be, but as the tea tray arrived at this moment, she thought it more prudent to let the woman regather her senses and strength.

While Miss Mellis dispensed tea, Sophie expressed her shock in a manner that had the effect of encouraging Mrs Delabole by having someone sympathise with her feelings.

"I cannot but admire your fortitude of mind, ma'am. For myself, I should by this have been prostrate upon my bed. But I have never been strong, you must know. Such terrible scenes as you have endured are perfectly disastrous for me."

"Very true," Ottilia cut in before Sybilla could wither her guest. The dowager had not taken kindly to Sophie's sickly constitution and had privately accused her to Ottilia of quacking herself. "But what occurred with the perpetrators afterwards? You said Miss Ingleby drew your attention?"

"She and he both." The matron was sipping her tea, but set down her cup in the saucer and leaned forward, looking now rather more elevated than distressed by what she had to relate. "For one thing, they were in dishabille and you would suppose embarrassment would cause him at least to withdraw. But no such thing. Would you believe it, he tried to get back into the bed with her! But she would have none of him."

Ottilia was obliged to wait for the comments to die down before asking for further enlightenment. "But you said, I think, that Miss Ingleby has gone?"

Mrs Delabole began to nod in as fervent a manner as she spoke. "Indeed she has. She swore at Mr Roy and knocked him back, shouting that she was leaving on the instant. Then she leapt from the bed and dragged a portmanteau from somewhere and began opening drawers and throwing things pell-mell into it."

"Did Mr Roy try to stop her?"

"No, it was I who did that. In vain did I beg and plead with her to remain. She showed me her wounds — and indeed they were severe for Tamasine had quite battered and bruised her — and demanded to know if I would remain in a like case, which I am bound to say I would not. The next thing I knew Mr Roy was demanding to know where she thought she was going to go, to which she had no answer. And the long and the short of it was he vowed to drive her somewhere and it is of no use to ask me where for I could not tell you."

Ottilia was much inclined to think it good riddance to both, except that she found it difficult to believe in this fairy-tale. "Do you tell me they did actually leave the house together?"

"Yes, for he went off to dress, although I have no notion whether he took all his belongings. She most certainly did not. The chamber was strewn with clothes still even when she had rushed out, calling for one of the footmen."

"Did you see them leave, ma'am?"

"No, for I was so put about and upset I could not bear it and I ran to my chamber to scramble into my clothes since I could scarcely reason further with the wretched woman only in my nightgown. I don't know what happened, but when I emerged, Hemp told me Mr Roy had driven Miss Ingleby away in his curricle. Which so overset me, I could think of nothing else to do but to come here to you, Lady Francis."

A faint hope the elopement might prove abortive stirred. After all, it was scarcely in Simeon's interests to leave with the companion when he meant to secure Tamasine's hand. Would he forego his sworn hope of that destiny? Besides, he must know Tamasine was unlikely to bear a grudge. In all probability, she would have forgotten the whole episode by the time she came back to herself.

"Perhaps Simeon took her only for the purpose of giving her time to recover her temper," she suggested. "I should strongly doubt he will in fact run away with Miss Ingleby. I own it would be an excellent thing if he was to go for good, but that young man has an eye to the main chance. I should think he at least will be back before long. Moreover, I cannot suppose he will allow Miss Ingleby to depart since he won't wish to manage Tamasine without her assistance."

Unfortunately this opinion found no favour with Mrs Delabole. She seemed determined to consider the case hopeless and wasted a great deal of time debating whether to pack her own bags and withdraw altogether from the debacle, or to hire another companion without more ado. Since she interlarded her musings with animadversions upon the disreputable conduct of Miss Ingleby and Simeon Roy, assisted in this endeavour by both Miss Mellis and Sophie, it was some time before Ottilia could have edged in a word, even had she made the attempt. She did not, her mind busy with possibilities.

Aware of Sybilla's narrow regard, she was rather glad than otherwise that it was impossible for her mother-in-law to

368

demand what she was thinking. She would have been hard put to it to answer. Her scheme of taking Willow Court by surprise to try to finalise her conclusions was effectively blasted. Impossible to engage in the battle she had anticipated when the attention of the household was concentrated upon Tamasine. Although, if Francis were here, she might persuade him to make the attempt without the culprit being present, a proceeding far more likely to succeed. It would take some explaining, should events prove her wrong, but Ottilia did not believe that would happen. The delay chafed her, but it could not be helped.

Mrs Delabole was just returning to what Ottilia supposed passed for normal in her temperament when faint shouts from without arrested everyone's attention.

The dowager set down her cup and saucer with a bang. "Oh, what is it now? Don't tell me they are bringing the fracas over here!"

Just then a voice a little nearer at hand could be heard, calling for "Miss Tam".

"That's Hemp, I think," Ottilia said, rising and going to the French window to look out.

The matron uttered a cry. "She must have escaped again! Oh, what have I ever done to deserve this?"

Sybilla was up, moving to join Ottilia. "Inevitable, I suppose, after all that fuss and bother. I could wish my house was situated elsewhere!"

Next instant, her sister-in-law was bobbing about by Ottilia's elbow, a frantic note in her voice. "Should we not lock all the doors, ma'am? By the accounts I have had from my sons, the girl could get in anywhere."

"Very likely," returned the dowager, "but since she has made a habit of entering by this way, I doubt it is necessary to go to such an extreme."

It was plain to Ottilia that Sophie was dissatisfied with this answer, for she argued the matter for several moments, only ceasing when she bethought her of the boys, commenting aloud her relief that they had gone with their father upon his errand. Ottilia caught Sybilla's eye before she could refute this statement, giving her a quick shake of the head. The dowager's brows rose, but she mercifully refrained from saying anything. They did not need Sophie in hysterics as well as Mrs Delabole.

The calling, which had continued unabated, receded into the distance. Ottilia opened the door and slipped out, moving into the garden and peering down towards the slope that led to the road between the two properties, at once feeling the chill through the thin sleeves of her gown. She could hear more voices, but it was impossible to tell from where they came, nor who was crying out Tamasine's name.

"Come back inside, Ottilia," commanded her mother-in-law, opening the door and leaning out. "It's cold and I want to lock it. If that wretched child is wandering about, the last thing I need is for her to come battering on this door."

Obedient to the common sense of this, Ottilia went back in and closed and locked the door behind her. Turning, she beheld Mrs Delabole once more in the throes, weeping this time all over Sophie. With an inward groan, she would have gone to the rescue, but Sybilla detained her.

"Let Mrs Hathaway deal with her, my dear, you have done enough." She added under her breath, "Besides, it will do her good to be thinking of someone else's difficulties for a change."

Ottilia smiled. "No doubt. I wish Tamasine had not escaped. I imagine the whole household is out looking for her. Else I would have gone across and consulted with Hemp, I think."

"No, you don't! You don't stir from this house until Francis is here to go with you. Good God, Ottilia, have you forgot how strong that girl is when she gets into one of her mad fits?"

"I have not, but I dare say she has calmed down again, if she has slipped out in the old way. She usually does so out of mischief rather than fury, if I am not mistaken."

"I dare say. Nevertheless, I will not have you risk your safety."

Sighing, Ottilia allowed herself to be urged back into the room. It irked her to be idle at such a juncture. On the other hand, she had promised Francis only the direst necessity would draw her forth.

The sudden sound of feet pounding in the direction of the house drove her back to the window, the dowager right behind her

"Don't open the door, whatever you do!"

By now the rest of the party had realised something was up and, although Mrs Delabole shrank back in her cushions, both Sophie and Miss Mellis came crowding round.

"Is it that girl again? Come away, do, Lady Francis, or she will be throwing stones again!"

"I hardly think she will do that, Miss Mellis. Besides, it does not sound like her steps."

No sooner had she spoken than a figure appeared at the window. A shorter one than Tamasine, with uncovered blond locks, who first tried the door and then knocked frantically on the glass.

"Auntilla! Auntilla!"

Sophie uttered a shriek. "Oh, heavens, it is Ben! What is he doing out there? Is she after him? Let him in, Ottilia!"

Ottilia's fingers were already turning the key. She wrenched open the door and her nephew flung through, seizing her arms and shrieking in a terror-stricken voice.

"Auntilla, you've got to come quick! The madwoman! She's got Tom!"

CHAPTER EIGHTEEN

For a heart-stopping moment, Ottilia could neither move nor think, but as pandemonium broke out around her, she came to her senses in a bang. Ben was moving towards his mother, who had given way to immediate hysterics, crying out her younger son's name and collapsing onto the sofa. Ottilia caught her nephew about the shoulders.

"Let be, Ben! Your mama has two ladies attending to her already."

"Where's Papa?"

"Out, but he will be sent for at once."

She found Sybilla at her elbow. "Go, Ottilia! I will despatch young Toby to fetch back both Doctor Hathaway and Francis."

Ottilia lowered her voice. "Keep Sophie from following, Sybilla!"

"Stay! You ought to take a cloak. It's freezing."

"There is no time. I will survive, never fear." Seizing the boy, she went quickly through the French doors, leaving her mother-in-law to shut them behind her. "Let us hurry, Ben! We have not a moment to lose. You may tell me on the way just what occurred."

Only now did it strike her that her nephew was dashing tears from his eyes. His voice was choked.

"It was my fault, Auntilla! I should never have suggested we go there."

"Yes, never mind that. What happened?"

The chill was penetrating, but Ottilia barely noticed, her concentration on setting one foot in front of the other safely even at speed. Her pulse was behaving in a distressing fashion and her chest was hollow, but her mind remained all too clear as she pictured the images Ben was painting.

"We never meant to do more than scout around the village, I swear, Auntilla, and we had got up a game of skimming pebbles on the pond with some of the boys hereabouts. Then that fellow Simeon came racing along in his curricle and he had Miss Ingleby up beside him. He was driving hell for leather, Auntilla, and she was looking like a nightmare! As they passed I heard her say she was never going back and they could all go to hell, for all she cared."

Ottilia grasped his hand. "A little slower, if you please, Ben. And you need waste no time telling me of that pair. Mrs Delabole has given me that story. What about Tamasine?"

Moderating his pace, Ben sucked in a distraught breath. "She went missing, Auntilla. Or at least they thought she had. Only she hadn't. She was —" He broke off, drew a sobbing breath, and tried again. "At first we just went on with our game, but in the end I said to Tom we should go and see what was up with the place, and I know I shouldn't have, but —"

Ottilia shushed him. "Keep on with the story, Ben. There will be time for regret later."

"Yes, well, we went and — and I only thought to find Hemp and ask him what was toward. Only by the time we got there no one was in sight. Nor was there any row or anything, no screaming like you'd expect. So we went to the kitchen and the cook said everyone was looking for Tamasine."

By this time, they had reached the roadside and Ottilia glanced across at the coming height she must climb. She was conscious of fatigue for the pace was faster than she was used to, but she ignored it, forcing her steps onward. Once on the Willow Court grounds, she urged Ben to continue.

"How did Tamasine get hold of Tom?"

The explanation came in staccato fashion, Ben gamefully saying his piece while remorse and anxiety still clearly held him too near tears for comfort. It appeared that, in a praiseworthy effort to help, the boys went all over the house, just in case Tamasine was not in the grounds where the rest of the household were out hunting for her.

"And she was — in the house, I mean. Only — only — it was horrible, Auntilla! Every time I think of it, I feel quite sick."

"Think of what, Ben? Come, hold it together, if you please. Just tell me."

Thus adjured, he sucked in another shattering breath and continued. "She was in her eyrie. Up in the attic. Only we didn't know. Couldn't see her. But — but when we peeped in, there was a — a body…"

Ottilia's throat constricted. "Oh my God! We are too late!"

Ben's gaze hunted hers. "What do you mean, Auntilla?"

"Never mind. Go on, Ben." The steps were beyond the rise ahead and her thumping heart warred with the dread. "Quick, for we are nearly there!"

"It was her. The fat, dumpy one."

"Oh, dear God! Mrs Whiting?"

"Yes, and she was lying near the window. We didn't know, Auntilla! She might have fainted or something."

Ottilia's brain was whirling, though the leaden feeling in her chest increased. Too late! Fainted? If only it were so innocent! She ought not to have waited. A bad misjudgement. Had she not known it might come to this?

Ben's voice thickened. "There was blood. That's why we went in. At least, I wasn't going to. But Tom ran forward before I could stop him. I shouted. But I was too late. The madwoman rushed out. She must have been hiding behind the door."

Ottilia's heart contracted, horror in her head.

"I saw Tom turn. He cried out. I tried to get in, I swear I did. But she slammed the door in my face. I heard the bolt go in." The boy was crying now and had come to a standstill right at the top of the steep flight of stairs. "I kicked the door and I screamed and screamed at her. I yelled to Tom to keep away from her. I yelled I was going for help. But I couldn't find anyone when I ran downstairs. I called and called for Hemp and Cuffy, but nobody answered me, Auntilla. And she's got Tom! She's got Tom!"

He threw his arms around Ottilia as she caught him close, murmuring words that in no way expressed her own feelings. "We'll get him back, Ben, we'll get him back. Never fear. She won't hurt him. She has no reason to hurt Tom. Come. Let us go and rescue him at once!"

Her words, brave as they sounded, were as empty as her heart. But they served their purpose. Ben straightened, dashed his hands across his eyes, sniffed and turned with resolute steps to stomp down the stairway.

Ottilia followed more cautiously, her whole being consumed with dread. Would Tamasine hurt him? She was eminently capable of it. And if she had killed once…

Reaching the flat again, she began to hurry, only to be brought up short by Ben standing stock-still, mouth open in a silent scream. Ottilia's gaze followed her nephew's pointing finger up to the roof and the breath stopped in her throat.

Tamasine was standing on the parapet, her arms wrapped about Tom's slight chest, holding him in a grip that looked like certain death.

An eon of time held Ottilia in thrall to sick horror, unable to move, unable to think.

In reality, it could not have been many seconds before the cogs began to shift and roll again. One salient fact hit her with violence. Tom was alive! She could yet save him.

Acting on sheer instinct, she moved towards the open front door, not pausing to wonder why it had been left thus, but grateful in a corner of her mind for the fact of it.

Her nephew was dogging her steps. Ottilia whirled on him.

"Find Hemp! I don't care how you do it, but find him! Quick, Ben!"

And then she was running, speeding through the door and clattering up the wooden stairs, her skirts held up so as not trip her. Somewhere in her head she thanked her stars for having found the way up onto the roof before this, but a litany was forming in her mind.

Don't let him fall ... don't let him fall.

She was out of breath before she made it to the top of the second flight, but she pushed on, refusing to abate her speed, the litany repeating over and again as she reached the last flight and halted briefly. Panting, she looked up the narrow stair to the open door at the top that let onto the roof at last, her ears strained to hear anything from that quarter.

No screams assailed her ears. That meant at least Tamasine had neither fallen, nor thrown her nephew to a shattering end. With renewed hope, she ascended the last stair, slipping quickly between the elevations and stopping just at the edge of the open roof space. A residue of caution kept her silent and still, listening out for any sign of life.

The soft sing-song came as balm at first, and then gave rise to a resurgence of dread. That was Tamasine. But what of Tom?

Ottilia peeped around the edge of the wall and lost her breath again. Tamasine was alone, still standing on the parapet and swaying dangerously.

Where was Tom?

Creeping, she slipped onto the roof, her back to the wall. Revulsion drenched her as she caught sight of the harsh streaks and spots of red stain down the front of Tamasine's white gown. Blood. Mrs Whiting's blood. The madwoman had taken her revenge.

A scrabbling above Ottilia's head drew the girl's attention. Shrinking against the wall, Ottilia formed an instant hope. She wanted to call out, to assure herself it was her nephew, but she did not dare. Tamasine had not yet seen her.

She held her breath. The girl seemed calm enough, even a trifle too calm. She watched as Tamasine raised a wavering hand and one of her high-pitched squealing laughs emerged.

"I see you!"

Had she noticed Ottilia? No, for her gaze was concentrated at a higher point. She crooked her finger towards it.

"Come, come, come, come ... dance with me! I am the sugar princess and I want to dance..."

So saying, she half fell, half jumped from the parapet, landing awkwardly and staggering several steps across the roof. Ottilia let her breath go very gently indeed, her eyes never leaving the girl's face. It was pallid, save for a splatter of blood spots which stood out against the shine on her skin.

Shine? Ottilia's mind leapt. Was she sweating? Unsteady on her feet too. The obvious conclusion came as comfort and misery both. She had overdosed on laudanum. Or had been given an overdose? Yes, that was it. Mrs Whiting had done her damnedest and been punished for it. The poor, demented child had seized her chance. Crazed indeed, Tamasine had taken her reckoning.

Even with the realisation, Tamasine seemed to recover herself. Of a sudden, Ottilia found the girl's china blue eyes, glassy with triumph, fixed upon hers.

"Lady Fan, Lady Fan, Lady Fan."

From above Ottilia, an anxious voice called out.

"Auntilla? Is that you?"

Without thought, Ottilia moved out into the roof space, keeping to one side to avoid Tamasine, but not close enough to the edge to put herself in danger. She flicked a glance upwards and saw Tom clinging monkey-like to the roof slates near a chimney.

On instinct, she called out. "Stay there, Tom! Hold on!"

Even as she turned, Tamasine came hurtling towards her, menace in her eyes, hands flailing. Acting on instinct, Ottilia seized hold of them as the girl reached her, gripping the cold fingers hard. The impact sent her backwards, but she rallied, realising Tamasine's ability to hold steady was impaired. Riding on sheer necessity, she raised her voice to a high pitch.

"Tamasine, Tamasine, Tamasine! Dance with me, Tamasine!"

The girl squealed, delight superseding the menace in the wide blue gaze.

"Dance with me, Tamasine," Ottilia repeated, and moved, dropping one hand and sliding into position by the girl's side as if she took a partner for the dance. "See, it is the minuet. Follow with me. Nice and slow now, here we go. And..."

She held the girl's hand high and, despite a fast-beating pulse, began a stately set of fleurets across the roof space, leading Tamasine along with her and counting as they went.

"Step and step and step, and then dip, my dear. Follow with me! There we go. Step, step, step and dip. Heel to heel on the dip. Very good. You are a natural, Tamasine."

The high-pitched laughter sounded as Tamasine picked up the rhythm, inexpertly, but well enough to manage a semblance of the dance, singing out as was her wont.

"I am dancing, dancing, dancing… I am dancing, dancing, dancing."

Ottilia thought fast as they approached the end of the available space.

"And now we turn. Nice and wide, my dear, and step and turn, and step and turn, and step and here we are straight again, and dip into our curtsy. Oh, lovely, Tamasine, you are doing so very well."

Tamasine released her hand for the purpose of clapping wildly. Or attempting to, missing as her fingers flapped past each other. She staggered slightly and Ottilia grabbed her hand again.

"Steady, now. Let us dance some more."

Nothing loath, Tamasine complied with her instructions to step and dip, laughing merrily as she went. The space ran out again and Ottilia made the turn, hoping to heaven she could keep the girl dancing long enough for the laudanum to do its work. Across the roof they travelled, turning at each end, until Ottilia's voice counting the steps and the rhythm began to feel hoarse, her calves and thighs aching from the unaccustomed exertion.

Still Tamasine danced, crying out now and then that she was dancing, but becoming momently more breathless, more readily losing her footing. Ottilia's heart bled for her but she had to keep her happily occupied if she was to bring herself and Tom off safe. There was no saying how far along the road to oblivion she yet was. And there was no sign of Hemp to relieve her.

"And step and step and step, and here comes the dip again, and off we go ... step and step and step..."

Again came the turn. Again the roof space proved too short. Ottilia did not dare change the rhythm to encompass a circle instead. Who knew what change might do? Tamasine's compliance must be solely due to the drug. But how much had she imbibed? Impossible to guess, although the girl's gradual decline indicated Mrs Whiting had been thorough.

"I am dancing, dancing, dancing..."

The song became plaintive, losing both volume and strength, and at last disappeared altogether as Tamasine's fingers slid out of Ottilia's clutch and the girl began to turn on the spot in the old way, raising her hands and watching her fingers wiggling against the light.

Ottilia made no attempt to recapture her. It was obvious Tamasine was spent. No danger remained for her strength was visibly ebbing as she turned and turned, her fingers twinkling in the light just as they had that far-off day when Ottilia first beheld her dancing in the snow. Time rolled back and all the horror of the days since receded in the well of compassion flooding her breast.

Then Tamasine stopped moving altogether. For a moment she stood as if petrified, like a statue frozen in time. Then she swayed.

Ottilia leapt to catch her, breaking her fall as the girl slowly sank, her knees giving way beneath her. The weight rapidly overburdened Ottilia and she was obliged to obey the dictates of her own body, ending on the cold stone with Tamasine captured in her arms.

She guided the fair head onto her knees, despite the awkwardness and discomfort of her position, and offered words as empty as the comfort she tried to infuse into them.

"There, there, my dear, it is over now. It is all over…"

The lovely countenance, pallid and still, blue eyes gazing fixedly at the sky, grew misty in Ottilia's vision as time seemed to stop, her whisper the only sound.

"Poor little fairy, poor little sugar princess."

Quite when Tamasine ceased to breathe she could not tell, but presently a waxy tinge began to overspread the pale skin. Ottilia's tears were still falling and the world felt far away.

CHAPTER NINETEEN

"Milady, let me come there."

Ottilia blinked back to awareness and looked up. Hemp, his features ravaged, was standing over her. Ottilia caught her breath on a sob.

"Oh, Hemp, I am so very sorry!"

He dropped to his haunches. With the utmost gentleness, he lifted Tamasine off Ottilia and caught her close to his chest, his gaze fixed on the dead face as he dropped to the roof floor and cradled the girl in his brawny arms. He said not a word, but Ottilia saw the tears begin to trace down his cheeks and her heart broke for him.

Not wishing to intrude on his grief, she pulled away and scrambled untidily to her feet, feeling her limbs protesting and a sudden penetration of cold. Looking up she saw Tom had slid down to the edge of the slated roof, sitting above the elevation.

"Look out, Auntilla! I'm coming down!"

Alarmed, Ottilia started forward. "Tom, it's too high!"

But her nephew dropped, rolled and sprang to his feet again, not a penny the worse. In body at least. As Ottilia reached him, he flung his arms about her and she caught him close, feeling the tremble as his limbs began to shake.

Ottilia released him and took him by the shoulders. "Come, let us go away from here, Tom."

"Yes, please, Auntilla."

There was a sob in his voice and Ottilia put an arm about his shoulders as she hustled him along the path between the elevations to the open door leading down into the house. As they reached the bottom of the flight, a deep-throated howl sounded from the roof.

Tom shuddered. "Is that Hemp?"

"Tamasine was his sister, Tom."

Tom stared up at her, open-mouthed. But Ottilia was too distressed to indulge in further explanations. Moreover, with the world coming in on her again, she was all too conscious of the dreadful aftermath of these appalling events still to be faced.

"Let us go down, Tom. You may tell me what happened on the way."

His teeth were chattering by this time, and he was shaking a little as he related his adventures. Much to Ottilia's admiration, it appeared that he had not lost his head when Tamasine bolted the door.

"Ben yelled he was going for help, and I knew she'd gone into one of her mad fits, Auntilla, so I kept back by the window. She didn't come at me and I kept my eyes on her and didn't look at the body, though it made me feel quite sick when I saw what she'd done to that fat woman."

"I am not at all surprised," Ottilia encouraged him. "How did you manage to keep Tamasine from hurting you?"

"The m-mattresses, Auntilla! I re-remembered how she liked to mess things up, and I started digging out straw and throwing it about."

"How very clever of you, Tom! Did she follow suit?"

"Straight off she did. She was shrieking with laughter, the way she does, you know, and she bounced about, throwing the straw everywhere. So I just kept on doing it and shrieking too, so she would think it was a game."

A macabre game with the blood-stained body of Mrs Whiting lying in the attic room, but Ottilia refrained from saying so.

"How did she come to get you onto the roof?"

"Oh, she said she would take me to her eyrie, which was funny because I thought that place was her eyrie. And she unbolted the door. I thought then I might escape, but she grabbed my wrist. Auntilla, she's so strong! Even Ben couldn't hold me that tightly!"

"Yes, your papa says abnormal strength is one of the aspects of that sort of insanity."

"Well, all I know is I couldn't get free, so I just let her take me where she wanted. I was afraid if I tried to pull away she would hit me over the head like she did that woman."

"Is that how she killed her?"

Tom shuddered again. "She did it with one of the bars from the window. And don't ask how she got it out, 'cause I can't tell you. But it was lying on the floor and it was all bloody and horrible."

They were approaching the main staircase when heavy footsteps sounded from below. Ottilia paused, catching Tom's shoulder to keep him still. In a moment, Cuffy came into view, taking the stairs at a run. He stopped short at sight of the pair in the gallery.

"Madame! You are safe?"

"Yes, Cuffy, and Tom too, as you see."

His gaze shot up as another howl, now distant, sounded from above. He threw a questioning glance at Ottilia. She gave him the word without embellishment.

"Tamasine is dead. Hemp is with her."

Uttering a low growl in a foreign tongue, Cuffy slid past and pounded off along the gallery and up the next flight. The heaviness in her bosom lightened a little. At least the footman might succeed in comforting his fellow. She set her hand to her nephew's shoulder again.

"Come, Tom."

The boy did not speak as they moved to turn into the main stairs. Just as they started down, a well-known tall figure raced through the front door, closely followed by her other nephew.

"Papa!" shrieked Tom.

Patrick skidded to a halt at the bottom of the stairs as his son tumbled down them and threw himself into his father's embrace. The ensuing cacophony of reunion, accompanied by Tom's hiccupping sobs and Ben's yelps of joy brought tears to Ottilia's eyes again.

Suddenly dog-tired, she sank down to sit on the stairs, clutching at the banister rail as she listened to the excited retelling of Tom's incarceration by the madwoman, as he insisted on calling Tamasine. She heard this time how he had managed to get away after the girl had dragged him onto the parapet, with a threat of jumping off.

"I don't think she would have jumped really. But she said we would jump and I said we should jump the other way first just to make sure we could do it. She started to turn and I managed to slip out of her hold. I ran along the wall and climbed onto the roof as fast as I could. I thought she would follow me, but she didn't. And then I thought she was going to fall, but she managed to keep her balance. And then Auntilla came and danced with her and she died and…"

Ottilia closed her eyes, the remembrance of Tamasine's last moments coming back with a vengeance. It was so unfair! The child had likely been driven even more demented by the application of increasing doses of laudanum. If only they had never brought her to England. Although, would that have served? Even then Mrs Whiting had the fixed intention of taking her life whenever she became too difficult to manage. Just so had she served the wretched Florine.

"Tillie?"

Her eyes snapped open to a sudden flash of déjà vu. An eon ago she had been sitting on the stairs at the end of the first such adventure and Francis had asked her to marry him.

"Oh, Fan, thank heavens you've come!"

He sat down beside her and drew her close against him. "I wish I'd never gone." His face changed. "Dear Lord, you're freezing, Tillie! Here, let me warm you up."

Hours passed before Ottilia was able to satisfy the hungry curiosity of the inmates of the Dower House. With the recovery of her faculties, a number of urgencies overtook her and she was obliged to enlist her spouse's services.

"Delaney, Fan. Or is it Lovell now? He must be sent for at once. The coroner too."

Francis released her and stood up. "I'll send Giles. He drove me back and should have gone around to the stables by this time. Come, Tillie. You will take cold sitting on the stairs."

She allowed him to pull her to her feet, holding together the edges of his coat which he had stripped off to wrap about her shoulders. Her mind was already busy with the next problem as she descended the flight.

"And Summerton too, I think. We cannot rely upon Patrick at this juncture."

But her brother, still holding his younger son in his arms, looked up at that moment. "Let me but take Tom and Ben to Sophie and I will come and take a look at the bodies."

"I'll look to Tom, Papa," said Ben, sounding decidedly grown-up. "You have duties here."

Ottilia's heart warmed. No trace remained of the desperate child who had run to her in fear of his brother's life. But the mention of bodies brought the other appalling happening to mind and she seized Patrick's arm as she reached the bottom of the stairs.

"Mrs Whiting must not be moved! The Justice ought to see her exactly where she is."

Patrick released Tom into his elder son's charge. "I'll see to that. Go to your mother, Tom, there's a good lad." He lowered his voice as the boys headed for the front door. "What about the girl?"

Ottilia's throat constricted for a moment. "Hemp is bound to bring her down. She cannot be left on the roof."

"Then I'd best instruct the footmen to put her in her bedchamber." He was gone on the words, taking the flight two steps at a time.

Francis slipped his arm around Ottilia again. "Will you sit in the parlour until I get back?"

"No, Fan, I will come with you if you mean to go through the servants' quarters. I must go to Mrs Whiting's room."

"What the devil for? Can't it wait?"

But Ottilia was already moving in the direction of the baize door at the back of the hall. "Too important, Fan. Do you get to the stables and catch Giles before he takes it into his head to come into the house. I don't think it would be good for him to see Tamasine, do you?"

Her spouse looked at once grim. "Decidedly not."

Ottilia slipped off his coat and gave it to him. "Take this, Fan. I am warmed up now."

He shrugged it on, told her he would join her in the housekeeper's room the moment he had sent Giles upon his errand, and departed down the long corridor leading through the domestic offices.

Ottilia followed more slowly, trying to dismiss from her churning mind the more lurid of the morning's memories. A clatter of pots and pans indicated the stirring events of the immediate past had not yet penetrated to the nether regions. The oddity of this heightened a growing sense of unreality. Even the fact of Mrs Whiting's murder seemed remote now.

She was glad to think it would be Patrick and not herself who witnessed Tamasine's handiwork. She was not normally squeamish, but she found it profoundly affecting to think of the child's vengeful act after holding her while she breathed her last. Poor little sugar princess indeed. It was hard to blame her, painful to think of the viciousness existing within that tortured mind. Better perhaps to remember the childish delight, the gleeful silvery laughter and the occasional amusement of her non sequitur utterances.

Her thoughts had brought her within sight of the housekeeper's domain and Ottilia hesitated on the threshold. She must do now what she had intended to achieve before the drastic happenings of the day. It had been meant to prevent them, but a sneaking sense of the kindness of providence could not but obtrude upon her regret. The child was at peace and Mrs Whiting could no longer answer in this world for her misdeeds.

She drew a breath and walked into the room. The door of the housekeeper's cupboard, which she had fully expected to find locked, was hanging wide. Confusion, shock and dismay attacked Ottilia one after the other.

Had Mrs Whiting left it thus? In the heat of this morning's debacle had she seized what she needed and rushed to the scene? Or had another broken it open and rifled some of the contents?

She moved to examine the lock. The wood around it was splintered, telling its own tale. Who in the house had forced it? Not Mrs Whiting. She had the keys after all.

Ottilia pulled the door wide and checked over what it contained. The ledgers were still stacked where she had seen them last when the housekeeper showed her the records of Tamasine's doses. There was no way to tell from memory if any were missing, but there was no gap, so it was safe to assume they were intact.

She shifted her attention to the various bottles and jars on the upper shelf. This was where the laudanum was stored. There was one full bottle and another standing open with its cork vanished. It was half empty. Had Mrs Whiting grabbed a dose in a rush? Ottilia looked around for a set of glasses and spied a measuring tub on the table with the errant cork nearby. In her mind's eye, she imagined the housekeeper dashing in, aware from the cacophony that a dose would be needed and hurrying to set one up.

But had the cupboard been broken open even then? Was anything else missing? She turned back to her inspection of the shelves. She readily recognised a collection of innocuous household remedies: Asoefetida drops, Turkey Rhubarb, Cream of Tartar and a variety of elixirs jostling one another, along with various unguents and a pot of Mercury pills. Nothing obviously missing. She checked further down.

The lower shelves contained various packages and boxes, but at once a tell-tale gap showed a hefty stack of uniform shape to be conspicuous by its absence. The size rang a bell with Ottilia and she had just placed it when her husband's voice drew her attention.

"Have you found whatever you were looking for?"

She turned to look at him. "Something is missing."

He came forward, eyeing the cupboard. "Do you know what it is?"

She returned her gaze to the gap. "I have a fairly good notion. What I don't know is who forced the lock."

Francis instantly cast his eyes upon the area where the wood was splintered and cursed. "For pity's sake! Another mystery is all we need."

A horrid thought struck Ottilia. "We must stop Hemp from taking Tamasine to her room!" Energised anew, she sped from the little room and hurried along the corridor. "There's a back stair, Fan. Quickly!"

A burst of excited whispering broke out behind her and she flicked a glance backwards. A couple of maids and a sturdy woman in a stained apron, who was holding a wooden spoon, stood in a cluster a few doors down from the housekeeper's room. Ottilia ignored them and hurried on.

Reaching the cross-corridor at the point of the door to the main house, she turned into it, pointing towards the stairwell now visible ahead. "There, Fan! Run up, if you please, and head Hemp off if he is on his way. Let him put the girl in any other room but her own."

Francis was already halfway up the first flight, but he acknowledged this with a nod and clattered on up the wooden stairs.

Out of breath already, Ottilia paused with her hand on the bannister.

"What is it, ma'am? What's happened?"

One of the maids had braved the scene. Ottilia waved her back.

"That you shall know presently. Stay down here, if you please." She bethought her of the butler. "Wait! Where is Lomax?"

The maid, a frightened-looking creature with a thin face, crept a few steps closer and dropped a curtsy. "He's still out searching far as I know, ma'am."

"Ah, then he was here when all the commotion started, was he?"

The maid's eyes rolled. "When Miss began a-screaming fit to bust herself, ma'am? I didn't see him, ma'am, but I heard he went up. I seen Mrs Whiting who went up straight."

"Did she come down again, do you know?"

The maid shook her head. "I seen her go up, but she ain't come back down since."

No, for she could not. Then she must indeed have seized a dose and taken it up with her. But who had broken open the housekeeping cupboard? She thanked the maid and headed on up the stairs, still pondering. On recalling the butler, she'd wondered if he was the culprit, although it was hard to think why he might have occasion to do such a thing. Then she recalled Mrs Delabole mentioning Lomax having helped the footmen to overpower Tamasine.

Instinct pointed her in one direction. If she was right, it would explain a great deal.

By the time she reached Tamasine's bedchamber, she was out of breath again, but was relieved when Francis came out of the room, looking exceedingly grim. Ottilia halted in the corridor, surveying him.

"You've found them!"

"If you mean what I think you mean, the remains are scattered all over the place."

392

Ottilia walked into the familiar bedchamber and halted on the threshold. The boxes lay everywhere, the empty packages strewn across the bed, the floor and clinging here and there to the curtains. She went to pick up one of the boxes, turned upside-down on the unmade bed. It was an exact copy of the box of sweets Tamasine had offered to Ottilia the day before and it was, like the rest, empty.

"She stole them. She must have been eating them all night."

"And you think Mrs Whiting gave her another dose?"

Ottilia sighed out a hopeless breath. "I should doubt of her being able to. I would not be surprised to find a vessel spilled on the floor in Tamasine's attic. She might have had a dose last night. But if she ingested five boxes of these wretched sweets, it is unsurprising she was maddened this morning. She might have been hallucinating."

"What, when she killed Mrs Whiting?"

"Who can say? I only know she meant to kill her — someday. Just as Mrs Whiting intended, at a suitable moment, to dispose of Tamasine. Only I don't think she did. Tamasine saved her the trouble."

When, at length, Ottilia expounded this view to Mrs Delabole, that lady burst into sobs, sitting plump down upon one of the parlour chairs where she had taken refuge as soon as she returned to the house.

"Thank heavens! I could not have borne it if the wretched creature had done such a thing. But does that Justice fellow believe you?"

"I have not troubled him with that tale, ma'am. He has enough on his plate coping with Tamasine's destruction of the unfortunate woman."

In fact Ottilia had abandoned as futile any attempt to explain her theory about Tamasine's revenge. The Honourable Mr

Robert Delaney, arriving along with the coroner in default of his colleague Mr Lovell who was still away, had no difficulty in believing Tamasine had committed the murder. The condition of her gown and the blood on her face were proof enough. Not to mention the weapon.

"For I understand from your good brother, Lady Francis, that the insane can display superhuman strength if they are in the throes of a mad fit." Horrified he might be, but he was inclined to think it a judgement upon those who knew no better than to allow an insane person to roam free. "What if the creature had bludgeoned some innocent instead of a member of the household? I can only suppose it a merciful dispensation of providence that she was found within the house since I understand most of the inhabitants were out hunting high and low for her for some time."

He considered the case as closed and gave leave for the dead to be buried as soon as may be, saying he would write up his report for the authorities, who would, he asserted, be perfectly satisfied with his judgement.

Ottilia did not doubt it and was glad to see the back of him at last. By the time he departed, the undertakers had arrived, closely followed by the unexpected return of Miss Ingleby and Simeon Roy. The ensuing uproar, when the events of the morning were divulged to the truants, was enough, Francis said, to wake both corpses from their rest.

He refused to allow his wife to become embroiled, and indeed Ottilia was relieved to leave the cacophony behind her.

"Though I feel sorry for poor Mrs Delabole."

"It is time and past she took charge of the situation. I only hope she will not feel it incumbent upon her to come crying to you at the Dower House whenever she can't cope."

The dowager, when informed of his hope, told him he was baying at the moon.

"Mark my words! The creature will be over here dragging us into the business before the cat can lick her ear. She can't leave until all is settled, I presume? How did you fare with Delaney?"

Since Sophie, attended by Miss Mellis as usual, had swept her sons upstairs with her, refusing to let them out of her sight, Ottilia had no qualms in relating what the Justice had said and her mother-in-law, doubtless querulous from the horrors of the day, animadverted on the man's character for several moments.

"Of course he has no notion," Ottilia said when she could get a word in, "for I did not feel it incumbent upon me to tell him, that Tamasine's attack upon Mrs Whiting was the culmination of her reckoning."

Sybilla, seated across from her on the sofa, cast her an eagle glance. "How so?"

"Mrs Whiting poisoned her mother."

This announcement was productive of a sudden silence. Lady Polbrook stared. Patrick, occupying the other end of the sofa, raised his brows. And Francis, in his favourite stance by the fireplace, one elbow resting on the mantel, bent a frown upon his wife. He was the first to speak, his tone reproachful.

"I dare say you have known that for days."

"Of course she has," said Sybilla on a scornful note. "You did not tell us that when you said you thought Mrs Whiting made those wretched confections."

Patrick raised an eyebrow. "That is what makes you maintain she intended to do the same by the daughter?"

"I am quite sure she did. If Tamasine had not broken into her housekeeping cupboard, I expect she would have fed her those sweets every day in hopes that her addiction to sugar would do her work for her."

"Along with the doses to quiet her? Yes, I must concede that would be enough to do the trick. Without time for the body to get rid of the poisons, the accumulations would inevitably result in coma, and very likely death. You could scarcely hope for an emetic to remove enough to keep her alive."

"You are certain it was Mrs Whiting feeding the sweets to Tamasine?" asked her husband.

"Who else? No one had access to those boxes except herself. Tamasine stole five from the cupboard and there may be more in there. I did not have time to make a thorough check."

"Do you mean to tell me," broke in Sybilla, evidently still struggling with the truth of it, "that the wretched woman had it in mind all along to dispose of that afflicted child?"

"Yes," said Ottilia baldly, "I do. What is more, I am convinced that the moment she realised how her machinations had helped to put paid to Sir Joslin, even though by accident, she found every opportunity to increase Tamasine's dosage in the hope the girl would succumb as quickly as possible."

"But how callous!"

"To her mind, I believe, she was performing a service. Just as she did for Florine, after it became clear the woman had become too violent. When I spoke of Tamasine suffering imprisonment, or perhaps hanging, Mrs Whiting was horrified and said she could not let them do it. She preferred to dispose of her in a fashion she thought humane. I suspect Tamasine's attack upon Phoebe sounded her death knell."

Francis's frown was direful. "Mrs Whiting did not bargain for Tamasine's scheme of revenge, I take it?"

"I doubt she even guessed Tamasine knew she had poisoned her mother. If she heard her speak of revenge at all, I imagine she took it for another manifestation of the girl's deranged mind, and never thought to be upon her guard. Only Miss Ingleby understood the streak of rationality that ran through Tamasine."

"That creature? I thought we had been rid of her at least!"

"Oh, I imagine you will be, Sybilla. I cannot suppose the rekindled passion between those two has as yet burned itself out. Although, I would guess Simeon will wish to remain for a while, in hopes of a share of Tamasine's fortune."

"For my part, they are welcome to each other," said Francis. "A more quarrelsome pair I hope I may never meet. As for that fellow, Lomax, he may go hang for all of me. What troubles me more is what is to become of those blacks."

"Won't they return to their native land?" Patrick suggested.

The dowager's eyes were afire. "To be slaves again?"

"No, no, they are both free men, Sybilla," Ottilia reminded her. "Tom and Ben discovered as much from Hemp and he said so himself to Mrs Delabole. Indeed, Hemp has some sort of competence. And I cannot suppose Sir Joslin, or even Matthew Roy himself, will have forgotten to provide for Cuffy."

Later, alone with Francis, Ottilia was more forthcoming when she broached a matter she had been turning over in her mind. "Fan, should you object to it if I were to offer Hemp a position with us?"

Her spouse stared at her. "A position? What in the world do you want him for?"

"He engages my sympathies, Fan. Only consider: he has spent his life in service to his father and his half-sister, for little or no gain. Now he will be adrift, with no purpose to fulfil and in a foreign country to boot."

Francis appeared unconvinced. "Well, he may not choose to remain in England. Besides, he said himself he is independent. I don't say he might take his place in society, but he may set himself up somewhere, if he so chooses."

"How, Fan? A black, in the climate that persists in this country? He is an intelligent man, and deserves to succeed. Besides, what level of competence is this? Will it be sufficient to enable him to support himself here rather than in Barbados?" She came to him, laying her hands against his chest and smiling up into his face. "Dearest Fan, I feel for him, indeed I do. He will be grieving for some little time, and perhaps it would help him to have an occupation."

"But what in the world is he to do for us? We don't need another footman."

"No, and I should not dream of asking him to take such a lowly position."

"What, then? It seems to me, Tillie, you have not thought this through at all."

"Indeed I have not. I freely confess it. I don't know, Fan. He may be my personal steward or some such thing. I am sure I shall think of something suitable." She read the condemnation in his face, and added on a coaxing note. "Pray indulge me in this, Fan."

"But, why, Tillie? I dare say the wretched fellow will not in the least wish to come to us."

"In which case, the matter will be instantly resolved."

To her relief, he looked to be thawing. He slid an arm around her and sighed. "I wish I understood what you mean by this, my love."

Ottilia stood on tiptoe to kiss him, and then leaned back into the circle of his arm. She tried to smile, but knew it went awry as her voice turned husky. "This has been a tragic episode, my dearest. I feel so badly, you cannot imagine."

"Oh, can I not? As if I did not know you well enough to be sure you have by this persuaded yourself the whole thing has been your fault from start to finish."

She gave a watery chuckle. "Not quite as bad as that, but you must see —" She broke off and drew a breath. "No, I will not tease you with my megrims. Only permit me to save a little something from the wreck."

"More than a little, my dear one. Giles and Phoebe have a hope of coming out of it relatively unscathed, once we can bring Randal to his senses. Which may appease Mama's temper at last. While as for my darling wife —"

She stopped him with a finger to his lips. "You need not say it. It has indeed served to divert me, despite the horrors we have endured. And if you will only allow me this one little thing, I swear I will not utter one word of complaint throughout the remainder of my pregnancy."

He gave a shout of laughter. "If I believed that, Tillie, I should be taken at fault within a week!"

She was obliged to smile, but she did not lose sight of her objective. "And Hemp?"

He hugged her. "Do as you wish, my darling. I admit I like the fellow. It is a small price to pay and you deserve a reward, if only for enduring the hideous madness of Willow Court."

Content to have won her point, Ottilia thanked him in a manner appropriate to the occasion. But her spouse seemed to have few illusions.

"Yes, it's all very well to play off your cajolery on me, but I warn you I shall not be encouraging you in any more such enterprises, my Lady Fan."

A NOTE TO THE READER

Dear Reader

The idea for *The Opium Purge* was a snatch of something I thought would be the start of a romance. A girl comes over to the new neighbours and pleads for sanctuary, but a brother comes to fetch her and tells the neighbours she is mad. In that scenario, the girl was being held against her will and was perfectly sane. That, as you have now read, did not materialise when it turned into Ottilia's next adventure.

Research for this one proved wonderfully satisfying. I needed a suitable poison that would have been easy to get hold of at the time. Google led me to Google Books where I found the most amazing contemporary source from the later eighteenth century. The book was digitized so you could read it online. It was a lengthy treatise written by a doctor on poisons and covered absolutely every possible poison you could think of, particularly poisonous plants and their derivatives.

Not only that, this doctor gave exact descriptions of the symptoms in several cases, explained how and in what timeframe the person might die, and went on to describe what the post-mortem would show and how tests might be made. For example, the contents of the stomach could be given to a frog and if it died, they knew the poison had been in the body.

I ploughed through a number of possibilities before I settled upon opium. That immediately led me to research about opium-eaters, and I found another digitized book about the confessions of an opium-eater. The data here augmented what I had already found out and gave me much information about how much opium would kill, depending how it was taken, whether as liquor or grains, or as a laudanum sweet. The symptoms of being high on the narcotic were described, and how it felt afterwards. A tremendously revealing read.

Of course I then had to put this all together, using only what was pertinent to my story, and making sure it all made sense and worked. A fascinating exercise, I can tell you.

What I enjoyed most about this story was creating the Willow Court household – literally a madhouse – with their cross-currents of passion and secrets. Like Ottilia, I found myself pitying the unfortunate Tamasine, condemned to a terrible malady in spite of her extraordinary beauty.

I hope you are enjoying the development of Francis and Ottilia's marriage, which, without giving any spoilers, is inevitably going to have its ups and downs. If you would consider leaving a review, it would be much appreciated and very helpful. Do feel free to contact me on **elizabeth@elizabethbailey.co.uk** or find me on **Facebook**, **Twitter**, **Goodreads** or my website **www.elizabethbailey.co.uk**.

Elizabeth Bailey

Sapere Books is an exciting new publisher of brilliant fiction and popular history.

To find out more about our latest releases and our monthly bargain books visit our website: **saperebooks.com**